Murder in Coral Bay

Dedicated to the memory
of Peter Whims,
singer, builder, outlaw,
above all, friend,
who loved the Virgin Islands
and who
gave much joy
to the many years we spent there

Cover Image © Wilson Roberts

Wilder Publications, Inc.
PO Box 632
Floyd Va 24091

ISBN-13: 978-1-62755-647-7

FIRST EDITION

10 9 8 7 6 5 4 3 2 1

Murder in Coral Bay

A Tale of St. John
By
Wilson Roberts

Wilson Roberts (signature)

To the Reader

AT TIMES, staring at the edges of things—perhaps the gap between the bottom of a cellar door and the threshold through which the darkness of the unlit basement is visible—if I relax my eyes I see that those edges are not firm; they shift and disappear for the briefest instant, reforming and fading, reforming, fading, as if I am on the threshold of seeing into a vast mystery. I could lose myself in such a moment, slide into a state where facticity slips away, where being-itself seems to evaporate. I struggle to avoid such notions and to perceive things as concrete and unwavering, sustaining my clarity of mind by adopting a faith in the solidity of the world.

The following narrative consists of a series of appropriations. In addition to my own experiences on the Caribbean island of St. John during the time in which the incidents recounted in *Murder in Coral Bay* occurred, I recorded interviews with everyone who played a principal role in those events, including those in prison and even those who have been presumed dead by some of my other interviewees. I also conducted an interview with myself. I transcribed the recordings with the intention of donating them to the St. John Historical Society so that chroniclers of the Island's history who might be so inclined would have them to draw upon as they sought to compile accounts of the Coral Bay community of St. John in the U.S. Virgin Islands during the second decade of the twenty-first century. I also wished to specifically supply information that might throw light upon the Coral Bay murders of that time.

In studying the interviews I realized that while they were of local historic interest, they were far more intriguing than a simple compilation of individual recollections. Each interview contained a unique take on a series of events in which I also was a participant. Accepting as inevitable the axiom that writers betray friends, lovers, acquaintances, to say nothing of the use they make of people they have never met, I rewrote each interview as a third person statement. I then wove them together into the tale that makes up this book.

The result is what appears to be a single story from an objective point of view. It is not. It is portrayal of what happened in Coral Bay constructed from the appropriated and rewritten recollections of many individuals, including my own remembrances. The seemingly objective narrator of this tale is a work of fiction, an invention. The people whose stories that narrator recounts have been filtered through my imagination. Yet, in some way, it all happened.

The facts underlying the events I have pieced together from the often contradictory accounts and interpretations of events I found in the many interviews that I transcribed and subsequently rewrote as I created this narrative may have sorted themselves out in the course of this experiment, although that was not my purpose in presenting its results here. I was seeking to convey a deeper truth. I hope you might discover it and that you will find the following tale more than an entertainment to be read on the beach and left behind on the free bookshelves at Dante's Landing, Skinny Legs Bar and Grill, Aqua Bistro, Shipwreck Landing, Miss Lucy's, Vi's Beach Bar, the Tourist Trap and other Coral Bay hangouts.

In keeping with Coral Bay tradition, I withhold my stateside name, as well as the Coral Bay nickname by which I was known during the period covered in this tale. As the maker of this story I have pirated from the recollections of my associates of the time, I give it to you under the more appropriate name of Pirate Pete.

As they say when setting your burger and fries on the table at Dante's Landing: Enjoy.

Pirate Pete aboard *Clair de Lune*
Canal du Midi
Agde, Languedoc-Roussillon, FRANCE

Part One

Dante's Landing

One

ROBERT PALMER BRACED himself to die. Through the window on his side of the 737 he saw a single-engine plane headed toward the jet as it passed Culebra, minutes from landing at the St. Thomas airport. He imagined his remains, mixed with those of his fellow passengers and the flaming shell of AmerAir Flight 243, scattered over the Caribbean and small islets surrounding the capitol of the Virgin Islands. Closing his eyes, he placed his arms tight on each side of his head, his hands clasped together at the nape of his neck.

So this is how it ends, he thought. And why not? Everything that mattered had been taken from him. Why not his life? Who would care? Since Maria left, taking their daughter Grace with her, nothing was important. Not his medical practice. Not his friends. Not the view over the western Massachusetts hills from the home Maria had designed and he had paid seven hundred thousand dollars to have built.

Bitter, even with death seconds away, he corrected himself; house, not home. The building at the top of Headly Ridge in Keetsville had ceased being a home when Maria walked out the door into a late October snowstorm.

Mingling with the roar of the jet engines and the certainty of sudden death, the memory of Maria's words howled through his thoughts

"I'm leaving you, Robert."

"Why?" Robert asked.

Maria looked away, her eyes quickly passing over the room. She opened her mouth, as if about to speak, but she said nothing.

"Why?" Robert asked again.

"You don't know?"

He shook his head.

Raising her eyebrows as if in disbelief, she spoke brusquely, "I need to be away from you."

"Why?" Robert's question was a whisper of pain.

She parted her lips to speak, closed them and looked at him in bewilderment. "You really don't know, do you?"

"I thought we were happy. I've got a good job, make good money. We have a beautiful home. We have a good marriage. We have Grace to think about."

"I'm not happy."

"Are you unhappy?"

Without answering his question, Maria turned away from him and stepped outside, the child, Grace, wearing a down jacket, held tight against her chest. She left the door open to the storm as she walked from the house. Robert hadn't argued. He hadn't tried to stop them. He hadn't called after Maria as she walked toward the garage where the car was already running and warming up. He hadn't reminded her of the vows she was breaking. He simply crossed the room and closed the front door.

His reminiscences were broken by a muffled shout. A flight attendant strapped into his seat near the rear of the plane had seen the small aircraft headed toward them and cried out in alarm. Suddenly the cabin was filled with cries from passengers on his side of the jumbo jet. At the same time the pilot pulled the plane upward. The 737 lurched abruptly. Opening his eyes, Robert saw the other plane disappear as it passed beneath the AmerAir jet. The speaker above him clicked twice and the pilot spoke in that voice of authority and self-importance that pilots all over the world have adopted.

"Everything's all right folks. This isn't an uncommon experience. Nearly all midair collisions occur during daylight hours and in VFR conditions." He laughed nervously. "That's visual flight rules for you civilians aboard. Most of those crashes occur within five miles of an airport, in the areas of greatest traffic concentration, and usually on warm weekend afternoons when more pilots are doing more flying." He chuckled. "Of course it's always warm in these islands, so leisure pilots taking up our airspace are pretty common. Fortunately, commercial airlines have see-and-avoid protocols that enable us to prevent collisions. That's what just happened. We followed protocol and nothing happened. Now relax. We'll be landing at St. Thomas in a few minutes."

"God saved us," the flight attendant yelled.

Many of the passengers applauded.

Robert did not.

AmerAir Flight 243 landed smoothly at the Cyril King Airport. Waiting for the ground crew to wheel the air stairs up to the plane's exit door, the passengers talked in excited tones about the near-miss. Robert looked out the window and did his best to ignore them. After what seemed a long wait, the plane was ready for passengers to disembark. Stepping from the air-conditioned cabin onto the top of the stairs, he was hit by hot moist tropical air mixed with the scents of vegetation, the sea and jet fuel.

At the baggage claim a porter loaded his five suitcases onto a cart and wheeled them to a nearby area where passengers from various flights crowded around a heavy West Indian woman wearing a red flowered dress and carrying a clip board.

"Where are you going?" She asked him after long wait.

"Someplace where I can get a few drinks and a decent meal, and get them fast."

She smiled and pointed to a row of vans idling nearby, each with seats for twelve passengers. "Go to the third one. Tell him to take you to Hook, Line and Sinker. It is a very good place."

The driver, a tiny, elderly West Indian man in a red and yellow flowered shirt, a hearing aid in each ear, piled Robert's bags in the rear of his van. He nodded silently when Robert gave him the name of the restaurant the dispatcher had mentioned. Thirteen people were crammed into the twelve seats.

"You can sit on the back seat between those two." The driver gestured with his thumb. There was one narrow place left to sit on the back bench. Bending over, Robert nearly had to crawl to get to it and squeezed in between an obese man and a woman doused with perfume. A local news broadcast blared from two radio speakers mounted in the van's roof. With the heat of the van's interior, the odors of perfume and the sweat of passengers crammed closer together than he believed human beings should ever be forced to sit, along with the smells from cardboard air-purifiers hanging in several places, Robert felt as though he would be sick at any moment.

"Open the windows," the obese man called when the driver got in and started the engine.

"They do not open," the driver said.

"Turn on the air-conditioner," a woman in front of Robert said.

"It is broken," the driver said and pulled onto the roadway leading from the airport.

Ten slow minutes later he stopped in front of a low building by the water, *Hook, Line and Sinker* on a sign above the door. Sailboats and motor launches bobbed at their moorings at the adjacent marina. No one moved as Robert crawled and pushed his way out of the van. The driver put his bags on the curb in front of the restaurant and looked at him.

"What do I owe you?" Robert asked.

"Twenty dollars," the driver said.

Robert looked at him in disbelief. "Twenty dollars for taking me a couple of miles?"

"You had five bags. Twenty dollars is the rate."

Robert gave him a twenty dollar bill.

"A tip is customary," the driver said, the twenty resting in his outstretched hand.

Robert slapped a five on top of the twenty. "Maybe you could help me take the bags inside."

"I am not a porter." The driver climbed back into the van and drove off.

"Welcome to paradise," said a tall heavy West Indian man who had been standing outside the restaurant smoking a cigarette. "That driver cheated you, mon."

"I guessed that."

The man grunted. "It should be seven dollars for one person, six apiece if there are more than one in the van. That driver saw you coming."

Rubbing his eyes, Robert said, "At least I'm here."

"There is that." The man smoked the last of his cigarette, exhaling slowly through his nostrils.

"And I need a drink and something to eat."

"This is the place." Flicking the cigarette butt into the water, he introduced himself as Jason O'Neal and picking up two of Robert's bags, carried them inside, putting them on the floor by the door. He sat on a stool and patted the one next to it.

Robert brought in his last bag and sat beside him. "I owe you a drink. What'll you have?"

"Water," Jason said.

Robert signaled the bartender. "A gin and tonic for me, water for my friend."

When their drinks came, Robert lifted his glass and clinked it against Jason's. "Thanks for the help."

"It is nothing."

"It was something to me."

Jason took a sip of water and set the glass on the bar. "Where are you staying?"

"I have a reservation at a hotel, the Dolphin."

The corners of Jason's mouth turned downward and he shook his head slowly. "That is not a good place."

"What's wrong with it?"

"It's a flea bag," said the bartender, who stood three feet away drying glasses,

"Their web-site makes it look inviting."

"It's quite inviting if you're a bedbug," the bartender said.

"You can do much better." Jason drank his water, his eyes meeting Robert's over the rim of his glass. When he set it back on the bar, he spoke softly. "My uncle has a room for rent in his house. It is just around the corner from here."

Robert looked from Jason to the bartender. "A flea bag with bedbugs?"

"That is the Dolphin," Jason said. "Not my uncle's place."

"A perfect description," the bartender said. "Of the Dolphin, that is."

"My uncle's place is very clean and very close to here."

Robert looked around the restaurant. "Here strikes me as a pretty okay place to be." He finished his drink and pointed at the empty glass. The bartender reached for a bottle of gin.

TWO HOURS later Robert paid Andrew O'Neal five hundred dollars for a month's rental. The one-story house was a small, clean and tidy Frenchtown frame building. The room Andrew showed him was big enough for a double bed, a dresser, two bedside tables with lamps and a large mahogany wardrobe that served as a closet. A window with a fan permanently fixed in place faced the street.

"It was good luck, me finding this place," Robert told Andrew.

"There is no such thing as luck," Andrew said. "God knows what he wants for us and he leads us to it."

"I'm not so sure about God," Robert said. "I don't think he has any plans that include me. I'll stick with luck."

Andrew smiled at him. "Ah, but what brought you to my son, Jason?"

"Luck and a deaf taxi driver."

"That could be true." Andrew smiled again. "If you need anything, let me know. You can use my refrigerator, except for alcoholic beverages. I do not care if you drink, but I do not want alcohol in my house."

"Thanks. This is more than I had hoped for."

Andrew raised a hand, as if embarrassed by Robert's gratitude. "One more thing. Should you need it, there is a Bible in the drawer of the bedside table closest to the window. I keep one in each room of the house."

Robert unpacked his bags and dropped onto the bed. Lying on his back, his head resting on his hands, he stared at the ceiling. This was as far from his life in Keetsville as he could imagine. He could change himself here. Do whatever he wished. Become whoever he wished to be. He would make a new life for himself in the islands. Everything was up to him, but for the present he would sit back and wait for things to happen. With the pressures of prep school, college, medical school and work, letting life take its own course was something he had never allowed himself the freedom to do. Later, perhaps, he would come up with a new plan for living.

He thought of Andrew O'Neal telling him that God had brought him here, and mentioning that a Bible was in the drawer beside the bed. Never a reflective person, Robert had not thought much about religion, accepting without examining the teachings he had been raised with. They were part of the conventions he accepted as he pursued the goals his parents had set for him, college, medical school, a career, a family.

Now, with Maria and Grace having walked out of his life, he suspected God was a delusion. He had seen the books, even read parts of them that claimed the world was a sphere where meaningless and random events buffeted men and animals alike. If that was so, man was a pathetic being cursed with awareness of his mortality, tortured by his knowledge of the futile yearning for a reality beyond the sad lives and deaths of other creatures. He hoped it was not so, but any faith he might once have had was gone, vanished as surely as smoke dissipates in a breeze. He was alone. It was up to him to create a meaningful structure for living.

He fell asleep, his mind buzzing. Several hours later he was jarred awake by an instantly forgotten dream, his body covered with perspiration in the hot tropical night. Disoriented, he sat up. Street lamps shining behind the mullions on the windows formed a broken pattern on the floor and walls. Slipping out of bed, he turned on the window fan and peered out at the still and empty street. The click from the movement of the second hand on a quartz wall clock seemed surprisingly loud. He stumbled across the floor and flopped back into bed, nearly knocking the coffee table over as he did. The drawer slid open and the Bible fell to the floor with a loud thump, landing in the shadow of the window fan. He picked it up, dropped it back into the drawer and shut it. Pulling the sheet over his head to block the streetlight, he slipped into an uneasy sleep.

Two

⁓

BETHANY WREN jumped when Hank Pearson put a hand on her shoulder. Holding a glass of vodka in the other hand he put his face close to her cheek. She had just finished her shift waiting tables at Dante's Landing in Coral Bay and was sitting at the bar drinking a glass of ginger ale and waiting for the hamburger and fries she had ordered. Tall, broad-shouldered and muscular, her long reddish-brown hair pulled back in a loose pony-tail, she half turned at his touch.

"I'm Hank," he said.

She gave him a disinterested grunt and sipped her drink.

"This is my first time on St. John. I sailed out of Nassau and I'm headed for St. Kitts." His speech was slurred and his eyelids hung at half mast.

She did not reply.

Hank tapped her shoulder a second time. "A man gets lonely on a long trip, especially at sea. You know what they say about sailors coming ashore."

She kept her eyes straight ahead, focused on a photograph of a donkey that Skipper Dan, owner of the Landing, had hanging above the cash register. It was standing with its rear to the camera and looking over its shoulder, the caption, *Bars are home to all kinds of asses*, written in bold letters along the top.

"What's your name?" Hank asked.

She turned her head and looked at him. "I prefer to be left alone."

Ignoring her dismissive tone and the hint of ice in her eyes, Hank eased himself onto the stool beside her. "I'm looking for a good time, if you know what I mean."

His grin reminded her of the expression on a stuffed fox her father had kept on a shelf above his desk in the gas station back home. She returned her attention to the picture of the donkey.

He draped an arm around her shoulder. "Come on. We could go to my boat, have a few drinks and see what happens."

Shuffing him off, she said, "There's no way that I'd go to your boat, but if I did—and remember, I won't—and you tried what I think you'd try, I'd have to punch you out and you'd have a black eye or a broken nose."

He leaned back and stared at her. "You think you're pretty special, don't you?"

"Everybody's special."

Hank stood, hands on his hips. "You're missing out on a good thing."

She turned on the stool and smiled. "Well bless your heart for caring so much about me missing out on such a good thing as you."

Skipper Dan, who was tending bar, set her meal in front of her. "Is there a problem?"

She shook her head. "Hank and I understand one another."

Skipper Dan looked at Hank. "Is that right?"

"Yeah, I guess we do." Walking across the room, he leaned on a railing and looked at boats anchored on the bay.

"Let me know if you need anything," Skipper Dan told Bethany.

She took a bite of the burger and spoke as she chewed. "You need a new daytime bartender. Since Rotten Cotton quit to do charter sails you've been working overtime."

"I've got some feelers out," Skipper Dan said.

After finishing her burger and fries, washing them down with a second glass of ginger ale, Bethany left the Landing and walked to the dock that led from the restaurant to the narrow slip where she tied her dinghy each day. She untied it, got in and yanked the motor cord. It started on the third pull and she headed out toward *The Saved Wretch*, the boat she had lived aboard for several years. She did not notice Hank following her in his dinghy.

He shut down his engine before she turned hers off and sat bobbing on the waves as she tied her dinghy to a clip on *The Saved Wretch* and climbed aboard. Minutes later she saw Hank try to step on deck. Before he could get both his legs over the gunwale she grabbed his arm and twisted it up behind his back. His face contorted in pain, he cursed and spat threats at her.

"I don't reckon you'll do any of those things," she said in her soft Carolina mountain accent, increasing the pressure on his arm as she spoke.

"You'll break it," he said, tears filling his eyes.

"Broken things heal if you treat them right." Her voice was cold.

He took a step down the boat ladder and she released his arm.

"Why'd you do that, let me go?" he asked, noticing for the first time her muscled forearms. "You could have walloped the daylights out of me."

"You stepped down."

"I could come back up."

"But you won't, unless I was of a mind to invite you up. If you tried I would have to hurt you. I don't let people hurt me or hurt them that I care about." She spoke and her voice was calm. A hard smile came across her lips. "You just weren't thinking clearly when you tried to board my boat."

"I guess I wasn't." Hank stood on the ladder and watched the smile broaden. It did not reach her eyes. They looked at one another, the boat rocking.

Hank broke the silence and pointed at her arms. "How did you get those muscles?"

"I've always worked hard. When I was a girl I held on to a plow and followed a mule over mountain hillsides, chopped firewood, hoed tobacco, helped my daddy hoist engines out of cars and trucks, did all kinds of hard labor. Now I carry heavy trays of food and drinks at the Landing, and my friend Andrea and I have some rental villas we maintain. Gardening with a heavy digging bar in this rocky land we've got here and working with a machete and a heavy weed-whacker will do a lot to keep a person in shape. Then there's hurricane season. When a storm's coming Andrea and I move all the outdoor furniture inside the buildings and put up hurricane shutters to protect the houses."

"You could be a lady wrestler." He leered at her. "Except you're a lot sexier than those female oxen they show on television."

"I don't care to look sexy."

"All women want to look sexy, even the ugly ones."

"You don't know much about talking to women, do you mister?"

"I've never had much trouble getting a woman to listen to me, or do anything else I want her to do."

"You're headed to trouble with me if you don't take care with your mouth."

Looking at her muscled arms, he raised his hands in surrender. "We'd be a pretty even match in a fight, and you've got the upper hand, seeing as how you're on deck and I've got a delicate perch on this ladder of yours."

"You ever been to church, mister?"

Hank gave her a look, one she saw often, one indicating that the person looking at her thought she was—as her mother would say—a tad peculiar.

"Not since I was a kid. My parents made me go to Sunday school and church every week. The organist, Mrs. Feaster, was our teacher. She was old with snaggley teeth and bad breath and she'd stand behind us and watch us color pictures of Jesus and his disciples. As soon as I was big enough to say I wasn't going there anymore, my parents let me stop."

"You stopped because you weren't big enough," Bethany said.

Hank shook his head. "And what does that mean? I was big."

"You were small, too small to be charitable toward that woman who was just trying to bring you to the Lord. From the way you just talked about her you're still small."

Hank took another step down the ladder.

"You afraid of me?" she asked.

"Afraid isn't the word. I don't get you. I came here with every intention of taking advantage of you and you start talking to me about religion. You're a piece of work, lady." He stepped down to the bottom rung. One more step and he'd be back in his dinghy.

"What's your full name, mister?"

"Henry Lewis Pearson."

"I'm Bethany Angelica Wren. Now you get yourself back up on my boat and sit quiet and I'll give you some iced tea and you can sober up a bit before leaving and maybe drowning yourself trying to get to your own boat."

"It's right there," Hank said, pointing to a nearby sailboat.

"And you're right here and you're drunk. That's no way to go out on the water. I've known sailors who drowned less drunk with no farther to go in a dinghy than you've got. Now get up here and sit down."

Hank obeyed. By the time he left he'd had three glasses of iced tea and promised Bethany that he'd attend services at the Coral Bay Christian Church.

The next morning, as they opened Dante's Landing, Bethany told Skipper Dan the story.

"He could have hurt you," Skipper Dan said.

"But he didn't, and if he had hurt me, Jesus would've taken care of him. Jesus always finds ways to punish hurtful people, even if he has to hire the work out to somebody else. Jesus can be fierce."

"I thought Jesus taught love."

"He does, but he's got no use for them that don't have love in their hearts. That's when he can turn to the sword, or find somebody else to wield it for him. Like he said, 'for all they that take the sword shall perish with the sword.' That's from the Gospel of Matthew 26:52."

"I don't think that passage means you should take up the sword."

"That's what I was taught."

"You worship a harsh god," Skipper Dan said.

"I believe you should love them that love Jesus and try to save them that don't love Jesus, and mete out severe punishment to the wicked. Those that will never learn to love Jesus deserve to be smitten and condemned to hell."

"There's not a person in Coral Bay that wouldn't shoot someone who hurt you."

"That man was just aching to be set right," she said. "I might could have had a chance to do that, but his boat was gone when I got up this morning. I don't reckon he'll be back to come to church with me."

Skipper Dan laughed. "Maybe not, but I'd wager that you scared the hell out of him."

"I hope so," she said, brushing her long auburn hair from her shoulder. "I surely do hope so, and he'd better hope so too. Scaring the hell out of someone is the next best thing to saving them."

BETHANY KEPT *The Saved Wretch* clean and orderly. She never used the term "ship-shape," and it would not have been an appropriate way to describe her boat, a hurricane damaged sailboat that she had bought for a few hundred dollars and rescued from the mangroves along the shore line of St. John's Coral Bay, where the storm-driven winds and waves of a late season Caribbean hurricane had left it listing in the muck, its mast broken off and the engine ruined by salt water. She paid a worker at the local marina another hundred and fifty dollars to patch several basketball size holes in the hull.

When the job was completed and the boat towed to a mooring in the middle of the bay, she replaced the bedding and appliances and ended up with a floating home at a fraction of the cost of housing on an island where the price of a roof over one's head was often far beyond what the average waitress and house cleaner could afford. Her furniture came from a thrift store on St. Thomas and the only luxuries she indulged in were a new queen sized mattress and two sets of five hundred count Egyptian cotton sheets and pillowcases. She cooked on a propane camp stove and read at night by the light of propane lanterns.

An inflatable dinghy with a 3.5 horsepower outboard engine provided her transportation from *The Saved Wretch* to shore, where she kept an ancient Suzuki Samurai, its front and rear seats long ago replaced with benches built of pressure-treated lumber she had salvaged from the island's transfer station.

She kept the Samurai parked under a large flamboyant tree next to the restaurant.

"It's a cool set of wheels, a classic island car," Skipper Dan had said once, when she talked about trading it for a well used 2005 Jeep Wrangler one of the car rental agencies was selling.

"It would be a lot nicer if it had a top," she replied. "The old one fell apart weeks ago."

"There's bound to be one around somewhere," he said. "That's the thing about St. John. People save everything, figuring somebody'll need it sooner or later."

Three days after posting a request for a used Samurai top on bulletin boards in the stores and bars of Coral Bay, Bethany had seven to choose from. One was ragged beyond use and she asked Rupert Gumbs why he had saved it.

"I keep it on top of my chicken coop," he told her when she went to look at it. "It helps weigh down that old blue FEMA tarp I got under it."

"And you thought I'd buy it from you?"

He shrugged. "Maybe I thought you had a chicken coop with a worse FEMA tarp than I got."

Dozer Larry, owner of a small excavating company, had the best top. He sold it to her for fifty dollars and a free hamburger, fries and beer next time he came to Dante's Landing. "I got a couple of front seats too," he said, looking at her Samurai's splintery benches.

Bethany patted the seats he showed her, rusty springs poking through their vinyl covers. "They're worse than the ones I threw away."

Dozer Larry laughed. "There's a good chance that they could be the very same ones. I picked them up at the dump, figuring maybe I'd need them someday. Most things got some use left in them, you know."

"Not those seats," she said, laughing with him. "You can't save everything."

Dozer Larry scratched his beard. "Ain't that the truth? There's things and people that are beyond any kind of salvation."

"Things maybe," she said. "People, I have faith in. There's hope for many of them."

"I've seen some damned souls around here that even God himself wouldn't look at twice."

"He always looks twice. Often three times. I believe he never stops looking for the good in people. Like I said, most times it's there and when it isn't..." She paused and putting her hands on her hips spoke with an icy tone that startled Dozer Larry. "When it isn't God knows what needs to be done and he knows how to get it done."

"Not always. Some scumballs lead wonderful lives."

"They seem to," she said. "People like that, I believe they fit into God's plan in some way we can't understand. She took a deep breath, drawing in her lips. Exhaling, she said, "But there are them that are pure rotten, evil, and we have to be on the watch for them and know what steps to take that will satisfy God by seeing to their ultimate punishment."

Dozer Larry looked away, Discomfited by a sudden intensity that crossed her face and filled her voice. He directed her attention back to the car. "So you don't want those seats?"

"Just the top," she said.

"It's never been used, you know. I bought it from Jimmy No-Legs when he left the island. I had me a nice little Samurai back then and figured the top would eventually go bad and I'd have this one for a back-up, but some kids got drunk and stole the car and totaled it. The police never did find who they were, or if they did find out, it could have come to be that the kids turned out to be their nephews, or maybe their own brats. You know how it works around here with the cops."

"Everyone knows that." She wrote the check for fifty dollars and handed it to him. "Come on over to the Landing and get your burger and beer any time."

"And fries," he said. "Don't forget the fries."

IT RAINED the first day Bethany had the top on her Samurai. She was driving to the Upper Carolina section of St. John where she and Andrea Hillborn were scheduled to clean a villa and get it ready for renters coming in the next day. Halfway up the long concrete road that wound around the hill, the rain stopped, the sun came out, and a triple rainbow stretched across the mouth of the bay. She pulled the car to the side of the road and got out. Below her, sunlight on the waves of the blue/green Caribbean glittered and danced. Sailboats, some with brightly colored jibs, moved swiftly in the wind. In the distance, a cruise ship rose above the horizon. Her eyes followed it for a few minutes, then dropped toward the middle of the bay where *The Saved Wretch* bobbed atop the bright waves.

Not trusting the car to make it up the steep and rocky drive to the villa, she parked along the side of the road and walked the rest of the way to the house. Andrea Hillborn was swabbing the villa's tile floors, a cigarette dangling from her lips. She looked up when Bethany, breathing heavily from her uphill trek, stepped onto the patio and pointed at the swimming pool on the lower deck.

"It's green again," she said. "Something must still be wrong with the pump."

"I thought you fixed it last week."

"I thought so too."

Andrea flicked her cigarette butt over the railing and pointed at a pile of leaves near the bottom drain of the pool. "That's the problem with people who rent for a week or two. They never clean the pool. If they'd use a skimmer net once a day the water would stay clear."

"I'll take care of it," Bethany said, and while Andrea continued cleaning the floors, she removed her sandals and stepped into the pool, the water slick from suntan lotion and rotting vegetation. Using the net, she scooped out the leaves, a greenish trail of slime further clouding the water behind each scoop. The pump seemed to be running smoothly, but the jet of water coming from it back into the pool was sluggish. She shut it down and removed the filter. It was green and clogged. Washing it with a hose, she set it out to dry and put a new filter it its place. That done, she turned the pump back on, dumped two bags of shock in the water and put a new chlorine tablet in the skimmer basket. When she checked the pool the jet stream from the pump was strong, rippling across the pool's surface and scattering the shock granules through the water.

Bethany smiled. "That pool will be crystal clear by tomorrow."

Andrea lit another cigarette. "Yeah, right, and the next renters will foul it up just like the last batch did and you'll have to clean it and shock it and take out the filter all over again. People make me so mad."

"If people didn't rent the place, we wouldn't have a job cleaning it after they leave."

"And if they took better care of the place when they rented it we wouldn't have to work so hard to clean it for the next people."

"We charge by the hour. If it was cleaner we'd have fewer hours to bill."

"Don't you ever get angry over how we have to struggle?"

Bethany smiled. "I wouldn't put it that way. I get frustrated, sometimes, but this is just a job, not a way of life."

"It seems like a way of life to me, cleaning up other people's messes so that people who can afford to fly down here in the winter and rent a place like this can come in and make another mess for me to clean up." Her eyes filling with tears, she sat on a stone planter at the end of the patio, smoke drifting from her nostrils.

"And I'm thankful that they can afford to come here and make work for us." Bethany sat next to her, leaning away and taking shallow breaths to avoid inhaling Andrea's tobacco fumes. "Cleaning houses and waiting tables is a means to a way of life for me."

Shaking her head, Andrea wiped her eyes with one hand, tapping ashes from her cigarette with the other. They fell into the planter, startling a lizard that had been sitting on the stalk of a small palm. "I wish I could look at it that way."

Bethany squeezed Andrea's shoulder. "I'll pray that you will."

Three

IN THE MID-AFTERNOON of a warm and sunny tropical day, Robert Palmer sat at the bar in Hook, Line and Sinker, his fourth gin and tonic half-full in front of him. He ran his thumb and forefinger up and down the sweat covered glass, making lines in the moisture as he slowly turned it. When he reached the spot where he had begun, the damp covering had reformed. He started clearing it again.

"You want anything to eat?" The bartender wiped the counter and raised his eyebrows.

Robert shook his head and smiled at his reflection in the mirror behind the bar. Forty-three years-old and he still looked good. Gregory Peck handsome, his mother had called him the day he graduated from Jefferson Medical College in Philadelphia. He rubbed his cheeks, wondering how he would look with a beard.

"You're in here almost every day," the bartender said.

"Not almost. I'm here every day," Robert said.

The bartender shrugged. "You never eat, just sit and drink."

Robert cocked his head. "So?"

The bartender shrugged again and turned away to wash glasses and set them on a rack to dry. "Just thought I'd mention it."

"I'm not a drinker," Robert said.

The bartender looked at the glass as Robert raised it to his lips. "You've got me fooled."

Lowering his drink, Robert set it back on the bar but continued to fidget with the glass. "I mean I never was a drinker."

"But something happened?"

Robert sighed. "Something."

"A woman?"

"It's nothing I want to talk about."

"So instead you drink like a broken-hearted barfly in a Merle Haggard song. Let me tell you friend, the bottle's going to let you down. It might not be tonight, like Merle said, but someday it'll let you down." Smiling at his comment, he lifted Robert's glass and wiping the bar with a damp rag, he set the glass back in place. "You wouldn't want to drink if you had a job like mine. It's sobering to watch pathetic losers fall off their stools and stagger down the street to sleep in places a rat would shun."

Robert drank and watched him work for several minutes. When he finished and asked for a fifth drink, he added, "Is tending bar hard work?"

"Only when my customers are rude."

"Like me?"

"You said that, not me."

"My life is falling apart."

The bartender looked at him with a knowing expression. "You're not exceptional. Stories of lives falling apart are old hat to every bartender I know."

"Let me clarify that statement. It's not falling; it fell apart." Robert's words were mingled with brittle laughter.

"These islands are good places to come to after life's played its dirty tricks on you." The bartender set another gin and tonic in front of Robert and grinned. "End of the world spots are like that. We kind of drift here when we don't have any place else to go. We don't have to pretend to be anything other than what we are in any given moment. There's no past and no future, just breathing and pretending that nothing matters but whatever we might be doing at any given moment. Drinking. Staring at the sea. Counting the knot holes in the wood paneling behind a bar. Maintaining some kind of equilibrium in spite of whatever it was that drove us to this particular end of the earth."

"You said end of the world a minute ago."

"No difference," the bartender said.

"Maybe." Without looking up, Robert moved his glass in a circular motion on the top of the bar. The moisture from it left a damp swirling pattern on the polished wood. "I get it, though, what you said about no past and no future. I'm nothing more than what I am right now, a man sitting at the bar having a gin and tonic. It doesn't matter what I was back in the world, and I don't give a rat's tail about anything I had back there."

"How about the future?"

Robert looked at the bartender. His dull eyes and downturned mouth were his only answer.

Again, the bartender wiped the bar around Robert's drink. "A lot of folks here are like the frost dripping off that glass of yours, running as far toward the bottom as they can get and pooling on the bar when they get there. It's the southern bottom of the world that we sink to." He lit a cigarette, took a deep drag and set it in an ashtray on the bar top, smoke curling and rising from its glowing tip as he continued dunking glasses in a sink of dirty water. "Patagonia, down at the tail end of South America, must be like that. I hear it's a pretty cool place, but who speaks Spanish?"

"Most Hispanics," Robert said.

They both laughed and the bartender said, "My job's no problem. All you got to do is pour booze from bottles into glasses and make sure that your customers can sit up straight. If they fall on the floor, you're obligated to stop serving them."

"Sounds easy."

"It's a living. You do have to learn the recipes for some special drinks. You get a few self-styled sophisticates that'll come in and ask for some kind of exotic new drink that you never heard of." He reached under the bar and pulled out a tattered paperback book with a coiled plastic spiral binding. "That's when you need this, *The Bartender's Bible*. The publisher claims it has 1001 recipes for mixed drinks."

"Sounds like a practical, down-to-earth title for a book," Robert said.

"This thing'll tell you how to make anything that drinkers have dreamed up through..." he paused and opened to the copyright page, "...through 1993. I'm sure dedicated boozers have come up with new drinks since them, but most people here want beers and shots, maybe a glass of wine, and a few simple drinks. It's rare that I have to make a drink more complicated than a Martini."

Robert emptied his glass and slid from the stool. Stumbling, he steadied himself against the bar and sat back down. "Maybe I should have a hamburger."

The bartender wrote the order on a slip and took it to the kitchen. When he came back, he leaned both elbows on the bar and looked at Robert.

"You've been around here long enough for us to know each other's names. I'm Dave."

"Robert." He held out his hand.

"Most people call me Gypsy Davy, after the old folk song" Dave said, shaking hands with him. "I play and sing a little, open mikes, things like that. What do you do?"

Robert dropped his eyes and sighed. "Nothing. I quit my job and came to the islands to start over, but so far all I've managed to do is drink and battle hangovers."

Gypsy Davy laughed. "A lot of people claim they came here to start over, and a lot of them haven't done much more than fall into a bottle." He pointed at the empty glass still sitting on the bar in front of Robert. "Looks like you've got a running start."

Robert spread his arms. "This is temporary, until I figure out what I'm going to do."

"I've heard that before."

"I mean it. I'll figure out something to keep me sane."

"You looking for work?"

Robert took a deep breath. Was he looking for work? What did he mean, saying he'd figure out something to keep himself sane? And how did that jibe with having no past and no future? The words had come to him without any forethought. And if by finding something he meant work, what kind of work? He did not want to practice medicine. He didn't want to do anything that reminded him of the life he left behind.

Days of working only to come home and sit alone in the house in Keetsville had worn him down. For weeks after Maria had taken Grace and walked away he would turn on the television and watch whatever might be on, drinking until he fell into a slumber that was as much stupor as restful sleep. Rousing himself by six each morning, he would take a cold shower, dress hastily, and drive to the hospital in time to be there for morning rounds. He knew he had to get away from Keetsville and its memories, but he had no idea how to do it or where to go.

One winter day a nurse told him about her honeymoon. "It was the middle of February and the lowest the temperature got was seventy-two degrees and eighty-six was the warmest the whole two weeks Henry and I were there. It was paradise."

Robert asked her where she had been.

"St. Thomas. That's in the Virgin Islands, you know."

"I don't know much about them," Robert had said.

"Paradise," she said again.

That night he looked up the Virgin Islands on the Internet. After staring at photographs of turquoise bays and mountaintop rain forests, he made up his mind to leave the western Massachusetts hills. He would go where tropical winds and Caribbean waters could blow over him and wash away the world he had known before Maria had said those words, "I need to be away from you."

It had taken seven months to close his practice and tell colleagues and administrators at Wessex Medical Center he was leaving. Indeed, it took more than simple telling; he had to convince them of his sanity and of his determination to go. His world was shattered, but he would not let people see the depths of his despair. There was no way to explain the dark and hollow thing his heart had become. Instead, he resigned his post as Wessex County's part-time medical examiner, sold his interest in the group medical practice to his partners, and rented the house in Keetsville to the new president of Graham Community College, including giving her an option to buy in the following two years.

With the exception of Raymond Wentworth, the closest thing he had to a friend among his partners, he told no one of his plans.

"Swear you won't tell anyone," he said to Raymond.

"Only if you'll keep in touch with me once or twice a year, and send me a little sunshine from time to time."

"It's a deal," Robert said.

Now his days were spent walking between his room and the bar and drinking. He never felt drunk, never felt the relief of alcohol borne oblivion. Nor had there been any meaningful conversations until Gypsy Davy broke the bartender/drinker compact of respectful distance and asked him if he wanted anything to eat, told him his name, and asked if he was looking for work.

"Work gets you outside yourself," Gypsy Davy said. "You seem like a man that's locked up pretty tight up inside."

Robert nodded in silence and pointed at his glass. Gypsy Davy refilled it just as Robert's hamburger came from the kitchen. He salted it and took a bite. It tasked fine and he ate quickly. "I suppose some kind of a job would be all right."

He spoke as he chewed, saying the words as much to placate Gypsy Davy as to open the possibility of taking some kind of job. He didn't need money. The proceeds from selling the practice, plus his savings and the rent for the house were enough for him to live comfortably. Still, he was bored; bored with himself, bored with his emptiness, bored with the narrowness of a life spent going between his rented room and the bar.

He felt like the man from the creeks in the old Robert W. Service poem, as though his soul had been looted clean of all that it once held dear. He did not know how to recreate himself.

Glancing around the room, the only familiar face was Gypsy Davy's. Interlocking his fingers, he tapped his joined hands lightly on the bar, raised his thumbs and rested the bridge of his nose upon them. Eyes open, he stared at the wooden surface, marred by cigarette burns, scratches and stains from years of spilled drinks.

Lost in his thoughts, Robert was startled when Gypsy Davy set a cup of black coffee on the bar in front of him. "I'm cutting you off the booze today. Drink this and sober up a bit."

Robert looked blank. He felt blank.

Gypsy Davy pushed the saucer holding the coffee cup closer to him. "My cousin, Dante, they call him Skipper Dan, runs a little place over in Coral Bay on St. John. He called me yesterday and said he wants me to leave here and tend bar for him."

"Will you?"

He shook his head. "I like things busy, lively, and I've got no desire to live on an island as laid back as St. John. Unlike a lot of my regulars here, you strike me as a smart guy that can handle just about anything, plus, you seem like a guy who needs to be someplace quiet where you can figure out just what it is that you need. I could tell Dante about you and suggest that he think about hiring you and forgetting about trying to convince me to leave St. Thomas."

Robert almost laughed. "I don't know how to tend bar."

Gypsy Davy tapped his fingers on his well-thumbed copy of *The Bartender's Bible*. "That's what this if for. It's got everything you need to know about the job."

"Except for exotic new drinks."

"So buy an updated edition."

"I'll think about it."

Gypsy Davy stared at him, his voice thick with sarcasm. "Sure you will. You sound like following my advice is the last thing in the world you'll think about."

"I might." Robert drank the last of his coffee. "Really, I might."

"Take my advice."

"I'll think about it." He paid the bill and left the restaurant by a side door.

The warmth of the afternoon sun was eased by a light ocean breeze and he walked unsteadily along the seawall leading to the adjacent marina. His shoulders slumped, his eyes on his feet, he was startled by a voice coming from the direction of a clump of bushes filled with bright red flowers.

"If you'd raise you head and look and around, you'd see the reflection of sunlit clouds on the surface of the water. It's quite lovely."

A pelican swooped down and plunged into the water a few feet away, rippling the surface and turning the reflections of the clouds into a moving kaleidoscopic seascape.

"And that made it all the lovelier," the voice said.

Turning, Robert saw a tall man standing near the bushes. He looked to be in his late sixties or early seventies and moved with the grace of an athlete as he walked toward him. His white beard neatly trimmed, he wore white linen trousers and a silk shirt decorated with images of palm fronds, hibiscus blossoms and bougainvillea. A finely woven straw fedora sat at a rakish angle atop a thick mass of white hair. With a smile, he pointed toward the horizon lined with thick dark clouds.

"Change coming," he said.

Robert nodded with a grunt.

"But things always change, don't they?"

"Not always for the best," Robert said.

"The beauty of being human is the ability to make the best of any change."

"The best may not be enough," Robert said.

"It's all we have. Look at that sky. It'll rain and the wind will blow and then it won't rain and the air will be still. Then there'll be wind and rain again, perhaps even a hurricane."

"That's a pleasant thought."

"Even hurricanes blow themselves out."

"And leave a mess behind."

"So?" The man spoke with a hands up gesture.

"So a mess is a mess."

"Until it's cleaned up. Often for the better. When we clean up a mess we tend to clean up the messes the mess we've set out to clean up is piled on top of. If things didn't change, even for the worse, people wouldn't have the opportunity to clean up the messes under messes that keep them from moving forward with their lives."

"I suppose," Robert said.

"No supposing about it. You look like a man in a mess, dragging yourself along here as though you would just as soon throw yourself in the water as walk beside it."

Robert wanted to turn away and head back to his room, but the man's eyes held him there like a spell. "I've had thoughts like that."

The man laughed. "That would be a dumb thing to do. Not only would you drown, which must be a terrible way to die, you'd be denying yourself the joy of cleaning up your messes."

"And just how do you propose I go about cleaning up my messes?"

"You'll have to figure it out for yourself. Of course that assumes you've got messes to clean up."

"Doesn't everyone?"

"It seems to be part of the human condition, although some messes a person can clean up just by doing it; other messes require massive efforts, like cleaning up after disasters, such as earthquakes, tsunamis, wars, disasters natural and man-made."

"And how do people do that?"

"It takes faith," the man said.

"Faith is something I don't have."

"Nonsense. Everybody has faith. There are endless varieties of faith, you know. Faith in one's self, faith in other people, faith in the future." He laughed. "Look at how long New England had faith in the Red Sox, and they came through."

Robert could not hide a smile.

The man continued. "Faith comes in many forms. Your faith in yourself may be buried under piles of messes, but it's there. A little digging can turn it up. You simply have to be willing to take up a pick and shovel."

Robert turned his eyes toward the horizon. The storm clouds were heavier, closer, but the sun was still bright and the water reflected its light. He looked back to where the man in the tropical shirt had been standing. He was moving away. Robert watched as he walked onto one of the docks jutting out from the seawall. He disappeared behind a sailboat. When he didn't reappear, Robert assumed he had boarded the boat.

Walking back toward his room he thought about Gypsy Davy's suggestion that he take the bartending job on St. John and the stranger's idea of cleaning up messes piled upon messes. Maybe it was time to clear away the rubble. Perhaps his life was not trashed, only temporarily blocked by mounds of trash that he needed to start sifting through in order to discard what was truly rubbish.

He stepped back into Hook, Line and Sinker.

"Coffee and food only," Gypsy Davy said.

Robert rapped his knuckles lightly on the bar. "Tell your cousin I'd like to talk to him about that job. And thanks."

"No problem," Gypsy Davy said.

FOR THREE DAYS Robert did little but study the latest edition of *The Bartender's Bible*. Memorizing recipes for drinks came easily to him after the demands of medical school where he had memorized every bone in the human body, knew the names and diseases of every organ and the place and function of every sinew. On the eighth of December he started his first stint as the daytime bartender at Dante's Landing.

"It's hard work buy I pay well," Skipper Dan told Robert when he hired him. "I keep open every day but one each year."

"Christmas?" Robert asked.

Tall and thin with a trim salt and pepper beard, Skipper Dan shook his head. "Christmas is a big day for business. I close on the Fourth of July for the St. John Festival. That's the biggest day of Carnival. All the action is in Cruz Bay; business gets so slack here in Coral Bay that I close for the day. To make up for the money I lose on the Fourth, I put on a pre-Fourth of July Festival party at the Landing the night before. I hire a band and a bunch of guys to dress up like jumbies and we have a dandy time. I sell a lot of food and booze that night."

"Is Carnival like a county fair back in the states?"

Skipper Dan laughed and shook his head. "Carnival lasts for a month and Festival on the Fourth is the culmination of it."

"A month long county fair?"

"It's nothing like a country fair. Carnival's unique."

"I guess I'll have to see for myself."

"That's the only way," Skipper Dan said. "Carnival is Carnival."

The Landing opened at ten. The sun was already climbing high, a white burning circle in a cloudless sky, the air still and heavy with moisture when Robert arrived at the open-air pentagonal building that housed Dante's Landing. A cluster of six men and two women stood outside Beth's Booty, a small clothing shop adjacent to it, several of them fanning their faces with open hands. They watched as Skipper Dan unlocked the wrought iron gate at the front of the restaurant. Once it was open, they jostled one another, passing by two large stuffed dummies dressed in tropical clothing by the door to Beth's Booty, one with a patch over its right eye and a multi-colored bandana around its head. Propped up on chairs outside the shop, the largest dummy held a *More Inside!* sign in its lap.

Once past the gate, Robert looked around at the bar and restaurant where he was about to start work. The building resembled a huge gazebo, its roof constructed of sailcloth suspended over heavy timber rafters that tied into a central pole and spread outward like spokes, each rafter resting on four additional poles, placed in concentric circles and painted the light blues, pinks, oranges and dark blues favored by Caribbean designers. At the center of the pavilion was the bar, also circular and surrounded by barstools. Cabinets containing wines and liquors were built around the central pole and secured by heavy padlocks. Beyond the bar, tables covered the floor, placed close enough to accommodate a maximum number of customers and yet allow the servers room to maneuver around them. Six fifty-two inch flat screen televisions hung around the pavilion, at least one visible from each seat in the place.

Once beyond the gate, members of the small crowd settled themselves on barstools and watched expectantly as Skipper Dan opened a line of wooden shutters that sealed the Landing off from the surrounding bush and the waters of Coral Bay. A forty foot dock leading from the pavilion out into the bay held half a dozen narrow finger docks, places for dinghies and other small craft to tie up.

"The usual morning crew," Dan told Robert. "The guy with the kerchief around his head and the black beard is called Teach. He keeps to himself and nobody knows much about him. Some say he got the nickname because he was a professor back in Michigan, others say he got it because of his beard. Captain Edward Teach was Blackbeard the pirate, you know."

"I don't know much about pirate history," Robert said, looking closely at Teach.

He was of middle height, muscular, with a thick black untrimmed beard and mustache. Barefoot, he was the only one among the men at the bar who wore long pants. His white short-sleeved shirt was open three buttons from the top and Robert saw a gold coin on a gold chain resting against the thick mat of hair covering his chest. A tattoo of a snake encircled his left arm, so well executed that Robert thought its yellow eyes blinked when

Teach moved his arm to lift a drink. Its mouth was open, as if to bite a victim and its long fangs dripped blood. The body was brightly colored, mostly reds and greens, with several patches of blue. It seemed to undulate, as if alive, whenever Teach moved his arm.

"A creepy guy," Robert said.

Skipper Dan made a light clucking sound with his tongue. "Where he got the name doesn't matter. He showed up here a year or so ago, took a place at the bar a few stools away from the others, and the next thing you know everybody was calling him Teach, not that he's got much to do with any of us. He's one weird guy." Skipper Dan shrugged and pointed at a small thin man wearing a cowboy hat, a tank top, cut-off jeans and sandals. "That's Pilgrim Jack. He says he's from Boston and claims his family came over on the Mayflower, but he's got a Texas accent and carries a Bowie knife and washes dishes at any restaurant that'll put up with him. I've fired and hired him at least five times.

"That skinny blonde woman with the tight denim shorts and a faded Rolling Stones t-shirt is known as Nutty Betty. She and Pilgrim Jack live in a tent somewhere in the valley below Bordeaux Mountain and walk here every morning at opening time. They say she was a lawyer in Russia, and she does have what sounds like some kind of eastern European accent, but who knows? Down here you hardly ever get a straight story about who people are and where they came from. For all I know, she could be from Detroit and faking the accent."

"Why the nickname?"

"She's a nutcase."

"In what way?"

Skipper Dan laughed. "She lives in a tent in the valley with Pilgrim Jack. That's nuts."

Skipper Dan filled Robert in on the other men sitting at the bar; Icebox Bob, who worked on air-conditioning systems and refrigeration units, when he was sober; Mechanic Mike, who Dan said had an almost magical ability to listen to a car or truck and diagnose whatever might be wrong with it. Barefoot, he wore his red hair pulled back in a pony tail. His thin arms and legs stuck out from his shirt sleeves and black cut-off shorts.

Skipper Dan gestured toward a huge man, who sat with his elbows on the bar, his shoulders hunched. "That's Durham Bull. He says he's from the northeast of England by way of Philadelphia. Whatever he says, the one thing we know is that he's a professional idler. Rumor is that he made a bundle in dot coms before the crash and hasn't worked a day since he got here. You don't want to get downwind of him."

Robert said, "I'm getting a whiff from here."

"He gets pretty odiferous. The guy next to him, the one with his head down, like he's asleep on the bar, we call him the Liquid Plumber, at least he says he's a plumber, but nobody's ever seen him lift a wrench."

Robert's eyes turned to the second woman. Tall, with long black hair and fine features, she wore a black t-shirt with a small rose painted over her heart, and a black skirt of thin cotton. As if suddenly aware of his attention, she looked up from her drink. Her eyes rested briefly on Skipper Dan, then shifted to Robert. Holding his eyes for a moment, she gave him a half smile. It lasted an instant and she returned her gaze to her drink.

"That's X," Skipper Dan said.

"X?"

"That's what she calls herself. Nobody knows her name."

"You got a lot of weird names around here," Robert said.

"People re-create themselves in places like this. They pick a name, or someone gives it to them, usually representing what they do, or how they look. You don't have to be tied to your past if you live in Coral Bay."

Robert smiled. "Interesting. She's called X, nothing else? Like Miss X, or Ms. X."

"Just X, like the letter," Skipper Dan said. "That's what she told us when she showed up four years ago and that's all anybody here knows about her, except that she can out drink any of the other regulars and never once slur a word or stumble on her way to the bathroom. I asked her one time what X stood for and she said it could be anything she wanted it to be: ex-wife, ex-singer, ex-cop, ex-con. 'Maybe even ex-human being if I get lucky,' she told me once. Teach stares at her a lot, like he's interested, but she hasn't given him a tumble. He's also got a thing for Bethany, my best waitress. I can tell by the sideways looks he keeps giving both of them. Odd looks, if you ask me."

"Quite a crew," Robert said absently, not knowing what else to say.

Skipper Dan said, "I make a good living keeping losers so drunk that they forget to commit suicide." He opened a beer and continued.

"Not only are they the morning crew, they're part of the afternoon crew as well, and you'll see most of them at closing time. Just listen to them and say as little as possible. They'll be easy, beers, shots and dark and diets—that's rum and Diet Coke —is what they mostly drink. Just make sure they pay each time you give them a refill. I don't run tabs for people. The price list is taped to the cash register."

He unlocked and opened a set of the shutters enclosing a cluster of cabinets behind the bar where the bottles of liquor were shelved. Slapping Robert gently on the shoulder, he rapped his knuckles on the bar and gestured toward the six men and two women who were now sitting at the bar, waiting for the drinks to begin flowing.

"Hey everybody, this is Robert, the new daytime bartender. Be good to him."

There were mumbled greetings, mixed with requests for drinks as Robert assumed his position behind the bar. While he took drink orders from the morning crew, Skipper Dan used a remote to click on the TVs, three tuned to ESPN and three to CNN, their sound muted and replaced by captions in black boxes with white lettering. He turned on a stereo system tuned to a satellite radio classic country music station.

Robert looked toward the speakers with a resigned expression. He disliked music. To him it was audible sewage, reeking from speakers, earpieces, stinking up elevators, stores, restaurants and bars, even telephone systems where robot voices put you on hold and you have to listen as music assaults your ear. Classical, country, rock, jazz, it was all a screeching mess. He could not understand what was wrong with people that they sing and waste their time building boxes with strings, and sticks and tubes with holes to blow into, all making a terrible clamorous din. When he was still practicing medicine, he insisted there be no music playing in the waiting room and he kept the radio in his car tuned to WAMC, the public radio station from Albany and WNNZ in Amherst. Both played talk programs all day.

The year before Maria left she bought a guitar, telling him that she wanted to be a singer/songwriter. Often he could hear her practicing in the living room as he tried falling asleep in the bedroom above. Several times he asked her to go into the den or the kitchen when she played, but she insisted the living room was more comfortable, especially in the colder months when she could sit beside the gas stove with the artificial logs. Resorting to ear plugs, he would pull the covers over his head and finally fall asleep.

He knew that music blasting from the overhead speakers would be the worst part of his new job, but he hoped that as the bar and restaurant filled up, the chatter of diners and drinkers would drown out the stereo.

Four

BETHANY CAME to work shortly before noon. Putting on an apron, she reached behind her back, struggling to knot the side ties as she crossed to the bar and slid onto the stool next to X.

"Hey, X," she said, her fingers fumbling with the ties.

"Let me do that," X said. She took the ties and quickly fastened them into a bow knot. "You meet the new bartender yet?"

Bethany shook her head. X gestured toward Robert, "Bethany, meet Bob. Bob, this is Beth."

"Robert," he said, nodding politely at Bethany.

X stuck her tongue between her lips and gave him a razzberry. "Oh, Robert. Excuse me."

Bethany laughed and shook his hand. "Bethany, not Beth."

X made another razzberry and laughing with her, looked at Robert. "You people are so fussy about your names."

Robert said, "If you can't control your name, what can you control?"

X winked at him. "Names are just a way the world has of making you be whoever your parents, or anybody else, for that matter, want you to be. Names, like faces, are an indication of who you are or who you might become."

"I like being Robert."

Bethany kissed X's cheek. "And I like being Bethany."

"I chose to be X. I don't like it or dislike it. I'm simply X. It's who I am. What I am, X, not anybody else's Annie, or Evelyn or Margie or Wanda or Marilee." I remade myself when I became X and everything else is ancient history that doesn't mean a thing to anybody."

"Nobody makes herself," Bethany said. "We're all made, created."

"Bethany has faith," X said, looking at Robert. "It can make her difficult to reason with."

"X is very cool," Icebox Bob said.

Bethany shrugged. Swiveling on the stool, she looked at Robert. "I guess we'll be working together."

Across the bar, Teach looked up, his eyes moving from X to Bethany and resting briefly on Robert, who noticed the attention and felt a slight involuntary shudder. He turned away, focusing his attention on Bethany.

"It looks that way." He smiled and was caught by her eyes, pools of blue/green sparkling with light. It was nothing more than reflections from the fixtures around and above the bar, he felt sure. Less than an inch shorter than he was, Robert's immediate attraction to her was dampened by the sight of a thin gold cross hanging from a chain around her neck.

X had turned and was talking to Icebox Bob, who slipped his arm around her shoulder and signaled Robert for another beer.

"Where are you living?" Bethany asked Robert.

"Frenchtown."

She frowned. "You come over from St. Thomas every day?"

"I just started today. I took the downtown ferry from Charlotte Amalie and hopped the VITRAN bus at the dock."

"Neither of them are reliable," she said. "The downtown ferry's expensive and they run it only when they feel like it, and the bus can and does break down and people end up having to get off and hitchhike. You should check the bulletin boards around Coral Bay for people with a room to rent, or somebody who needs a house sitter."

X, who had been listening to their conversation while she talked with Icebox Bob, turned back toward them. "Bethany's a professional rescuer. She's got to take care of everybody. If I were you, Robert, I'd turn my life over to her. She'll find you a place to stay, help you buy a cheap car that runs well, and cook you the finest fish and chips in Coral Bay." She touched the shoulder strap of Bethany's apron. "There's them that say she could feed all the down and outers of Coral Bay on her fish and chips."

"Ignore her," Bethany told Robert. "X is a good soul, but she's full of bananas."

Wiping the bar with an already dirty rag, Robert shook his head and looked from X to Bethany. "I appreciate your advice, both of you, but I can take care of myself. This is only my first day at Dante's Landing." He glanced at his watch. "My first two hours, actually. I'll commute from St. Thomas for a while. If the job pans out I'll look for a place to stay."

"You can crash with me anytime," Icebox Bob said. "I got a nice little house trailer out on King Hill Road, just before it starts up the mountain. Ten bucks a night, if you need it."

X snorted. "It's a nice place if you don't mind donkeys pawing the ground and making their hideous noises all through the night, and roosters and goats waking you up before the sun rises. I stayed there one night when I first came to the island and that old goat of a rooster sitting right here next to me this morning was worse than all those animals put together with their braying and cockadoodling and bleating outside the window."

"I didn't hear no complaints about the breakfast I fixed you," Icebox Bob said.

"Breakfast was fine." X touched his cheek. "And you're not a bad old coot."

Bethany jumped from the stool, pointing at the clock. "It's going to get busy here any minute. This place will be swarming with tourists and snowbirds and regulars from now until closing time."

"I get off at six," Robert said.

"Unless Boozie doesn't come in." When she saw his eyebrows go up, Bethany said, "Boozie's the night shift bartender."

Robert chuckled. "Having a bartender named Boozie doesn't seem to make good business sense."

Icebox Bob slapped the bar. "The good thing about him is that he really knows his drinks."

"A good skill for a bartender," Robert said.

"They say he makes the meanest margarita on the island." Icebox Bob emptied his beer and raised it toward Robert. "Another, please."

With raised eyebrows, Bethany said, "Boozie surely does know his drinks, and that's good for Skipper Dan's business, but there's a downside, one that always comes with alcohol. He loves to drink them. Sometimes he'll come in late, or he won't come in at all and then the day bartender has to stay until Skipper finds somebody to fill in for him, which he can't always do."

"He never mentioned that."

"Would you have taken the job if he had?"

Robert looked around the building. On the bay side, the waters were deep blue, small waves rippling out from boats that moved in and out of the harbor. A pelican dove into the waters at the end of the dock and heard the splash over the sounds from the stereo. Above, frigate birds circled, soaring on wings that reminded him of pictures in a dinosaur book he had owned as a child. He thought they looked like jagged cracks in the sky.

"I suppose I would have taken it if I'd seen the place."

Suspended on a thin wire hanging from the beam was a mobile made up the battered soles of sneakers, flip-flops, shoes and sandals. A sign on the wire read, *The Lost Soles of Coral Bay.*

Seeing Robert looking at it, Bethany said, "I picked them up on various beaches and put that thing together. It's amazing how many of them you can find on the rocks and under the sea grapes and palms along the shoreline."

A recycled telephone pole on one side of the bar, one of several supporting the roof, was covered with business cards from all over the world. Across the room, another bore photographs, including ancient and faded Polaroid shots of tourists, some with a young Skipper Dan, many hoisting beer cans and plastic cups, presumably filled with drinks, all smiling as if having the time of their lives. A chalk board to the left of the bar listed sandwiches, dinners and desserts, the swipe of an erasure mark beneath the price list of each item, evidence of recent changes in the cost of a meal.

A dart board hung on the opposite wall. A few feet below it and to the right was a five step staircase leading to a grassy yard with picnic tables and a small covered stage, the slogan *Hear the Music of Paradise*, painted in colorful letters on the fascia board. Reading the words and chuckling at what he regarded as a contradiction in terms, Robert pointed at a bony kitten with a notched left ear. It had crawled out from beneath the stage, dragging its left rear leg as it moved across the yard.

"Somebody ought to put that poor thing out of its misery," he said.

Bethany took one look and was down the stairs in a single leap. Scooping up the kitten, she held it close to her chest, stroking its head and speaking to it in soft tones, almost chanting, as she carried it back into the bar.

"It'll be fine with some food and TLC," she said.

Laughing, X said, "There she goes, saving something again. Bethany always has to save something, like it's her mission in life to keep people and critters from suffering."

"Only if they deserve it." Bethany's voice was sharp, and Robert noticed a hard glint in her eyes.

X said, "Last year she kept an old West Indian fisherman on her boat for a month while he recovered from a heart attack, which he never did, by the way. She came back from work one night and found him dead, lying on the deck with an empty hook on a line next to him." She looked at Robert. "And you know what? She paid for his funeral."

"Of course I did," Bethany said. "He was from St. Kitts and didn't have any family here. What did y'all want me to do, toss him overboard and let the fish have him?"

Icebox Bob said, "That's what I would have done. Hey, he got fish his whole life; it'd be right and proper for the fish to get him in the end."

Bethany waved her free hand at him and tsked several times. Then she went to a storage room and returned with an empty cardboard carton. Padding it with rags, she set the kitten inside and hand fed it a small bit of hamburger she took from a refrigerator behind the bar.

"You'll be just fine, kitty," she whispered to it.

"Another helpless useless critter," X said.

"An innocent one," Bethany said.

Robert thought her smile was radiant.

Five

SHORTLY AFTER NOON, two men in flowered shirts came in and sat at the end of the bar. They spoke in loud voices that got louder as afternoon gave way to the long shadows of early evening. An hour after Robert's shift was supposed to be over, Boozie had not shown up and he was still behind the bar when a woman complained to him that one of the men had approached her in the hall outside the rest rooms in what she described as a threatening manner.

"It's not the first time he's done something like that, and he's big and scary," she said. "Those two have been coming in here for days, harassing women. They followed my friend Liza to her car one night and that same one that just bothered me pressed up against her so hard that she had a bruise on her back from the hood ornament."

"I'm just a bartender," Robert said.

The woman's nostrils flared and her eyes narrowed. "You could throw them out."

"It's not my place. I just work here."

She snorted. "You could stop serving them; tell them they're flagged for the night. Listen to them, practically screaming at the football game on the TV."

"I could ask them to quiet down."

"And to stop harassing women. That big one especially."

He shrugged and was about to speak to them when Boozie, the evening bartender, arrived an hour late. Bethany introduced them and Robert explained the problem and turned it over to him.

"I'll keep an eye on them," Boozie said, looking at his watch. "If they don't leave in an hour or so, I'll tell them to cool it."

Robert shrugged and turned away. With his shift over and Boozie behind the bar, he needed a drink or two before catching the bus back to Cruz Bay where he would hop a ferry to St. Thomas.

Boozie was accompanied by a small West Indian woman who looked at him with a worried expression. Putting on an apron, he took his place behind the bar. A thin wiry man in his forties, with dark hair and sunken eyes, he wore a sleeveless t-shirt. His left arm had a tattoo of Pooh and Christopher Robin, each holding a balloon. Batman glared from beneath his cowl on the right upper arm. In spite of looking as though life's hard deals weighed heavily on him, adding years to his appearance, his mustache and beard gave the scraggly impression of the first growth on an adolescent's face. Jaundiced, his skin a sickly yellow, his eyes yellow and watery, Robert instantly diagnosed him as a man with serious liver disease.

"Do not let these people run you ragged tonight," the West Indian woman told Boozie, looking worriedly over at the two men. The larger of the two stood with his arms folded over his chest, staring at two women who were walking toward the rest rooms. She sat on a stool beside the cash register and waved to Bethany, who came over and kissed her cheek.

"You come to watch over your man?" Bethany looked at Robert. "This is Gloria, Boozie's wife."

"His keeper be more like it," Gloria said, giving Boozie a stern look. "No drinking on the job tonight, you understand? I cannot stay here all night while you work. It should not be my job to keep you on the straight and narrow, you understand me? When I go home you got to behave yourself. Understand, me mon?"

Boozie, his lips drawn, nodded and flashed a narrow smile.

Wearing a blue dress with small white dots, and a round straw hat that barely covered the top of her head, Gloria had a yellow hibiscus in her hair over her right ear. A string of artificial pearls hung around her neck. She leaned toward Boozie. "And move slow. These drunks can wait an extra thirty seconds for their fix without you killing yourself to wait on them. You understand?"

Boozie smiled and nodded a second time.

Gloria sighed and turned back to Bethany. "That man. He drinks too much and he will not go to church with me and he works too hard trying to fix our house that got caught in the landslide after the last storm. He is killing himself."

"You just have to do your best by him and pray. When all else is said and done, we alone are responsible for our condition."

"Lord knows I pray," she said, and laughed. "I pray and I work with him and I work on him, and I watch over him."

"Sometimes I think she believes she's God," Boozie said.

Gloria's head whipped around, her eyes stabbing him. "That is not funny, mon."

Boozie's face tightened. "You're right. Sorry."

"I don't think he meant it," Bethany said.

"It does not matter if he meant it or not. It is blasphemous."

Bethany moved her head slightly and smiled at Gloria. "You can't force people to have faith. All you can do is live according to your beliefs and be an example to them. If they're ready, you'll touch their hearts. If they're not, you can talk to them until you're blue in the face about the Gospel and God's love and they'll never hear you. Boozie will be ready when he's ready or he'll be damned and burn in hell for all eternity."

There was a tone of harsh satisfaction in Bethany's voice as she spoke of Boozie's potential damnation.

Boozie's looked from Gloria to Bethany, his face red.

"As far as that man in concerned, sometimes I believe I am exampled out," Gloria said, and shook her head in frustration. "Look at him, all yellow skin and yellow eyes and so thin that sometimes I cannot see him when he turns sideways. He gets thinner and sicker every day." She lowered her voice. "What am I going to do?"

"You love him," Bethany stated.

"I do."

"Then take him to a doctor," said Robert, who stood at the bar between Gloria and Bethany, a gin and tonic in his right hand. Boozie had moved to the far end of the bar and was taking orders from three middle-aged men. They were talking loudly, insisting on top label liquors in their drinks.

Gloria's shoulders sank. "And pay the doctor with what? Everything we got goes into fixing up the house."

"I can't answer that," Robert said.

"I can lend you some money," Bethany said.

Gloria shook her head. "I cannot take your money, girl."

"Borrowing isn't taking. It's a loan, not a gift."

"He would not go to a doctor anyway. The man says doctors do not know everything."

Boozie, who had come back at the end of the conversation, coughed and held his chest. "She's got that right," he said.

"They can't know everything," Robert said. "But they're pretty good at what they do know. For instance, I can look at your skin and eyes and tell you that the kind of jaundice you have could be an indication of cirrhosis or hepatitis."

"You a doctor?" Gloria asked.

Robert was about to say he was, then hesitated and shook his head. "I had an uncle who died of cirrhosis. He looked like your husband."

"He must have been an ugly uncle," Teach said. Nutty Betty, sitting several stools away, beside Pilgrim Jack, laughed and lit a cigarette, coughing heavily as she inhaled.

It was the first time Robert had heard Teach speak. His voice was deep and rasping. Studying his face, pale and blank of expression Robert thought briefly of creatures that lived deep beneath the earth, moving in a netherworld where the sun never shines. It was not a face one expects to find on a tropical island. With a second chill of discomfort, he looked away and noticed X watching him.

The instant their eyes met, she picked up her drink and turned to speak with Nutty Betty, who was still coughing, her cigarette dangling from her lips. Robert considered approaching her and starting a conversation, but it was nearly time for the next bus to Cruz Bay. He was about to leave when a young woman wearing a brightly colored sarong cursed and slapped the taller of the two men in flowered shirts.

"Scum," she said, and raised her hand to slap him again.

Laughing, he grabbed her wrist and twisting her arm behind her, forced her to her knees. The second man leaned over, pushing his face close to hers. "Don't mess with the Bear."

"He touched me," she said, her voice tight with fury.

"Listen to Sonny," the man called Bear said.

X left her stool and crossing the room, disappeared.

"Consider yourself lucky," Sonny said. "The Bear likes to give hugs. Most women would be grateful for a little loving from Bear."

"That's enough." Surprised at himself, even as he did it, Robert quickly moved toward them and put his hand on Bear's arm. "Let her go and enjoy your drink."

Still laughing, the Bear increased pressure on her. At the same time, he swung his leg out and tripped Robert. He fell to the floor, his head crashing against the side of the bar.

"See," the second man said. "Don't mess with Bear."

Robert tried to sit up, but Bear pushed him down with his foot. "Like I said, listen to Sonny," Bear told him.

"Bear's the man," Sonny said. "Nobody messes with the Bear and gets off easy."

"Ignore him, Sonny," Bear said. "He's an idiot trying to be a hero. Don't waste your time trying to make him understand."

Abruptly releasing his grip on the young woman's wrist, Bear grinned at Sonny. She fell to the floor, her head next to Robert's. He tried to get up, but she gently pushed him back down. "Not now," she whispered.

X returned with Skipper Dan who was swinging a raised baseball bat.

"You boys better leave right now," he said.

His hand in his pocket, Sonny took a step toward him. Bear rested a hand on his shoulder. "Not now, pal. Save it for later. Let's go."

The two men went to the exit for the dock and walked out into the night. A few minutes later Dante's Landing was filled with sound of twin diesel engines roaring across the bay.

Robert sat up, his head bleeding from a cut where it had hit the corner of the bar. The young woman sat next to him.

"Thanks," she said.

"I didn't do much."

"You tried. They're gone."

Skipper Dan helped Robert to his feet. "They came in a few days ago on that Cheoy Lee motor yacht you see moored out off Calabash Boom, the seventy-eight footer. I thought they'd have sailed on by now, but they seem to be hanging around for some reason."

"Probably waiting on a drug deal," X said.

Robert asked, "Why didn't anybody call the police when this started?"

Pilgrim Jack signaled Boozie for a refill. "There ain't no police in Coral Bay. They know better."

"He's right," Skipper Dan said. "A few years ago V.I. Police Department opened a sub-station at that little shopping center around the corner from here, by Aqua Bistro. They closed it after the cops they assigned to it said it was too far from everything and too dark at night. They were frightened, their union rep said."

"Frightened of what?" Robert asked.

Boozie's grin revealed a mouth with one front top tooth and three bottom teeth missing. He spread his arms wide, as if to encompass the entire pavilion. "Us. All of us. We scare the daylights out of cops and bad guys."

"They're not scared," Nutty Betty said. "They don't want to work. The local police are worthless."

"She's got that right," Icebox Bob said.

"They're not all bad," Bethany said. "I believe most of them are right sick over the bad apples in the department."

"That looks like a nasty cut on your head," Skipper Dan told Robert, ignoring Bethany's comment.

Robert touched it and gave him a dismissive grunt. "It's superficial. Scalp lacerations often look a lot worse than they are. Just wash it with a little vodka and tape a napkin over it."

Skipper Dan dabbed at the cut with a vodka drenched rag.

"That's the best use for alcohol," Bethany said, gesturing toward the bar. "Look at what it does to them." Pilgrim Jack, Nutty Betty and Mechanic Mike, bleary-eyed and slumping, rested their elbows on top of the bar, their heads hanging, drinks clutched in their hands. The Liquid Plumber snored, a half empty glass still in his hand.

"It pays my bills," Skipper Dan said. "Yours too, what with what I pay you and the tips you get from serving them."

She sighed. "It does, but it grieves me something fierce."

"Fierce enough to quit?"

Waving at him, she smiled and shook her head. "Not yet, Skipper. Maybe someday, but not yet."

Robert touched the bandages. The wound was sore and he winced slightly. "I've got a ferry to catch."

"You've missed the bus," Skipper Dan said.

Bethany took Robert's arm and pointed at the one empty table in the place. "You sit down. I'm ordering you a hamburger and a soda and a chef's salad. My treat. Then I'll take you to Cruz in time for the ten o'clock ferry to Red Hook."

Skipper Dan said, "And I'll pick you up in the morning. I've got to be in town to pick up a load of supplies that's coming on the early boat from downtown. If you're on it, we can have breakfast and I'll bring you out to Coral Bay."

"Sounds like a plan," Robert said, and let Bethany lead him to the table.

Six

LOOKING AT THE pressure-treated wooden bench that served as the Samurai's front seat, Robert rested a hand on the canvass top of Bethany's car. The car was streaked with moonlight coming through the branches of the huge flamboyant tree under which it was parked. "This is one of the most beat up unreliable looking cars I've ever seen."

"It runs," she said. "It'll take you to Cruz Bay as quick as any car on St. John."

"I'd guess that's because the roads here are so narrow and twisting that nobody can get up any decent speed on them."

"That's the truth, Mr. Robert, but that doesn't mean that my car should be disrespected."

He felt his face flush. "No disrespect intended."

She laughed. "I was teasing you."

Robert's flush deepened. "Sorry. I'm not used to being teased."

"My gracious, Mr. Robert, have you led an overly serious life?"

"I'm afraid I have."

She climbed in the Samurai and turned the key. The engine started immediately and ran smoothly. "Sounds real good, doesn't it?"

Robert slid onto the bench. "No seat belts?"

She shook her head. "There's nothing to bolt them to; the undercarriage is almost completely rusted out. I just get in, start it up and drive with faith in my heart."

"You mean you have imaginary seat belts."

She spoke through tight lips. "I wouldn't put it that way, Mr. Robert."

He thought he heard ice in her voice and changed the subject. "How does it pass inspection?"

"It's an island car. People understand island cars. They pass inspection."

"Things certainly are different here," Robert said.

"Where are you from?"

"Massachusetts," he said in a deliberately vague manner. "You?"

"A little town in the North Carolina mountains that nobody has ever heard of in a little county that nobody outside of the mountains has ever heard of."

"Try me."

"Newland. It's the county seat of Avery County, North Carolina with a population of a little less than seven hundred people, according to the 2010 census."

"Never heard of it."

She laughed. "I told you that not many people have, and especially you Yankees."

They were pulling out of the parking area behind Dante's Landing when Robert noticed light and the sounds of singing coming from five arched windows in a large building with a pyramidal roof.

"That's the St. John Singers getting ready for a concert," Bethany said. "They're always looking for recruits. Do you sing?"

"I'm tone deaf," he said, knowing that mentioning his dislike of music could challenge people to argue and attempt to save him from what Maria had called a deprivation of the spirit. "Music is the celebration of the soul," she once told him.

"That's the Emmaus Moravian Church," Bethany said. "It was built in 1872 and is one of the most beautiful buildings on St. John. We could stop in and listen for a while, if you'd like."

"I wouldn't like."

She glanced at him, her eyes sad. "You sound bitter, Mr. Robert."

He did not respond as he struggled to ignore an unexpected wave of bleak futility. He could not banish the sudden memory of that October day when he had stood in his doorway, the house empty behind him, watching the snow of an unexpected autumn storm drift into Maria's departing footprints.

Driving past the church, light streaming from its arched windows washed over Robert's head. Bethany recognized the look on his face. She had seen it often on the faces of Coral Bay, a place where people came after leaving behind the pains and heartbreaks and misdeeds that plagued them in what many of them had come to call the real world. "Welcome to paradise," was the typical greeting they gave newcomers and returning friends, the words often tinged with irony. For Bethany, Coral Bay was more purgatory than paradise; a place of absolution where people came to wash away the residue of the world they had known before setting foot on St. John. Where she had come.

She drove, both hands on the wheel, her eyes on the road. She slowed to a stop as they came abreast of three adult donkeys with two colts. From a bag on the bench between them, she took a handful of carrots and held them out to the colts. A large male lunged forward. Slapping the end of his snout, she reached down to the colts, giving each of them several carrots. That done, she emptied the remains of the bag's contents on the ground for the adults and drove off, the donkeys chewing on carrots and watching the rear lights of the Samurai disappear around a bend.

"Do you always do that?" Robert asked.

"Only when I have a bag of carrots or something else they like."

"It's a nice thing to do."

She looked over at him, but responded with only a small smile, wondering how long he would last at Dante's Landing. Taking the downtown ferry from St. Thomas in the mornings would be relatively simple, but there was no evening downtown boat. The ferry to Red Hook was a short trip, but for Robert to get home to Frenchtown necessitated a long and expensive taxi ride after the ferry docked. Most people who commuted from St. Thomas to St. John, West Indians and Continentals, came over early and left St. John either on the last downtown boat at 3:30, or on the five o'clock ferry to Red Hook, where they had parked their cars and trucks.

"If you're of a mind to keep on working at the Landing, you might should find a place to live on St. John," she said.

Smiling inwardly at the sound of her Carolina accent and phrasing, Robert nodded and closed his eyes, the memory of the moment of Maria carrying Grace away still on his mind. He was shaken from his thoughts when Bethany swerved to avoid a small deer that ran in front of them.

"That was a close one," she said, her hands tight on the wheel.

Robert, startled, watched the deer's white tail disappear into the thick bush along the road. "You've got quick reflexes."

"I couldn't sleep if I hit a critter. Back home, I killed a dog once and you know, Mr. Robert, that poor thing haunted my dreams for a year or more. I got out of the car and it was just lying there, taking its last few breaths, and it turned its head and looked at me with the saddest eyes I ever have seen. I reached town to pet it and say I was sorry, and you know what that dog did?"

"Of course, it bit you."

"It licked my fingers, Mr. Robert. My lord, I'd killed that poor innocent creature and before it died, it licked my hand. It forgave me."

"Maybe it was trying to bite you and didn't have the strength. What you took to be a lick was a failed attempt at biting you."

She shook her head. "You know it when you're forgiven. There's no mistaking the miracle of forgiveness. That dog forgave me and came as close to kissing my hand as I believe a dog can come."

"You're very fortunate," Robert said, the words automatic, without feeling.

Bethany glanced over at him. They were passing through an area where thick jungle grew on either side of the road, the heavy canopy above them blocking the stars and moon and he appeared to be nothing more than a dark shadow on the bench beside her. She turned on the radio. Beethoven's Ninth was playing on WVGN, the St. Thomas public radio station. They rode the rest of the way to Cruz Bay with Bethany humming the "Ode to Joy."

Bethany stopped by the entrance to the Cruz Bay ferry dock just as he boat crew was pulling up the gangplank. "You better run," she said.

Robert jumped from the Samurai. Racing toward the ferry, he waved and called his thanks back to her and leapt from the dock to the ferry just as the boat was pulling away. A crew member grabbed his arm to steady him.

"Easy, mon," he said. "I got you."

Winded, Robert collapsed into a seat. Minutes later, the cabin—despite being open to the sea—was filled with the odor of diesel smoke. Rallying his strength, Robert climbed the ladder to the upper deck. It was empty and he lay down on a seat, his hands behind his head, and looked up at the stars, the sky almost pale with moonlight.

He thought of Boozie's jaundice and how close he had come to revealing his medical training. The last thing he wanted was for people to come to him, seeking information on their ailments and injuries. That was his past, saving people from the indignities of illness and pain. He had no idea about the future. He imagined that it could mark a return to medicine, someday, but no time soon, perhaps not for years; then again, perhaps never. The future held nothing. There was no promise. There was no hope. There would be tomorrow, and another ferry ride to St. John and another shift at Dante's Landing, but that was as far ahead as he wanted to think, indeed, as far ahead as he could think.

Up until today, his life in the islands had been little more than waking up in his room, wandering down to Hook, Line and Sinker, drinking until he was numb before wandering back to his room and sinking into a mystery novel of the sort that in his earlier life he would have never considered reading. He would finally fall asleep, the book on his chest, his bedside lamp burning. He would wake up at least twice through the night, but each time he would turn on his side and lie there for long minutes before falling off again. He would leave the light on, banishing any shadows that might otherwise surround his bed.

Today had been a welcome break in a routine that was already growing old. He looked forward to another day at his new job. Even on the first day, the Landing had given him a sense of place. He felt as though he had taken ankle deep steps in a journey that could take him below the surface of island life, to where people lived in a community that bound them together. Dante's Landing in Coral Bay was unlike anyplace he had ever been, and he liked the way he felt after a day of working there. He looked forward to going back.

He awoke as the ferry docked. Later, jammed into a passenger van with sixteen other people, he endured the ride from Red Hook to Charlotte Amalie, and finally to the small house in Frenchtown. The house was dark, the old man snoring in his bedroom. Once in his own bed, Robert studied *The Bartender's Bible* for half an hour, then picked up the mystery he'd been reading, sure that the depraved characters in the novel were the products of the author's fevered imagination and could never exist in the real world.

He dropped off to sleep. As he expected, he awoke several times through the night, tossed in the bed and fumbled with his covers before falling back to sleep. He did not know if he dreamed. Given his troubled sleep, he assumed that he did, and that his dreams had not been pleasant. But if there were dreams, he did not remember them.

Seven

BETHANY WAITED to see if Robert made the boat. When she saw him jump aboard, she returned to the Samurai and drove back to Coral Bay. Dante's Landing was closing when she parked beneath the flamboyant tree. Bear and Sonny had returned and were following two women to their cars. They hovered over them, laughing and poking their shoulders. Bethany picked up a handful of rocks and threw them at the two men. They turned away from the women they had been taunting and charged her. The women jumped in their car and sped from the parking area. Bear and Sonny gave Bethany menacing looks as they moved toward her.

She ran into Dante's Landing. Boozie was wiping the bar and Skipper Dan pushed a hand-truck carrying a stainless steel beer keg across the floor. Teach, Pilgrim Jack, Mechanic Mike, Icebox Bob and Bull Durham were still sitting on their stools, nursing their last drinks. Nutty Betty was asleep, her head cradled in her arms. The Liquid Plumber had awakened enough to order and drink one last beer and shot of whiskey. There was no sign of X.

"Those two bullies from the Cheoy Lee are after me," Bethany called and ran across the floor. Bear and Sonny came through the door, a jagged tear on Bear's right cheek where one of Bethany's rocks had hit him. Blood dripped from his face onto his flowered shirt. He saw Bethany and moved quickly toward her, his huge hands balled into tight fists.

Skipper Dan set the hand-truck upright and reached for the baseball bat still leaning against the wall outside his office. Seeing him raise it in striking position, Bear laughed, swerved away from Bethany and bore down on Skipper, his arms outstretched, his fists open, his fingers in a claw like formation raking the air.

"You're a dead man, Babe Ruth," Bear cried.

Skipper Dan swung the bat. Hit on the side of the head, Bear dropped to the floor.

"Home Run," Boozie called. "Skipper Dan's rounding second and headed for third and there's nothing to stop him."

Bear raised himself on an elbow for a moment, then sighed and fell back down. "I'll sue you for this," he said. "This bar and everything else you've got will be mine."

"That's right, Bear. It'll all be yours." Sonny's head popped up and down with each word.

Bethany laughed. "You look like one of those drinking birds that ducks up and down over a glass of water."

"Get him out of here," Skipper Dan said to Sonny.

"You'll be sorry," Sonny said to him. "Bear will bury you."

"Get him out," Skipper Dan repeated.

"I'll need help," Sonny said. "He's too big for me."

Without speaking, Bull Durham and Pilgrim Jack left their seats, picked Bear up and carried him out to the dock. Sonny went ahead and stopped at a boat with twin outboards. "That's his dinghy. Just put him in it and I'll take him out to the boat."

"Some dinghy," Bull Durham said.

"There's folks in Coral Bay that could take a tarp and live on a boat like that," Pilgrim Jack said.

They dropped Bear with a thud into the bottom of the dinghy. Sonny jumped in and tried to start the engines. "I don't have the key," he said.

"It's in my pocket," Bear said, his voice a barely audible mumble.

"Not there," Sonny to Bear said after several minutes of looking. "Maybe it fell out when Babe Ruth sideswiped you with his bat."

"So go look," Bear said.

They all looked, but the keys seemed to be lost.

"What should I do?" Sonny asked Bear, but Bear had fallen asleep and was snoring. Sonny tried to wake him, but Bear turned over and snored louder.

"Looks like you boys are going to spend the night on your dinghy," Skipper Dan said.

"We got no blankets or anything to keep warm with," Sonny said.

"Ain't that a shame?" Mechanic Mike grinned. "I guess you're just going to have to paddle out to your yacht using your hands."

"I can't do that." Sonny's voice was small, like that of a bewildered child.

Pilgrim Jack looked at Mechanic Mike. "Yeah, ain't that a real shame."

"Sleep well," Skipper Dan said. "And don't come back to Dante's Landing again. You two are permanently flagged."

Back inside, he and Boozie and Bethany continued shutting the Landing for the night. Skipper Dan took the cash register into his office where he placed it in the safe along with the day's receipts. Everything done, they shooed out the remaining drinkers and closed and locked the iron gate. Teach was the last to go.

Skipper Dan had kept the baseball bat with him. He said to Bethany, "Before I take Boozie home, he and I are walking you to your dinghy."

"You don't have to, but I'd like it if you did," she said.

"I want to make sure those two don't cause you any trouble."

"You home-runned the trouble out of that Bear guy," Boozie said.

Looking from Boozie to Bethany, Skipper Dan smiled. "And I want to make sure you don't pull one of your classic Bethany good deeds and get all tender-hearted and take those two out to their yacht in your dinghy."

"I'd be a fool to do that," she said.

"But you'd do it."

She shook her head. "Not a chance."

"You've done things almost as stupid; you and your forgiving ways."

"But I wouldn't do anything for those two. Some people don't deserve forgiveness."

Skipper Dan looked at her with surprise, but said nothing.

"They're bad news," Boozie said.

Skipper Dan nodded. "They're dangerous, especially Bear."

"I'm going straight to my boat and to bed," Bethany said. "Those two can rot in their dinghy for all I care."

TEN MINUTES LATER she climbed up the boat ladder to the deck of *The Saved Wretch.* Yanking the pull cord on the generator she kept to run her cube refrigerator, a few lights and a small television set with aluminum foil on its rabbit ears antenna, she opened a can of root beer and flopped into a folding canvas chair. It was moon noon, the moon's silver path on the Caribbean leading away from Coral Harbor toward the British Virgin Islands. For a moment she thought she could hear music coming across the water from *The William Thornton,* a floating restaurant and bar on an old schooner anchored off Norman Island, but realized it probably came from one or more of the houses on nearby hillsides.

She had been to the *Willy-T* once. Bobby Carson, a Coral Bay charter boat captain, took her over one Saturday afternoon. She found it charming, the food good and the location idyllic, until several charter boats sailed in and tied up to the *Willy-T's* floating dock, and the bartender and waiters provided free drinks for each woman who would climb to the deck above the captain's cabin, strip to her undershorts, and to the accompaniment of men chanting and rhythmically clapping their hands, dive into the water below, swim to the dock and climb aboard, either feigning indifference to, or reveling in the men's leers and comments.

"Those women have no respect for themselves, and the men in this place surely have no respect for those women," she told her date.

Carson argued that everyone was just having a good time.

"You let that happen when you take charters out?" she asked.

"People do what they're going to do. They pay me for food, drink and to take them around the islands so they can have a good time. They most decidedly do not pay me to monitor their behavior. I don't tolerate violence on my boat, but almost everything else goes."

She had tried to make him understand her objections to such goings on, on both religious and moral grounds, but he had shaken his head and laughed at her, saying she was an old-fashioned prude.

"There's no shame in being an old-fashioned proud," she said. "If finding that kind of behavior disgusting makes me a prude, then I'm a proud prude."

They had laughed together at her self-description, but he never asked her out again and she was relieved. When they ran across one another, as is bound to happen often on an island as small as St. John, they would hug and chuckle together over how their cruise to Norman Island had ended any chance of them getting involved. It was just as well, she knew. She was not destined for romantic entanglements.

She finished the root beer and stood up. Across the bay, anchored a hundred feet off Calabash Boom, she saw the hulk of the Cheoy Lee outlined against the moonlit water. There were no lights aboard and she thought with some pleasure of Sonny and Bear sleeping on the open motor launch docked by Dante's Landing. Serves them right, she thought, and it served Bear right to get conked on the head with Skipper Dan's baseball bat. People need to be punished when they do bad things. Some people deserved eternal punishment, she believed. Perhaps Bear and Sonny were two of them. She decided she would probably never know, but she smiled at the memory of Skipper Dan with the baseball bat, pleased by the thought of Bear having a headache for days, glad that both he and Sonny would spend the night shivering at dockside, their launch banging against the pilings of the dock every time a wave came up or a passing boat sent its wake to break against the hull.

Going below, she put on her pajamas, brushed her teeth and pulled back the covers on her bunk. Making sure her digital book was fully charged, she went back on deck and shut down the generator. A sailboat was coming down the middle of the moon path, its sails full. She rested her hands on a railing and watched as it moved closer. As beautiful as the mountains of home were, she was elated by the sight of sails on moon path, of the distant stars burning in the night sky, lights from boats and those from homes and business on the land, all reflected in the night time waters surrounding St. John. She believed they were among the most beautiful sights in creation.

She did not move until the passing sailboat stopped at a mooring and she heard the flapping of sails being lowered, the clanking of standing rigging and halyards against the aluminum mast and human voices echoing across the water as the crew called instructions back and forth. Then a generator went on and lights shone from the boat and she turned and went below, where she lay down and picked up her electronic book, returning to an Agatha Christie novel she had been trying to finish for several days.

After reading the first paragraph three times, she let it fall to the blanket and was surprised to find herself thinking of the new bartender. Robert. He never mentioned his last name. She smiled. He may not have been down here very long, but already he was reticent about his life before coming to the islands. It was a sign that he might truly belong in Coral Bay. "Massachusetts," he had said when she asked where he came from. Not Amherst, or Boston, or Northampton, or any town, any place that had a particularity about it. Just Massachusetts.

His vague reply fit with the hollow look of his eyes, the rare smile, the absence of lightness about him. Loneliness. She thought there was a deep loneliness about him. Loneliness for true human contact was something she understood, something she often saw in the faces at Dante's Landing, but she sensed something deeper in his loneliness, a desperate solitude. Seeing that in him made her want to reach out to him. She wondered if she might find a way to touch his soul before his heart hardened and he was lost.

For she believed that was her mission, her *raison d'être*; she smiled, recalling the phrase from her French courses at Appalachian State. She was meant to bring deserving people to God and to do all she could to ensure the wicked were punished, and she knew God's punishment to be unforgiving and harsh. In her mind, the Old Testament was God's word.

The New Testament belonged to Jesus, but Jesus, she was sure, was God made man and God made man had mankind's flaws, including the weaknesses of having too much compassion, being too easy to forgive. Jesus' word was love, but God's word was law, a law above all other laws. She had internalized every letter of it, the words *Thou Shalt Not* burned into her mind. In her way of thinking, God's punishment outweighed Jesus' love

The bay was calm and *The Saved Wretch* bobbed gently. Her thoughts slowed and her eyelids grew heavy. She began to sleep, briefly roused by the sounds of rigging and halyards on nearby boats echoing softly from across the water. Finally falling into a deep sleep, she dreamed she was singing in a choir, surrounded by men and women in brightly colored robes, songs of faith and praise in perfect harmony as they rose into the cloudless heavens, the sun a brilliant orb shedding its golden light over the earth.

She was awakened by the roar of an outboard coming from shore. It passed less than ten feet from *The Wretch* and set her boat rocking in its wake. Torn from her dream, she sat up, shaking from the sudden disruption. Going above deck, she stood by the railing and looked toward the island. Most homes along the hillsides were dark and she pushed the stem on her watch to light the dial. It was 2:36. The outboard stopped and she heard a thud as it bumped the hull of a boat. The beam from a flashlight lit up the stern of the Cheoy Lee, and the sound of someone scrambling up a boat ladder carried across the water. Moments later the light was gone as whoever had boarded the Cheoy Lee went below. The moon had set and she could see nothing move in the bay. Yawning, she went back below and stretched out on her bunk. The wake had dissipated and the waters of the bay had calmed. *The Wretch* barely moved.

Shutting her eyes, she rolled onto her side and fell asleep.

Eight

AS PLANNED the night before, Robert took the early morning downtown ferry from St. Thomas. Skipper Dan met him at the Cruz Bay dock on St. John and they had coffee and toast, bacon, eggs and home fries in Cruz before driving out to Coral Bay in Skipper Dan's pickup. Upon arriving at the parking area outside the pavilion, they unloaded the truck and began carrying the cartons they had picked up at the ferry. At the entrance to Dante's Landing, they found the larger of the two dummies from Betty's Booty lying on the ground near their chairs.

Bear's body had been carefully placed where the dummy once sat. He had been killed by a single shot to the head. His arm was draped around the smaller dummy's shoulder. The entrance to the shop was on the bay side of the building, away from the road, the body hidden from the line of sight of anyone driving or walking by.

Robert touched Bear's neck and briefly lifted his arm. "Judging from the state of rigor and lividity, he's been dead for at least six hours."

Skipper Dan clucked his tongue. "Were you a cop back in the real world?"

Robert shook his head. "I read a lot of mysteries. We need to call the cops."

"The local cops are a pain in the butt and many of them are as crooked as a dog's hind leg. I'd rather put him in a dinghy, take him a couple of miles out to sea and toss the body in the water. With the cops nosing around I won't be able to open until at least after lunch, and with my luck, they could keep me closed all day. We don't have many murders on St. John. The cops won't have any idea about what to do. An informal burial at sea could save them a lot of trouble, and us the trouble of having them snooping around Coral Bay." He looked at the horrified expression on Robert's face, barked a nervous laugh and shook his head. "Rats. As much as I'd like to, we can't dump him. Somebody'd be sure to see us."

He dialed the police department on his cell phone and was put on hold. After fifteen minutes of waiting, he was shifted from one office to another before he managed to report the murder. Disconnecting, he clucked his tongue again. "You'll learn about the local cops soon enough," he said to Robert. "A lot of them are incompetent, corrupt and dangerous." He looked at his watch. "I'll bet you all your tips for the day that they won't even get out here for at least an hour. There was a proposal a few years back to have the Feds come in and run the Police Department. It came to nothing, but there were a lot of people who thought it was a great idea."

An hour and a half later two police SUV cruisers pulled into the parking lot, their sirens blaring, their blue lights flashing. Before examining the body, the five police officers from the cruisers cordoned off the area with yellow plastic crime scene ribbon. That done, they stood in a circle around Bear's body, hands on their hips. A small crowd gathered, including the Landing's regulars Robert had met the day before. They stood elbow to elbow with the cops.

"We got to wait for the medical examiner," said a cop who introduced himself as Sergeant Preston, much to the amusement of the Landing regulars. "Who killed this man?"

"That's your job to find out," the Liquid Plumber said. "Mine is to have a drink as soon as possible." He looked at Skipper Dan. "You've got to open soon."

Skipper Dan shrugged.

Sucking his teeth, Sergeant Preston gave the Liquid Plumber a dismissive glare. "Do not you worry, mon, we will find the killer, and perhaps you will not be so happy about that."

The Liquid Plumber looked longingly toward the locked and shuttered bar and turned to Icebox Bob. "We should head over to Skinny Legs. They open at ten."

"You will stay here," Sergeant Preston said. "You are witnesses to a crime."

"We didn't see a thing," Icebox Bob said. "He was dead when we got here."

"You try to leave and I will have to arrest you," Sergeant Preston said.

"I'm awful thirsty," the Liquid Plumber said.

Sergeant Preston sucked his teeth again and said nothing.

Fifteen minutes later, an ambulance pulled to a stop next to the cruisers. A tall heavy-set West Indian man got out of the passenger's seat. Wearing a gray suit with a white shirt and somber necktie, he carried a small satchel. Pinned to his jacket was a rectangular blue plastic badge, its white lettering bearing the name Willis G. Penn, Jr., MD. He nodded in the direction of Sergeant Preston and smiled at Skipper Dan, who walked up to him, hand extended. The two men shook and smiled at one another.

"What happened here, Skipper?" Penn asked.

Skipper Dan tilted his head toward Bear's Body. "We found him a little while ago when we came in to open the Landing."

"Do you know who he is and who killed him?"

"All I know is that he's called Bear. He and a friend have been hanging around the Landing for some time, annoying women and being generally belligerent. I had to kick them out last night. If I had to guess, I'd say it was his friend who did him in."

Willis Penn's voice was even. "Why?"

Skipper Dan shrugged. "Nobody here knew him or cared enough about him to kill him."

"Killing a man is a funny way of caring about him. Besides, you said he was annoying people."

"Annoyance isn't usually a motive for murder."

Willis Penn sighed. "Sometimes just looking at someone in the wrong way is enough to get you murdered." He stepped over the yellow crime scene tape and leaned down to look at the body. "Small caliber entry wound, a .22 I would guess." He turned to Sergeant Preston, ordering him to take some pictures. Nodding to the ambulance driver, who stood beside him, he said, "Grayson, as soon as the sergeant finishes with the pictures, get the bodies to the morgue at the clinic."

"Thanks for that, Doctor Will," Skipper Dan said. "I was afraid he'd be here all day."

"We do not want that to occur in this heat," Penn said.

"He's already been here for at least six hours," Robert said.

Penn gave him a suspicious look. "How do you know that?"

"I looked at his state of lividity and rigor."

"Are you a physician, sir?" Penn asked.

"I read novels about police procedures," Robert said.

Penn nodded in a distracted, disinterested manner and looked at Sergeant Preston, who had finished photographing the scene and stood idly a few feet away.

"Sergeant, help Grayson get the body in the back of the ambulance."

Sergeant Preston ignored him and turned to the small crowd of onlookers. "Did any of you hear shots last night?"

Teach laughed. "These island cars around here are always backfiring, so how can you tell if shots have been fired?"

"I could tell the difference. It would be no problem," Preston said. He glanced at each person standing in the small area between Betty's Booty and Dante's Landing. Folding his arms over his chest, he stood with his legs spread, his face expressionless.

Willis Penn pointed at Bear's body. "The corpse needs to be removed, Sergeant."

Preston gestured to one of the other police officers. "Mookie, help Grayson with the body."

Mookie shivered. "I do not touch the dead."

The other three policemen backed away and looked toward the waters of the Bay. The surface was crisscrossed by the wakes of small craft that buzzed in the background, moving among and between larger boats and the shore.

Robert smiled at Grayson and nodded toward the body. "I'll give you a hand."

Before putting him on stretchers, Grayson looked through Bear's pockets, finding a driver's license identifying him as Stanfield Paul Crowley of Toms River New Jersey. Crowley's wallet and pockets were stuffed with hundred dollar bills.

"I count over four thousand in bills." Grayson looked from Willis Penn to Sergeant Preston, waving the handful of money at them.

"Theft was clearly not the motive for the murder. Count it and write down the full amount. Then give it to me." Willis Penn turned to Skipper Dan and spoke quietly. "Unless I have both Grayson and Preston sign off on the amount and I take custody of it, that money will disappear into the depths of the police station never to be seen again."

"Not much faith in your fellow man?" Skipper Dan said.

"The only faith I have is in the good Lord. Grayson is a good cop, but Sergeant Preston is another matter altogether." Willis Penn lowered his voice. "I have heard rumors."

Skipper Dan raised his eyebrows. "About?"

Willis Penn pursed his lips, his forehead creasing. When he spoke, his voice was just loud enough for Skipper Dan to hear. "He is being investigated."

"For arrogance and stupidity?"

The medical examiner laughed and shook his head. "It is far more serious. The word is that he is involved in some criminal activity with a former colleague who now works as an enforcement officer for the Department of

Planning and Natural Resources."

"Criminal in what way?"

Taking a deep breath, Willis Penn looked away for a moment, then resumed his normal speaking voice. "It is of no matter to civilians. I have said too much. You may read about it in the paper some day."

"Sounds like a juicy story," Skipper Dan said.

Willis Penn smiled but said nothing, shifting his eyes to where Grayson counted the money Bear had been carrying. We he finished, the two men lifted the body into the back of the ambulance. Grayson signed the paper and passed it to Willis Penn, who handed it and a ballpoint pen to Sergeant Preston. Preston gave him a disdainful look, but signed the paper and gave it back.

"Can I open the Landing now?" Skipper Dan asked.

"Please," the Liquid Plumber said.

Preston shrugged and got into his cruiser.

BETHANY TIED her dinghy to a piling at the dock outside Dante's Landing.

"You missed the excitement," Skipper Dan said when she came from the supply room, tying the strings of a clean apron behind her back. He told her about the murder.

"He was not a good man," she said.

"Nobody deserves to be murdered," Skipper Dan said.

"You want me to pray for him," Bethany said. It was not a question.

"He's beyond prayer," Skipper Dan said.

"It's never too late for prayer," Bethany said. "It all depends on what you pray for. It might could be that I'd pray he gets the eternal punishment he deserves and burns in hell forever."

"Eternal punishment is worse than murder," Skipper Dan said. "If there's a God, he should allow for people to be purged of their sins."

"The fallen away may be purged of their sins, but not the truly fallen."

"There's a difference?"

Bethany closed her eyes and spoke as though reciting. "It's blasphemy to think that an evil person should suffer the judgment of God because of his sin only until he is found worthy to be with God. It's like saying that Jesus' atonement for our sins by suffering and dying on the cross is insufficient and must be completed through the suffering of the sinner until the sinner is ready to enter into Heaven. The truly wicked have rejected Jesus' sacrifice. There should be no end to their suffering and despair. It must go on eternally. That is the proper punishment for sin." Her voice grew harsh as she spoke and her final words sounded to Robert as though she were growling.

Skipper Dan smiled and lightly tapping her shoulder, looked at Robert who had just set a beer and shot of Jack Daniels in front of the Liquid Plumber. "She's a little crazy, you know."

Bethany whirled, her face crinkled in false rage. "Skipper Dan is a fool."

Robert raised both hands in surrender. "I'm keeping my mouth shut."

"Good move," Bethany said.

"Excellent move," Skipper Dan said.

"The Cheoy Lee is gone," Bethany said. "I woke up at sunrise as it was sailing out of the harbor and veered left toward British Virgin Island waters."

"Probably taking whoever killed that Bear away from the Virgin Islands," Teach said.

"Good riddance," said Mechanic Mike. He yawned and signaled for a refill.

"That's it? If the killer's on that boat, he's just gone and that's the end of it?" Robert asked.

Skipper Dan leaned on the bar opposite Robert. "There've only been a handful of murders in the twenty years I've been on St. John, one right here in Coral Bay. Either the killers are caught and turn out to be related to a cop or a judge or a member of the Legislature and end up getting the back of their hands slapped, like two I could name; or they're never caught, like the one here in Coral Bay. Of course, we all know who it was that did it, but no one was about to squeal, and if someone did, there was no way to prove it."

"Jesse James was an evil man," Bethany said.

Robert almost laughed. "Jesse James?"

"We called him that because everybody knew he was a thief and that he carried a gun under his shirt," Icebox Bob said. "Then one night he broke into a house up on the hill. He beat up on the old woman who lived there, left her for dead and stole over a thousand dollars. We knew this because the next day he showed up here with a pocketful of cash and was buying drinks for everybody in the place. The day after that they found his body, face down in the mangroves, his neck broken."

"And that's all right with you?" Robert looked from Bethany to Skipper Dan, to the regulars sitting at the bar.

Bethany glanced away, but Skipper Dan nodded, his face grim. "He was just another dead white man as far as the police were concerned. There were one or two articles in the paper, and it was forgotten within weeks, like Bear will be forgotten. They won't break any speed records in trying to find his killer."

"We look after our own," the Liquid Plumber said, taking a sip of his drink.

"It's not the best way," Pilgrim Jack said. "But sometimes it's the only way."

Robert shook his head. "There are laws. Civilization is built on law and the rule of law."

"There are laws and there are laws," Skipper Dan said. "There are Federal laws, and state laws, territorial laws, municipal laws. They're all built around carefully defined codes. And then there's the law of self-protection, and that goes for individuals and for the communities they live in. When codified laws don't work, when the state fails people, for whatever reason, the law of self-protection has to take over. That's what happened with Jesse James."

"Don't forget, he broke God's laws," Bethany said, but no one paid her any attention.

"And you think that's what happened with Bear?" Robert said. "That whoever killed this Jesse James killed him?"

"It couldn't have happened that way," Pilgrim Jack said. "The guy that killed him left the island less than a year later."

"Bear wasn't a nice guy," Skipper Dan said, "but we don't know if he deserved what happened to him."

"We held a beach party and raised enough money for the guy who killed Jesse James to fly back to the States and get started over once he got there," Pilgrim Jack said.

"We've got a mystery on our hands," Bethany said.

X clapped her hands. "I love mysteries."

Nine

ROBERT MOVED to St. John two weeks later. Without telling him, Bethany had contacted the owners of Coral View, one of the villas she looked after. A wealthy couple from Stone Mountain, Georgia, they used their island home for six weeks each year and were glad to have a permanent resident in the small apartment under the main section of the house. Located in Estate Carolina, a section of the island that included part of Coral Bay, Coral View was less than a mile from Dante's Landing.

"I found you a place to stay," she told him when he came to work for the fifth day.

"I've got a place."

"How's the night time commute to Frenchtown working out for you, Mr. Robert?"

"Not great."

"How's the job at the Landing working out?"

Robert smiled. "Pretty well."

"Wouldn't it be working out better if you could be home five minutes after finishing a day's work?"

"Probably."

"And if you move to St. John you won't have to pay for a ferry and taxi ride to get home. Plus, the people who own the villa where your apartment is aren't asking for rent. All they want is that you look after the property, pay the utilities and make sure the cistern is kept full. He's a retired doctor and she was a professor at Emory University in Atlanta."

"My apartment?"

"It could be."

"Are you a guardian angel?"

Bethany's chuckle sounded like rippling water. "I like to help people who I believe deserve it."

Teach spoke in a growl. "The stupid girl likes to help people, critters, beat-up old cars and anything else that she figures she can lead to some kind of improvement."

"You haven't looked at me closely. I haven't been a girl for a good many years." She flashed him a smile, speaking in a sweet voice tinged with steel.

"You're as pretty as one," Icebox Bob said.

"That's a fact," Pilgrim Jack said, turning to Robert. "If you wonder if she's an angel now, wait until you hear her sing at one of the open mike nights here."

"I've got no plans to do that again anytime soon," Bethany said.

"You'll do it," Pilgrim Jack said. "A person with a voice like yours who can play guitar like you do can't keep from doing it for any length of time. You owe it to yourself."

Bethany laughed and gave him a friendly dismissive wave as she tapped Robert's shoulder. "We should look at the apartment I found for you."

"We should?"

"You might not like it."

"And if I don't?"

"Then I'll have to find another place."

He sighed. "I guess I'm moving to St. John."

"You've got no choice," X said. "Next thing you know you'll be a full-fledged member of Bethany's congregation."

Robert turned to Bethany with a startled look. "Are you a minister?"

Bethany shook her head vigorously.

"She's more and less than a preacher," Durham Bull said, a hand-rolled cigarette hanging from between his lips. "She helped start a church right here in Coral Bay. Not that any of us go to it, you understand."

Bethany whirled and pointed at him. When she spoke there was no trace of humor in her voice. "And it won't be due to any fault of mine when you burn in hell, Mr. Durham Bull."

"She fixes things and people whenever, wherever she can," Skipper Dan said, pulling the cigarette from Durham Bull's mouth. "No smoking in Virgin Islands places of business, remember?"

"I like to help my friends." Bethany said.

"You hardly know me," Robert said.

"You're a fellow worker at Dante's Landing," she told him. "What else do I need to know? Now, let's go look at your apartment."

Robert looked around the bar. "Do I have a choice?"

"Probably not," Skipper Dan said.

"THIS IS SURELY a pretty fierce mile to walk after a hard day's work," Bethany said as she drove him up the steep road leading to Coral View's even steeper driveway. "You might want to get yourself a car of some sort."

"Like that heap of yours?" Robert laughed.

"It's reliable."

Coral View was a large home consisting of three separate buildings, all of reinforced concrete, its stucco covering painted white. Elaborate stonework planters and a stone archway covered the walk from the great house to the master bedroom, complemented by stone trim around the arched windows and doors of the pods, each of which contained two bedrooms and two baths.

Sitting on a large lot, the great house had a verandah that stretched along its full length. Robert stood on it and looked out over Coral Bay. To the left, he could see the southernmost string of the British Islands, from Norman Island, the closest, all the way to Virgin Gorda. The sea sparkled in the mid-morning sun.

"It's lovely," he said.

Bethany took his hand and guided him from the verandah to the patio behind the great house. "Wait until you see your rooms."

The apartment took up half of the area below the living room and kitchen of the great house, and included one bedroom with a bath and outdoor shower which was surrounded by a stone trellis covered with tropical vines and flowering bushes. There was a large living room with several couches and chairs, an entertainment center with shelves stacked with CDs and DVDs. An arched doorway led to a kitchen big enough for a dining table. Each room had French doors opening to a second verandah below the upper one, with an equally stunning view of Coral Bay and the BVI.

"Like it?" Bethany asked.

Robert said, "How could I not?"

"When do you want to move in? I could take my car in the barge to St. Thomas anytime and we could pick up your things."

"I can manage my stuff on the ferry."

She shook her head. "It will be much easier if I drive you over and back. Then you won't have to juggle your things in a taxi, the ferry and the VITRAN bus out here. Plus, you'd have to carry it all the way up here since the bus will drop you at the bottom of the hill."

Robert spread his arms and sighed. "I could do it tomorrow."

She shook her head. "I have church tomorrow."

"All day?"

"Morning services, followed by Sunday school, which I teach, and then

Bible study and evening prayer. The rest of the week is mine, except for Wednesday evening prayer meeting."

"At the church Durham Bull said you started?"

"I had help. You could come to it, you know."

Ignoring the invitation, he said, "How about after work on Monday for moving me?"

"Monday it is."

BY LATE MONDAY night he was sitting on the upper verandah at Coral View sipping from a glass of vodka over ice, his feet propped on the railing, his chair resting on its rear legs. Bethany sat in a chair beside him, a diet cola in her hand.

"What's great about this is that you have full run of the house except when the Chandlers are here." She took a sip, set her glass on the railing and walked from one end to the other of the verandah. Returning to where Robert stood, she leaned against a railing and let her eyes meet his. "Now, Mr. Robert, what is your story?"

Robert watched in silence as a cruise ship crossed a large stretch of the horizon. He was not ready to tell anyone his story, to share the humiliation he still felt when recalling that cold October storm that had invaded his heart the day he watched Maria's footprints fill with snow as she carried Grace away from the home they had shared.

"I thought the Coral Bay tradition was for people to let their pasts lie quietly in the past."

She nodded. "It is."

Robert cocked his head as he looked at her.

"You can let it remain there. That doesn't mean I can't ask."

"I understand."

"And I understand you're in pain. Anytime you want to share your burden with me, just blurt it out. I won't ask again."

"Thanks," he said.

She finished her soda and stood. "I've got to go. You'll find it an easy walk downhill to work in the morning. I'll drive you home until you get a car."

"So, I'm getting a car?" he said, laughing.

"I predict that you will."

"You can read the future?"

She did not laugh as she replied, "Sometimes I can."

Ten

X SAT AT the bar, a frozen margarita in front of her, slowly exhaling cigarette smoke through her nostrils. Skipper Dan was in town and Robert pointed to a small framed poster provided to Dante's Landing by the Virgin Islands Department of Health.

"No smoking," he said and read aloud the full warning on the poster.

X took another deep drag and blew the smoke toward him.

"Ah, Mon, let the lady smoke her cigarette in peace." The speaker was a tall West Indian known as Moonie, due to his round face and shaven head. A jack-of-all-trades, he made a living fishing, doing electrical wiring, small construction jobs, driving a safari bus for his uncle and, from time to time, doing landscaping work. Known around the Coral Bay area as a fine cook, he often filled in at various local restaurants when the regular cooks were unavailable. His true love, however, was wildcrafting—harvesting and selling local plants. He sat several seats away from X, a cigarette hanging from his lips, smoke curling around his head. Beside him, the Liquid Plumber downed a shot of whiskey and sipped from a bottle of beer.

"If an inspector from the Board of Health comes in and sees you two smoking, they'll close us down for a week," Robert said.

Looking genuinely alarmed, X snuffed her cigarette out in a wadded up napkin and dropped the butt into her purse.

Moonie sucked his teeth and shook his head, "Too many rules, too many people telling other people what to do." He finished his drink and slid off his stool, tapping the Liquid Plumber on the shoulder.

"Want to go out with me while I check my fish traps? I have a case of beer and a bottle of Jim Beam on my boat."

"Does a bear like honey?" The Liquid Plumber upended his bottle and drained it.

Moonie shrugged. "I do not know, mon. There are not many bears on St. John."

Standing, the Liquid Plumber swayed for a moment before finding his balance. "They're big hairy animals that go growl." He made the word growl into a low growling sound.

"I have seen pictures of them," Moonie said. "We should go before the day gets too hot." The cigarette still smoldering, he walked out to the dock, followed by the Liquid Plumber. They got in *The Redfish*, the small wooden boat he used for fishing.

"Moonie's right about there being too many rules," X said, the sound of Moonie's outboard quickly fading as he and the Liquid Plumber moved out into the deep waters of Coral Harbor.

Robert shrugged, his eyes following her as she picked up her drink and walked out of the building and onto the dinghy dock. She sat at the far end dangling her toes in the small waves from Moonie's wake watching his boat shrink in the distance. Setting her drink on a nearby piling, she took the cigarette from her purse and relit it, her hand shaking as she raised it to her lips. She steadied it with the other hand and inhaled deeply, holding the smoke in her lungs until they felt as though they would burst; exhaling with a spasm of coughing that racked her body.

"You've got to quit these things, girl," she said to herself, taking another drink from her margarita.

She'd tried to quit smoking before and once made it for eighteen months. Bethany warned her about the danger of tobacco every time she saw her light up. X knew she was right but she didn't care enough to fight the addiction.

"You're right, you're right," X would say. "I just don't want to; got no reason to."

"They'll kill you," Bethany had said.

X had laughed. "So who'd care?"

"Me," Bethany said. "I'd care. A lot."

"I wouldn't," X said. "And nobody where I come from would."

"And where's that?"

"Long Lake, New York, a town of a little over seven hundred people in the middle of the Adirondacks."

"That's you and me, just women from towns of seven hundred. I wonder what that means?"

"Probably nothing."

Sitting at the end of the dinghy dock, X recalled that conversation. It was the most she had ever told anyone on St. John about her life, and she remembered clamming up as soon as she said it. Bethany had pumped her for more, but X said nothing.

"Somebody must care," Bethany had said. "You've got a beautiful house with a great view."

"And we all know how I came by it. You've got to promise to forget everything I just said. I don't want anybody to know where I came from or why."

"You haven't told me why," Bethany had said.

"And I won't."

Startled from the memory by several small fish nibbling at her toes, X lit a new cigarette from the remains of her old one. Tossing the butt into the water, she watched it bob on the waves. Something struck at it, then swam off, leaving the remains of her cigarette to float away, the paper and tobacco to decompose, the filter to linger for years in the sea or wherever it might wash up onto the shore.

Closing her eyes, she thought of Long Lake, a world away from St. John. Both seemed like end-of-the-world places where drink and depression were the central facts of life for people like her. Fishing, both on the open lakes and streams, as well as through holes in the winter ice, along with legal and illegal hunting, snowmobiling and guzzling alcohol were among the main activities in the north woods. Fishing, boating, lazing on the beach and guzzling alcohol among those in the islands of the Caribbean. Her father, a logger, died at forty-five from cirrhosis; her mother, Gladys, worn down by the same age, taught fifth grade at Long Lake Central School and waitressed at the Adirondack Hotel to make ends meet, to feed and house and clothe the five children Lacy St. Pierre had left her with when drink finally killed him.

"If it wasn't for my friends at the church I'd've blown my brains out after your father died," Gladys often told her children, referring to how members of the Long Lake Wesleyan Methodist congregation were there for her when times seemed too much for her to handle.

Determined to live where life was easier, warmer, as well as to be as far from her mother and brothers as possible, Christine St. Pierre and Bobby Bean left Long Lake in his ancient, rusted '88 Chevy the day after their high school graduation.

"Christine," he told her—refusing as he always did to call her by her nickname, Chrissy. "We're gonna live like millionaires where the air is warm and we can walk on a beach beside the ocean every day."

They spent July and August working in Beach Haven on the Jersey Shore, where Bobby waited on tables and she clerked in a package store. They left in late September as the air cooled and summer jobs dried up. Moving south, they stayed just ahead of the fading season, working for short times in Oxford, Maryland and Myrtle Beach, South Carolina, ending up in St. Petersburg. They rented a decrepit Airstream that sat on cement blocks in a trailer park and found jobs at a marina. This time it was Christine who waited on tables in the evenings at the marina's upscale restaurant. Bobby worked days around the docks, repairing boat engines, replacing sails and riggings, delivering provisions from the marina's chandlery to boat owners and charter clients, sweeping the docks and checking the water and electricity lines that ran along them for boat hookups. One night, he picked her up after work, and was driving back to the trailer park when their car was T-boned by a pizza delivery van. Bobby died in her arms, his last word simply, "Christine."

"I'm never going to let anybody call me that again. You're the last person I'll ever hear say that name." She closed his eyes with her thumb and forefinger and held his cheek close to hers until the police arrived and an ambulance took him from her.

Instead of going back to her job, she wandered around Florida, from the Gulf Coast to the Atlantic, coming finally to Cooley's Marina in Fort Lauderdale, where there were public restrooms and showers. There she heard tales from sailors about St. John and especially, Coral Bay, a place many of them described as where the broken in spirit, the broken in heart, could settle and find ways to either heal or to sink into their miseries without others judging them, their sorrows lessened by the warmth and ease of the tropics. Determined to reinvent herself as a cipher, she hitched a ride on a boat named *Bunyan's Dream* and sailed to the Caribbean. The couple that took her on seemed puzzled that she insisted they call her X. They tried giving her different nick-names, but she would answer only to X. After a month of sailing, the *Dream* came into Coral Bay. Almost as soon as her feet touched land, she walked into Dante's Landing and became a regular at the bar.

A few weeks later she took a job caring for an elderly widower who died two years later and left her his home, Paradise Found, and an endowment big enough for her to maintain it and lead a relatively Spartan life without having to work. She could have rented rooms, or opened a bed and breakfast in the villa, but she preferred living alone with minimal responsibility.

Sitting on the dock and smoking, she shivered as a wind, chilly for the islands, began to blow. She wrapped her arms around her shoulders, and after flicking her fourth cigarette in the sea and watching it float away, she went back to the bar and ordered another margarita.

"That makes six since noon," Robert said.

"Do I look or act drunk?"

"Not a bit."

"I don't get drunk."

"I've noticed that."

"So why are you counting my drinks?"

"I don't like to watch people kill themselves. You may not seem drunk, but the booze still goes through your liver and whether or not you feel its effects, it does its damages."

"Who made you my doctor?"

Robert nearly choked. "Nobody. I'm not anybody's doctor."

She smiled at his discomfort. "Kinda scary, thinking of a bartender trying to be a doctor."

"Yeah," he said, and looked away. Fixing her drink, he slid it across the bar.

Reaching for it, she said, "You make an awful good margarita."

Robert recovered his composure and gave her a slight bow. "My pleasure is to serve."

She raised the glass to him and drank. "And mine is to be served."

A sudden sharp gust rushed through the open building, clattering the mobile of the lost souls of Coral Bay. Bethany steadied it as she passed and came to the bar to place an order for a table of loud tourists.

"It'll be cold and bumpy on your boat tonight," X said.

Bethany shook her head. "Bad weather doesn't worry me."

X laughed. "You've got a naturally sunny disposition."

"I can see the best in people, but no one can ignore the evil in the world. I just don't believe that weather can be evil, so it can't worry me. Some things you simply have to bear because they are. True evil is what bothers me and I will fight it to the death." Her jaw tight, her eyes narrow, she spoke in a quiet, urgent tone, emphasizing each word. "God's plan is for the truly righteous to be as unrelenting and merciless in meting out punishment to the truly wicked as the truly wicked are unrelenting and merciless in their mission of spreading sin and evil throughout the world. It's war all the time and I am a soldier in the army of righteousness."

X and Robert looked away for a moment, neither of them able to respond to Bethany's words and the fervor with which she spoke. After a brief, awkward silence, X cleared her throat.

"So hurricane season doesn't worry you?"

Bethany looked from X to Robert, as if expecting them to react. When they didn't, she took a deep breath. "I know how to take precautions. I bought an outboard and I know where to put my boat when a storm's coming, and how to secure it to best protect it. God gave us a brain so that we can figure such things out and take care of ourselves."

"And if you take all the precautions and your boat is destroyed, what does that say about God?"

Bethany laughed. "It doesn't say anything about God. It says that I didn't take enough precautions because I didn't understand the severity of the storm."

"So you're at fault?"

"Me and the storm. It isn't God's fault."

"I'm not so sure of that," Robert interjected.

"I'm positive of it," Bethany said.

X's voice trembled. "You two can argue all you want about God's responsibility or lack of it for your problems. I say, what god? Everybody's got a different god or goddess. Allah, Rama, Thor, Zeus, Athena, Hera, Kali, and that's just a start. As far as I know, they're all just the stuff of stories, nothing more than made-up imaginary friends, as someone called them."

"I'm talking about the God who gave us Jesus to save us from despair and sin and give those of us who truly deserve it the possibility of eternal joy."

"God," X said, turning the word into a three syllable exclamation dripping with sarcasm. "There's no more a God or gods and goddesses than there is a Wizard in Oz, no more heaven or hell than there is Oz."

Bethany smiled. "He'll come to you, someday when you least expect it, trust me."

"He hasn't come to me," Robert said.

"He's always with us," Bethany said. "His ways are beyond our understanding."

Robert shook his head. "If I believed in him, I wouldn't like him, couldn't like him. I've got no faith in his good will toward us."

"I don't believe in any God or gods or goddesses," X said.

"I'll pray for you both," Bethany said. "I'll pray that God will open your minds, save you from evil and sin and fill your hearts with joy."

"I say that we agree to disagree on this subject and get on with things," Robert said.

X nodded and drank.

"I'll keep quiet for now, but I won't agree to disagree on such an important topic," Bethany said. "Anytime you want to reopen this discussion, you'll find me ready to do it."

X grinned at her. "And you pray for us?"

"Of course."

Robert said, "That's nice, thoughtful of you."

"You might as well blow smoke into the wind," X said.

Bethany replied, "Smoke in the wind blows around and disperses and means nothing. Prayer is solid. "

X rolled her eyes.

"She's being considerate," Robert said.

Bethany said, "You really believe that prayer won't do any good?"

Robert looked at his fingernails. "But it can't do any harm."

Bethany took a deep breath and smiled. "This conversation is over. For now."

Skipper Dan came from his office, his words drowning her final comment as he said, "I just heard on my scanner that a British Virgin Islands police boat stopped that Cheoy Lee and arrested that Sonny creep. They've turned him over to the U.S. Coast Guard."

"That should settle our murder case," X said.

Teach looked up and sneered. "Sounds too easy to me."

"Something else on the scanner," Skipper Dan said. "There's been another murder on the island. Last night a tourist was killed. Somebody slashed his throat and left the body on the beach beside the ferry dock in Cruz Bay."

Eleven

THE FERAL DONKEYS of St. John wander freely over the island, occasionally blocking the roads, often seeming to be studying the goings-on of humans. They stand in small groups, barely moving as life goes on around them. Many West Indians regard them as living symbols of emancipation, and they are left free to roam wherever they choose, with the exception of carefully tended and fenced gardens. Once beasts of burden, they were beaten and starved by plantation owners who used them with the same calloused disregard for their well-being as they did the enslaved Africans who worked the hot and rocky hillside terraces where sugar cane grew. With the end of slavery and the plantation system, the owners and their overseers left St. John, abandoning the former slaves to survive or die on the rugged island, its topsoil long before washed into the surrounding seas.

The descendants of the Africans used the donkeys, as they developed a culture built around small farms and fisheries. In 1916 the Danish government sold the Virgin Islands to the United States, but for years little changed. It was a time of close kinship relationships and an economy of trade and barter, traditions that were slowly eroded by the rediscovery of St. John by people who saw it as a tropical paradise, promising warmth and relaxation far from the cold, gray snow-bound cities of the north. In the early 1950s, Lawrence Rockefeller bought over six thousand acres on St. John, which he donated as a National Park. Roads, once nothing more than donkey trails, were widened and paved. Private villas sprung up on the once terraced hills where cane had been cultivated with cruelly forced labor, and donkeys began to lose their utilitarian value to the West Indians living on the island. They wandered off to live as best they could, and are today one of the unique features of St. John life, along with many feral chickens and cats, all enjoying a relatively trouble-free existence.

Five donkeys, one a newborn, were standing in the yard when Bethany parked at the end of the drive beside Coral View. Robert held a carrot out to one, a mare with a dead milky eye and what appeared to be a long bloody gash on her rump.

"Most people with villas that have gardens think of the donkeys as pests, better shooed away, even better shot," she said.

"They remind me of myself," Robert said. "Left behind to fend for themselves with nobody really caring about them.

"I found you a car." Bethany turned off her engine and walked toward the mare, looking closely at the gash. "Surely does look like she got hit by a car or truck." Gently probing the area around the wound with one hand, she petted the mare's snout with the other, cooing to it as she did. After briefly shaking its head, the donkey stood still. The others watched, slowly chewing as they did.

"It's not so bad," Bethany said. "You got any rubbing alcohol, Mr. Robert?"

He shook his head. "Vodka's the only alcohol on the place."

"That'll do. Fetch it for me, please."

"Vodka isn't cheap."

"You want me to clean this wound, or leave it to fester?"

Robert sighed. "If you put it that way."

"The vodka please. Helping this poor critter might could be the best use for it."

Robert shrugged, went to his apartment and quickly returned with a bottle of vodka and a roll of paper towels. Bethany soaked a handful of the towels with alcohol.

"Save some vodka for me," he said.

"She needs it more. In fact, she needs it, you don't. Nobody needs to drink this stuff." She placed heavy emphasis on the word, needs.

Still talking softly to the animal, she cleaned dried blood, gravel and mud from the cut on the mare's rump. "It's not deep, just a nasty abrasion," she said to Robert.

The donkey flinched once, flicked her tail several times, then lowered her snout and licked Bethany's hand.

"You'll be just fine, mama," Bethany said, scratching the donkey between its ears. She patted it lightly on its uninjured rump and the donkey trotted over to join the others. Soon they all moved off into the heavy bush surrounding the villa and disappeared among the trees.

Robert watched until they were gone and turned to Bethany. "So, you found me a car?"

"It's an island car," she said, gesturing toward her jerry-rigged Samurai. "It's got lots of character."

Robert thought briefly of the matador red year-old Lexus LS 450 and the lovingly restored blue '63 Corvette convertible sitting in the barn behind the house in Keetsville. "What color is it?"

"Mostly rust and Bondo. It was a rental Jeep at one time, but it's been through a lot of owners and a lot sorrowful treatment over the years."

"How old?"

"Maybe a '95, '96. I couldn't tell by looking. You can find out when you make an offer on it. I reckon you might could get it for five hundred. The seats are gone, so you'll have to build a bench out of lumber, like I've got in the Samurai, and there's spots on the floor where it's rusted through that you'll have to patch. Moonie claims it drives real good."

"It's Moonie's car?"

Bethany shook her head. "He bought it from a guy that was leaving the islands. He does that, you know, buys cars from folks that've got to sell and leave quickly. Then he doesn't fix them up, or do anything with them except move them to his place and sell them for fifty to a hundred dollars more than he paid for them. Five hundred isn't bad for a car that'll get you up and down this hill to work and back and into Cruz Bay from time to time. It's not like there's any long distance traveling to do on an island that's got less than twenty square miles of land to drive around on."

TELLING ROBERT that he was his favorite bartender, Moonie sold him the Jeep for four hundred and fifty dollars, and even threw in three two-by-fours and several planks of pressure treated lumber that had been lying under the deck since he built his house twenty years before. With Bethany's help, and the use of her tools, Robert spent his day off building a bench seat and padding it with half a dozen stained and faded throw rugs someone had left hanging on the side of a roadside dumpster.

When they finished, she stood with hands on her hips examining the Jeep. "I reckon you owning this car and having it fixed up like it is makes you a *bona fide* St. Johnian, Mr. Robert."

He rested a hand on the right front fender. It was loose and rattled noisily. "If I were to judge by most the cars parked outside Dante's Landing, I'd have to say that you're right."

"Now I think you need to get yourself a date and take her somewhere other than to the Landing for dinner."

Robert laughed. It felt good to laugh. He imagined he could count on one hand the number of times he had genuinely laughed since coming to St. John.

"Where do you want to go?" he asked her.

She blushed. "I didn't mean me, Mr. Robert. I was thinking of X. I think you should ask her to go to dinner with you. She's very lonely, you know."

He shook his head. "I didn't know. She's not someone I pay close attention to."

"You know when you think she's been drinking too much."

"That's part of my job, making sure people don't get stumble-fall-down plastered and then get in their cars and kill themselves, or other people."

"X doesn't get stumble-fall-down drunk."

"I know."

She laughed and pointed at him. "See, you do pay attention to her."

"Not close attention."

"Close enough to notice that she drinks a lot and doesn't get drunk. Why do you think that is?"

"Must be something about her metabolism, or she's got an iron-clad liver."

"I mean how did you come to notice that she drinks a lot but never gets drunk?"

"I'm a bartender."

"How much does Teach drink?"

Robert smiled and shrugged. "I don't have a clue."

"And why is that?"

"I've not noticed."

She folded her arms over her chest. "But you've noticed X."

"She's better looking than Teach."

"She's beautiful."

Robert nodded again. "She is. So are you."

"But she'll go to dinner with you."

"You won't?"

"That's not open for discussion."

Robert felt his face stiffen. "I'm important enough to pray for, but not good enough to go out on a date with?"

"That's not what it's about."

"Then what's it about?"

"This conversation is over. For now."

"That's the second time you've said that."

"To you. It's the second time I've said it to you. I've said it many times before. There are things I don't wish to discuss." She flashed him a smile so bright that it left him dazzled and confused.

"You're a mystery," he said.

"I am. I hope that doesn't make you angry."

"You couldn't do anything to make me angry."

"Yet you're angry at God."

"I'm angry, but not at any god. I never said that."

"You don't have to say what I can see." She took a deep breath. "Now, how about asking X for a date?"

"I'm not ready for that."

"You wanted me to go to dinner with you."

"You're the only friend I have on St. John."

"I'm not your only friend here."

"Who else is there?"

Her face clouded for a moment, as if she were terribly sad for him. "Mr. Robert, you'll just have to figure that out for yourself; when you're ready you'll understand."

"What I'm not ready for is dating. Going to dinner with you is a way of saying thank you for all you've done for me, finding me this apartment, finding the Jeep, helping me fix it up. You've been my angel here on St. John, so it would be friends having dinner, not a date."

"Shipwreck Landing would be a good place for dinner."

"You'll go with me?"

"It's just friends for dinner, not a date, right?"

"Friends for dinner."

She touched his hand and turning, walked toward her car, calling behind her as he went. "I'll meet you there at seven."

When she was gone, he took a quick shower, shaved and dressed in his cleanest tee shirt and shorts. He read in the online edition of the *Graham Enterprise*, the Wessex County daily newspaper, that a blizzard had swept into western Massachusetts. Fallen trees and heavy snow knocked out power lines and blocked roads, necessitating wide-spread school closings throughout the area. He sat on the verandah, feet on the railing. Watching boats sail and motor into Coral Harbor, he was surprised by a sudden realization that he was as content as he had been in a long time. Work had never been this satisfactory, although he had liked being a doctor and had enjoyed the prestige that came with the profession. He thought his marriage had been one of contentment, but Maria had clearly been discontented. He had to accept that his sense of satisfaction with their life together had rested upon false premises.

Looking down at the Caribbean over eight hundred feet below, watching the comings and goings of boats, the valley lush and green, the Trade Winds warm as they gently tousled his hair, he realized he was comfortable, that he felt he was in control of his life, and comfort and control were certainly part of contentment, weren't they? This was surely a good place to be. It amused him to hear people refer to it as paradise, and the word sounded very different coming from the lips of locals than it did when tourists said it.

There was always a trace of sarcasm when St. John's residents used it. The coming of a hurricane would always be met with a "welcome to paradise," as would a week-long spate of rain that undermined roads and sent parts of some cliff-side homes sliding downhill, or the news of a member of the VI Legislature caught looting a fire damaged shopping center or sexually abusing his daughter, and never being charged with a crime. "Welcome to paradise," someone would be sure to say, adding, "We make Boston Camden Chicago Las Vegas Philadelphia Harlan County Miami [choose one or all] look like paragons of civil government."

Tourists, on the other hand, gush as they say the word. "Paradise," they sigh as they lean against the railings of an overlook at the edge of Bordeaux Mountain, the view extending up Drake's Channel to the furthest reaches of the British Virgin Islands. "Paradise," they say as they sit on the island's beaches, the blue/green Caribbean waters lapping at the shore, pelicans diving and splashing, frigate birds soaring above. "Paradise," they say after hiking to the edge of Ram Head on a full-moon night, the light bright enough to read by.

Paradise. Robert shared both senses of the word. The island's beauty was overwhelming and the people he worked with at Dante's Landing and those who frequented the place, were friendly and funny and they all looked after one another. That qualifies for paradise, he thought. But his introduction to this paradise was a brutal murder, still unsolved. "Welcome to paradise."

He wished the word did not exist in his lexicon. The idea of paradise held too much promise: the promise of happiness; the promise of peace; the promise of divine perfection; the promise of promise. He feared the world was nothing more than a lovely rock circling a minor star in a universe devoid of any consequence beyond what poor stage props of meaning the fallible minds of human beings managed to conjure up to make their lonely hours of strutting and fretting seem significant. Yet the panorama below was beautiful beyond words and it was his to look at, to consider, to enjoy anytime he wished when he was not working at Dante's Landing, and even when he was at work he could see the Caribbean a few feet away, hear it lap against the pilings of the dinghy dock, catch glimpses of boats in the harbor and feel the breezes that swept through the open-air building.

If this was as at ease with life as he would ever be, he would accept that. It was time to move on, and Bethany was right, X was intriguing and lovely. He wondered what her name was, had been, and wondered if he could ever get close enough to her to find out. It was worth a try.

Twelve

IMAGINE A GARGOYLE, one of those grotesque demonic figures found crouching on the high reaches of medieval churches and cathedrals, personifications of evil designed, some say, as a warning that malevolent forces and beings exist all around us and only in the church are people granted safe haven from such flesh-rendering, soul-eating monstrosities. Now, think of that gargoyle squatting on its haunches atop an outcropping of volcanic rock on Bordeaux Mountain, the highest point on St. John, its pitiless eyes surveying the earth and sea below. If you can see its snarling face, twisted by hate and rage, you will know how Teach looked, smoke from the smoldering cigarette in his left hand rising in thin dark streaks. It curled around his head in a film that darkened his vision.

A red bandana on his head, he wore a leather vest and torn dungaree shorts. His chest, legs and arms were covered with thick and wiry hair, and the curved and chipped nails on his toes looked like claws. The gold medallion that hung from the thin chain around his neck caught the light, reflecting it onto a nearby tree, like a laser beam from a sniper's rifle. From the stony perch on the mountain he looked over Coral Bay, his gaze sweeping across the surrounding hills, along their narrow and rutted roadways, down to the valley where the ruins of a plantation era sugar mill glimmered in the pale yellow orange of the setting sun.

He looked down on goats grazing on the playing field next to the Guy Benjamin elementary school, cars slowing down for the speed bumps on the narrow road running between the school and Sputnik's Bar and the adjacent Donkey Diner. Shifting his eyes to the right, he watched as Bethany's Samurai turned off Centerline Road onto the road leading to Salt Pond and Lameshur Bay. The circular roof of Dante's Landing sat to the left of that road. Bethany turned into the drive and parked beneath the flamboyant. He saw her get out and walk into the restaurant.

The cigarette burned down to his fingers but he did not move. It was as though he felt nothing when the glowing core of tobacco singed his flesh, the odor from his burning skin sharp in the still air. After two hours of watching the scene below, unsure of what he had been waiting for, he saw a hawk circle and suddenly swoop down into the bush and come out of it grasping a small mongoose. Rising again, the creature struggling in its talons, the hawk passed through the first wave of bats flying in wavering patterns as they came from their nests to assume their dominion over the coming night.

His body as still as a granite gargoyle, only Teach's eyes moved as he watched the hawk and bats weave through the gathering dark of the world below. Shadows moved over the valley as the sun disappeared behind Bordeaux. Even with the fullness of night upon him, Teach remained motionless. The hawk would be in its aerie by now, the mongoose torn into small shreds of meat. At the thought, he smiled and slowly rose. Slipping into a pair of flip-flops, he moved along the path leading from rocky outcropping toward his small house, a two room frame cabin at the edge of a small clearing surrounded by a thick stand of trees and vines.

Inside, he sat at his desk and wrote in his notebook, describing what he had seen from the mountainside, recounting in detail the flight of the hawk and his imagined vision of its talons sinking into the mongoose's flesh as it attacked and rose high in the air with its terrified and screeching prey, envisioning in detail the feast that ensued as the hawk, its mate and offspring tore the creature into pieces and devoured its flesh.

He smiled as he wrote, "A fitting end for a member of such a foul species, known for its enmity to snakes and lizards. The hawk is among the most noble of creatures. If I had been able to choose a name by which people on this isle knew me, it would have been Hawk, and certainly not the stupid 'Teach.' Still, if it must be Teach, it's better that they think of calling me that after Blackbeard than because of my having been a teacher."

Closing the notebook, he sat back and took several deep breaths. In the time since he had come to St. John, the hawk that dwelt within him had been quiet, restless, always restless. Now its wings, once clipped, had grown again and were ready to soar. That fool in Dante's Landing had stirred the hawk and it had spread its wings and flown. Now the fool was dead. No loss to the world, Teach thought. And the tourist in Cruz Bay. Another idiot, staggering drunk from a nearby bar, slurring and slobbering as he asked him for money, *Jus' a coupla bucks for another drink or two. I guess I lef' my wallet back at the campground.* Teach smiled again. Thinning the herd. It was his calling.

Born Thomas Andrew Edmunds, trained as a wildlife biologist, with an undergraduate degree from the University of Pennsylvania and a Ph.D. from Harvard, Teach had spent seven years in the field, observing the lives of animals. He never lost his amazement over the efficiency with which they killed for survival, going after the weak, preying on creatures undeserving of the right of reproduction; creatures whose genetic lines needed to end so that more superior creatures could rise to fill and dominate the realms the weak threatened to overrun.

It thrilled him to see Darwinian Theory in action, the survival of the fittest, the extinction of the unfit, so different from the human world in which he was forced to live. The world of human institutions was one in which people attempted to undercut and rewrite Darwin's laws. Those most hateful to him were the churches, with their schools, colleges, seminaries, all preaching love for one's fellow man. He believed the mission of religion was to lift up the weak. The church exalted the weak, promising that they would inherit the earth. Edmunds was convinced that many among his fellow men, the weak ones, did not deserve to live and that the churches with their prattling of God's love for all, their mewling about the meek inheriting the earth, was a crime against what he believed to be the laws of nature.

For years he had ignored the hawk growing within him, denying the reality of the initial stirrings of its wings. Finally he could take it no more. The hawk was released; preying on the weak, clearing the way for the strong to prevail. He flew and joined the many like him who scoured the world, removing the weak, the undeserving, who would, were it not for warriors such as him, inherit the earth.

He had questioned himself but once and he cried out in the night, who am I to play God? It was before he had first allowed the hawk to swoop down, beginning its attacks on the most worthless examples of humanity, the walking rubbish of the species. Don't be a fool, the hawk had answered in his mind. The strong rise and evolve by feeding on the weak, by destroying the weak so that the strong can take their places. He stood and spread his arms. "I am the hawk," he said aloud.

And when he had realized releasing the hawk was something he must do, he had soared and preyed. For ten years he carried out what he believed to be his mission, the advancement of the genetically strong, the improvement of humankind. But the weak, he knew, had their own defenses: laws and police forces created to protect those who could not protect themselves. Slowly, the authorities seeking to abort his mission gathered information from his kills and pieced things together.

Eventually they were closer to finding him that he could allow, not when he was coming to realize who and what he was, whose agent he had become, a belief that grew in spite of his earlier rejection of anything that defied human reason. His mission was far greater than the improvement of humanity.

He packed his bags and flew to St. Thomas and moved on to St. John, convinced that a few quiet years would be good for him. His work had been hard and he had earned a rest. He moved onto the mountain, hid among other people, the weak and the strong, and relaxed. It had been a fine time and he enjoyed himself more than he had thought was possible.

Then, once again, the hawk moved its wings.

Teach rose and stood, his feet firm on the rocky hillside. He knew he had to keep those wings as still as possible. St. John was a small island and he would not be able to avoid detection for very long if he pursued his mission there, but quiescence would not be easy now that he had once again tested his power, felt the thrill that came only when he struck and rose into the sky, his prey struggling against the grasp of his talons.

A drink would be a fine thing at this moment.

"HIYA, CAPTAIN Teach." The Liquid Plumber smiled as Teach took his seat at the bar. He gulped down a shot of whiskey, followed by a long swig of beer. X sat two stools away.

Teach gave him a silent look, nodding barely perceptibly. He could never understand what the pathetic drunk had to smile about. For that matter, he could not understand what possible value there was in allowing such a wretch to take up space on the earth.

Robert looked at Teach. "The usual?"

Teach said. "A dark and diet."

"How much rum?"

"A shot."

Bethany touched his arm. "Nothing to eat?"

Each hoped the other was unaware that they winced slightly as they touched.

Teach said, "Maybe I'll have a burger and fries."

She wagged a finger at him, her tone one of mock scolding. "Maybe or definitely? I have to know. I can't give a maybe order to the cook."

"Definitely." Teach answered abruptly and turned to Robert, who stood behind the bar. "And I've changed my mind about the drink; make it a double shot of dark rum."

"Did you hear about that tourist they found dead in Cruz?" X asked.

Teach did not look at her as he shook his head.

"Somebody cut his throat," the Liquid Plumber said. "The paper said that he was propped up against a palm tree with beer bottle in his hands."

"Terrible," Teach said.

"Evil," Bethany said.

Teach nodded. "Some might so describe it."

"That's two murders right close together," Bethany said. "That man here and the one in Cruz."

"I doubt if they're related," Teach said. "The one who called himself Bear was shot, and you say the one in Cruz Bay was killed with a knife."

"They probably don't have anything in common," Bethany said over her shoulder as she took his order to the kitchen.

Robert slid the drink toward Teach who let it sit untouched as he stared at a football game on the television set hanging above the bar, the announcer's comments scrolling in black and white across the bottom of the screen. For several minutes the only sounds were Jimmy Buffett's voice from the stereo, the racing of outboard motors nearby, and the crash of waves stirred up by the boats sloshing against the dock's pilings.

X broke the silence. "Related or not, two murders in one year on St. John is scary."

Robert nodded. "The town I come from hasn't had a murder since 1873, and some say the victim in that case was killed in self-defense."

"A peaceful place," X said.

Robert paused for a moment before responding. He took a deep breath. "I used to think it was peaceful, but a man's peace can be disrupted by things other than murder."

"And a woman's." She smiled and spoke softly.

"Of course." Robert felt a flush surge up his neck into his cheeks. He was not sure if it was the result of X's mild rebuke, or from seeing Bethany, who was standing behind X, gesturing at him and silently mouthing, 'Ask her out.'

Wiping the top of the bar with a damp rag, he worked his way toward its far end where Nutty Betty sat beside Blowitup Barry, a former Navy SEAL who had turned his demolition skills to civilian use, helping blast building sites on steep hillsides.

"What's up with Bethany?" Nutty Betty asked.

Shrugging, Robert kept his eyes on the rag he was using.

"She was trying to tell you something," Blowitup Barry said.

"And you're sweet on Beth," Nutty Betty said.

"Bethany," Robert said as he met Nutty Betty's eyes. "I'm that obvious?" Nutty Betty laughed and nodded.

"She's not interested," Robert said.

"X is a babe," Blowitup Barry said. "I'd bet Bethany would think twice if you dated X."

"Come on, Bob," Nutty Betty said. "You're a good looking guy and you don't get drunk every night, like most of the guys around here. Beth's sure to get jealous if you and X start hanging together."

"Bethany," Robert said again. "She's Bethany, not Beth, like I'm Robert and not Bob."

"See, he's sweet on her," Nutty Betty said in a loud voice. Blowitup Barry looked over at Robert and gave him a thumbs up.

"She's my friend, that's all there is and that's all there's going to be," Robert said.

Bethany brought Teach's burger and fries, placing them on the bar in front of him, asking, "Anything else you need, Mr. Teach?"

"Nothing here," he said.

Robert looked from Teach to Bethany, his eyes resting on X. She is lovely, he thought.

THAT NIGHT, sitting on his verandah, Robert watched the wave-borne motion of mast lights in Coral Harbor. X filled his thoughts. He was lonely, but skittish of any romantic involvement. Having cut off all contacts with acquaintances and colleagues from his life in Wessex County, he had no way of knowing whether or not Maria had filed for divorce. Lacking such knowledge, he believed he had to assume that she was still his lawful wife. Even though she had walked out on him, taking Grace with her, he was unsure what complications could arise if he began a relationship with another woman.

He and Maria had taken vows to love, honor and cherish one another. She had broken her vow. Did that free him from his? He hoped so. With a sigh that became a groan, he raised his head and looked through watery eyes at the sky, watching as thin traces of wispy clouds raced over the new moon holding the old moon in its arms.

Thirteen

"BEAR WAS my friend. I didn't kill him or nobody else." Sonny's eyes were heavy with the tears. "I woke up in the dinghy where them scumballs at the bar had dumped me and him and the Bear wasn't there. I figured that he was still drunk and maybe had gotten out of the boat and was wandering around. That maybe he'd fallen and hurt himself or something. I looked all over and finally found him dead in that dummy's chair. I freaked out and went crawling all around the dock area and finally found the key we thought was lost, started up Bear's dinghy, high-tailed it back to Bear's boat and got out of there."

Sergeant Preston leaned against the wall of the interrogation room at the Cruz Bay Police Command. His arms folded, he watched Sonny's face as two detectives, Roland Marsh and Eddie Penn questioned him.

"Who killed him if you did not?" Detective Marsh asked.

Sonny shrugged. "How should I know?"

"He did it," Sergeant Preston muttered. "He probably killed that tourist in Cruz Bay."

"That would not surprise me," Detective Marsh said.

"I didn't kill Bear and I didn't kill nobody else and you got no proof that I did," Sonny said. "I been on Bear's boat since I found him dead. There's no way I could have gotten into Cruz and killed anybody."

"That remains to be established," Detective Penn said.

Detective Marsh nodded. "Indeed, we cannot yet prove you are the murderer, but we will hold your passport and driver's license and impound the boat until we find out who did kill Mr. Crowley."

"I got rights. You can't do that."

Detective Marsh leaned into Sonny's face. "You are not in the States down here. You are in our islands and we say what we can and cannot do. We have already taken the steps we believe necessary to solve this murder." Removing Sonny's passport and driver's license from his jacket pocket, he waved them in the air in front of Sonny's face. "The BVI police confiscated these when they arrested you sailing illegally in their waters. They gave them to us when they turned you over. In addition, we have disabled the engines on the Cheoy Lee and its dinghy and we have both boats locked to a mooring chain. You are going nowhere."

Burying his face in his hands, Sonny sighed. When he looked back up he said, "Where am I going to stay?"

"That is not our problem," Detective Penn said.

"Do not worry," Sergeant Preston laughed. "Sooner or later you will be going to jail for murder and then you will have a place to stay."

Sonny reached into his pocket. "I got no money. I had a couple hundred dollars and it's gone. Them goons on Tortola took my money."

"The BVI police had the right to do that," Sergeant Preston said. "You were sailing in their waters without going through their Customs and Immigration. You were fined."

"They arrested me, took my passport and driver's license, and stole my money and said it was a fine, and you've impounded the boat and now you're going to turn me loose without no money and nothing else. How do I live?"

"That is not our problem," Detective Penn said.

Half an hour later, Sonny walked out of the police station. Blinking in the sudden brilliant sunlight, he stood on the narrow sidewalk at the edge of the street and was nearly hit as an open-air taxi filled with tourists snapping photos veered off the road.

Frightened, he jumped back and stood in the shadow of the three story police building. Just downhill was a bar, its patrons spilling over the sidewalk and into the street, forcing cars and trucks to move slowly around them. He wanted a drink, but had no money. Turning away from the bar, he stuck out his thumb and started walking uphill, hoping that someone would give him a ride before he had walked the eight hilly miles to Coral Bay.

Half a mile on, Bethany picked him up.

"I know you," she said when he slid into the passenger's seat. "I wait tables at Dante's Landing. You were there with that man that got killed."

Sonny nodded. "We was pretty drunk that night and the Bear, he can get obnoxious when he's drunk."

"You were pretty unpleasant yourself," she said.

Sonny looked out the window. After a long silent moment, he said, "Yeah, well I can get pretty obnoxious too when I've had a few drinks, but being obnoxious don't mean Bear should've got himself shot and killed and it don't mean I should be stranded on this god-forsaken place with no money."

"There's no such thing as a God forsaken place," Bethany said.

"Sure seems like it's that way here."

"It's not," Bethany said. "And you're right, being an obnoxious drunk doesn't mean somebody should be murdered for it."

"Maybe I am god-forsaken," Sonny said, and told Bethany what had happened to him since he found Bear's body and fled St. John in the Cheoy Lee.

"It might could be that you've forsaken God," she said when he had finished his story. "People that do that get what they deserve."

With a dismissive grunt, he said, "All that matters is that I got nothing going for me right now."

She looked over at him and through his side window she saw that they were passing a roadside dumpster piled high with black and white plastic bags of trash. Someone had left three rusting beach chairs leaning against the side of the dumpster. She stopped and threw them in the back of her Samurai.

"I never know if I'm saving something worthwhile, but I reckon somebody'll get some use out of these things."

"You talk southern," Sonny said.

"I am southern. North Carolina."

"I'm from Worcester, Massachusetts. I don't have much reason to meet southerners."

"You've met one now," she said.

He shrugged. They rode along without talking for another mile or two, Bethany's hands on the steering wheel, her eyes on the road. Sonny stared out the passenger's side window, his hands on his lap as he fiddled with his thumbs. They passed five donkeys grazing along the side of the road. She tooted her horn and waved at them, but they kept their eyes down and chewed, their tails swishing back and forth.

"What're you going to do?" she asked him. "You said you've got no money and you can't even get on your boat."

"Sleep on the beach and fish, I guess."

"What will you fish with? Without money you can't afford to buy fishing equipment."

He shook his head and snorted. "You're bumming me out, lady."

"I'm trying to help."

"It don't seem that way to me."

"What kind of work can you do?"

"I ain't worked in a couple of years. Not real work. Bear kept me around to pick up after him. He'd make a mess and I'd clean it up, you know, push people around that had got him mad at them, things like that. His thing was to act like a tough guy and I was the tough guy that backed him up. When I was a kid I used to mow lawns, trim bushes for people, things like that."

"Think you could still do that kind of work?"

Sonny looked at her and spoke with a sneer. "I don't like to sweat and break my back working."

"But could you?"

"Any idiot could do that kind of work."

"Maybe I could use you."

Sonny looked at her, but said nothing.

"I help manage a couple of properties. I could use somebody to do the outside work; mowing, weed-whacking, trimming bushes, stuff like you said you used to do. I could give you some work."

"You don't even know me. Why would you do that?"

"Because you need money. Can you do it?"

"Yeah."

"Do you want to do it?"

"No."

She looked at him, a faint smile at the edges of her lips. "Will you do it?"

"What choice do I got?"

"Sleeping on the beach and trying to catch fish with your bare hands."

"That ain't much of a choice, is it?"

"I don't reckon it is."

"Then you got yourself a hired hand, lady."

"Fifteen dollars an hour is the going rate for that kind of work."

"That beats minimum wage."

"It costs more to live on St. John. Everything here's more expensive than it is back in the States."

At the Dante's Landing parking lot she shut off the engine. Taking three twenty dollar bills from her purse, she gave them to Sonny. "Here's an advance on your first four hours. You start tomorrow. Meet me right here at six-thirty in the morning."

"Why are you doing this?"

"I've got work I need to have done."

"You could've hired somebody you know."

"I hired you."

Sonny closed his eyes and rubbed the back of his neck. "Yeah, but why pick a guy that you saw drunk and nasty just a couple of nights ago?"

"Because you're in need."

"I still don't get it."

"It's what I do."

His brow furrowed and he briefly looked away. "Like those piece of junk chairs."

"Something like that."

"Thanks. You just might've saved me from a few nights of hell, sleeping on the beach and eating God knows what."

She touched his arm. "Like I said, it's what I do."

Sonny got out of the car, the sixty dollars in his pocket. He would not meet her the next morning at six-thirty. Why bother? He had enough money for a few drinks and a burger or two and he didn't have to work for it. Besides, how bad could it be to sleep on the beach of a tropical island?

Fourteen

X LOVED her villa. Wendell Trout, a retired banker from Boston, had been a difficult man when she went to work for him. His wife, Sandra, had died several years before. Childless, the couple's lives had revolved around one another and when Sandra Trout died, Wendell fell into a deep depression. Unable, or unwilling to care for himself, he let the villa fall into neglect. A 2,500 square foot white masonry home, its rooms spread over four buildings with arched windows topped with stained glass inserts, and Spanish tile roofs, Paradise Found sat on six and a half acres of mountaintop land.

With Wendell ignoring the place after Sandra's death, it began to fill up with filthy laundry, piles of plastic bags filled with rotting garbage, and more piles of unread mail: letters, magazines, catalogs, newspapers, unpaid bills and urgent requests for long overdue payment, bank statements. The gardens had grown wild, and the patios and lawns were covered with leaves and fallen branches. The swimming pool was filled with thick dark water.

After four months, Skipper Dan grew increasingly concerned that he had not seen Wendell since Sandra's funeral. One Sunday afternoon he drove to the villa and found him drunk and filthy in the midst of what Skipper Dan later described as the most horrific mess he had ever seen. He loaded Wendell into his Jeep and took him to the island clinic.

"It was like those hoarder houses you see on TV," he told X a few hours later as she sat at the bar. "The only things missing were refrigerators filled with dead cats and rooms overflowing with junk from tag sales. The garbage, trash and accumulated filth were bad enough."

"He needs someone to care for him," she said. "My mother's sister was like that. She died and they actually did find her house filled with cats, alive and dead. Some were in boxes; some really were in the refrigerator and the freezer. Most of them were lying under her bed, as well as under couches, chairs and in one case on the pillow of her bed. The floors were several inches deep in garbage and cat droppings and urine soaked trash was strewn everywhere. Nobody should have to live like that."

Skipper Dan pulled in his lips and shook his head. "Wendell's place is a mess, but not nearly that bad. He's going to be at the clinic for a few days, and I convinced him to pay someone clean up the place and look after it and him when he gets home. Bethany suggested you. Are you interested?"

"I need a job," she said.

The next day she and Skipper Dan visited Wendell at the clinic. He agreed to hire her and when he returned home, she had the house, gardens, lawns and pool spotless. She stayed with him for three years, living in a small guest cottage near the entrance to the property. Cranky and demanding, Wendell expected breakfast to be ready when he woke in the mornings, no matter what time. Lunch was at eleven-thirty and dinner at six. Each Sunday he prepared a menu for the rest of the week, including instructions on how each item was to be cooked, for how long it was to be cooked and how it was to be served. He rarely smiled and spoke to her only to bark orders.

When he had a heart attack in the swimming pool, she jumped in, towed him to the edge of the pool and managed to get him out of the water and onto the deck.

He looked up at her, his face twisted in pain, and said, "The least you could do is cover me with a beach towel before the ambulance gets here."

"I haven't called the rescue squad yet," she said. "I was too busy keeping you from drowning."

"Get to it. I don't pay you just to sit in the sun, you know." He smiled weakly and died, leaving her the house, the six and a half acres of land and a mutual fund with enough income for her to live comfortably. The rest of his estate went to a cousin in Maine.

Paradise Found was a home far grander than anything Christine St. Pierre had ever dreamed of owning. The green one-story cottage where she had grown up on Walker Road in Long Lake had three small bedrooms for eleven people. She and one sister slept on a pull-out couch in the basement beside the oil burner. Here she had four large bedrooms, each with a bath and a balcony that looked over panoramic views of the north shore. She slept in a different one each night for the first year she owned the place, finally settling into what had been the master suite.

"You were good to him," Bethany said when X first told her of the inheritance. "You were kind and loving and he returned it in the only way he knew, by giving you material things, his home and an income. Love begets love."

"I didn't love him. I worked for him. I worked hard and I made his life livable, maybe even pleasant."

"And why did you do that?"

"It was my job."

"Cleaning and cooking for him was your job. Making his life livable, maybe even pleasant wasn't what you were paid for."

"I saw it as part of my job."

"A lot of people wouldn't look at it that way."

"Well, I did."

"That's called being kind and loving."

Sitting in the great room of her home, petting the calico cat that sat purring on her lap, she listened to Mozart's piano symphonies and thought of how she came to own Paradise Found. Although she would never say it aloud, she had loved the old man. His cantankerous ways reminded her of Lacy St. Pierre, and although Lacy was a poor drunken logger and Wendell was a rich drunken lawyer, they had been alike in their love of a good story, a full meal and in appearing to the world as petulant, demanding and short-tempered cranks, qualities that hid from most people a generosity of spirit that may have been at the heart of who they truly were, or may have been the result of the loss of inhibition that can infect some drunks. Either way, there was a spirit in her father and Wendell that made it possible for her to overlook their weaknesses and belligerent ways.

The cat leapt from her lap when the phone rang.

"It's Robert from the Landing," the voice from the receiver said when she answered. "You left your blue sweater here."

"I don't have a blue sweater."

"I found one on the back of the stool you were sitting on after you left."

"It's not mine."

"It smells like your perfume."

"You know my perfume?"

There was a pause on the other end before he said, "It probably smells that way because it was there when you sat down and the odor got transferred to it."

"You picked it up and smelled it," she said with a tinge of laughter.

He did not reply.

"You know my perfume," she said again.

"It's distinctive."

"I get it in Paris every spring."

"You go to Paris every spring?"

She laughed. "I just said that."

"Every spring, really?"

"No. But I go some springs."

"How often?"

"Once. Two years ago for the first time. I want to go more often, and talking about it makes it seem more possible."

"You lied to me."

"I fantasized. Fantasy is creative. Lying is bad."

Robert cleared his throat. "So it's not your sweater."

"It's not, but it was nice of you to think of me."

There was a silence on the line, broken only by the clicks and hums of the island's phone service.

X asked, "You still there?"

"I have been thinking about you," Robert said.

"And what do you think?" Her words took on a teasing tone.

"I was thinking that it would be nice to see you for dinner."

"I often eat at the Landing. I'll see you there tonight." She hoped the smile playing on her lips could not be heard in her voice.

"I was thinking of something a little different from that."

"Different, how?"

"We could drive into Cruz Bay, have dinner there."

"Maybe we could go hear some music. We could take the ferry to St. Thomas and get a cab to Latitude 18. They have some great music."

"How about just a nice quiet dinner?"

"When?"

"I have Wednesdays and Thursdays off."

"Thursday then?"

"That's tomorrow."

"I know," she said.

They made arrangements and Robert rang off.

X walked outside. Placing her hands on the top railing of the verandah, she leaned toward the distant water below. Robert wasn't the first man to ask her out. Pilgrim Jack had tried at least twice, and she had quickly rebuffed the Liquid Plumber before he could get his request fully spoken. Rotten Cotton, ironically nicknamed because of his sweet friendly nature and white hair, when he was working at Dante's Landing had once suggested dinner at Shipwreck, a mile or so down the road from the

Landing, but she had laughed and told him that she was too nasty for such a nice guy.

Now she had surprised herself by accepting Robert's invitation without hesitation. She had no idea why she had taken him up on his offer and hoped it would not turn out to be a disastrous mistake.

ROBERT SET the phone in its cradle beneath the bar and gave Bethany a thumbs up.

"Good job, Mr. Robert."

"I don't know if it was a smart move."

"You're lonely," she said. "God doesn't want people to be lonely."

"So you say."

"He cares about everything, like in that old song." She sang the chorus of "He's Got the Whole World in His Hands."

"You believe in all that?"

"Beyond a doubt."

The expression on Robert's face mirrored his skepticism. "No one can know that."

"I do."

"How?"

Instead of answering, Bethany sat on a stool opposite where he stood behind the bar. "How were you hurt? Who hurt you and why? And why do you still carry your pain around?"

He grinned at her. "This conversation is over."

She laughed at his use of her phrase. "For now, you mean."

"Over," he said.

MOONIE LOVED Bordeaux Mountain. Sparsely populated, he knew every inch of it, the rises and falls of its land, the guts through which water ran in times of heavy rain, the places where wild plants grew. He had read many books on wildcrafting and was proud of the ethical manner in which he practiced harvesting wild plants from their natural habitats. Mostly he took only the fruit or flowering branches good for eating or useful for medicinal purposes. He would sell or trade them to the few other West Indians on St. John and St. Thomas who still carried on the traditions of their ancestors. He knew which species were endangered and carefully avoided injuring them. Whenever he took a whole plant, generally for sale and transplantation in the gardens of the many private villas on St. John, he would be sure to carefully plant seeds from the plant in the place from which he had taken it, and he never took more than one or two plants from any given spot.

His favorite place to hunt for plants was high on the side of the Bordeaux where his cabin stood, an area bathed by the first rays of each day's morning sun. Teach's frame cabin was nearby and Moonie would often see him working in his yard or resting in a beach chair from which he could easily see the view over Coral Harbor. Property boundaries on St. John are often unclear and Moonie was not sure if the land he had roamed over since boyhood, land from which he had harvested wild plants for almost as long, was part of Teach's land or his. Moonie was always careful to keep out of his neighbor's line of vision. It would be ruinous for his wildcrafting way of life if Teach did have legal title to the land and decided he didn't want Moonie trespassing on his property and taking plants from it.

Sometimes he would hide in the bush for an hour or more, watching, waiting to see if Teach was around. If he was, Moonie would go elsewhere, or wait for him to leave so that he could get to work. He would sit on the ground, resting his back against a tree, reading a book or writing in a notebook he had filled with sketches of plants and information about them he had garnered over his years of wildcrafting.

Once, within his memory, all the land on this side of Bordeaux had belonged to his family and there had never been any question about his right to hike over it and take whatever it had to offer. For years members his large family, his grandparents and parents, aunts, uncles, first, second and third cousins had argued over how best to use the undivided acres of land they all claimed in part. Forty years ago they made an informal agreement to sell off parcels of the never surveyed land. Teach's cabin was on one of those parcels. Moonie did not know if Teach owned the place, or if he rented it. It wasn't a fine distinction in his mind. Either way, if Teach knew he was intruding he could legally tell him to leave.

Moonie kept an eye on Teach's coming and goings in order to safely harvest his wild crops without Teach knowing. At times, when Teach was gone, Moonie would steal into his cabin, using a lock pick he had fashioned by hand using old bandsaw blades. Once in, he would take a beer from the refrigerator and drink it as he snacked on crackers with peanut butter, always careful to take only one beer and two or three crackers, an amount he was sure Teach would not miss. He cleaned up after himself to assure that there would not be a crumb remaining to betray his presence, and he always took the empty bottle with him when he left.

Fifteen

ROBERT COULD REMEMBER having but a few dreams over the course of his forty-three years. He could not recall their content, remembering little more than awakening, troubled by vague images from what must have been dreams, lost as the light of day touched his opening eyes. That changed when he awoke the morning after his dinner date with X.

It had been a fine evening. They dined at table in a Wharfside Village restaurant overlooking the Cruz Bay beach, light from the half moon was reflected from the nearby sea. Shadows from palms swayed in the breeze, sweeping over the patio and adjacent beach and harbor.

"Even a quarter moon gives off almost enough light to read by," X said when Robert remarked on the beauty of the evening.

"No wonder they call this the American Paradise," he said.

X took a sip of wine and dabbed her lips with a napkin. "Don't take that too literally. There's as much corruption in these islands as there is in the States, or anywhere else. Living with corruption is the human condition and we have to ignore it or fight it every minute of our lives. I prefer to ignore it."

"Are you successful?"

She sipped again. "Most of the time I manage to live in willful ignorance."

"And the rest of the time?"

Resting her hands flat on the table, she tilted back in her chair. "The rest of the time I'm angry at the terrible things I see in the world—and I don't have to look far to see them. Aaron Mathews comes right to mind."

Robert grunted. "He's the guy who keeps getting elected in spite of having been caught looting that shopping center after a fire, the one that sexually abused his daughter?"

"And he was never charged for doing any of that and doing who-knows-what other rotten deeds. That's just as wrong as can be."

Robert forced a smile through narrowed lips. "It surely isn't good."

"Terrorists are worse. Spreading fear throughout the world." Her jaw rigid, her eyes moist, she let her chair settle on its four legs and sat upright, clapping her hands softly together. "Enough of that; I say we ignore it and enjoy dinner and one another's company."

Robert raised his glass. "To willful ignorance."

Lifting hers, she clinked its brim to his. Behind them the ferry from St. Thomas crossed the moon path and glided into the Bay, coming to rest beside the nearby dock, waves from its wake lapping softly on the beach a few feet away.

"I don't know much about you," X said.

"I don't even know your name," Robert said.

"Have you ever been married?" She spoke quickly, as if to avoid his question.

"I may still be married. I don't know what Maria has done about that."

"Maria is a lovely name."

"X isn't even a name."

"It's who I am."

Robert shook his head. "It's what you've chosen to think you are. You have a name, even if you won't tell anyone what it is."

She looked toward the harbor, pointing toward the ferry. "I love the lights and the sounds of water and halyards, all that goes with boats sitting at their moorings. I even like the smell of diesel engines mingling with sea breezes." Turning her eyes to Robert, she said, "Did you dump Maria, or did she dump you?"

"I took my marriage vows seriously."

X nodded and gave him a sad smile. "She dumped you."

"Why do you call yourself X?"

"I would never tell a man that on the first date."

They both laughed.

"We should talk about the food, or gossip about the people back at Dante's Landing," Robert said.

"My salmon is delicious," she said.

"My steak was tough."

"How were the garlic mashed potatoes?"

"Excellent. Your rice pilaf?"

"The rice was overcooked."

"Are we going to spend the rest of the evening like this?"

"It's a lovely evening. The sky's clear and the island looks beautiful in the moonlight." She pointed toward a man and woman standing in the water, looking toward the lights of St. Thomas, their arms around each other's waists.

Robert leaned forward as he spoke. "We really are going to spend the rest of the evening like this, aren't we?"

She made a sound almost like a giggle and resting her elbows on the table, cupped her chin in her hands and smiled at him. "It's a first date, Robert. First dates should be light and easy if there's to be a second date."

"Should we have a second date?"

"Most definitely. And perhaps a third and fourth. I enjoy your company."

"I may still be married."

"It doesn't matter. Going out to dinner and perhaps spending part of an evening dancing is innocent enough. Besides, she dumped you."

"I didn't say that."

"You didn't have to say it, exactly."

"And I don't dance. I don't like music."

She laughed. "Everybody likes music."

"No me."

She looked at him in surprised silence before saying, "I've never heard of anyone who disliked music."

"You've met me."

"Why?"

"I tend bar, you drink at one."

She laughed uncomfortably. "Really, why don't you like music?"

"It's frivolous, distracting and unpleasant."

"That's not why you don't like it. Why do you think it's frivolous, distracting and unpleasant?"

"This is too serious for a first date." He fiddled with the salt shaker. "It's something we should save for the sixth or seventh date. Do you want dessert?"

"Is the sky blue?"

He looked up at the moon and stars. "No tonight."

"It's still blue. We just can't see it at night."

"I don't trust what I can't see."

She heaved a deep breath and slowly shook her head. "Me neither. Isn't that sad?"

"Maybe it's the saddest way a person can be."

She gave him a bright smile as the waiter pushed a dessert cart to the side of their table. "Here comes something that isn't sad."

She had a slice of key lime pie topped with drizzled chocolate, which she could not finish. Robert ordered a double fudge brownie and a huge scoop of vanilla ice cream topped with thick chocolate syrup and blueberries, and ate the remainder of X's key lime pie, washing it down with a cup of coffee. X drank decaf.

Their conversation the rest of the evening touched on local politics, gossip, reviews of their dinners. He dropped her at Paradise Found.

"So, another date?" he asked.

"I'd like that."

"Next Thursday?"

"We could take a ferry to Red Hook. There's a nice Italian restaurant there."

He agreed and shook her hand. Once back home, he read for several hours, then lay in bed staring into the darkness before falling into a fretful sleep.

He woke with a jolt at first light, shaking, sweating, images from the dream that startled him awake as clear as if he were seeing them for the first time. He could not chase away their memory or the dread they had aroused in him; the moon-borne shadows of a ruined sugar plantation sitting near the edge of a steep cliff overlooking the Caribbean, waves breaking against the rocks below. He looked up at a windmill tower. Ringed with jagged rocks, it rose high above where he stood. Behind him the cliff dropped to a white-capped sea. The rocks along the rim of the tower looked like broken teeth ready to snatch and devour the hundreds of bats flitting around it, their small bodies outlined against the moonlit sky.

Vines reached through the rocky soil touching his feet and ankles as they grew visibly larger with each passing second, threatening to wind around him and pull him to the earth where they would grow ever larger and tear the life from his struggling body. He would step away from them and they would follow, as if aware of his fear and determined that he should not escape their grasp. One step back he would go, one step closer the vines would creep. He backed up until he stood at the edge of the cliff, sea spray from the breaking waves below soaking his clothing.

The vines moved quickly, as though leaping toward him and he took a step back, his left heel striking against a rock as he fell backwards into space. The last thing he saw as he plummeted to the rocks and raging sea below was a shadowy figure standing atop the tower and pointing at him. Despite the shadows obscuring its face he knew he would recognize it should he ever see it.

He woke before plunging into the rock-bound sea.

Unlike any many dreams, he was unable to forget this one. Even at work, in the late afternoon of the day, its images remained with him. He could not banish them: the tower with its teeth and the dark creature standing on top of it; the sounds of waves breaking against the rocky bottom of the cliff as he fell backwards; the vines grasping for him; the bats with their skriing cries looking like jagged rips in the brightly moonlit sky.

At six, when Boozie relieved him at the bar, he walked to the end of the dinghy dock. The sun was still shining. Sailboats came into Coral Harbor, their jibs brightly colored as they bounced on the waves. Bending over and using both hands, he scooped up sea water and poured it over his head. It jarred him from the half-dazed state he had been in since morning and he spread his hands, embracing the beauty of the island and the sea. A pelican swooped down and perched on a dock piling, blinking as it looked at him.

"Hello, bird," Robert said.

The pelican blinked two more times and took off. Soon it was soaring high above him, circling the harbor. Robert thought it one of the most beautiful and graceful things he had ever seen.

Sixteen

A WOODLAND TRAIL runs through the mangroves between the beach at Francis Bay and a salt pond several yards inland. After several tenths of a mile, the trail turns inland along the top of the pond, eventually leading uphill past the ruins of a plantation era home sitting in the shadows of the surrounding jumble of bushes and trees, its walls of coral, brick and stone encircled by thick vines which give the crumbling ancient structure a measure of stability.

In the middle of the twentieth century squatters had propped tin roofing over several rooms at the rear section of the ruined building. Now rusted, with a number of holes that allowed rain to fall through, the roof still provided enough shelter that Sonny, broke and without work, could sleep there, using for bedding towels and clothing left hanging from trees or lying in the sand at Francis Bay by absent-minded beach-goers.

He survived by eating breadfruit, mangos and papayas he found growing in the nearby bush, and by creeping to the beach during the days where he would slip sandwiches and drinks from the backpacks and coolers of tourists swimming in the surf, always careful not to take but one or two things from any single group. In spite of the leaking roof, the lizards, rats and spiders he shared the ruin with, and his makeshift bedding, it was not a totally unpleasant life. It provided a respite from the turmoil of life with the Bear and the problems he caused for both of them wherever they set anchor, but he knew it could not last. He would have to settle matters with the Virgin Islands Police, convince them that he had nothing to do with Bear's death or the murder of the tourist in Cruz Bay, and get them to return his wallet and passport. He would have to write off the money the BVI customs people took, but he had to have his driver's license and credit cards if he was going to get off the island.

The problem was how to prove his innocence. Perhaps, he decided, it would help if he could appear to be settling into a normal life. After a week of sleeping in the ruin and foraging in the bush and on the beach, the novelty was wearing off and one morning he hitched a ride to Coral Bay, approaching Skipper Dan as he opened Dante's Landing for the day.

"You probably think I'm a worthless piece of garbage," he said.

"Your words, not mine." Skipper Dan turned a key in the lock and pushed the door open. Sonny followed him inside.

"Me and the Bear did spend a lot of time drunk, stoned on weed, and coked up. That's not a good job recommendation, I know."

Skipper Dan laughed. "Are you asking me for a job?"

"Yeah, I guess I am," Sonny mumbled and gave him a hope filled look.

"You and your friend caused trouble in my restaurant and he got himself killed here. And the cops still think maybe you did it."

"Bear was my friend. I wouldn't kill a friend." Sonny coughed and tried to give him a smile. It looked more like a grimace. "I wouldn't kill nobody. I'm sorry I caused trouble for you, but I was messed up and I'm straight now. No booze, no drugs since they day they found the Bear dead."

Without speaking, Skipper Dan looked at him. His clothes were mussed and dirty, his face and hands covered with scratches.

"I really need a job," Sonny said. "For a little while, until I can clear things with the cops. Then maybe I'll be able to get away from here."

"Bethany said she paid you in advance for a job that you never showed up for."

"That was then," Sonny said.

Skipper Dan nodded, "And you're saying that this is now, that it's different this time?'

Nodding, Sonny puffed his cheeks and exhaled slowly. "I know I look pretty bad. I been living in some kind of broke down old place in the jungle. There's all kinds of lizards and spiders and weird looking little animals that look like they'd like to bite you finger off, and there's vines that like to take the skin right off a man."

"Mongooses and catch-and-keep. They brought the mongooses in to kill the rats but forgot to take into account that rats do their work at night and mongooses are daytime animals. Catch-and-keep's the vine. It's nasty."

"I don't care what you call them; I want to get back to my life."

"Seems like St. John's never going to be able to get rid of rats."

Not knowing how to respond, Sonny blinked and rubbed the back of his neck.

Skipper Dan laughed. "After what you did to Bethany, I can't believe you've got the nerve to ask me for a job."

Sonny's voice cracked as he spoke. "I'll do anything, clean toilets, take out trash; I'd even lick your floors to wash them if it'd mean I could earn a little money and maybe get off this crumby island."

Skipper Dan looked at Sonny's clothes and scratches, his watery eyes, his thin face and shaking hands. He'd helped sadder looking cases, but when he thought of Sonny and his friend, Bear, harassing people, especially the women, and customers at that, he wondered if a few more weeks of living in the bush and barely surviving might serve him well.

He pulled at his beard, torn between his natural inclination to help people who seemed up against the wall and his disdain for Sonny. "Why should I help you?"

"You got no reason to, I know." Sonny's eyes fell to his feet. "But I need help." There was desperation in his voice and on his face.

Skipper Dan clucked his tongue and rattled his lips. "And you'll do whatever work I give you?"

Sonny nodded, his eyes brightening. "Yeah, like I said. I'd even lick your floors clean."

"You won't have to do that, but I've got things that need doing that I wouldn't ask my regular workers to do."

"I'll do them."

"My septic system's failing. There's sewage running out of the pipes in the leach field and pooling behind the building. I need someone to dig a couple of thirty, forty foot trenches for a new leech field, lay some perforated pipe, then dig out the septic tank and connect the new pipes up to it. It's dirty, smelly work. You'll be trudging around in blue mud."

Sonny rolled his eyes, a disgusted look on his face. "That's all you got for me?"

"That's it. Fifteen bucks an hour. Most people get twenty for that kind of work on St. John, but I'll give you fifteen and a hamburger and fries and slaw for lunch each afternoon and for dinner each night you're on the job, that is if you clean yourself up before coming in to eat."

"And where am I going to wash up?"

"There's a hose down by the marina."

"I got no clothes but what I'm wearing."

Without a comment, Skipper Dan went to his office. He came back waving a pair of faded and torn denim shorts. "Wear these to work in, change into your regular clothes after you hose off."

"You got yourself a sewer worker, not that I got any real choice right now," Sonny said.

"Septic tank worker. There aren't any sewers in Coral Bay."

"Whatever," Sonny muttered.

Skipper Dan took a bottle of #8 SPF sun block from behind the bar. He thrust it and the shorts into Sonny's hands. "Put these on and get to work."

"Yeah, boss."

Skipper Dan's face flared red. "I don't want sarcasm, and one more thing."

Sonny looked at him but said nothing.

"You'll pay Bethany back the sixty bucks you took from her, twenty bucks a day for the first three days."

THE FAILING leach field was in an area between Dante's Landing and a small boat yard that shared the dock. It was littered with trash, rusting oil cans, broken glass and rotting vegetable matter and torn shreds of paper. Several fifty-five gallon drums were filled with foul-smelling and viscous liquids Sonny could not identify and feral chickens and cats chased one another through the razor sharp grass that grew in clumps on the hard-packed red and rocky ground. Two bone-thin brown dogs roused themselves from time to time to snarl at Sonny whenever he moved close to them. Broken wires hung from electrical poles, dangling a few feet above the ground. Afraid some might be live, Sonny gave them wide berth as he worked.

After the first hour of digging his long unused muscles ached, and by the end of the second his damp, greasy hair flopped over his face and eyes and the sun burned his shoulders and back in spite of the sun block he had smeared over them. At the end of three hours of sweating and cursing in the midday tropical sun, working with a shovel and heavy forged five foot steel pry bar to move heavy rocks, Sonny had managed to dig a trench eighteen inches deep and three feet long. The ground over the old leach field was covered with a layer of foul smelling blue and red mud created by leakage from the septic tank and it oozed slowly into the new trench, the stench causing his eyes to water.

He would pry with the bar, freeing rocks which he flung aside, then dig until he hit another one. Roots from nearby trees were another problem. He would cut through them with the shovel's end, battering them over and over until they broke apart. He would then have to reach down and pull them from the tight hard soil until they were removed from the area he was trenching. As he worked, he thought of life on Bear's Cheoy Lee, of the coolers filled with beer, the Altoids tins full of cocaine and the steaks they would cook on the grill at the boat's stern, laughing and drinking with men and women they met as they sailed from island to island.

He leaned on the shovel's handle and looked around. Off to his left the waters of Coral Bay rippled quietly. A bikini clad girl on a paddle-board passed, her sun bleached hair tossing in the breeze. He watched her for a long time. She did not look his way. Turning at the sound of a motor, he saw a couple on a Harley bouncing down the pot-holed gravel drive leading to the Coral Bay Marina. He watched them disappear behind a thick stand of hibiscus and low bush palms beside which a donkey, its head lowered, munched on a thin patch of grass. A sudden breeze blew over the leaking tank and surrounding contaminated soil, the heavy odor of human waste hitting him like a physical blow.

He threw down the shovel. It clanked against the digging bar and he kicked at them, stubbing his toe. Crying out in pain, he spat at the tools and stomped toward the marina and the hose outlet where he had left his shirt and pants. Once he was a clean as he could make himself, he dressed and walked back to Dante's Landing. Inside, he sat on a stool at the bar next to Pilgrim Jack.

"Hot day," he said.

"Especially if you've been working like I saw you doing out there," Pilgrim Jack said.

"Yeah, well I'm done." He looked toward the office where Skipper Dan sat at a desk, his back to the door. "Hey, boss," he yelled.

Skipper Dan turned and raised his eyebrows.

"You owe me forty-five bucks and burger," Sonny said.

"You can't be finished already," Skipper Dan said.

"Finished as I'm going to be. I quit. Like Johnny Paycheck said in that song, take your job and shove it. Ain't nobody that should have to work like you got me working down there, especially in such stinking muck"

"Somebody's got to do that kind of work," Pilgrim Jack said.

"Not this boy," Sonny said, his voice soft and guttural.

A few seats away, Teach had been drinking alone, his shoulders hunched as he listened to the conversation. Curling his lip, he turned his back to Sonny. Draining his glass, he set it down with a loud sound. "I'm ready to settle up," he said to Robert and placed a twenty dollar bill on the bar.

Robert picked it up and put it in the cash register.

"How far did you get?" Skipper Dan asked Sonny.

"See for yourself. I got forty-five dollars and a hamburger far, and that's far enough for me."

Teach swept up the change Robert put in front of him and stood. Pushing away from the bar, he looked at Sonny for a moment and turned to Robert with a smile. "Some people aren't worth the space they take up on this green earth." Saying nothing else, he walked to the far side of the room, sat at a table and looked toward the harbor.

Sonny swiveled on his stool, his mouth open to respond, but seeing something in Teach's eyes, he turned back to the bar. "Fries with that burger," he told Robert.

"You didn't finish the job." Skipper Dan was back from looking at the result of Sonny's work. "I'll pay you thirty bucks for the time you put in. That trench you dug should've taken no more than an hour, so I'll pay you for two, given that you probably aren't used to hard work. I figure at least an hour of that three you claimed that you worked you spent about looking around, leaning on the shovel, and feeling sorry for your sorry self. Thirty bucks is what you'll get and the burger and fries will come out of it. Take it, shut up and be glad I didn't keep it all for Bethany. Before you get anything, give me back the sun block. I don't want the shorts after you've worn them."

Sunny frowned but said nothing. He took the bottle of sun block from his pocket and slammed it down on the bar. "How much for the burger and fries?"

"Twelve ninety-five," Robert said.

Sonny glared at Skipper Dan. "That'll leave me seventeen bucks and a nickel." He looked sideways at Robert. "Don't expect no tip from me."

Robert shrugged and walked to the other end of the bar where Moonie sat with the Liquid Plumber. Raising two fingers in the air, he signaled for refills on his dark and diet and the Liquid Plumber's beer and a shot of whiskey.

"Make that burger and fries to go," Skipper Dan called to the cook and tossed a twenty on the bar in front of Sonny. "Keep the change. Like I said, you're lucky to get it, given what you owe Bethany."

"I want a beer," Sonny said.

"Seven bucks," Skipper Dan told him.

Sonny made a spitting sound. "Forget it. I'll get a beer for a buck-fifty at the Love City Mini Mart down the street."

"Good choice," Skipper Dan said.

Sonny shook his head, but said nothing. When the cook brought his burger wrapped in aluminum foil, Sonny grabbed it from his hand and walked out of Dante's Landing, stomping his feet as he went.

"Scum of the earth," Teach said, coming back to his stool once Sonny was gone.

"I don't think he'll be back," Skipper Dan said.

"For sure he won't be back here again," Teach said.

Seventeen

"GOT A LIGHT, sailor?" X asked Robert, an unlit cigarette in her hand. It was a warm tropical night and they sat on the top deck of the ferry pulling into Cruz Bay, returning from an evening on St. Thomas; a movie followed by dinner at the Italian restaurant in Red Hook.

He shook his head. "I don't light cigarettes for anyone. There's a reason they call them coffin nails."

She put the cigarette back in its pack and dropped it in her purse. "I suppose you think a good breakfast is granola with soy milk."

"I'm more of a bacon and eggs man," he said.

"That's a relief."

"In moderation, of course. For me it's bacon and eggs once or twice a month, at most. It's the cholesterol, you know." He licked his lips. "But I do love them. And ice cream too, and extra cheese on pizza, rare steak, all those tasty cholesterol laden things."

"I know cholesterol's bad for you, but don't really understand what it is," she said.

"It's a part of animal cell membranes that's essential to establishing the right level of membrane permeability and fluidity."

She pretended to choke. "That's more than I can handle. I don't understand HDL and LDL, no matter how many times I read about it."

"HDL, that's high density lipoprotein, is the good stuff. LDL, low density lipoprotein's the one that's bad for you."

"Why?"

"You want to keep LDL low so it doesn't build up in the walls of your arteries and form plaque that reduces blood flow. Reduced blood flow is very bad and can increase the risk of cardiac problems."

"Bacon and eggs," she said.

"Bacon and eggs." He raised a finger in the air. "And don't forget the ice cream and extra cheese and the delicious tenderloin."

"And the high stuff?"

"High density lipoprotein helps keep your LDL down."

"I'd wager that if I asked you why, you'd be able to tell me."

"I would."

She gave him a quizzical look. "What did you do back in the real world?"

He affected a teasing tone. "And what was your name back there?"

"Not X." Extending her forefinger, she poked his shoulder. "So, what did you do?"

"Not tend bar."

"I like you," she said.

"I like you."

"We don't know anything about each other beyond who and what we are in Coral Bay."

"We don't. Maybe we don't need to."

"Not yet," she said.

He smiled. "Not yet?"

Blushing, she smiled back. "It is only our second date."

The ferry docked and a few minutes later they were wading along the beach in front of the Wharfside Village shops and restaurants. Halfway along, she slipped her hand into his. He took it, giving it two quick squeezes. She returned them and they walked without talking to the end of the sandy area, climbed to the street and walked to the lot where Robert's car was parked. On the way to Coral Bay they stopped at the Bordeaux Mountain overlook. Robert parked and they got out to gaze at the starlit Caribbean, the British Virgin Islands rising from the moon-washed sea in darkened masses. Again, she took his hand, this time raising it to her lips and quickly kissing his fingertips. Reaching over with his free hand, he caressed her hair and dropping his arm to her shoulder, he pulled her close. They stood there until a car rounded the bend, the glare of its headlights breaking the mood.

Back in the car, she said, "You know a lot about cholesterol."

"You must know about a lot of things that I don't."

"Probably." She let her head fall back against the headrest. "This is fun."

"It's been a nice evening."

"That too, but I mean trying to figure each other out. It's a game where the stakes are surprises, getting to know you in the present, without any baggage."

His voice dropped and he sighed. "The baggage is always there."

"Maria," she said.

"See, you already know more about me than I do about you."

"You're probably more interesting."

"I doubt it." He pulled the car to a stop in front of Paradise Found.

"We'll have to have a confessions date."

"Or a revelations date."

"Date three?"

"Seven," he said.

"Why seven?"

Robert shrugged. "Why three?"

She touched the back of his hand. "Because that's our next one."

"I like the guessing game. Let's keep it going a little longer."

"And what's your guess about me?"

"The X gives it away. You were a spy." He spoke with a soft deep tone that was nearly a whisper, "The mysterious Madame X slipped away from the shadows of the Kremlin clutching a bag filled with American dollars, an Israeli made pistol equipped with a silencer resting in her purse."

Her laughter echoed in the night. "Not even close. I'll give you one clue. I've always lived near the water."

Pretending to think for a moment, he snapped his fingers. "No doubt about it, you were a spy for the Navy. A knife gripped between her teeth, the mysterious Madame X swam around the pier as she fastened plastique explosives in several locations on the hull of the Iranian tanker, the bodies of the sentries floating in the sea around her, blood oozing from where their throats had been slit."

"Good night," she said and leaned over to kiss his cheek.

He turned toward her and their lips met briefly. She touched his cheek and left the car.

By the time he reached home a light rain had begun to fall and when he dropped into bed it was pouring steadily. Usually the sound of rain was comforting; a steady soft drumming that would gently edge him into sleep. This night he lay with open eyes, his head cradled in his open hands as he stared upward into the darkness below the ceiling. He willed himself to stop thinking, but his mind would not rest.

He had been largely successful at building a wall between his old life in Massachusetts and his current life in Coral Bay, tending bar and living from moment to moment with little reflection and no commitments. Now, lying in the dark, his head resting in his hands cupped upon the pillow, he thought how much his success at walling himself off from his previous life came from drinking and working at Dante's Landing. Perhaps Skipper Dan's bar and restaurant was a way station for him, a place between what he had been and what he might become, as if he were on a journey with an unknown, as yet unfathomable destination and it was up to him if that journey was to be one of progress or one of dismal failure. Work was the best part of it, drinking the worst. He would focus on the best and do what he could to mitigate the worst.

He fell asleep thinking of the light touch of X's lips on his.

SONNY HAD a bad night. He lay on his rough pallet in the ruins of the plantation great house. Despite having doused himself with cold water from the marina's hose, the stench from Skipper Dan's leaking septic system still seemed to cling to his skin. Shuddering with rage and despair, his arms were taut and his veins felt as though snakes slithered through them. Something skittered over his outstretched bare arm, a lizard, he hoped, a spider, he feared. In the surrounding bush, the tiny tree frogs of the Caribbean began to sing in the light rain, the noises from the small creatures unbelievably loud.

Just beyond the broken walls of his shelter, he heard the rattling of stones on the ground and the rustling of leaves and branches; probably a donkey passing by he thought, although he had heard rumors of wild boars living in the bush. Sitting up and leaning against the wall, he put a cigarette in his mouth and touched his lighter to it, the flickering flame reflected in the eyes of a bush cat sitting atop the wall opposite him. Startled, he reached to the floor, grabbed a small rock and threw it at the eyes. The cat howled and jumped down, hissing and spitting as it ran off.

He cursed it, then loosed a torrent of curses and obscenities in general at the world, in particular at the Virgin Islands Police, at Skipper Dan and at the Bear: the police for leaving him stranded without his wallet, with his license, credit cards and passport; Skipper Dan for giving him an impossible task and cheating him when he could not complete it, and the Bear for bringing him here and getting them both in trouble with the locals and then getting himself killed, leaving Sonny to deal with the mess.

Bear had always left the messy stuff for Sonny, but he was there to take care of things if anyone needed to be paid off. Bear was the mess-maker and Sonny the mess-cleanser, but the Bear was the true fixer, if removing the mess meant somebody's hands had to be greased. "How much?" the Bear would ask. Sonny would tell him and Bear would open his wallet, always packed with large bills, and pass him the necessary amount. "Take care of it," the Bear would say.

Now Sonny was alone; broke, sleeping in a lizard, spider, rat, mongoose and scorpion infested pile of rubble surrounded by feral donkeys, chickens and cats, perhaps even wild boar. He cursed them all, and he cursed himself for his weakness. He would not be in this position had he not attached himself to the Bear. He should have stayed in Worcester, satisfied with the small time drug deals and petty thievery that had stood him in good stead before the Bear came along.

"I'll be reading about you in the newspaper police logs," his step-father said when he kicked Sonny out of the house the day after his sixteenth birthday.

Over the next fifteen years Sonny was arrested many times. He served three six months sentences in the Worcester County Jail and one five-year term at Cedar Junction, the state's maximum security prison where he met the Bear, who promised him an easy ride if he would come to work for him when they got out. The Bear finished his five-year sentence on the same day Sonny was released two years early for good behavior. Life was easy for him after that, if cleaning up the Bear's messes—and there were a lot of them—didn't bother him, and it did not.

When the Bear figured out how to launder the fortune he had made in the drug business through banks in the British Virgin Islands, he bought the Cheoy Lee and retired to cruise the tropical seas. Knowing he would still need someone to pickup after him, he took Sonny along. The arrangement worked out well for Sonny, until they came to St. John.

Sonny cursed Skipper Dan again. He might not be able to get at the police, and the Bear was beyond his reach, and besides, if the Bear hadn't screwed Sonny by getting murdered, things between them would still be fine. But the lousy low-down smug cheating owner of Dante's Landing would pay for giving him a disgusting job and short changing him. He'd pay for the Bear's death, if for no other reason than it had happened just outside his crumby restaurant.

A chicken clucked nearby, then another one a little farther away, followed by the noise of a cluster of chickens clucking and jumping from limb to limb. A rooster crowed once. Again, Sonny heard rattling stones and the rustling of branches and leaves. He sat still, listening to each sound. There was a sudden deep cough. The noises from other creatures ceased abruptly, the result he was sure, of there being a wild boar outside, pawing the ground and terrifying those living in what he had come to think of as the jungle beyond the ruin.

He stood, picked several large stones from the loose wall, and went outside, armed to chase away whatever lurked there. He did not see Teach step from the shadows behind him. When the rope was slipped around his neck and quickly tightened, he had no time to get his fingers under it and ease the pain as he choked. He was unconscious in seconds and dead in but a few more.

Eighteen

EARLY ON A Sunday morning Robert leaned against the shelves behind the bar, Skipper Dan sitting on a stool in front of him. Aglow with orange-gold light from the morning sun, the room glistened with turquoise sparkles reflected from the waters of the nearby harbor. They had come in to do the monthly liquor and food inventory and were drinking coffee and eating chicken and mutton pates Skipper Dan had brought from Hercules Pate Delight in Cruz bay. A greasy white paper bag holding several more pates sat on the bar between them

Skipper Dan poured a generous helping of bourbon in his cup and waved the bottle at Robert. "A little hair of the dog?"

"No thanks," Robert said.

"Too early in the day?"

"I need to ease up on my drinking."

Skipper Dan smiled. "I like that. I wish you could convince Boozie to do the same thing. Non-drinking bartenders are always good for the bottom line."

"I paid for all my drinks." Robert's voice snapped like a whip.

Skipper Dan raised his hands, as if to fend off a blow. "I didn't mean it that way. There are places on this island where the owner never knows when and if a bartender's going to make it to work or lie home drunk or hung over or both. I never questioned your honesty, or Boozie's."

The sound of heavy footsteps came from the front deck and they looked up as Sergeant Preston walked into the Landing, his chest puffed out.

"Whatever you are eating smells good." He came to the bar and looked in the bag. "From Hercules, I assume?"

"Take one," Skipper Dan said.

Sergeant Preston already had his hand halfway in the bag. Without a word, he stuffed a pate in his mouth. Skipper Dan and Robert watched his cheeks fill, the wet sounds of his chewing mixed with grunts of appreciation.

"They are the best breakfast in the world," Sergeant Preston said as soon as his mouth was free enough for speech. He did not seem to notice a quick look of amusement pass between Skipper Dan and Robert.

"There has been another murder," he said, swallowing the last of the pate.

"A tourist?" Skipper Dan asked.

Sergeant Preston sucked his teeth, a classic sigh of disdain for the other two men. "Not exactly. This one was the companion of the first one killed. The one called Sonny. A retired airline pilot and his wife went to Francis Bay for their morning swim and found him. He was lying on a towel, his head resting on a small mound of sand. A cigarette hung from his lips."

"How was he killed?" Robert asked.

"He was strangled with a thin rope. It was still around his neck." Sergeant Preston sucked his teeth again. "This is three murders in a very short time. That creates a great deal of unpleasant work for the police. You would do well to consider that this killing, like the first, comes back to this place."

"A coincidence," Skipper Dan said.

Sergeant Preston looked at him with blank eyes. "Perhaps, but the first one was found just outside your door and they both had been in here the previous night and, from what I have heard, they had been causing trouble for you."

"They were," Skipper Dan said. "But there's no such connection to the second killing."

"Perhaps not," Sergeant Preston said. "And perhaps there is a connection and we just have not seen it yet."

"Why did you come here?"

Sergeant Preston smiled. "I wanted to see what was in your face when I told you about the murder."

"And what did you see?"

Sergeant Preston shook his head. "Nothing and I am very good at reading people's faces. You are either a very good actor, or you are innocent of this particular murder. Whether or not you are also innocent of the first murder remains to be seen."

"I've got nothing to do with either one," Skipper Dan said.

"Perhaps not." Sergeant Preston glanced at Robert.

"Don't look at me," he said.

"I will look at anyone I choose to look at. I am a policeman and it is my duty to follow each and every lead in a case."

"There are no leads here," Skipper Dan said.

"I will find the killers," Sergeant Preston said.

"I surely hope so," Robert said.

"This could be bad for tourism, and whatever's bad for tourism is bad for my business," Skipper Dan said.

"That is not my concern." Sergeant Preston sucked his teeth one last time, took another pate from the bag and left.

"Like he's going to find the killers," Skipper Dan said. "From what I hear, Preston could be in jail long before anybody has a real clue as to who the killers are."

"Killer, singular," Robert said. "And what's up with Preston?"

"I'm not sure, but Willis Penn, the Medical Examiner, told me that Preston and another cop of some sort are being investigated. Too many of the VI Police are crooked. Some people think the Feds should come in and take the department over, clean it out and retrain the honest cops that are left."

"Could that happen?"

"It could, but it won't. The idiots in Washington would quiver at the thought, believing it could too easily be interpreted as politically incorrect."

"But the cops are really corrupt?"

"At the very least a huge minority of them are. Others just beat up their wives and girl friends and turn their backs when relatives or friends break the law."

"That's a little scary."

"It is," Skipper Dan said, and changed the subject. "What makes you say there's only one killer?"

Robert briefly looked toward the harbor as he gathered his thoughts, and in his replay was again careful not to reveal too much about himself. "As I said to the ME when they found Crowley's body outside here, I like to read police procedurals, both fictional and non-fictional."

"And that tells you what?"

"It's obvious. All three murders were staged for effect. The Bear, Crowley, or whatever you want to call him, was found sitting on a chair just outside here with a dummy on his lap. The one in Cruz Bay was sitting propped up against a palm tree holding a beer bottle. Now they find Sonny lying on a beach towel with a cigarette. That's a pattern."

"Why didn't you say anything to Preston?"

"Upstage the local police would not be a clever thing to do. He'd be all over me."

Skipper Dan sipped his coffee. Cutting the last pate in half, he passed one of the halves to Robert. "You're right. At best, he's a little man who's smug because he's insignificant, and if what Willis Penn said about him being investigated is true, he's a loose cannon. Remember how disdainfully Willis treated him at the time they were investigating the first body?"

"I remember. Sergeant Preston could be a dangerous man to antagonize."

"Like I said, anyone on the Virgin Islands Police force would be dangerous to antagonize. It's a group not famed for honesty and non-violence."

"But very efficient I take it?"

Both men laughed.

THE ISLANDS of the Caribbean are graveyards of broken dreams, filled with the remains of grand projects begun by statesiders who fail to understand the difficulties inherent in trying to conduct business according to the practices they had followed and the habits they had developed in doing business up north. During the year since its founding, the Coral Bay Christian Church had been housed in a former restaurant, a masonry structure built to look like a plantation great house. By failing to understand the culture of Coral Bay, boasting that they were bringing culture to a backward community, the owners of the restaurant, Expeditions, had offended the locals and ended up bankrupt before the end of their second year in business. Until Bethany and a young minister rescued the building and turned it into the church, the former restaurant sat empty for ten years, looking increasingly like a ruin of the great house it had been designed to resemble.

The eaves along the front of the verandah had cracked and hung loose, broken by three large palm trees that blew against it during a hurricane, the rotting trees resting where they had fallen. Sheets of roofing had been torn off and never replaced. The remaining roofing was rusting and covered with debris. Window shutters hung askew, the broken windows behind them an invitation to the birds, bats and other small animals that entered and built nests inside the deteriorating building. In many places along the exterior walls the stucco had cracked and fallen off revealing the gray cement block walls beneath, a construction far less attractive than the rock, coral and brick used in building the plantations that are now in ruins. The grounds, untended since the restaurant closed were covered with weeds, grass and small trees. Thick stems of thorny catch-and-keep crept along the foundation and wound around iron-work trellises that once held brightly flowering tropical vines. The Expeditions sign hung from a single chain. The broken chain that had held up its other end lay on the ground beneath it.

Bethany and Garry Jensen, a tall, lean visiting pastor from a mission church in a small town on the the Keweenaw Peninsula, the northernmost part of Michigan's Upper Peninsula, struck a deal with the lawyers representing the creditors for the former Expeditions building. Garry had already convinced his missionary group to support him in leasing the building and opening a mission on St. John. After months of renovations, mostly done by volunteers, the Coral Bay Christian Church had opened a year before. Garry moved his family to St. John and became the church's first pastor.

"We were delighted that the Lord called us away from the waste lands of the north," he said during his first sermon, comparing the flat forests and abandoned copper mines of the Keweenaw with their piles of waste and treacherous pits to the palms and beaches and green hills of St. John.

It was a small congregation, mostly a mix of a few West Indians uninspired by the formalities they associated with the older, more established churches on the island, and three or four aging Coral Bay hippies, tired of drink and drugs and lonely carousing, people looking for something to fill the emptiness they felt had come to dominate their lives.

On this Sunday morning, not wishing to disturb the worship services already underway, Bethany slipped into the rear entrance to the church and sat on a bench near the door. The congregation was singing "Will There Be Any Stars in My Crown," accompanied by a tall West Indian woman playing an acoustic guitar and two teenagers, one lining out the rhythm with a tambourine, the second playing a small silver flute in harmony to the congregation's melody. Leaning forward, Bethany rested her arms on the bench in front of her and raised her voice in song, "When I wake with the blest in those mansions of rest; will there be any stars in my crown?"

She glanced around, smiling as she saw the altar that stood at the front of the room where the restaurant's bar had once been. Its centerpiece was a mahogany pulpit carefully hand-crafted by a member of the congregation, Wendell Lettsome, a West Indian fisherman locally sought after for his boat building skills. He had also built a simple cross that hung behind the altar, as well as benches for the worshippers, who were now clapping and swaying as they sang.

The service over, Garry stood at the door shaking hands and conversing with anyone who wished to speak with him. Merry, his wife and their children stood beside him and chatted with members of the congregation, many of them seeming as eager to visit with Merry as they were with Garry. Bethany approached Merry, slipping an arm around her shoulder.

"I love hearing you sing," she said.

"Your singing is inspired." Merry reached up and took Bethany's hand. "I feel blessed every time I walk into this church and think how you were instrumental in saving the building from falling completely into ruin so that we could worship here."

Bethany laughed. "I reckon we've got a mutual admiration society going here."

"You two could do a lot worse than admire one another," Garry said. "I sure admire the both of you."

Bethany and Merry shook hands. "We've got him fooled," Bethany said.

Merry said, "I've had him bamboozled for years. He says I'm a saint for putting up with him. And you know what, he could be right. At least I was a saint to follow him to the Upper Peninsula." She hugged herself and mimed shivering. "I was raised in Atlanta and met Garry in college. When we ended up in Michigan I was sure I'd died and gone to Hell. I'd never been in such a backwoods place, and a cold snowy one at that."

"And then I brought her here," Garry said. "From a backwoods place to a backwater one."

Merry took his hand. "There's no snow here and I don't miss that one bit. If I never see another snowflake as long as I live I'll die happy, so thank you dear for bringing me here."

Bethany gave them each a hug and walked off. Waving, she got into her Samurai and drove to the beach at Maho Bay.

A line of dark clouds was advancing from the north and a strong wind blew over the surface of the water, the full tide sending waves into the single line of seagrapes that separated the end of the beach from the adjacent road. She parked and walked to the water line. It was still early, with only a few scattered beachgoers on what little open sand remained as the swells blew in from the north. Taking off her shoes, she waded into the surf and lifted her skirt high enough to keep the hem dry as waves broke against her legs.

"I wonder if I'm doing enough here," she said, half aloud, thinking of how tired she often felt at the end of a day.

A pelican plopped into the water a few feet away. Bethany watched it dunk its head, its tail end bobbing up and down as it searched for food.

"Hey pelican," she said as the bird raised its head. It seemed to ignore her. "Hey pelican," she said again.

This time the bird turned toward her and blinked. "You know what you have to do," it seemed to say, but its beak never moved.

"You do choose the strangest ways to talk to people," she said. "Most people would say that I'm flat out crazy to think that I'd believe you were talking through a pelican, and they'd surely bring out the white jackets if they heard me talking back." She smiled at the bird. "It's a good thing there aren't many people on the beach today."

The pelican blinked again. "Would you ignore me if the beach was filled with people?"

"Of course not. I just meant that because of the weather, there weren't many people here to think I was crazy. But then I suppose those clouds and the waves and the wind were your idea."

This time the pelican seemed to say, "Everything is my idea. The world was my idea and people would do well to remember that."

"And those that don't, those that deliberately ignore it must be punished."

She was sure the pelican replied, "You've always known what you have to do."

She closed her eyes and said. "I've been doing just like you told me to do, but I've probably disappointed you."

"You've done as well as you could."

"Is that enough?"

"Nothing you could do would ever be enough for me. There is no one on earth who could do enough to please me."

"I try."

She opened her eyes to look at the pelican, but it had already spread its wings and flown off. She looked up and saw it soaring ever higher; circling the bay looking for food just like the other pelicans it had joined in the air. Another one plopped into the water a few feet away and dunked its head, its tail end bobbing up and down as it searched for food.

Reaching down and cupping seawater in her hand, she let it fall over her head. The moment with the pelican was both her question and its answer. There could never be enough to do in a world filled with loneliness and pain and evil. There were challenges for her, tasks ahead in this funny little corner of the world. She had come to love Coral Bay and its people. She would do whatever she could for them, because that's what Bethany Wren did. That was what she was meant to do, give succor to those in need and see to the punishment of evil. It was a two-fold mission she had long pursued, convinced there had to be both comforting and avenging angels. It pleased her to know that she was both: that it was her mission to love who properly and dutifully loved her God, and to assure that the horrors of Hell rained down upon those who failed to live up to His—and to her—notions of obedience.

There was nothing crazy about that, she was sure.

Nineteen

THE LIQUID PLUMBER sat at a table a few feet from the bar, near the exit leading to the dock. Three empty glasses were in front of him and he tapped his fingers on the table top. Robert was away from the bar helping the cook restock the beer taps. No one was watching to see if he needed another drink and the first tendrils of sobriety were sneaking around the outer corners of his brain. He wanted to snuff them out as soon as possible, before the reality of his life began to show through the clouds that covered his thoughts.

Her tray heaped with sandwiches and drinks, Bethany passed him on her way to deliver them to a group of tourists gathered around a table at the far side of the room. Talking in loud voices, the men wore bathing suits and flowered shirts, straw hats and baseball caps, the women had thrown thin cotton shifts over their bathing suits. All had the red skin that comes from spending too much time on a beach with too little sun screen for protection.

The Liquid Plumber raised his finger and gestured toward Bethany, pointing at the empty glasses on his table.

"You're killing yourself with booze, you know," Bethany told him.

He did not look at her. "Your job isn't to keep people from drinking."

She nodded. "I get paid to sell drinks and food but that doesn't keep me from trying to save people from themselves when I see them drowning in the alcohol they buy from this place."

"I'm doing just fine."

"No, you're not. You come here first thing in the morning and sit drinking all day. That's not fine. Not in any way is it fine. It's slow suicide."

"If it's suicide, it's my suicide and my way of doing it."

Bethany bit her lower lip. "It's like John Donne said, 'No man is an island...each man's death diminishes me, for I am involved in mankind.' That means all our lives would be lessened if we let you kill yourself."

Teach cleared his throat and turned on the stool. "'Therefore, send not to know for whom the bell tolls. It tolls for thee.' That's foolishness, you know."

"I know nothing of the kind."

His lip curled, his nose quivering, Teach shook his head. "Why bother trying to save this idiot here from killing himself with alcohol? He's smart enough to know what booze does to a man's liver and his brain and the rest of him. If he chooses to drink the way he does, it's his business, not yours. When he dies the world will be better off, not lessened."

"Listen to the man," the Liquid Plumber said.

Bethany stared at Teach. "He may be smart, but not smart enough to save himself."

"So you're going to save him?"

The Liquid Plumber said. "If you're determined to save me, then get me another drink. That's all the salvation I need."

Her eyes still fixed on Teach, she ignored the Liquid Plumber's remark. "I'll do what I can to save almost anybody." She paused, then added in a pointed tone, "Except them that don't deserve salvation; them that are damned at birth."

Teach made a spitting sound. "Don't you ever get tired of interfering in people's lives? If the man wants to drink himself to death, let him do it for Christ's sake."

"It's for Christ's sake that I try to stop good people from harming themselves and others." Bethany's voice trembled with anger.

Teach's eyes narrowed and he spoke so softly that she had to lean close to him in order to hear. His breath reeked of tobacco and beer. "All men are islands and the sea is rising and it will cover them all and there's nothing you or anybody else can do about it. Each man's death doesn't mean anything to me other than giving me the satisfaction that's there's one less worthless human being taking up space and wasting the earth's resources. Let the bell toll. I don't give a rat's tail who it tolls for as long as it's not tolling for me."

"It's our responsibility to do whatever we can to keep the seas from rising," Bethany said. "And it's a responsibility I choose to take on."

Teach jerked his thumb at the Liquid Plumber. "And he chooses to drown in alcohol. We all make our choices."

"It's a totally different kind of choice," she said, her voice filled with sympathy. "You're a sad and bitter man."

"I'm not at all sad. As far as being bitter is concerned, I've got a better poem for you than that treacle of John Donne's."

"It's not treacle," she said, her voice still tinged with anger.

He shrugged. "This one's by Stephan Crane. It's perfect and beautiful."
He raised his voice and nearly chanted Crane's poem:

> In the desert
> I saw a creature, naked, bestial,
> Who, squatting upon the ground,
> Held his heard in his hands,
> And ate of it.
> I said: "Is it good, friend?"
> "It is bitter-bitter," he answered;
> But I like it
> Because it is bitter
> And because it is my heart."

Teach's eyes burned and he bared his teeth. "Now, that's the truth of the human condition."

"That's not poetry. It's the worst kind of venom, Satanic verse."

"Think whatever you wish," Teach said.

Bethany pointed to the mobile of the soles of sneakers, flip-flops, shoes and sandals. The sign on the wire holding it suspended from the beam caught the breeze. The words, *The Lost Soles of Coral Bay*, spun slowly above them. "That's you, Mr. Teach, just another lost soul in Coral Bay spinning in the wind."

"I'm solid." He said. "The only thing spinning around here is your brain."

Picking up the tray upon which she had put the Liquid Plumber's empty glasses, she touched Teach's arm in passing. "You don't have to be the way you are," she said.

He recoiled and brushed her hand away. "I am the way I am because it's the way I am, the way I am supposed to be."

"I don't believe that."

"You have faith," he said.

"I do."

"Then have faith that I am exactly what I am and what I wish to be."

"Then I pity you."

"Don't."

"I can't help it."

"Neither can I." His lips turned upward but there was no warmth in the smile that he put upon his face.

Twenty

"WHAT IS IT about you and music?" X asked.

She and Robert had hiked the trail that runs along the shore line from the ruins of the Annaberg Plantation to the far end of Leinster Bay where it becomes the Johnny Horn Trail, leading uphill to where a short jaunt away from the main trail a secondary trail ends at what had once been the Leinster Bay Estate House. Situated on Windy Hill, a ridge above the bay, the ruins of the estate house overlooks the Mary Creek section of St. John and opens to views of the British Virgin Islands. It was Robert's day off and he had packed a picnic lunch and stowed it in his backpack. When they reached the ruin, he set the pack down behind the remains of a wall where the sun would not shine directly on it.

Standing atop a broken wall, Robert reached for X's hand as they looked at the view, the British islands in the background, the sky filled with puffy sundrenched clouds that were reflected in the sea, its surface mottled with their shadows. The surrounding islands and small cays rose from the Caribbean. Lush with vegetation and edged with white sandy beaches, they were so unlike the snow covered hills of western Massachusetts that he felt as though he was in a world apart from the one he had always inhabited. A world, he was beginning to feel, where almost anything might be possible, one where he might free himself from the disappointments and sorrows of the past.

"It's lovely up here," he said.

She squeezed his fingers.

"What's your name?" he asked, avoiding her question about his feelings regarding music by asking one equally intrusive.

"It is lovely up here," she replied.

"It is."

"There's something in your eyes that makes me think your story must be a sad one."

"Sometimes people see their own unhappiness in others."

"You're avoiding the question."

"As you avoided mine."

"Fair enough," she said. "We can avoid our questions a little longer, but you do know that we will have this conversation at some point."

"I know." His voice was soft, barely audible over the light breeze drifting uphill from the sea below.

"That is, we'll have it if we're going to be anything other than bartender and customer who have dinner together and take occasional hikes to look at beautiful ruins and views."

He nodded.

"But not today, I guess," she said.

"Soon," he said. "Maybe."

Releasing her hand, Robert walked to the edge of the ruin, kicking pieces of crumbled brick, loose rock and broken coral ahead of him as he scuffled over the rubble. X followed and stood beside him. She gestured toward Drake's Channel which ran between the United States and British Virgin Islands.

"It looks like you could swim to the west end of Tortola from here."

"They say some of the slaves did that, swam over there to get away from the brutality of life on St. John's plantations. They also say that a lot of them drowned."

"Was the life you're running from as brutal as that? So brutal that you'd risk drowning to get away from it."

"Not in any way. Yours?"

She shook her head. "Thinking of how the slaves suffered on the plantations here makes my miseries seem foolish and petty."

"Misery swells to fill any space you have that it can find to pour itself into, no matter how inconsequential that misery is."

"I don't think I could in good conscience use the word misery for what I carry with me. Grief and the sorrow that come from it are what I left behind, not a life of bondage, hard labor and despair."

Robert's breath caught in his throat but he said nothing.

X said, "We could start talking about simple things; sort of break the ice for that conversation we know we're going to have."

"It we're going to be more than friends, you mean."

She smiled. "So, tell me something about yourself before you came to St. John, anything, no matter how trivial."

He chuckled. "I grew a beard in college."

"When did you shave it off?"

"In medical school." As soon as the words were out, he grunted in disgust, shook his head and ran his hands through his hair.

"You didn't mean to say that, did you?"

"I didn't." He kept his eyes on the water. He could almost feel the thrumming from the diesel engines of a green and white Tortola ferry. Sailboats with brightly colored spinnakers darted about and small motor launches crisscrossed around them. He thought how deceptive it was that their formless wakes seemed to create patterns on the surface of the sea.

"My name's Christine," she said to break the silence that had fallen between them.

He laughed. "Mine's Robert, and I did go to medical school. The last name is Palmer, by the way."

"I knew your first name."

"It could have been an alias. There are a lot of aliases in Coral Bay. "

"But it wasn't an alias."

"No."

"I won't ask if you graduated from medical school."

"Thanks. We have to save some things for the conversation that we're not having now but will have."

"Soon, I hope."

He turned toward her. Placing a hand on each of her shoulders, he pulled her close. She stayed that way for a moment. She pulled away with a gentle motion and looked back over the channel, "I wondered why you knew so much about cholesterol."

"Everybody should know about cholesterol and watch what they eat."

"But they don't, do they?"

He answered with a negative grunt and again they stood for a long moment without speaking. The ferry passed beyond sight, the sound of its engines fading until Robert and Christine could again hear waves breaking against the rocks far below.

"Did Bethany tell you to ask me for a date?" Christine said.

He nodded.

"She told me to ask you for one if you didn't ask me."

"That woman is determined to make sure that everybody she meets is happy."

"Do you think she's happy?"

"I don't believe she thinks about her own happiness," he said.

X nodded. "If I had to guess, I'd say that she uses religion to keep her mind occupied on things outside herself. It's her wall against the world."

"It's a harsh faith. She seems as determined to see some people suffer for eternity as she is to save others."

X cleared her throat and turned to face him. "You can call me Christine, if you want to, but only when we're alone."

"I'd like that, Chris."

She wagged a finger at him. "Christine. Not Chris. Never Chrissy. Never Tina. Only Christine."

"You have a last name, I assume."

"Did you finish medical school?"

"Ah," he said, laughing. "That discussion."

"I guess you're really not ready for it."

"Not yet." He took both her hands and held her at arm's length. "Are you?"

"I think I am." She spoke quietly. "But we don't need to rush things."

The wind blew through her hair and rustled the fabric of her blouse. Her eyes were brown and clear, her lips full, even when spread in a smile. He opened his mouth to tell her that he thought her beautiful, but stopped himself before he could utter the words. They would have expressed more than he was ready to say, promising as much to himself as to her that other words could follow. The thought frightened him.

Christine said, "You looked like you had something more to say."

"It's for later," he said. "For the conversation."

"It seems as though we're saving a lot for later."

"Does that bother you?"

Her eyes glistened and raising her hand, she shielded them from the sun. "No. I think it's sweet. We're like a couple of kids slowly testing the waters."

He looked at the sea below them. He could hear waves breaking against the rocks. "Testing the waters is a smart thing to do if you don't want to drown. There are deep places and dangerous things down there."

"I've come already close enough to drowning. I won't plunge into treacherous waters again."

"I think I did drown." Robert's voice was as flat and dull as his eyes. "I think I may be dead."

"You're no zombie or vampire," she said. "You've got too much of a sense of humor."

He sighed, laughed and slapped his head with the heel of his hand.

"What I am is a melodramatic jerk. I should have said that I'm still coming through a bad time. I'm not miserable and I'm not drowning and I'm not dead. I'm just cautious—wary."

She gave him a bright smile and affected a light tone. "Me too, so let's stop talking and acting like we feel sorry for ourselves."

Crossing to where the backpack sat, she picked it up and took out a red and white checkered tablecloth, spreading it on the floor of the ruined estate house. Before she could finish, a breeze lifted one end and folded it over. While she picked up several small rocks to weight it down, Robert took the sandwiches and drinks from the backpack. Once they were seated, he opened the tabs of two soda cans, handed one to her and tapped his to it.

"Here's to you, Christine X," he said.

"And to you, Doc."

"Robert," he said.

She rested a hand on his cheek. "Here's to you, Robert."

"I told you my last name," he said.

She lowered her hand and looked across the channel toward Tortola. Clouds surrounded its highest peak. "There a rain forest up there," Christine said, pointing at the misty summit. "We could go there someday, take a boat to Tortola, rent a car and drive up to the trail head. We'd hike through the forest and have lunch back at the trail head where an old Brit expatriate has a rundown restaurant."

"I'd like that," Robert said.

She leaned over and kissed his cheek. "It's St. Pierre. Christine St. Pierre."

Part Two

The Pit of Hell

Twenty-one

BETHANY WAS UNAWARE that for two weeks Teach had watched her closely, noting her habits and schedule. Her presence filled him with rage, in part due to the pity she had expressed for him, but also due to her piety. He believed her show of decency and kindness was a cover for her true nature, one as unforgiving as his own. It contrasted with all he felt within himself, the joy of creating chaos, wreaking havoc, the pleasures of being an agent of death whenever the hawk moved its wings.

A week of following her had more than doubled his wrath. Beyond her work at Dante's Landing, her villa cleaning activities, and her attendance at church—Sunday services and Wednesday prayer meetings—he saw no clear pattern to her comings and goings, and thus no path by which he might fly down and pounce upon her.

She occasionally went to a beach, but when and to which beach was unpredictable, other than that she tended to go at the height of the day when the beaches were filled with people. She seemed to favor Maho Bay, but she would go to all the North Shore beaches, as well as Salt Pond and Lameshur. She would set a chair up on the sand just inside the water line and read as the surf swirled and foamed around her feet. Populated beaches presented no opportunities for him to vent his fury.

She and Amanda Hillborn were always together at the villas they cleaned, making it too risky to go after her while she worked, if going after her was what he was going to do. Bethany was not like the others. She was a threat. She was his opposite, yet strangely, his twin; both of them determined in their beliefs that the unworthy must be rooted out. Teach imagined that like him with his hawk, within her was a brightly colored songbird with sharp teeth.

He thought her an abomination, but unlike his other kills, her death would give rise to a public outcry and action that the deaths of people like Crowley, the drunken tourist and Sonny never would. If the hawk were to soar and take her, there could be no trace of its talons, no marks from its beak. She would have to disappear, or perish in what people would assume to be an accident. It was a removal that would require all his skills.

He had done it before but she would be his most difficult elimination. He would have to plan carefully and be ready to take advantage of any opportunity. Only vigilance and a willingness to act quickly and the ability to cover his tracks would lead to success. The two weeks he had spent watching and noting her movements were the beginning. He would have to be ever ready to take advantage of any sudden opening, any unexpected move on her part.

SOMETHING WAS WRONG. In retrospect, Bethany realized she had felt it since before Bear Crowley's body was found in the chair outside Dante's Landing. Many recent mornings she had awakened long before dawn from dreams that left her shivering; dreams filled with shadowy images of broken and burning towers, of forests laid waste, fallen trees rotting into a barren land littered with the dried carcasses of deer, elk, wolves, bear, all the many creatures of the shattered forests where no birds sang or flew through the air where once the fallen and decaying trees had stood. There had been a sensation of menace lurking behind the dead trees and animals, their bones visible through the dry hides of their carcasses.

During the days she managed to ignore the disquiet to which the dreams gave rise, but at night, lying in bed, she would have to steel herself against them, willing herself to sleep despite fearing that another night of uneasy dreams lay ahead. There were nights free of dreams and nights filled with them. At bedtime, slipping under her covers and waiting for sleep, she had no way of knowing which lay ahead, dreams or peaceful slumber, and that unknowing itself was enough to lessen the peace of her sleep.

Following a Wednesday night prayer meeting, she took Garry Jensen by the arm and led him to a quiet corner on the church verandah. Someone was playing "Island in the Sun" on a steel drum at the nearby Aqua Bistro restaurant. The soft tones of the melody carried through the air to where they stood in the shadows of palm fronds on the trees members of the congregation had planted to replace the dead ones that had once leaned against the building.

"There's evil in the air," she said.

Garry took a deep insuck of breath and cleared his throat. "What is it?"

Bethany clasped her hands to her breast and raised her eyes to meet his. "I don't know, but whatever it is, it is very close."

"Are you in danger?"

She arched her hands, lightly bouncing the tips of her fingers together. "I think so. It feels that way. But I don't know how, or from where. It's just a sense I have of something, or someone, hovering nearby, waiting to strike." She shivered. "Whatever it is, it unsettles me."

"Of all the people I know, you are the one with the least to fear from evil."

"Everyone should fear evil." She willed her voice to be strong, in spite of the tremors she felt in her hands.

"Evil cannot prevail."

"Evil is strong. We must fight it with all our might. There can be no pity, no mercy for those who are truly evil." She looked toward the water. Lights on masts bounced in the moonless night as boats rocked in the light waves at the edge of the harbor. "Back home there was a man, Edd Byrd. Everybody knew he killed his wife and baby daughter, but it couldn't ever be proved. The sheriff even arrested him, but the district attorney wouldn't prosecute him. There wasn't enough evidence, she said. Then Edd Byrd went and married a woman from Stony Creek over in Tennessee and a few years later, she disappeared. He claimed she ran off with a holiness preacher from Johnson City and said he'd heard they were living somewhere in Alabama."

"That should have been easy to check out."

"The sheriff made a couple of phone calls and found out that a preacher was missing from that holiness church in Johnson City, but nobody knew where he went."

"You think this Edd Byrd killed both of them, her out of meanness and the preacher, as an alibi?"

Bethany sucked in her lips and popped them. "That's exactly what I think?"

"And the sheriff?"

"He told me he was too busy busting meth labs and burning down stands of marijuana to go off on a wild goose chase."

"Why did he tell you that?"

She looked away, her hands trembling. When she turned her face back to his, her lips were narrowed and she spoke in a clipped and determined manner. "Because I asked him to do something about that vile murderer."

"Why?"

"The first wife that he killed was my sister. She was the middle one of the ten of us brothers and sisters, ten years older than me." She closed her eyes, her face twisted as if she were in pain. "It's nothing I want to talk about."

"There are a lot of things that people in Coral Bay don't want to talk about."

"That's why a lot of people stay here where nobody bothers them."

"And they don't have to talk about their pasts?"

"Not if they choose not to."

"What happened to Byrd?"

"After the second wife disappeared, he got married again, to a fifteen year-old girl that lived back in a holler in the hills outside of Newland. When she was eighteen they found her drowned, lying face down in a creek, an empty bucket lying beside her. The sheriff wrote it up that she must have slipped when she went out to fill the bucket with water. Nobody believed it, including the sheriff, but he told me he couldn't prove anything."

"So nothing happened to Byrd?"

"Something happened." Bethany smiled. "Somebody stabbed him while he was sleeping, got him right through the heart with a knife that was almost as big as a sword. It happened a few weeks before I moved down here. Whoever it was that killed him, she snuck into his house, held a knife over him and brought it down with such force that it pinned him to the bed. She climbed up, put her knees on him and held him in place until his last breath came rasping out of him. He died hard, just like he should have. When they found him his eyes were open and his face looked like he'd just seen the devil come to snatch his soul away."

"Evil did not prevail," Garry said.

"It did not." Her voice rang with satisfaction.

Garry clicked his teeth. "He's rotting in Hell now."

"He is. Too often the world lets evil people evade punishment. It takes a special kind of believer to make sure that they are called to judgment, someone who has no doubts about the righteousness of her actions." Once again looking out over the harbor, Bethany sighed deeply. The impounded Cheoy Lee was moored close to shore, a dark hulk on the night sea.

"Many people of faith have moments of doubt."

She turned quickly and looked into Garry's eyes, replying in a voice that rang with conviction. "Never. I may have a flawed human memory, but I never doubt my faith."

"But you're afraid of something, or someone, hovering nearby, waiting to strike."

"I didn't say I was afraid. I said I had a sense of it, a feeling. What I'm worried about is what might happen to other people around here. There've been three murders already. Robert, the bartender at Dante's Landing, believes they're related."

Garry shook his head. "I don't understand why you work at that place. It's a haven for drunks and lowlifes."

"Who needs saving more than they do?"

"Do they seek salvation?"

She laughed. "What is a pastor's job? Do you tend only to the flock that comes to you, or do you go out and ask others in to join us?"

"I have to tend to the flock I have."

"And the others?"

Garry sat on the verandah's railing, his back to the sea. "That's the hard part."

"No doubt about that." Keeping her voice neutral, she flashed him a sly smile.

He coughed. "It's not easy for me to go into places where sinful things take place and try to spread the Gospel to the people sinning there."

"But that's your job."

He nodded. "It is. I do the best I can. I'm a limited creature. The human being is a limited and flawed creature, even the best of us."

"That's why God came to us as Jesus, so he could understand just how limited and flawed we are. As Jesus, he shared our limitations and flaws."

"I was taught that Jesus was pure and perfect."

She shook her head. "He was God made man. How can any man be pure and perfect? God knows our limitations and flaws because for a short time he shared them and felt them and was controlled by them. Then he went back to being God and now he knows who to punish and why." Her eyes narrowed and her nostrils quivered. "Them that revel in their flaws and limitations and don't repent will be forever tortured in the burning pits of hell."

"That a fierce way of looking at things," Garry said.

"We're all limited, but our mission is to try to overcome our limitations and go out and spread the Gospel, no matter how hard a job it is to do."

"I do it to the best of my ability."

She briefly touched the back of his hand as it rested on the railing. "And I know that you do. I see it every time I'm with you, but people like us are called upon to extend our abilities beyond any boundaries we believe we have."

"Do you think I'm failing in my ministry here?"

She raised her hands to his face, cupping his cheeks. "This church couldn't function without you, but that doesn't mean you couldn't be a better pastor. We can all always be better than we are."

"I can't be perfect."

"Neither can I. No human is perfect, but knowing that we can't be perfect shouldn't prevent us from striving for perfection."

"I can't go out and preach in bars," Garry said. "I know it's a failing in me, a weakness, but I also know that I'm not capable of doing it."

"No one expects you to preach in bars. But if you did, your ministry would grow, and you'd grow as well."

He smiled at her. "They'd beat me up, you know. If I went out and tried to preach in the bars around here, I'd have black eyes and bruises."

"And you're afraid of that?"

"I do my best, and you say it's not enough."

"I know you do your best, but that doesn't mean you shouldn't do more."

"Like preach in bars."

"If that's what you're called to do."

"I'm not called to do that. So what do I do?"

"You wait until you're called to do something else."

"And when will that be?"

She heaved her shoulders in a massive shrug. "When it happens. When you're called upon. I wait everyday for a call."

"Does it ever come?"

"Sometimes." Her gaze shifted, her eyes seeming to look into a past that she found unbearable.

Garry shook his head with a rueful laugh. "And I'm supposed to be the pastor here."

"You're a good one," Bethany said.

"I hope so."

"Every one of us can be better than we are. We forget that and we fail God and he will punish us."

"Are you going to let me forget?"

She gave his chest a light poke with her forefinger. "Never."

Their eyes met and Garry was the first to look away, a light shudder chilling his soul.

Twenty-two

MECHANIC MIKE came out from under the hood of Bethany's Samurai and clucked his tongue. He and Bethany were standing beneath the branches of the large flamboyant tree where she regularly parked, a few feet from the entrance to Dante's Landing.

"You could use a new engine," Mechanic Mike told her.

"Is this one dead?"

"Not dead, but not in good shape. If I was to fix it up you'd be wasting your money. Better to get a new one."

"Where do I do that?"

"Brand new, nowhere on this island. If I was to go down to Isaiah Lettsome's junk yard, I might find one in better shape than this one is, but if I was you I'd take this old wreck down there and sell it to Isaiah for the few bucks he'll give you for it, and then I'd go over to one of them car rental companies on St. Thomas that's getting a new fleet and buy one of them five or six year old cars they're getting rid of to make room for the new ones. That's what I'd do."

"But I wouldn't have salvaged this one, and I love this old car."

"Want me to get a used engine from Isaiah?"

She patted the Samurai's right front fender. "How long can you make this one last?"

"For a hundred bucks, maybe a hundred and fifty, it'll be good for at least six months."

"Do it," she said.

"It's your money."

"I can't give up on it."

"Maybe I could rebuild the engine."

"At what cost?"

He grinned at her. "If I was to buy a used engine from Isaiah, I could dismantle it, take the good parts and put them in your engine. Of course I might have to put one or two new parts in it as well."

"How much?" she said again.

"Maybe five hundred."

"You could do that?"

"Easy."

"Wouldn't that just be like replacing my old engine with a used one?"

He shook his head. "I'd be rebuilding yours, giving it a new life."

"You'd save it?"

"I would."

With a pleased expression, she looked from Mechanic Mike to the Samurai. "It'd be like it was reborn."

"It would be reborn. It might take a while, though. A job like this isn't easy or quick, especially if I got to order parts."

"I surely do understand that. I've got a couple of similar projects going that are taking a long time."

Looking confused, he said, "What are you rebuilding?"

"It's complicated. Nothing mechanical."

Nodding, without understanding, he said, "You'll be stuck in Coral Bay, or have to hitch-hike and take the bus to get anywhere."

"How long?"

"No way of telling. Depends on getting the right parts."

"Let's do it," she said.

"I'll need a hundred bucks now, to go down to Isaiah's and buy a used engine and other parts."

She took out her checkbook and wrote a check. "I'm putting my faith in you."

"I'll save your engine. It'll be as good as new, maybe better." He pointed at the Samurai. "Of course that won't do the rest of this rust bucket any particular good."

"Of course it will," she said. "The engine is the heart of a car. If the heart is reborn, it doesn't matter how beat up the rest is."

"Your engine will purr like a kitten when I'm done with it."

"What more could I ask for?"

"Maybe a new car."

"I love this one."

"It's an island car, that's for sure."

She tore the check from her checkbook and handed it to him. "Save my car."

ROBERT OPENED a bottle of Heineken and set it on the bar in front of Teach, who grabbed it and took several long gulps.

"You look like you needed that." Not for the first time, he noticed Teach's sharp and dirt caked fingernails.

Teach looked at him with empty eyes.

"There's plenty more where that came from," Skipper Dan said, sticking his head up from beneath the bar where he had been installing a fresh keg of draft beer.

"Having a hard day?" Robert asked.

Skipper Dan took a crescent wrench from a tool box sitting beside the bar's cash register.

Teach answered with a grumble and groan as Skipper Dan disappeared below the bar, the sounds of the wrench against the metal keg accompanying his work

"I'll take that for a yes," Robert said. "What's wrong?"

Teach said, "I've got a project going that I can't quite figure out."

"Tell me about it. I'm pretty good at solving problems."

Teach picked the fingernails on his left hand with those growing on the right hand fingers. They were long, yellowed and thick. Robert thought they looked more like talons than normal human fingernails. Bethany came to the bar with a drinks order.

"I've noticed that X is drinking less," she said. "She's smiling more. Are you two spending a lot of time together?

Before Robert could reply, Teach turned to look at her. He asked in a harsh tone, "What's wrong with drinking?"

Bethany gave him a sharp glance. "I don't touch the stuff." Her eyes briefly rested on the Liquid Plumber whose face was lowered to the gleaming surface of the bar. "I suppose it's all right for some people to have a drink every now and then, as long as it doesn't dominate their lives."

"You ought to think it's all right." Teach's voice was a cold rumble and his nostrils quivered as he spoke. "The more drinks customers have, the bigger your tips, so why would you whine about people drinking too much?"

She handed the order slip to Robert, gave Teach another biting look and walked back to the dining area where she stood at the side of a table, order pad in hand.

"You were a little hard on her," Robert said.

"She's a pious goody-goody."

"I like her."

Teach said nothing and returned his attention to his fingernails.

"You don't like her," Robert said.

"I didn't say that." Teach did not look up from his fingernails.

"You didn't have to say anything. It's obvious." He spoke as he wiped down the bar. "She's been a good friend to me since the day I walked into this place."

Teach emptied his beer and asking for another, mumbled a reply. "I don't have to like her. I don't have to like anybody."

"You don't," Robert said. "Nobody has to like anybody."

Teach inclined his head in the direction where Bethany stood taking orders. "But goody-two-shoes over there probably would say everybody's got to love everybody; that love is a Christian's duty." His upper lip curled in a sneer and he continued in a scoffing tone, nearly spitting his words. "Christian duty, indeed. Now there's a fool's idea for you. The only duty we have is to ourselves, to do things that give us pleasure. No duty but pleasure."

Listening to Teach, seeing the void behind his eyes, Robert felt cold and hollow. For a fleeting instant he once more saw Maria walk into the blank swirling snow, Grace in her arms. Did he look as bleak, as devoid of feeling and love as the dark vacancy behind Teach's eyes revealed? Shuddering, he looked across the room toward Bethany. Her voice, tinged with laughter, carried to where he stood behind the bar.

"Another beer," Teach said.

Robert opened one and set it on the bar. Teach's hand struck out and grabbed it.

Robert said, "All I can tell you is that Bethany's the kind of friend anyone would be lucky to have."

A low wordless rattle came from deep in Teach's throat.

Changing the subject, Robert asked him, "What's the project you're having trouble with?"

Teach looked away from Bethany, fixing his eyes on Robert. "Nothing much."

"Maybe I could help you."

"I don't need help. I'll figure it out." He finished his beer and left the Landing.

"What was that all about?" Bethany said, coming back to the bar.

Robert dropped Teach's empty bottle in a plastic barrel and wiped the bar in front of where he had been sitting. "You've got me. It was almost like he was attacking you."

"He was attacking me."

"Why?"

Her face looked strained and pale. "I wish I knew."

"Someone must have hurt him."

"It was more like he wanted to hurt someone."

"Why strike out at you?"

She forced a laugh. "If you figure it out, be sure to tell me."

Robert took a deep breath before speaking. "He called you a pious goody-goody and a goody-two-shoes."

She laughed again. "I suppose I seem to be a goody-goody."

"He was right about that."

"If having faith and loving God makes me a goody-two-shoes, that's fine with me."

Robert tapped the bar with his fingers. Looking beyond Bethany toward Coral Bay, he watched a small motor boat roar from the harbor, its wake widening behind it. When he spoke his voice was low and she had to strain to hear his words.

"I thought I had faith, once."

"What happened?"

"I lost it." He looked into her eyes. "Actually, I probably never had it. I just gave it lip service like I was taught to do."

"Why?"

He shook his head and spoke quietly. "I don't want to talk about it."

"I knew it the first time we met," she said softly.

"How?"

Running her open hand over her lower face, she raised her eyebrows. The action pulled her eyes wide open. "I just know things, Mr. Robert."

"Sometimes you sound as weird as Teach."

"What do you know about him? You must talk about things when he's sitting at the bar."

"If he talks at all, it's about the weather, the condition of the roads after heavy rains, the problems with donkeys and goats running around the island. He claims to have killed and eaten a donkey."

She grimaced and hugged herself. "He ate a donkey?"

"That's what he told me."

"That's disgusting." She looked off toward the waters of Coral Bay.

Robert made a half laughing sound. "Lately he hasn't talked much except to express meanness, as if there's a nasty well of hatred roiling his depths and rising up to a place where he has to spew it out."

"I see that," Bethany said. She turned her eyes away for a moment, as if looking into a different world. Then smiling at him, she said, "On a completely different subject, are you planning on going to the Festival on the Fourth of July?"

Glad of the distraction, Robert smiled back. "I hadn't thought about it. I'll probably be exhausted from working Skipper Dan's pre-Fourth of July Festival party the night before."

"Then you're probably the only person on St. John without a plan for Festival. I'm surprised X hasn't mentioned it to you."

"She could have and it slipped my mind."

"The peak day of Carnival doesn't easily slip from someone's mind."

"Skipper Dan mentioned it to me when I started working here, and he's brought up that fact that he'll need both Boozie and me at work for his pre-Fourth bash, but I don't know anything about Carnival itself."

She raised her right forefinger in the air. "Wait here a minute." She left and returned with a copy of *Trade Winds*, St. John's weekly newspaper. Laying it on the bar, she pointed to the front page photograph of costumed people, several on stilts, partying in the Cruz Bay waterfront park. "Read all about last year's Festival. It's part of living here."

"Are you going?"

"I haven't missed one since I came to St. John."

She was about to sit on a stool opposite him when a group of tourists came in, their loud voices and beach-drenched laughter filling the room.

"Back to work," she said.

"Back to work," he repeated, but there was no one at the bar and he picked up the paper.

Carnival, he read, *was first held in 1912, when the Danes still occupied St. John and the other Virgin Islands. Discontinued during the First World War, it started again in 1952. A month long gala that combines food, fun and fantasy, with a celebration of the end of slavery and the coming of emancipation and independence to the island's West Indian people, Carnival culminates with the merriment of Festival Day on July 4th.* The article discussed the Festival with its calypso competitions, the Ms. St. John Pageant, the food fairs and the booths at Festival Village, which was newly erected each year and torn down at the Festival's end.

There were photographs of the celebrations, of musicians, of the food booths, of crowds filled with happy looking people dancing with raised hands and broad smiles. A side-bar discussed the mocko jumbies central to the Carnival Festival parade.

A supernatural, ghost-like shape-shifter that has its roots in West African mythology the jumbie is believed to come in the dark of night to wreak havoc upon those who have misbehaved. Jumbies, the article said, are thought by some to be fearsome and vengeance seeking demonic figures. Others see them as colorful and reassuring beings, embodying the continuity of ancestral beliefs that were ancient long before Arab slave traders raided West African villages and sold their captives as slaves to be taken in the brutal Middle Passage to the Caribbean and later into the United States.

The side-bar article was accompanied by a photograph of a mocko jumbie, a man on stilts wearing clothes of elaborately tailored and colored silks and satins.

Twenty-three

TEACH DID NOT mind hard work. He picked an excavation site in the clearing near his house, where he dug in the early mornings and in the evenings before the sun went down. He passed the hot hours of midday at Dante's Landing, drinking beer and watching Bethany when she was working. If she was aware of his glances and the way his eyes followed her when she was turned away from him, she gave no sign of knowing. Determined not to draw attention to the burning contempt she ignited in him, he carefully avoided any conversation with her beyond ordering burgers and beer when he sat at one of her tables. Most of the time he sat at the bar and Robert quickly noticed Teach's attention to Bethany's comings and goings.

"It's a little creepy," he told Skipper Dan after describing his observations.

"Maybe he's got a thing for her. She is a fine looking woman," Skipper Dan said.

"You're probably right," Robert said. "Too bad for Teach. She's not interested in romance."

Skipper Dan agreed, and both men shoved the subject of Teach and Bethany to the backs of their minds.

Teach dug on. It was hard work. Having been depleted during the sugar plantation era, the top soil was thin on the mountainside. Much of what remained had washed down hill into Coral Harbor. Beneath the remaining soil were rocks and more rocks, intertwined with thick roots from nearby trees that spread their reaches wide in the need to find water in the dry and rocky ground. Digging holes on the island's hillsides requires more work with pry bars and machetes than it does with shovels. Teach had to dig and pry loose many large rocks, chopping roots with his machete as he dug. When there was too much loose rock, soil and broken roots in the hole, he had to reach down and pick them out. As the hole grew deeper, he had to squat inside and toss them to the ground above. He sweated and cursed, but toiled on.

Working only in the cooler hours of the day, the job took weeks, but when he was finished Teach had a hole ten feet deep and eight feet square. He lined the rim with a single layer of concrete blocks and capped it with rusted tin roofing he found in the bush, blown from someone's roof in a hurricane. On it he spray-painted the words: Pit of Hell

"We'll see how Miss Goody-Two-Shoes likes the place I've made just for her." He muttered the words aloud, as if speaking to an invisible entity, perhaps one he was eager to please with the results of his labors.

"I'D LOVE to go to Festival with you," Christine said. "I was waiting for you to ask and I was going to ask you to go with me if you took much more time doing it."

They were sitting on towels under a clump of sea grapes lining the beach at Francis Bay. A group of children played at the edge of the surf. Their shouts and laugher carried on the light ocean breeze and settled over the beach.

It was Robert's day off. Earlier he had convinced her to take a walk. Parking by the beach at Francis Bay, they jogged down the paved road leading from Francis to the Annaberg Plantation ruins, Robert carrying a small back pack. From Annaberg they followed the seaside trail to Leinster Bay and hiked back up to the ruin where they once again picnicked.

"You're getting quite fit," Christine said as they walked back to Francis Bay. "I'm exhausted and you look like you could run all the way to the beach, back pack and all."

"I was turning into a self-pitying lump," he told her. "I've cut way back on my drinking and I'm exercising some every day."

"It looks good on you," she said.

Back on the beach, they spread their towels a few feet from the gently breaking surf and lay beside one another. Christine reached over the space between them and touched the back of his hand. He turned it over and wrapped his fingers around hers.

"I've been out of circulation for a long time," he said. "I still feel awkward asking you for a date."

"But you manage to do it."

"I do."

She rolled onto her side and propped herself up on an elbow. She watched him for a time and thought about what he had said and decided to use his words to segue into a conversation she had wanted to broach since their first date. "You just said, 'I do.' Those are loaded words and it makes me wonder, why are you still legally married?"

He frowned. "I don't know."

Christine nodded and spoke softly. "She did leave you."

"She walked out the door into a blizzard, taking my only child with her." Describing the scene and the despair he had felt that day, Robert was relieved that it was as though he were talking about someone else. For the first time he had a sense of the distance between him and the pain of that day.

"You haven't heard anything from her or about her since coming here?"

"Nothing."

"Not even about your child?"

"Not a word, not a photo, nothing."

"I'm sorry." She squeezed his hand.

"It doesn't feel as important as it once did. She could have divorced me by now."

"She probably couldn't get a divorce without you knowing about it, so I'd guess you're still married."

"It hasn't been a marriage for a quite a while, maybe even before she left."

Biting her tongue to keep from asking for details, she said only, "And after she left you came here."

"To St. Thomas at first. Dante's cousin at Hook, Line and Sinker told me about this job."

"The one and only Gypsy Davy," she said.

"A good guy. He turned me onto the job at the Landing as well as onto the *Bartender's Bible*. He and that book saved me."

She smiled and squeezed his hand again. "Then I guess we both owe him a lot."

"Is he responsible for you coming over here?"

Smiling, she said, "No."

"So why do you owe him?"

"For you being here."

Robert squeezed her hand in return.

She asked, "Do you want to know if she wants a divorce?"

"What good would come of knowing that?"

"Maybe it would free you from the past. Maybe it would mean that we can be more than friends."

"We are friends, aren't we?"

"We are," she said. "Is that enough for you?"

"I don't know." He carefully withdrew his hand from hers. Sitting up, he began digging in the sand between his legs. She lay back on her towel and closed her eyes. They stayed that way, quiet for a long while, the only sounds the lapping of the surf and the voices of the children playing in the water. The moment's peace was broken by the sound of a plane flying over the water and they looked up to see a single engine Cessna. They watched until it vanished on the far side of the island

"Is being friends enough for you?" he asked.

She sat back up and laughed. It was a strong sound. "I'm very patient. You know what they say about the chances women have who are looking for male companionship on St. John."

"Nope. I don't travel in that company."

"There are more single men than there are single women in Coral Bay," she said.

"I've noticed that."

"That makes the odds pretty good that a woman will have no trouble finding a man."

"That's logical. So what do they say about women looking for men?"

She clucked her tongue. "They say that the odds are good, but the goods are odd."

He grinned at her. "I'd say that's a fair statement. Am I odd goods?"

"Only in that you don't know whether or not you're still married and you don't seem to want to know. That's a little odd."

"I don't think about it often. I suppose that's why I haven't tried to find out."

"If she hasn't already filed, she may want a divorce."

"True," he said, nodding.

"Do you have any way of finding out, besides getting in touch with her?"

"Maria," he said. "Her name was Maria."

"I remember. And it was Maria? Past tense? That sounds like wishful thinking."

"She's dead to me."

"She's the mother of your child."

"Daughter. Her name is Grace."

Christine smiled. "Grace is my middle name. Christine Grace my mother always called me. Not just Christine and never Grace. Always Christine Grace. Whenever she called me that it sounded beautiful, like she was singing my name, singing to me. Everybody else except my boyfriend,

Bobby, called me Chrissy. To him I was always Christine."

"Where is he now?"

"He died. Killed in a car wreck in Florida." Before Robert could say anything, she added, "It was a long time ago, a long time." She picked up a handful of sand and let it slowly fall through her half open fist. "Is Grace dead to you as well?"

Robert's eyes lowered his face, slowly shaking his head as he did. "I dream about her. Sometimes she's a newborn and sometimes she's a grown woman with children of her own. It's like she's lived a whole life in my dreams, but in real life she's still a little girl."

"So, I ask again, is there anyone you could call to find out what Maria has done regarding your marriage?"

Robert thought of his former partner in the medical practice, Raymond Wentworth, and nodded. "Yeah, there is."

"Why don't you call him?"

Robert felt suddenly ill, his vision blurred, his heart pounding, his breath coming in short quick gasps. It was the beginning of a panic attack, something he had not experienced since medical school. He lay down and tried to control his breathing. Christine saw his face turn pale and heard his labored breathing.

Immediately, she was on her knees at his side, her hands on his chest.

"Are you having a heart attack? Should I call 911?"

"Panic," Robert managed to wheeze as he struggled for breath.

"I'm not panicking. Just tell me if you're having a heart attack." Christine's voice was calm and she had her cell phone out of her beach bag and was dialing 911 with her thumb. When she saw she had no service, she tossed it onto her towel and began doing compressions on his chest.

"Panic attack," he managed to say as he slowly began to calm down. "I'm having a panic attack. I haven't had one in years, but I know the symptoms."

Lying flat, his hands digging into the sand on either side of the towel, he counted backward from a hundred and finally controlled his breathing. Color returned to his face and his vision cleared. Slowly, his heartbeat returned to normal. A few minutes later, he sat up and drank a cold soda Christine took from a small cooler she had in her beach bag.

She leaned over and kissed his cheek. "You seem all right now."

"It's passed," he said.

She forced a small laugh. "I guess you'd better forget about calling your friend."

"I don't want to hear any voices from the past."

"You have a pretty scary way of showing that."

He took a long drink from the can. "I suppose I could write Ray and ask."

"Only if you really want to know," she said.

After a long pause he mumbled, "I think I do."

Back at Coral View after dropping Christine at Paradise Found, he wrote a long email to Ray Wentworth, asking what he might know about the recent events in Maria's life, inquiring about her health and that of Grace. His hand shook as he typed and he was forced to delete typo after typo. He did not mention where he was or what he was doing, but he assured Ray that he was well and living comfortably in a climate far superior to that of western Massachusetts.

He let it sit on the screen, reading it over several times as he asked himself if he really wanted to know the details of Maria's life. His message seemed overly informal, too chatty, and he decided he did not want to mention anything about his current life, no matter how brief and sketchy. He and Ray had been cordial partners in the group practice, but they had never been close friends. He deleted the entire email and wrote a much more abbreviated message:

Hi Ray: I hope this is not a bother. Have you heard whether or not Maria has filed for divorce? Also, do you have any news about our daughter, Grace? I hope you are well. Sincerely, Robert Palmer.

He hoped that the message was not so terse that Ray would be offended by its tone and delete it without replying. Maybe he should delete this one too. He stared at the computer until the letters seemed to blur and dance on the screen. He left the desk and went to the kitchen. Taking a diet cola from the refrigerator, he spread peanut butter on a plateful of crackers and took them outside. The night was warm and still. Below, he stared at mast lights in the harbor, barely moving on the calm and wind free water.

The carbonated soda seemed to enliven his taste buds and mixing with the peanut butter he thought it had been a fine treat. When he drank the last of his soda and ate the final cracker, he went back inside and looked at the email. It would have to do. There was nothing else he wanted to say. Ray could respond, or he could delete it and forget that Robert had ever existed. Indeed, he might already have forgotten. Robert did not care. He wanted to know whether or not he was still married. And he wanted word of Grace. If Ray didn't come through with the information he would try another way to find out.

Why he cared about the state of his marriage confused him. Was it for himself? Was it because Christine wanted to know? Probably both, he thought. And what of Christine? Did he want to get serious with her, or was she simply a diversion, a pleasant and attractive companion to spend time with in order to punctuate the string of lonely hours that constituted his life when not working at Dante's Landing?

He knew he cared about Grace. Since she had been taken from him he had felt bereft. He did not fully understand why. She was a toddler when she had been carried out into that blizzard, but from the moment she was born and he had held her in his arms, she had filled his heart in a lovely and mysterious way.

He hit SEND. The screen blinked and the email disappeared, becoming nothing more than a stream of ones and zeros that would almost immediately be reconstituted into the words of his message in the inbox of Ray Wentworth's email on his computer in Graham, Massachusetts.

Robert went back out into the night and rested the palms of his hands on the railing of the verandah. He looked up at the stars just as a meteorite streaked over waters of Coral Bay. He took a deep breath, hoping that Ray would reply quickly.

Twenty-four

BETHANY WAS ENDING her shift at Dante's Landing when Mechanic Mike came in and sat beside Teach at the bar. She tapped him on the shoulder.

"Any progress on my car?"

He rubbed his stubble of beard and looked at her with watery eyes. His hands were shaking and he turned toward Boozie. "A dark and diet." As the bartender poured his drink, Mechanic Mike turned his attention back to Bethany. "I'm having trouble getting a few parts."

"What kind of trouble?"

"There's some I can't find nowhere here or over to St. Thomas. I got to send to Miami for them."

"How long will that take?"

He shrugged. "No way of telling. If they got them at the place I order from, maybe a week or so. If they don't then it could be a lot longer. It's an old car and some of them parts I need maybe nobody makes no more and I'll have to do a stateside junkyard search."

"I can't afford to send you up to find parts for my car."

He laughed. "Won't have to. All that stuff is on line from junkyards all across the country. Still, you won't have a car for a while yet."

"You warned me that might happen."

"I did."

"Do the best you can," she said.

"I always do." He gave Teach a playful tap on the shoulder. "I fixed your set of wheels up real good, didn't I?"

Teach rolled his eyes and spoke in a low growl. "You did all right. The windows are still jammed shut, except on the driver's side and the shocks are shot. Every time I go over a bump it sounds like it's going to bottom out, but at least it's still running.

"See," Mechanic Mike said to Bethany. "Another satisfied customer."

"I have faith in you," she told him.

"I'll get you fixed up soon as I can."

"I know." She smiled quickly and walked to the office to fill out her time slip. When she finally left the Landing, Teach was leaning against his car, a cigarette dangling from his lips.

"While you're waiting for that idiot to fix your car, anytime you need a ride and I'm around, I'll be glad to be a chauffeur," he said.

Startled by his offer, she nodded and answered with a non-committal thank you.

Teach sensed her wariness. "I've been pretty cranky with you of late."

"You have super cranky. Nasty, I'd put it."

"I'm sorry about that. There's been bad news from up home and I've been taking it out on the people around me."

"You've been harsh."

He put on an abashed look and ran his fingers through his hair. "And, like I said, I'm sorry about that."

She let her voice soften. "Things can get a person down, especially if they don't have a faith to sustain them."

"I've got faith," Teach said.

"I'm glad to hear that. You should come to our church sometime."

"I might do that." Teach thought his words sounded as if they had been pushed through a tight and narrow opening, coming into the open air begrudgingly.

Bethany seemed not to notice. "I'll look forward to seeing you there."

Teach replied with an affirmative grunt and said, "Don't forget, if you need a ride somewhere and I'm around and I'm headed anywhere near where you want to go, I'll take you along."

"Thank you. That's a right thoughtful thing to say."

"You going anywhere right now?"

She shook her head and looked at her watch. "I was going to take a walk, but it's late and I'm tired. It's been a hard day. I think I'll go back to my boat and collapse."

Teach touched his forehead. "Well, good night then."

He watched as she turned around and went back into Dante's Landing and walked across the floor to the exit for the dinghy dock.

TEACH RETURNED to his home on Bordeaux Mountain. Sooner or later he'd get her into his car and into the Pit of Hell. He lifted the make-shift roof from it and looked at its dark walls. The smell of damp earth rose from the hole and he was pleased, thinking of the pleasure he would feel when he lifted it to drop Bethany in. She eventually would die in there; die of starvation, of exposure, perhaps, he hoped, of despair, assuming, of course, that he could refrain from killing her with his bare hands. Lowering the roof back in place, he weighted it down with ten concrete blocks.

This was going to be the grand finale of his time on St. John. He would not kill Bethany as he had the others. She was going to die slowly, within earshot of his bedroom. It would, he was sure, be delightful. He would go to sleep, lulled by the sounds of her whimpering as she prayed to her God for release. She would beg him to let her go each time he lifted the roof to look in at her, to toss her a small plastic bottle of water, or just enough food scraps to keep her from dying before he was ready. He would become like a god to her, holding the power of life and death, the one who could answer her prayers or leave her to die in the pit, cold, alone and wondering why she had been abandoned and allowed to suffer so. She would cry for relief and release and he would laugh, knowing that his unalterable choice for her was death.

He would tease her from time to time. I'll let you go if you curse God, he might say to her, to that Goody Two Shoes, to that pious little twit. How quickly she would ditch her faith and piety in order to save her skin. She might not give in immediately, but after two or three nights in his Pit of Hell and she would question her beliefs and soon she would be willing to say anything, do anything he might demand of her, if he would only let her go.

And he would promise anything she wanted, as long as she turned away from her mindless religiosity and worshiped him and cursed God and Jesus and the angels and Heaven itself. Curse Heaven, he imagined himself saying to her. Curse Heaven and worship me. I am your only savior. Like any sane person, she would turn her back on her God. To save herself she would turn her back on everyone and everything she held dear, if only he would reach down, take her hand, and raise her from the Pit of Hell. The promise would be easy to make.

Of course, he would never do it. Oh, he might extend his hand into the pit just far enough for her to stretch as high as she could, straining on the very tips of her toes to touch her fingers to the ends of his, but he'd never reach down far enough for her to grasp his hand. It would be pure meanness and it struck him that there was no real pleasure in the world but meanness. He had no idea where that thought came from, but it was a good one and he smiled. This grand finale would be his masterpiece.

He removed the concrete blocks, lifted the roof and once again looked into the Pit before raising his head and glancing around his land. A ladder leaned against the side of his cabin. He lowered it into the pit and climbed down. It was dank and much cooler at the bottom. Running his hands over the walls, he found them smooth with no hand holds she could use to work her way out. He stood in the center of the excavation and looked up.

Night was falling, the first stars faintly visible. He tried to imagine the terror Bethany would feel the first time he lowered the roof over her as she stood alone in the center of her new world, and he could almost hear her voice asking him why he was doing this, telling him that she would pray for him if only he would relent and release her. She might even offer to pray with him. It would be a fine moment. Perhaps his finest. He climbed out. After pulling the ladder up, he stood again staring into the dark hole and smiled.

The other deaths he had caused had been public. He had arranged them for public display and enjoyed the public's reaction to his handiwork. Bethany's death would be private. It would be his alone to know of, to witness and to enjoy in the seclusion of his home on this remote patch of Bordeaux Mountain land with its view of the sea and British Virgin Islands. It presented a lovely and perfect backdrop for this. It would be his St. John masterwork, perhaps his ultimate work of genius, a *tour de force*. And engineering Bethany's death would be much safer than the other three he had killed since coming to St. John, risking being exposed by having to do his work where someone might see him. This time he would have privacy. He needed to savor Bethany's death in isolation, far from any prying eyes. When it was accomplished, he would leave St. John and settle somewhere else for a few years.

With each public display of death the police could draw closer to discovering him and he knew it was time to move on. He always knew when the time was right. It was if someone sat on his shoulder and told him to protect himself, to get out of Dodge. He rubbed his hands together and smiled. This was going to be a good one. The best.

Putting the roof back onto the Pit of Hell, he replaced the concrete block weights and headed to the house. He had no idea that Moonie watched him from a behind a thick clump of catch-and-keep, where kneeling he dropped a handful of seeds on the spot from which he had taken a plant that his wildcrafting father had called the Kittie McKwanie bush. Moonie's father had warned his young son about the plant when he was training him to follow his own wildcrafting ways. He urged Moonie to be especially careful when harvesting the bright red and black poisonous seeds from the plant. More commonly known as jumbie beads, the seeds of the Abrus Precatorius are prized for necklaces, bracelets, brooches and other ornamental uses, and they are believed by older West Indians to ward off jumbies. Handling them can be dangerous. Once out of their shells they are many times more deadly than ricin. One ground up seed will easily kill an adult human.

Carefully covering the six seeds he had planted, Moonie put the remaining ones in his pouch and waited quietly behind the catch-and-keep until Teach went inside. Then he headed back to his place to string the seeds and make necklaces and glue them to cardboard as decorative pins that he would sell from a card table he would set up at the bend in Centerline Road where the tourist buses stop at the Bordeaux Mountain Overlook.

He was puzzled by Teach's project. In his absence he had examined it close up. Seeing the writing on the roof, *Pit of Hell*, he had stood scratching his head. After lifting the roof and seeing nothing inside he was even more confused. Whatever Teach was up to, Moonie was determined to find out.

AT THE END of a long and tiring day Bethany sat on the deck of *The Saved Wretch*, the boat rocking in the wakes of passing motor launches making their way in and out of Coral Harbor. Watching as the lengthening shadows of early evening crossed the harbor and crept up the surrounding hillsides, she allowed the movement of the boat on the water to erase the tensions and pressures of work.

Her day had been begun early. Skipper Dan had called her cell phone before seven am, telling her that not only he was out of hamburger rolls, but he was low on several other staples and he needed her to go St. Thomas on the eight o'clock barge with his truck to pick up enough supplies to last until the next weekly delivery. Groggy, she climbed into the dinghy and pulled the on the outboard motor's starter cord. Nothing happened. She pulled it again. Still nothing. After the fifth try, she gave up and rowed to shore.

She rushed to Cruz Bay and was the last person to drive on to the eight o'clock barge. Back at Dante's Landing by one-thirty, she immediately plunged into her regular afternoon shift. The restaurant was busy. It was a cruise ship Wednesday. Every hour or so, safari buses disgorged loads of hungry and thirsty tourists from the seven huge cruise ships docked in St. Thomas who had been ferried over to St. John for a tour of the island and sights of the National Park, including a brief lunch in Coral Bay, considered the most unique of the island's communities. She had answered truthfully when Teach had asked her if she wanted a ride anywhere, but at day's end, as she sat on the deck of *The Saved Wretch*, she became increasingly unnerved by her earlier conversation with him.

The more she thought about his apology for the unpleasantness of his attitude toward her, the more false it rang; the forced, unnatural sound of his voice as he spoke seeming almost as if someone, or something had spoken through him. She would have to face him, deal with him at work. He was, after all, a regular customer at the Landing. Beyond that, she would have nothing to do with him, and she certainly would not accept a ride from him, for any reason.

She was not afraid of him. Bethany could not recall ever being afraid. She had been scared before: by someone hiding behind a door and jumping out yelling; or by horror movies before she stopped watching them, having decided not to subject herself to their gory manipulations; by the ghost tales and jump stories of the old mountain storytellers she knew as a child; and most chillingly—as a small girl—she was frightened by the Brown Mountain Lights her father and mother had taken her to see from Wiseman's View, not far from her home in Newland.

The lights were the most mysterious things she had experienced as a child. Brown Mountain is a low ridge in nearby Burke County where, during the night, usually in autumn, mysterious glowing orbs can be seen to rise up off the mountain, hover and wobble about fifteen feet up in the air, and then disappear. The Cherokee believed the lights to be the souls of Cherokee women searching for their men who had died in a great battle that took place on Brown Mountain between the Cherokee and the Catawba. Other legends say that the lights are the ghostly echoes of lights that appeared during a search for a murdered woman in the 19th century. Even today, with all the advances of modern science, no one knows what they are and they remain a great unsolved mystery.

While Bethany's first reaction to the lights was to be frightened, as she matured and gained perspective, she came to regard them as symbolic of the unknown world that remained inaccessible to science and reason. To her, they were not something to fear. To her they were awe inspiring, a sign of the immense mystery of Creation, a mystery the human mind must appreciate but will never understand. It was part of the larger mystery that formed the basis of her faith. Her mission was to witness it, to declare it and to convince others that it was real in order for them to feel it in their own lives, or suffer the tortures of Hell.

The feelings Teach provoked in her were puny compared to that. He was scary, surely, and perhaps he could be frightening, but he did not threaten the sanctity of her soul. Still she would avoid him. That would only be prudent.

She went below deck and crawled into her bunk. Sleep came easily and she soon fell into a dream in which she was hiking a trail that went from the north to the south side of the island. Halfway, the trail crossed Centerline Road, St. John's closest thing to a highway. Using a walking stick, she pushed her way through a thick growth of catch-and-keep and stepped onto the paved surface of the road, her face and arms bleeding from the tiny thorns that covered the vines. As she started to cross the pavement a car roared around a bend and stopped in front of her. A glistening black sedan, it was long and low, the engine rumbling like thunder as it idled by the side of the road, the sound vibrating through her body.

"Hop in," Teach said from behind the wheel. He wore a black suit with a white shirt buttoned all the way up, but with no necktie. A soft gray fedora sat squarely on his head.

"I'm not going your way," she said.

He fashioned a smile that did not go beyond his lips. "Everyone is going my way."

"Not this woman," she said.

"Time will come." His voice was expressionless. "You will go my way, no matter what you may think right now."

"I hope not. Your way is not mine."

"Oh, my dear, you are so deluded. We are not so different, you know." He touched the gold medallion that hung from the chain around his neck. "We are different sides of the same coin. We need one another."

"I know nothing of the kind." Her voice was indignant. "And I suffer no delusions."

"That is your greatest delusion, but the time will come when you will realize the truth of it and you will have to act on that knowledge." He flashed her a quick wave of his right hand, little more than a momentary wagging of his fingers, and drove off, the sound of his car rumbling in her ears.

She woke with a start. The boat rocked in suddenly heavy seas, waves lapping against the side of *The Saved Wretch*. She went above to make sure everything was secure and was standing in the open air when the first drops of rain began to fall. Seconds later she stood in a downpour, the rain splattering against the deck. Raising her head, she caught raindrops with her tongue and swallowed them. She thought nothing she had ever tasted was as cool and sweet.

Twenty-five

THE FOLLOWING AFTERNOON, his shift at the Landing over, Robert went home. Turning on his computer, he found Ray Wentworth's reply to his email. He read it several times before the meaning of the words sank fully in.

I've checked around, Ray had written. *No one I know seems to have any idea what your wife has done regarding a divorce. Sooner or later in a town as small as Graham, everyone knows everyone else's business. If she had been in a lawyer's office, a secretary or another client would certainly have mentioned it to someone and the rumor mill would have been fed.*

Robert, I hate to be the one to tell you this, but there is another kind of bad news. It is quite clear to many of us that Maria has moved on. She and your little girl are living with John Harris. You may remember him. He owns the jewelry store, Good Old John's, on Main Street across from the Court House, the one that is always advertising that they buy gold watches and other jewelry, taking advantage of people hard up in this economy. You may remember seeing his ads on television, him wearing a five gallon Stetson and using a phony Texas accent urging people to come on down to Good Old John's to sell their valuables.

Maria is very open about their living arrangement. My wife and I often see them at various restaurants around town, holding hands across the table and gazing into one another's eyes. That should give you justification to file for divorce if that is what you want. It's what I would do. I am sorry to be the one telling you this, but you asked and I could not lie just to spare your feelings.

I hope things are going well for you and that you are finding life more satisfying than what life in Graham, Massachusetts had become for you.

There was nothing more. After reading it through for the fourth time, Robert pressed the delete button and watched as Ray's email disappeared from the screen. He scrolled through the contacts on his cell phone and called Jeannette Evans, a lawyer in Graham who had successfully represented him in an ugly and capricious malpractice suit.

"I need a divorce," he said after they had exchanged the pleasantries required of people who knew one another as professionals in a small town.

"I generally don't do that kind of work," she said. "It's exhausting and depressing."

His sigh was loud. "I'm depressed."

"That's no wonder, given what I've heard about Maria and John Harris."

"Does everyone know?"

She laughed. "Hey, it's Graham, not Boston or New York. Everybody here knows everybody else's business."

"Ergo, my need for a divorce, and notice, I said I need a divorce, not that I want one."

"Because everybody knows?"

"Because I know."

"Where are you? I know you left the hospital and skipped town."

"Is this confidential?"

"I've represented you in the past, so that makes me your attorney."

"The Virgin Islands." He left it vague, not ready to tell anyone in Graham, even his lawyer, exactly where he was.

She whistled. "Send me some sand and sun. The islands are a great place to be. Eddie and I honeymooned on St. Thomas." After a pause, she added, "You do understand that you'll have to come back up here at least once or twice if you hope to get a divorce."

"I don't ever want to set foot in Graham again."

"You'll need to appear in court if you want a divorce from Maria on your terms."

"I don't want a divorce. I need to get one."

She sounded surprised. "So you said before. Have you tried reconciling with her?"

"Do you think there's any chance of that happening?"

She did not answer immediately. He heard her breathing over the line before she cleared her throat and said, "Not from what I've seen."

"She's tight with good old John?"

"They're quite the couple around town, out almost every night eating at one restaurant or another, huddling in a booth or holding hands over a table."

"And gazing into one another's eyes, I hear."

"You have spies."

"My daughter, Grace, is she with them in the restaurants?"

"Not that I've ever seen."

"I need that divorce, Jeannette." He was surprised by the sound of desperation in his voice. "I really need it."

"It shouldn't be a problem. Massachusetts is a no-fault state."

"But it's her fault that our marriage fell apart."

"Nothing is ever just one person's fault when a marriage breaks up."

"It's her fault because she never told me things were bad. She just walked out. We never talked about it, never saw a marriage counselor. She was in the house one day, gone the next."

"Things weren't bad in your eyes?"

"We didn't talk a lot after she got pregnant with Grace, hardly at all after she was born. I slept in the guest room so Grace could sleep in our bed with Maria. She said it made it easier to feed her and change her diapers during the night."

"And that didn't tell you anything about the state of your marriage?"

Robert took a deep breath and let it out slowly. "It was nothing I wanted to hear. I suppose I was in denial."

"You suppose? Friend that is deep denial."

"We vowed to love and care for each other forever."

Jeannette's voice softened. "Sometimes people fall out of love."

"I didn't. But even if I had, I'd've had a responsibility to fix things, make myself fall back in love. Falling in love, being in love, they're different from loving someone day to day, being responsible minute to minute, no matter what."

"Not everybody feels that way. Clearly, Maria didn't and doesn't."

"So I need a divorce, even if I don't want one. She's gone and I need to move on with my life and then there's the matter of custody of my daughter. I want to get Grace back into my life."

"Is there someone else?"

Robert grunted, then said, "There could be. There isn't yet, not exactly, but I need to be free in order to find out."

"Most men today wouldn't say that. They'd just jump into another relationship, or have a series of affairs."

"I'm not most men." He almost whispered into the phone. "You'll do it for me, get me a divorce?"

She sounded resigned. "Yeah. It's not my cup of tea, divorces, I mean, but you're an old client and you're too far away from Graham to start over with a lawyer you don't know."

She asked him a series of questions about income, property, the history of the marriage and who brought what into it. At the end of the conversation, she reminded him that he would have to return to Graham for hearings.

After hanging up, he sat on his verandah and stared at the sea, the shadows lengthening into evening.

An hour later, he walked into Dante's Landing. Christine was sitting at the bar listening to the Liquid Plumber ramble on in slurred English.

"I was just telling X 'bout this movie I saw last night," the Liquid Plumber said, looking up as Robert approached him.

"What was it?" Robert said.

"Can't remember the name of it," the Liquid Plumber said. "Been trying to but it just slips out of my mind each time I think I got it."

Boozie reached over the bar and patted Robert's shoulder. "Gin and tonic?"

"Diet Coke," Robert said.

"Dark rum?"

"Just the cola." He walked around the Liquid Plumber and sat on a stool beside Christine. "Hey," he said.

"Hey yourself."

"I've got a lawyer."

She looked alarmed. "What have you done?"

"I mean back home, or what used to be home. For a divorce."

"I've been divorced five times," the Liquid Plumber said.

"That's sad," Christine said.

"I'm not sad," he said.

"You're drunk all the time and you always look sad..."

He grinned and leaned toward her until their shoulders were touching. "Wanna marry me?"

"The goods are too odd." She pushed him away, poking his shoulder with her forefinger.

"My third wife lasted a month."

Christine smiled at Robert. "That must be some kind of record."

The Liquid Plumber nodded vigorously. "The other shortest one was eleven months."

"You clearly don't take marriage seriously," Robert said.

Boozie said, "He takes it real serious. Why else would he get married five times?"

"I like getting married," the Liquid Plumber said. "There's always a good party after a wedding."

"He just don't like being married," Boozie said.

The Liquid Plumber took a long drink. "I think I like being married. My wives don't like being married to me."

Boozie laughed. "No wonder. How many of them ever saw you sober?"

Ignoring the comment, the Liquid Plumber chugged his drink and pointed at his empty glass. "Wish I could remember the name of that movie."

Robert picked up his and Christine's drinks and led her to a table overlooking the harbor. "I'll have to go back to the States for court hearings," he said when they were seated.

"Divorce is a big step," she said. "Are you ready for it?"

He pursed his lips, smacked them and played with his glass. "I never thought I'd get divorced, you know. That's what other people do, people that can't honor their commitments."

"You're saying that breaking up wasn't your idea; it wasn't what you wanted."

"It wasn't." He sipped on his drink and waved to Bethany. When she came to the table he ordered a hamburger.

"What else do you need, Mr. Robert?"

"Cole slaw, fries and a new life."

"I see you working on the last part. I'll get the cook working on the first part." She wrote the order down and tapping on the table three times with the eraser end of her pencil, she left to take the order to the kitchen.

When they were alone Christine said, "She broke your heart."

Robert looked down at his fingers. Tenting them, he bounced their tips against one another several times. Lost in his thoughts, it seemed like a long time before he looked back up at Christine. "Maybe it's my fault. Maybe I broke Maria's heart and never realized it. I was always busy with my work and maybe she needed more from me than I could give her. That would make it my fault, right?"

"Things like a broken marriage are rarely just one person's fault."

Robert smiled. "My lawyer said something like that. I'd like to believe it."

"Then believe it."

"Just like that? Decide to believe it?"

"You can do that. We all make choices about what to believe, or not believe for that matter. Belief is always a matter of choice. We choose what we need to believe."

He sighed and looked back down at his fingers. "I don't know. I don't know what to believe about anything."

She took his hand and held it to her cheek. "Are you okay?"

Raising his eyes to her, he nodded. "I will be."

"Things take time."

Stirring the air around them, Bethany walked by the table with a tray of sandwiches for a couple on the far side of the room. Robert looked from her to Christine.

"I think I'm going to be just dandy. In a way it's a relief to know that things are really over with Maria. I've been tortured about it for a while, blaming myself, wondering what I could do to change things and now I know. Nothing. Absolutely nothing. It's out of my hands. Life with Maria is over. Finished. Kaput."

"And that's good? Dandy?"

"It will have to be good, and dandy."

She giggled. "Nobody says dandy anymore, you know. Cool, groovy, wicked, but not dandy."

"Dandy is different. It's not cool it's not groovy. I like dandy."

"What about your daughter?"

"I'm hoping that getting divorced from her mother will be a first step in getting Grace back into my life."

"You're lucky, you know?" Setting his hand back on the table, she stroked his fingers.

"Because my marriage went belly up and I'm going to be divorced?"

"Because you have a child. I never did."

"Do you want children?"

"I always thought I'd have a bunch of them." She held up her glass. "No kids, but lots of good booze over the years."

He did not respond.

"The right chance never came for me," she said.

"Maybe it will."

She met his eyes. "I haven't given up hope."

Twenty-six

CHRISTINE St. Pierre did not sleep that night.

Robert had left the Landing after finishing his soda, saying that he was tired and had a double shift the following day, filling in for Boozie who had an appointment at the veteran's hospital in Puerto Rico. She returned to her stool and ordered a martini. Next to her the Liquid Plumber was asleep, his head resting in his folded arms.

Boozie set her drink down. "How come you never seem to be drunk?"

"I wish I knew. It's not for lack of trying."

"Me, I smell the stuff and I'm tanked. Just ask Gloria."

"Bethany would say that maybe I'm not supposed to drink and this is the Lord's way of telling me." She leaned forward. "She's a little crazy, don't you think?"

Boozie shook his head. "What's crazy? She believes something, somebody else don't. Which one's crazy? Gloria thinks I'm crazy because I drink and I think she's crazy for God. I don't know what crazy is. Maybe that's why I drink, to keep from worrying about such things."

"Why do I drink if I'm still feeling lousy and sober after doing it?"

"You like the taste?"

She made a face. "Not at all."

Boozie looked around. There was no sign of Skipper Dan and he poured himself a shot of vodka. "Gloria says I'll live forever because of all the booze in me. She says that there's so much alcohol in my veins that I'm already embalmed and since I'm still able to stand up and walk around I'm probably halfway to becoming a living jumbie."

Christine sat on the stool, looking first at Boozie, then at the Liquid Plumber. He was snoring softly, his snores punctuated with a quiet whimpering. She thought it sounded as if he were weeping in his sleep. Wondering how he had come to be such a hopeless alcoholic, she was filled with sudden pity at the thought of what a sorrow-filled and wasted life he led. Tears began to build in her eyes, distracting her from her thoughts as she glanced around the restaurant. Teach was sitting in a shadowy corner on the far side of the room, light from a nearby television screen casting a blend of colors over his face. They changed as the images on the screen moved and shifted. He looked up briefly. She thought he was scowling at her, but he lowered his eyes and she convinced herself that she had imagined it. She hoped she had imagined it.

Speaking in a near whisper, she said to Boozie, "Does Teach creep you out?"

"In a major way." Boozie hugged himself and mimed a shiver. "That guy is one evil dude."

"That may be a bit of an overstatement," she said.

"Gloria, she's the one that said it first, and she knows what evil is. 'That mon is a demon,' she says. If she sees his car parked outside she won't come in here, even to pick me up after work, or to drop me off at the start of my shift. She honks and waits outside for me." He grinned at her. "Crazy, hunh?"

Christine stared at him in silence. Sure, Teach creeped her out, but he was a creepy guy, not some kind of demon hell-bent on destruction. Still, at that moment he resembled a creature that was anything but human with the multi-colored lights from the TV screen sweeping over his face and hands, glowing on his skin,.

"Teach is Teach," she said after a time, not sure what the words meant other than to deny Gloria's description of Teach as a personification of evil. He was, she was sure, nothing more than a man. Shaking her head, she pushed her martini glass, still full to the brim, toward the bartender. "Do you want this? I haven't touched it."

Boozie's eyes were wide. "You sure you don't want it?"

"I'm finished. Drinking hasn't done a thing for me, except waste my money."

"You didn't drink none of it?"

"Not a drop."

"Pinky swear?" Boozie held out the little finger of his right hand.

"Pinky swear." Christine laughed as she gripped it with her little finger.

"I don't want no germs," Boozie said. "You can get germs from drinking out of other people's glasses."

"Not if they haven't been drinking out of it, and I haven't. I pinky swore with you."

Boozie picked up the martini and drank it in two gulps. "I better not get germs. I get germs and I won't never trust you again."

"I'm trustworthy," she said and left Dante's Landing.

After an hour in bed, struggling and failing to fall asleep, she got up and went to the kitchen. Maybe, she thought, maybe I don't get drunk but perhaps the booze helps me sleep. Opening the liquor cabinet, she poured a glass half full of vodka and topped it off with ice and orange juice. She carried it to the living room and turned on the TV, flipping through the channels until she found a marathon of old *Twilight Zone* reruns. The glass sat untouched on the coffee table in front of her as she watched "The Howling Man," the story of a man named Ellington who unwittingly releases the Devil from his cell in a monastery where he had been imprisoned by Brother Jerome, the leader of the order.

When Satan attacks his liberator, Ellington realizes what he has done, telling Brother Jerome that until then he did not believe the abbot's contention that he had locked up the Devil. Brother Jerome says, *I'm sorry for you, my son. All your life, you will remember this night. And you'll know, Mister Ellington, whom you have turned loose upon the world.* Ellington replies, *I didn't believe you. I saw him and didn't recognize him,* to which Brother Jerome tells him that man's weakness and Satan's strength is man's inability to recognize evil.

Surprisingly unnerved, Christine grabbed the remote and turned the TV off before the show ended. She picked up her drink, still untouched, and walked out to the patio behind the house. Boozie's words came back to her, *Gloria, she's the one that said it first, and she knows what evil is. 'That mon is a demon...'* She shivered, in spite of the warm tropical night. Had the bartender's wife recognized something authentic about Teach, something deep and menacing, something...she mentally paused before allowing the thought to fully form...something evil? Or were Gloria and Boozie deluded? After all, without Skipper Dan seeming to notice, Boozie, in his sly way generally managed to consume as much alcohol as the Liquid Plumber. With his brain addled by drink, it was likely that his imagination was warped. He could well be hallucinating, seeing demons and Martians everywhere.

The Tiles on the patio were damp and she realized a light rain had fallen earlier. The songs of tree frogs broke the quiet of the St. John night. Chasing thoughts of demons and aliens from her mind, she dumped the vodka and orange juice into a planter and looked at the night sky. The Milky Way was clear, and she half believed that with a pair of binoculars she would be able to count the stars.

She thrilled to the night sounds and smiled, recalling how she had come to the island, filled with despair after Bobby Bean's death in Florida, sailing with the couple who owned *Bunyan's Dream*. They had been kind and good companions over the time they had sailed through the Keys and Bahamas, and were more than happy to take her suggestion that they moor in Coral Bay once they got to the Virgin Islands. Joan, the woman, had tried to convince her to sail on down island with them, to St. Kitts and farther, but Christine was determined to stay in Coral Bay, enraptured by the tales she had heard at Cooley's Marina back in Fort Lauderdale about how it was a place for the broken in spirit and the broken in heart.

Things had slowly turned around. Bethany took her under her wing and before Christine had truly thought about it, she realized she had found a home. She listened without paying attention when Bethany would talk to her about the Coral Bay Christian Church, urging her to come to prayer meetings and Sunday services. It reminded her of her mother insisting that she attend the Wesleyan Methodist Church back in Long Lake. Bethany was unfazed by the woman she knew as X's rejection of her entreating, and went out of her way to introduce X to the local residents. Far from the frozen lands of the central Adirondacks, Coral Bay became her community, filled with people Christine had grown close to and was content to be around. Then she met Robert Palmer and to him she was no longer X, but Christine once more, surprising herself by her candor with him and her hope he would become equally open with her. Perhaps the time was drawing near when she could once again become Christine to everyone.

A MILE AWAY as the pelican flies, fifteen minutes by road, Teach sat cross-legged on the roof of his Pit of Hell, a half-empty bottle of Cruzan dark rum on his lap, a pile of stones next to him. His eyes were fixed on a fire he had built on the ground before him, a bare patch covered by soil he had tossed there as he dug the pit. As the sound of the tree frogs rose, he picked up a stone and threw it into the surrounding bush, yelling as he did. The frogs grew quiet for a few minutes and when their noise rose again, he tossed another stone, yelling louder this time.

The second stone nearly hit Moonie. He had seen Teach drive up the Bordeaux Road and filled with drunken bravado, consumed by curiosity about what the man was up to, he cut through the woods and took up his perch by the catch-and-keep. Crouched behind the clumps of vine, its stems and leaves covered with sharp barbed hooked spines, he peered through the darkness of the night and spied on Teach's place. After an hour in hiding, Moonie saw him came out of his house, light the fire and climb atop the tin roof over the Pit of Hell.

Nothing seemed to happen. Teach sat there, throwing stones into the bush and yelling at the tree frogs. When the stone came so close that Moonie could feel the wind from its passage, he crouched lower. He froze when Teach spoke, his voice a deep rumbling sound heavy with rage and malice.

"I know you're out there," Teach said.

Moonie held his breath and lay still on the ground for what seemed to be a long time. Unable to hold it any longer, he took a deep breath and let it out slowly, silently.

"I saw you cut through the woods when I drove by. I know you're out there somewhere watching me, wanting to know what I'm doing. If you know what's good for you, you'll crawl back to that hovel you call home and never set foot on my land again."

In spite of the darkness, Moonie felt as though Teach's eyes were burning through the bush, staring at him though the thick tangles of catch-and-keep. He imagined the man could hear him breathe.

"I'd be within my rights to shoot you," Teach called. "Sneaking through the woods outside my home like you are."

Moonie began to slowly inch backwards, careful to not make a sound as he crept away from his hiding place behind the snarl of barbed vine.

Even though the tree frogs had stopped singing when Teach started to growl, he threw another stone into the clump where Moonie had hidden. "I could put a bullet through your heart and no court would ever convict me. You hear that?"

Moonie did not say a word. As soon as he thought it safe, he stood and ran back toward the road. Teach fell silent and Moonie was suddenly convinced the man was following him, walking several inches above the ground, almost gliding above it, a jumbie who would destroy his body and eat his soul. Once back in his small frame house, he locked the door. He took from the wall a small wooden cross he had made out of a piece of satinwood and sat in the dark, holding it over his chest. If the jumbie came through his door, he was prepared. He'd hold the cross up and the jumbie would turn and run. Tomorrow he would make crosses to nail to the frames of both doors and all four windows. Only then would he feel safe.

He was finished spying on Teach. Whatever that man was doing on his property suddenly was no longer of any interest to him. He was up to no good, no doubt, but no good would come to Moonie if he persisted in peering through the catch-and-keep. Let that man dig all the holes he wanted to and paint whatever he felt like painting on their roofs. It would not matter to Moonie. Nothing Teach did was any of his business. Maybe, if he stayed sober he could keep his nose out of Teach's affairs and keep his feet from walking across Teach's land, maybe then Teach would not shoot him.

Teach remained on the roof of his Pit of Hell until the fire died down and the bottle of Cruzan rum was empty. When only pale embers remained, he poured a bucket of water over them and went inside. His house was sparsely furnished. Lit by a single bare bulb in a plain white porcelain ceiling fixture, the living room held little more than several rusty beach chairs and a chaise lounge with torn fabric he had found by the side of the road near a dumpster and repaired with duct tape. Upended plastic milk cartons served as side tables and two others, piled atop one another against a wall, their open sides facing the room, served as a desk and held old newspapers, a few magazines, and several battered paperback mysteries he had taken from the free shelf by the front door of Dante's Landing.

He rifled through a cardboard box he kept in one of the milk cartons and found a black Sharpie felt tipped pen. On several pieces of paper he lettered the words:

Keep Off!
No Trespassing.
Trespassers Are Subject to Being Shot. This Means You.
Keep Off!

Grabbing a hammer and a handful of nails, he tacked the signs to trees that Moonie would have to pass were he to sneak again onto Teach's land.

Back in the house, a beer in hand, he went to the bathroom and took a bottle of aspirin from the medicine cabinet and stared into the mirror on the cabinet door. The face that looked back at him snarled, its yellow teeth bared, its eyes half open.

"You have not finished your work," it said.

"Soon," he replied.

"You know what you have to do," the face said.

"I do."

"When?"

"At Carnival. On the night of Festival I shall fill the Pit of Hell."

Teach felt his skin around his mouth and cheeks stretch as the face in the mirror smiled.

"The stilts are ready?" the face asked.

"And I'll have the rest of the costume soon," Teach told his reflection.

"And the fool who watched you from the bush?"

"If necessary, I'll kill him."

"Try not to," the face in the mirror said. "Another death could expose us."

Teach rubbed his chin. A hand rose and stroked the chin of the face in the mirror.

"Bethany should be the next and the last on St. John," Teach said.

The face in the mirror smiled again. "Let her Jesus try to save her from this."

Intending it as a laugh, Teach barked, the sound deep and malevolent. "She'll die as her delusions collapse around her."

The face fell silent, but Teach continued to stare at it. It was a face he had seen in mirrors for as long as he could remember; his face and not his face, it was a face that reprimanded him whenever he faltered in his mission. He smiled at it. He was not sure if the face smiled back.

He chewed the aspirin and swallowed it.

THE FOLLOWING morning, Bethany woke with first light. She heard the songs of tree frogs fade and those of morning birds rise. A dove murmured outside her window and an Elena sung nearby. Their sounds mingled with those of other birds, including a wild rooster living in the bush behind the house. She stepped outside. A buck and two does grazed in a clearing and five donkeys stood in her driveway, watching as she filled her bird feeders, their eyes leery. The largest of the five galloped away from her, the others following it down the driveway, their hooves clomping against the concrete surface.

"Silly things," she called after them. "I was going to feed you after I fed the birds."

Her eyes wandered over the world around her and she thought it beautiful; the palms moving in the light breeze, the red leaves of the bougainvillea, hibiscus blossoms abuzz with honeybees and hummingbirds, the pergola heavy with thunbergia vine, known as the scrambling sky flower. The three deer stood in the clearing, their eyes fixed upon her.

"I suppose you want something to eat," she said.

The deer did not move. She went to a storage area below the house and opening a gunny sack, filled a bucket with dried kernels of corn that she carried upstairs across the patio and tossed over the fence. The deer moved cautiously toward it and were soon munching it down.

Back on the patio she again looked over the surrounding landscape; green hills dotted with homes, the sea below, its colors varying shades of turquoise close to shore, gradually receding into a lovely deep blue farther away from the land, its tranquility on this perfect day broken by only the white water foaming around several reefs that lay well off-shore.

Sitting on the patio, she read her Bible for half an hour and then fixed breakfast and watched the morning news. When the broadcast ended, she washed the dishes and settled back into a chair on the patio to read when she heard Andrea Hillborn's car come up the driveway. They had a same day turnaround at Bayview, a ridge top villa owned by a couple from Massachusetts, and she was scheduled to start waiting tables at Dante's Landing at five that afternoon. It would be a difficult day, especially if the current tourists at the villa, who had rented the place for a week, were late in checking out. They were due to leave by ten in the morning and the villa had to be ready for new guests by two that afternoon.

Andrea waved as she walked to the house. "Ready for another day of cleaning up the messes people leave for us?"

"I'm just agog with excitement."

"Then I've got good news," Andrea said with her thumbs up. "I drove past Bayview on my way here. They've already left. All the beds were stripped, the sheets and towels were piled outside the laundry room, and the trash was bagged and sitting at the top of the drive."

"Well bless their hearts, that'll make life a tad easier."

"Even the pool looked as though they'd skimmed it before leaving."

"There are people who go beyond what you expect of them."

Andrea grunted. "And there are people so rotten to the core that the Devil would bar the door against them, to keep them from taking over Hell."

"There are." Bethany's face was grim. "I think we've got one of them right here in Coral Bay."

"Let me guess, you're talking about that Teach guy that hangs out at the Landing, right?"

Bethany's face filled with surprise. "You know him?"

"I wouldn't say I know him, but I've watched him when I've been in the restaurant while you're working. Girl, he looks at you in the weirdest way, like he wants to reach right into your chest, tear your heart out and eat it."

A chill ran up Bethany's spine. "Sometimes I manage to convince myself that it's all in my imagination."

"But you've noticed it?"

"He actually apologized to me the other day."

"For what?"

"For his attitude toward me, but his eyes were as empty as a dried salt marsh when he said it and his voice was mean even though his words were apologetic. Then he offered to give me rides while my car is in the shop." She shuddered. "I wouldn't take a ride from him if I was blind and both my legs were broken."

"You'd be crazy if you did. There's something dangerous about him, especially where it involves you."

Bethany exaggerated her Carolina accent. "Well, honey, crazy is one thing I'm flat out not. The day I get into a car with that Teach is the day I'll agree to have my head examined."

Part Three

Jumbies

Twenty-seven

AT 7:30 AM, Sergeant Preston parked his SUV cruiser in front of the Cruz Bay Police Command. Certain he had solved the recent series of murders on St. John he was sure this would be the biggest day of his career. He put the cruiser into PARK, the engine idling as he listened to the police radio. Reports and requests from central dispatch along with chatter from other cruisers came through the static and crackle, but nothing interested him; not the merchant at one of the upscale shops in Mongoose Junction who had filed a complaint about credit card fraud; and not the hungry teenager who had been caught stealing a package of hamburger from a grocery store.

He ignored all the messages, even the report of a possible drowning in the surf at Waterlemon Cay. Always eager to perform heroic rescues, he normally would have backed out of the parking lot, blue lights flashing and roared along North Shore Road, the cruiser's klaxon horn clearing the way. Today he had more important business. Lesser officers than Sergeant Preston of the St. John Command of the United States Virgin Islands Police Department could handle those situations.

Sergeant Preston thought of himself as the master of major cases. He loved the way being a central player in drug busts provided cover for his own illegal activities. A major pleasure was corralling illegal immigrants, Haitians, Dominicans, refugees from the volcano on Montserrat, people desperate to find a first step into American territory. A few years before, there had even been a wave of Chinese who waded ashore at the east end of the island. Rounding them up had given him singular pleasure.

Drunken tourists driving the island's twisting roads were a source of entertainment for Sergeant Preston. On a remote island in the Caribbean, far from their usual continental stomping grounds, they were often frightened when he turned on his lights and blasted them with his klaxon. On more than one occasion, had been offered substantial sums of money by Statesiders eager to avoid arrest. In the panic of the moment, especially at night, they would watch through their rearview mirrors as he swaggered toward them, the strobe effect of blue lights from the cruiser distorting and exaggerating his movements. In such situations, he counted on the fact that the drivers, their minds clouded with alcohol, might overlook the fact that the Virgin Islands was a US territory, subject to Federal policies and laws.

Many of them had seen movies and read novels in which naïve Americans were arrested and thrown into fetid jail cells in third world countries. Envisioning themselves in the hell-hole of a foreign prison they would do almost anything if he would let them go. He would pocket their money and arrest them, taking them to the holding cells at the police station. Another officer working with him would tell them that bail had been set and as soon as they paid, they could walk out. Later, the charges against them were either dropped, or the tourists ignored pending charges and breathed sighs of relief when their planes took off from the airport on St. Thomas, flying them back to the comfort of their homes in the States.

The bribes and bail money would disappear into Sergeant Preston's pockets and those of his fellow officers in the Police Department. Rarely did anyone report the extortion. On the few occasions when someone did, the complaint moldered in the department's filing cabinets. The tourists, their vacations over, would go home, relieved that they were not sweating in dark and airless dungeons. Safe in the States, their stories of arrest and brief confinement could gradually be refined into extravagant tales with which to regale family and friends.

Today none of this mattered to him. Today he, Sergeant Preston, would present the Commander of the St. John Police Command with the solution to three murders. A promotion would certainly follow. He turned off the cruiser's engine. The radio fell silent. Getting out of the cruiser, he stood as erect as possible, his chest puffed out, and walked into the police station, sure the news he was about to present to the Commander would soon create shock waves throughout the department. With brief nods to his fellow officers, he walked down the hall and rapped three times on the Commander's door.

"Sir, I have a suspect in our murders," he said, strutting into the Commander's office and standing at attention before his desk.

Commander Alexander Whatley glanced up from the papers on his desk and looked wearily at Sergeant Preston. If he could, he'd transfer the man to St. Thomas. He had tried several times, but the Chief, whose office was on the other island, always denied the requests, saying he preferred that Preston remain on St. John. "He will cause less trouble there," he would say.

"Less trouble for you is too much trouble for me," Commander Whatley replied, arguing that Sergeant Preston would not be as noticeable on St. Thomas. On St. John he was a member of a much smaller division of the Virgin Islands Police Department, therefore much more of a public figure. The Commander did not like the idea that Sergeant Preston was such a visible representative of his division. It would be especially embarrassing if the FBI investigation into his activities proved fruitful. A police sergeant being arrested for drug dealing would stain the department's reputation and curb a sideline he and many of the other officers found quite profitable. None of this mattered to the Chief.

"Who is your suspect?" Commander Whatley asked.

Sergeant Preston said, "I could arrest him today, if you give me the go ahead, sir."

Whatley looked at him through half-lidded eyes. "Who is your suspect, Sergeant?"

Biting his lower lip, Sergeant Preston looked at the picture of the Governor hanging on the wall behind the Commander.

"Who?" the Commander asked for a third time.

Sergeant Preston cleared his throat and looked at the top of the Commander's desk, avoiding his eyes. "I do not know his real name, sir."

The Commander rapped his fingers on the desk. "I need a name in order to get an arrest warrant."

"He is called the Liquid Plumber, sir."

Commander Whatley covered his mouth with his right hand, hoping that Preston had not seen his quickly suppressed smile. "What evidence do you have?"

The Sergeant looked up. "He has no alibi for the times of the three murders, sir."

"And how have you ascertained that, Sergeant?" The Commander spread his fingers enough to allow his voice to come through clearly.

"I asked around, sir. Everyone I questioned told me where they were during the time frames of the murders. Only this Liquid Plumber could not."

"Did the others' alibis check out?"

Sergeant Preston returned his gaze to the Commander's desk top. "I did not think that necessary, sir. This man has no alibi. He will not or cannot tell me where he was or what he was doing during the times in question. That makes him my prime suspect."

The Commander's fingers closed. He believed that he had never uttered the term, prime suspect. "This Liquid Plumber, does he strike you as a dangerous man?"

"Often, sir, dangerous men do not appear, when we first meet them, as being dangerous."

The Commander sighed and spread his fingers again. "Perhaps you should question him further, Sergeant. I suggest we hold off on getting an arrest warrant until we know more."

"As I said, sir, he has no alibi."

"About alibis, Sergeant; I want you to investigate the alibis of the other suspects, the ones you seem to have discounted simply because they gave you alibis."

"Yes sir." Sergeant Preston felt heat rush up his neck. Had the Commander just insulted him? There was one way to find out.

"You want me to conduct an investigation, sir."

Commander Whatley lowered his hand and threw his troublesome policeman a bone.

"That's exactly what I asked you to do, Sergeant. I want you to thoroughly investigate everyone's alibi."

Straightening his back until his spine hurt, Sergeant Preston saluted the Commander. He had just officially been handed an investigation. "You can be sure that I will be quite thorough."

"I have no doubt about that, Sergeant."

"And I will bring you enough evidence to have an arrest warrant issued for the Liquid Plumber."

The Commander hoped his smile looked sincere. "Be sure to get his real name. You know how those Coral Bay people are about names. Frequently they do not know the true names of their closest friends."

"I will serve the Liquid Plumber to you on a platter, sir, tied up and ready for persecution."

"Prosecution, Sergeant. We prosecute people. We do not persecute them." The Commander saluted Sergeant Preston. "Dismissed, Sergeant."

Sergeant Preston clicked his heels and returned the salute.

When he was sure Sergeant Preston had left, he punched in the number for the extension of Detective Roland Marsh. "You will not believe this, Detective," he said when Marsh picked up. "We have a problem."

"I saw Preston go into your office, sir."

The Commander filled Marsh in on his conversation with Sergeant Preston. "I need you catch up with him and tell him I assigned you to work closely with him."

"Sir." Detective Marsh's voice nearly wailed the word. "I am quite busy, you know."

"Preston must be watched. He could bring disaster down on the entire department. I could explain more if we spoke in private, Detective, but I am sure you understand what I am talking about."

"I understand fully, sir. There is no need to discuss it farther."

"And much safer," the Commander said.

"Much safer, sir."

DETECTIVE ROLAND MARSH slid into the passenger's seat of Sergeant Preston's cruiser. "Whatley wants me to work closely with you on this Liquid Plumber case."

Sergeant Preston's voice was testy. "I do not need help."

Marsh nodded. "And I do not want my attention taken away from my own cases. I am almost ready to arrest a bunch of drug dealers, one of them your cousin Arthel."

"I should warn him."

Marsh shook his head. "If you do that he will tell the others and I need a good bust on my record of accomplishments. However, since Arthel is a member of your family I suggest you find an excuse to keep him out of Cruz Bay Friday night."

"No problem." Sergeant Preston started his engine. "Are you coming with me to Coral Bay?"

"You go on. If Whatley asks anything, we will tell him we are cooperating on the case." Marsh got out of the cruiser and lightly patted it on the roof. At the signal, Sergeant Preston backed out of the lot and turned east on Centerline Road, whistling tunelessly.

WHEN ROBERT and Skipper Dan opened Dante's Landing the next morning, Nutty Betty, Mechanic Mike and the Liquid Plumber were waiting by the door, the Liquid Plumber with a can of beer clasped between his knees.

"A cop followed me here today," the Liquid Plumber said.

"No wonder if he saw you driving with that beer in your hand," Nutty

Betty said.

The Liquid Plumber looked at the beer and took a swallow. "No way. I bought it at Love City Mini Mart just before coming here and I didn't open it until five minutes ago."

The three followed Robert and Skipper Dan inside and sat on their accustomed stools. Robert turned on the television that hung directly over the bar and the screen was filled with images of destruction in an Oklahoma town, the news announcer talking about a tornado unprecedented in its size, wind speed and destructiveness.

The Liquid Plumber banged his beer can on the bar top as Bethany entered the Landing. "Tornados, hurricanes, tsunamis, earthquakes, volcanoes exploding, the world is nothing but a machine of destruction. If there was a creator it sure wasn't any God, it had to have been a devil, a demon. The whole world is nothing but an outpost of Hell."

"That's the most stupid thing I've ever heard," Bethany said. "We live in a fallen world and have ever since Adam and Eve ate that dratted apple. The Bible says that when they sinned all of nature was cursed because sinful humankind cannot possibly live in a perfect world, in a paradise, and that's why all of nature is cursed and that's why terrible things happen."

The Liquid Plumber drank. "And why does God let people do evil things?"

"Because he gave them free will, you ninny."

"So God lets people get swallowed by the earth and blown away in storms so he can punish them?" Robert said.

"Y'all don't know much about God, do you?"

"And you do?"

"God is the great mystery, Mr. Robert. What I do know is that God doesn't create natural disasters, but he could prevent them."

"Why doesn't he?"

"I don't know, Mr. Robert. Nobody can know God's mind. But there are things we can learn from disasters and other forms of human suffering."

"You've thought a lot about this haven't you?" Robert said.

"I'll have a shot and another beer," the Liquid Plumber said. "And a round for Nutty Betty too. This is too much for me to think about. I don't much like to think about things, and especially about religion. It's all a load of baloney."

Robert scratched his head. "So why does he let them happen?"

Bethany never took her eyes from Robert. "It's one of the most important things a person can think about and pray about. Disasters have lessons to teach us."

"Some things I'd rather not have to learn."

Bethany ignored his comment. "Disasters and other miseries teach about us the uncertainty of life. Who knows what's going to happen today? Any one of those fault lines connected with the Puerto Rico Trench could act up and all of us on St. John could be swallowed up before we could blink an eye and if there were any survivors they'd be swamped by a tsunami. We all could be eaten by the earth or be drowned rats ten minutes from now."

Nutty Betty shuddered and took a long drink. "I'd hate being swallowed up by the earth."

Bethany patted her shoulder. "It's probably not going to happen, but it could."

Nutty Betty gave her a weak smile. "I hope not."

"There'll be unimaginable disasters come the end of time. The disasters we know about, like that one on the television, they're a preview of the natural disasters that will befall the earth when Jesus returns to take the righteous homeward to Heaven."

"If you believe that stuff," Robert said.

"I do, and so should you, Mr. Robert. But disasters, diseases, accidents, none of them can increase the amount of death on this earth. Everybody is going to die. It's the way they die that causes grief in those of us left behind. Time is short and eternity is forever, Mr. Robert. Time is short both for each of us individually and for the world. Any day Jesus could return. He will gather the faithful in his arms and bear us on up into Heaven."

"God, if he is there, doesn't give a rat's tooth about me and, if he is there, I don't give a rat's tooth about him. He abandoned me and let my wife and daughter, Grace, walk away from me."

Bethany looked at him with a sad face. "Think about Job, Mr. Robert. He lost everything and his wife told him to curse God and Job replied, the Lord gave, and the Lord hath taken away; blessed be the name of the Lord."

"So?" Robert spread his hands and looked at her.

Bethany wagged a finger at him. "Job shows us that we can worship God, even without explanations. We can't begin to understand the reasons and those who worship him are blessed." Her face hardened, her eyes narrow and her lips thin. "Those who don't will burn in Hell, screaming in agony for all eternity, and God will look on their suffering with pleasure. It's no real pleasure in this world but contemplating the suffering of those who turn away from God."

"It wasn't taught like that when I was a kid in Sunday School at the Episcopal Church back in Graham, Massachusetts."

Bethany put her hands on her hips and grinned at him. "Well it's surely taught like that in my Sunday school class at the Coral Bay Christian Church. You should stop by sometime."

Realizing that a world without God was as comforting to him as the world with God was to Bethany, he gave her a non-committal smile and began to clean the top of the bar with a damp rag.

The Liquid Plumber emptied his beer and held up a finger to ask for another. "I spent some time in a seminary."

Nutty Betty's jaw dropped and everyone turned to stare at him. "You're a preacher?"

He shook his head. "I never got that far. The more I read the more questions I had. God eluded me; the very idea of God eluded, eludes, me. I walked away. Taking a job as an apprentice to a plumber, I worked at it until I couldn't stand it anymore. I fumbled around for a while and then I came here." He held up an empty beer can. "This is my job now, to stay as stinko drunk as I can and not think about questions that don't have any logical answers."

"God is above logic," Bethany said. "Martin Luther called reason a..." she blushed and paused. "He called it what some people call a fallen woman."

"Oh go ahead and say it," Skipper Dan told her, but she shook her head and ran a thumb and finger over her lips, as if to zip them shut.

The Liquid Plumber ended his part in the conversation by picking up his bottle and the shot glass Robert had given him. Walking across the room, he leaned on a wide railing and looked out over Coral Harbor.

Skipper Dan pushed a button on the TV remote and switched to a channel showing a soccer game in Italy.

"Not a good choice if you're trying to avoid disasters," Mechanic Mike said. "Soccer fans in Europe riot and kill one another at in and out of the stadiums."

Skipper Dan shrugged and put down the remote. "At least they have some idea of what they're getting into when they buy a ticket."

"That's more than the rest of us have going for us by being born in

Bethany's fallen world," Robert said.

"Laugh if you want, but laughing's catching." Bethany turned to Mechanic Mike. "What's going on with my car?"

"Not much. I'm still waiting on parts. My guy in Miami had to order them from someplace farther up north and it'll be a while."

"A while? What's a while?"

Mechanic Mike gave her a weak smile and raised his shoulder slightly. "I wish I could tell you. Maybe two, three weeks."

"I don't reckon there's anything to be done about that," she said.

"Just wait."

"I need my car."

"And you'll have it, soon as I get the parts and stick them in."

Bethany was about to mention being nervous about Teach, but a group of six loud adults and three louder children came in and sat down.

Twenty-eight

TEACH HAD LUNCH on the open air verandah of a restaurant overlooking Veteran's Drive and the Charlotte Amalie waterfront of St. Thomas across the way. Sitting on the floor beside his chair were several bags containing clothing and a wig for the jumbie costume he planned to wear at the Festival. Cars, trucks, busses and safari jitneys inched their way through the gridlock of downtown traffic, horns honking, brakes squealing and diesel fumes from the busses filling the air. Aside from the view of the waterfront and the huge cruise ships harbored there, he thought he could just as easily be in Camden, Newark, or any other of the crowded and unlovely New Jersey cities clumped around New York and Philadelphia.

Across the road the water glistened in the sun. A red imitation pirate ship tied up by the wharf bounced with the waves and wake from other boats. He pictured himself on deck, a sword in his hands, a blue kerchief around his head, barking orders at cowed seamen. He was born too late. The days of piracy on the high seas would have suited him. He would have loved making men walk the plank into waters thick with hungry sharks, slashing them with his sword, raiding other ships and slaughtering their crews and stealing their cargos of gold and jewels. It would have been a wild and wondrous life. The only thing wild about his life before discovering his mission was the tagging and marking and record keeping of a wildlife biologist.

He ate three hamburgers and two orders of fries that he washed down with several bottles of beer. Glancing around the room he looked briefly at a boy who appeared to be in his late teens sitting alone at a nearby table. He looked at the kid with disgust. Hair cut into spikes that were dyed red, green and orange, he wore a nose ring and had a stud on his lower lip. Another stud stuck out from the side of his left nostril. His thoughts idly wandering, Teach played with the idea of where he would place the kid's body and how he would position it, if he decided to kill him.

Not that he would follow through. All his energy was focused on Bethany, his grand finale in the Virgin Islands. Weeks from now he would be setting himself up somewhere thousands of miles from the Trade Winds and tropical waters. He supposed he would miss the climate and the open air living possible on St. John, but he would not risk his mission being interrupted, perhaps even ended, by the discovery of his activities that was inevitable if he stayed in the islands.

Reaching down, he picked up the bags and set them on the table. As he watched, the boy's mother came in and the boy stood up and gave her a hug and a kiss. He left the restaurant with her, his right arm locked with her left arm. A woman with an unlit cigarette dangling from her lips came over to their table and scooped something into her pocket. Leftover food, Teach assumed.

Each one of his bags contained part of his jumbie costume. One held a blonde wig, the hair pale and stringy. In another was a black hooded cloak. A third contained a pair of yellow trousers, the legs long enough to cover the eighteen inch stilts he would wear. In still another bag was a light blue tee shirt emblazoned with a bright red heart in the center of the chest. The heart was torn in two. At the places where it was ripped it appeared to bleed a darker red. The final bag held his make-up, a jar of white face paint and a stick of black lipstick. Each item had been bought at a different store to make the purchases less obvious, less memorable, than they would be if he had gotten them in one place and set the whole pile on a single counter in front of a single cashier.

He smiled with pleasure at the thought of his cunning when a voice at his side startled him and he saw the boy with the dyed spiky hair standing by his side.

"Hey mister," he said, pointing at the table he had left, his dishes and used napkin still on it. "I'm sorry to bother you, but did you see anybody over there after I left?"

"No," he said.

"I left my cell phone sitting on the table and it's now gone. I asked the manager, but he said he couldn't help me, that I should've been more careful. Are you sure you didn't see anybody?"

'Nobody," Teach said, his eyes quickly taking in the woman standing just outside, the cigarette lit. She'd be another fine one for him to take care of. It was a good thing he was leaving the islands. If he stayed, things could too easily to get out of control.

"You're an idiot, kid, leaving your phone on the table. What've you got inside your skull that substitutes for a brain? What keeps it from sounding hollow if you get hit on the head?"

The kid gave him a malicious grin. "Silver bells and cockle shells and pretty maids all in a row. What's inside your head mister? Ground glass soaked in monkey vomit?"

Teach stood. He towered over the boy. He leaned down toward him, and with bared teeth breathed into the kid's face as he spoke in a near whisper. "Boy, you don't want to find out what's inside my head. Nobody should want to find that out."

"Do you know what you are, mister?" The boy backed away, his eyes wide and frightened. Under his breath, he cursed Teach and turned to leave the restaurant.

Teach called after him, "I know exactly what I am."

ROBERT KISSED Christine once on each cheek. He thought they felt magically smooth and cool as his lips touched them. He had come to Paradise Found to pick her up for dinner at Aqua Bistro, a mile down the road from Dante's Landing.

"What was that for?" she said, laughing.

"It's in honor of your French heritage. The French kiss one another on the cheek as a polite greeting."

"It's a nice tradition, Doc."

"I've filed for divorce," he said.

She touched her right cheek where he had kissed it and nodded in silence.

"I don't mean I'm doing it physically. My lawyer back in the States is handling it, but I can't stay in a marriage that isn't a marriage anymore. Maria's with somebody else."

"And that makes you sad."

"Not anymore."

"Then how do you feel?"

"For her, not much. I had a life that included Maria, and Grace and my work and living in Keetsville, Massachusetts. Now I don't have that life."

"You're angry?"

He chuckled. "No. I was angry and depressed for a long time, but there's nothing to be gained by staying angry at the past, yelling and screaming about what's done and over."

"What about your daughter?"

"I'll find a way to get Grace back into my life. Maria can't fight me on that, according to my lawyer. She can make things difficult, but she can't change the fact that I'm Grace's father. I may have to wait until she's a little older before I can bring her down here for summers and for school vacations, but that will come."

Christine breathed deeply, as if bracing herself for what she had to say. "If you moved back up north you could start seeing Grace every day, get shared custody of her, you know, have her every other weekend, maybe some days through the week. And it could start as soon as you got back up there."

"I could do that," Robert said. "But there's a selfish part of me that won't. I don't ever want to see another snow flake as long as I live."

"If you were back in Massachusetts you could practice medicine again."

"If I want to practice medicine, I can do it almost anywhere. I could do it here."

"Do you want to?"

His brow wrinkled and he tapped his thumbs and forefingers together. "Sometimes I think I would. Other times I'm happy tending bar."

"Were you a good doctor?"

"I was an excellent doctor."

She laughed. "No false modesty there."

"Modesty is false if you know yourself well."

"And you know yourself?"

"I do, as far as my knowledge of medicine and my skill in practicing it; other aspects of my life, of life in general, I'm not so sure of."

"Since you never want to see snow again, you're going to stay here?"

"That's one reason."

"There are others?"

He did not answer immediately. Instead, he said, "We need to get moving. We've got reservations at the restaurant for seven-thirty and it's already quarter after."

They got in the car and rode for a while in silence. Near the intersection of Centerline and Salt Pond roads, Robert spoke a single word. "You."

"What about me?"

"You. You're one of the reasons I'll stay on St. John."

"That's a good answer." She ran the back of her hand down his cheek.

The Hot Club of Coral Bay was playing at Aqua Bistro, a trio consisting of a man with a mandolin, a woman playing a battered looking acoustic guitar, and a thin, almost cadaverous man leaning over a stand-up bass. The music was unamplified but loud if one was standing close to the musicians.

"Seat us as far away from the music as possible," Robert said. The maître d', who turned out to be their waiter as well, led them past the empty tables in the courtyard and showed them to seats under a canopy near the restaurant's small kitchen. Handing them each a menu, he stood beside the table, a pencil and pad of paper in his hands.

Christine ordered a glass of Pinot Grigio. "And you, sir?" the waiter asked Robert.

"A Diet Coke."

"Light or dark rum?"

"Just the Coke," Robert said.

With July 4th only a few days away, the high tourist season was long over and there were less than ten diners sitting at scattered tables. Music drifted throughout the open-air restaurant as the trio near the entrance played a mix of tunes; thirties jazz pieces, forties swing, fifties rock and roll, music from many eras. They segued from Benny Goodman's "Sing, Sing, Sing," with the mandolin taking Goodman's clarinet lead, through the Beatle's "Eleanor Rigby," to Kurt Cobain's "The Man Who Sold the World," into the old Appalachian folk tune, "Shady Grove."

"That's amazing," Robert said.

Christine made a question mark with her eyebrows. "The music?"

"Especially the guy on the mandolin. He makes beautiful sounds."

"I thought you didn't like music. You told me it was audible sewage."

"Maybe my hearing is changing."

"Maybe you're changing," she said.

"That's a lot to hope for."

"It's not your hearing. You hear just fine. Your hearing when you said you didn't like music is no different than it is right now."

"You are physiologically correct, madam."

Laughing, she said, "So what's different?"

The waiter brought their drinks and he fiddled with his glass, running his thumb and forefinger up and down its frosty side, his eyes staring at the ceiling. Finally, he looked at her and said, "Hey, how about them Red Sox?"

"Red Sox? How did we get on to baseball?"

"It's a New England code. Back there, whenever you're involved in a conversation that's getting uncomfortable and you want to change the subject, just say, hey, how about them Red Sox? Or even simpler, how about them Sox? It's a game changer."

Christine groaned. "That wasn't quite a pun, but it was almost as painful."

"Do you like puns?"

"It works, doesn't it?"

"Puns?"

"No, your, how about them Red Sox line."

"Every time."

She reached across the table and took his hands in hers. "I'm glad you liked the music."

"I think I did. I hope I wasn't deluding myself." He looked toward the musicians, then slowly shook his head. "It's more like I didn't detest their music."

"It's a change."

He shrugged. "Whatever it means."

She grinned. "Whatever."

Twenty-nine

THE NEXT MORNING, after a disappointing few hours on the water and only a handful of fish to show for his time on a choppy day at sea, Moonie shut down the outboard on *The Redfish* and, poled the small wooden fishing boat close to the rocky shore in Coral Harbor. Securing the engine to the boat with a chain and padlock, he disconnected the gas line and waded ashore, the red gas tank in one hand, a rope from the boat in the other. After tying it to a sea grape tree, he sat on a rock, gloomy over his unproductive morning, irate over the cause of his meager catch.

Someone had emptied his fish traps, probably his cousin Samuel. If he went after him, confronting him with his suspicions, they would probably get into one of their fights. If so, he knew both his and Samuel's mothers would hold it against him. With both women it was always, "Poor Samuel. He's not quite right, you know and everybody takes advantage of him." As Moonie saw it, Samuel was the one taking advantage. He avoided hard work by taking advantage of people seeing him as "not quite right." Moonie understood how Samuel's mother might be taken in by his cousin's act, but his own mother should be different. Instead, she stood by her sister rather than her son. It frustrated him.

Beyond knowing what Samuel was probably up to, there was nothing Moonie could do about it. It was just the way things were in his family. Nothing would change the fact that there would be no fish to sell today. He put on the shoes he had left under a large sea grape before setting out to check his traps and got ready for his next undertaking. Working under his uncle's electrician's license, he was wiring the house his brother's wife's father, George, was building in the countryside near Nanny Point. This was the day he had to have all the receptacles and switches in place for the electrical inspector. Tomorrow, his brother, Thomas, was scheduled to put the dry wall up in the house's interior. There would be no time for wildcrafting today.

He had recently bought a twenty-five year-old Toyota pickup from a builder on Ajax Peak who had fixed it up for sale after buying a ten year-old truck. He put the boat's gas tank in the truck bed and tied it to the side to keep it from shifting around and spilling. After trying several times to start it, he finally got the engine to turn over and drove off, the truck creaking and rattling. The tailgate, rusted loose from the pickup's bed, was held in place with rope. It banged against the truck body and seemed about to fall onto the road with each pothole he hit. Passing Dante's Landing, he decided to stop in for a quick lunch. Working in his brother's father-in-law's unfinished house on a midsummer day would be like being confined to a sweat box. Putting it off for a little longer felt like a treat.

He took a seat at a table a few feet from the bar. Bethany smiled and set a menu in front of him.

"Hey Moonie, y'all doing good?"

He told her he was and ordered a hamburger and a glass of ice water.

"Give him a beer and a shot on me," the Liquid Plumber called from his bar stool. "His brother, Andrew, stopped and helped me when I had a flat tire on Centerline Road last week."

Moonie waved his hands at him, pushing the words away. "Just ice water," he said.

Bethany wrote down the order. Looking at the Liquid Plumber, she told Moonie, "Water is a lot better for you."

"But you sell the booze, don't you?"

"Skipper Dan sells the drinks; I just bring them to peoples' tables."

Moonie looked surprised. "You do not drink?"

"Never have," she said. "My granddaddy used to make liquor. He and his brothers would truck it down the mountain from Boone to North Wilkesboro for sale, but that was back when all the counties around us were dry. The tourist business changed all that."

"I no longer drink alcohol," Moonie said.

The Liquid Plumber turned on his stool and laughed. "That'd be like running a truck without gas."

Bethany flashed him a 'shut your mouth' look and turned to Moonie. "I hope you know that our church over in the old Expeditions building is for everybody."

"My aunt Wilma and her cousin Mary go there. My mother and her sisters do too, sometimes."

"I've seen your mother there," Bethany said. "You could come too, you know."

Moonie nodded and looked toward her order pad.

Seeing the direction of his glance, she said. "I'll put it right in," and turned toward the kitchen.

Moonie's voice stopped her. "I have seen things that frighten me. When I drink they fill my mind and do not let me rest. So I will no longer drink."

"What kind of things did you see?"

Moonie thought about Teach's Pit of Hell and heard again in his mind Teach telling him he would be within his rights to shoot him. He was terrified of Teach and what he might do if Moonie told people what he had seen him doing up on Bordeaux and by doing so brought trouble down on the man. Instead, he said with a low mumble, "Jumbies."

Bethany understood. She was familiar with such things. The Carolina hills of her childhood echoed with tales of haints, those fearsome revenants of the dead, and she had heard of witches, both men and women, that could turn themselves into black cats and stalk you through the night. As a child, she had wakened many times from dreams of the little devils that played poker with Jack in the old tales, and of the horrifying Firedragaman that Jack followed to the underworld where he outwitted the creature and saved the lives of three girls the monster had imprisoned beneath the surface of the earth.

She remembered all the terrors of the world where she grew up in the mountains of North Carolina. The world—that of the mountains and the larger world as well—was filled with demonic creatures. People deluded by reason might deny their existence, but Bethany Wren believed they were real and lurking in every corner of the earth, no matter what they were called. Devils or jumbies or Old Firedragamen, men like Edd Byrd who had been pinned to his mattress by a long knife with a smoothly polished wooden handle, they were all spawn of Satan, and she was sure they were out there and they were waiting to eat the souls of unsuspecting and sinful humans and that it was her calling to do something about them whenever she could.

MINUTES LATER, Sergeant Preston walked into Dante's Landing. Standing in the doorway, he pointed at the Liquid Plumber who sat beside Moonie, the two men talking quietly.

"You, come over here," Sergeant Preston said.

The Liquid Plumber tapped his chest with four fingers and looked questioningly at the policeman.

Moonie shrank down on his stool, making himself as small as he could, hoping Sergeant Preston wouldn't see him. They were second cousins and the feelings between them had always been difficult. As children, the larger Preston had taunted him, and on several occasions he had beaten up the younger and smaller Moonie. It would be better not to attract his attention.

"You," Sergeant Preston repeated, still pointing at the Liquid Plumber, his right hand resting on the butt of his pistol. "Come over here now."

The Liquid Plumber stood and moved slowly across the room, exaggerating his state of drunkenness by walking as though his toes might shatter if he took a misstep.

"You have no alibi," Sergeant Preston said when the Liquid Plumber reached him.

"I'm a drunk. That's my story, my reality and my alibi. What specific alibi are you talking about officer?"

"I am a Sergeant, not a mere officer." Sergeant Preston was not amused by the Liquid Plumber's dismissive tone.

"Sorry, Sergeant," the Liquid Plumber muttered. "What is it I need an alibi for?"

"The murders that have occurred here recently."

The Liquid Plumber slowly moved his head up and down, struggling not to laugh. "You think I may have murdered someone?"

"Three someones." Sergeant Preston took a notebook from his pocket and opened it, reading names of the murdered men and the dates of their deaths. "I would like to know where you were on the nights before these men were killed."

"So would I." There was no trace of humor in the Liquid Plumber's reply. He leaned against the wall and looked across the room toward the bar, his unfinished drink sitting in front of his stool. "I know why I would like to know, but I don't understand why you do. I would like to know because there are too many things I lose, too many things I can't recall."

"I would like to know because you are a person of interest in the murders." Sergeant Preston carefully enunciated the words "person of interest," as if they were a magical incantation that once spoken elevated him professionally.

His eyes still on his drink, the Liquid Plumber opened his arms in a gesture of futility. "I don't know, Sergeant. I just don't know where I was. Probably drunk or asleep, or both."

"So you could have killed those men?"

"Anybody could have done that."

"I could not have."

The Liquid Plumber looked at him in silence.

Sergeant Preston waited for him to say something. When he did not, the policeman clenched his teeth and gave him a slow, calculated smile.

"I am warning you, do not stonewall me. If you truly cannot remember where you were or what you did those nights, why would it be wrong for me to assume that you are the guilty party?" He saw the words, 'guilty party,' written in capital letters in his mind's eye.

"Because I woke up in my own bed hung-over and without any blood on me."

Before Sergeant Preston could form a response, his cell phone buzzed.

"The Commander wants to see us," Roland Marsh said when Sergeant Preston answered.

"I am busy questioning a suspect."

"It won't wait. The ferry from Charlotte Amelia has gone aground on a reef off Little St. James Island. All hands, police as well as fire and St. John Rescue are needed." Marsh rang off.

Sergeant Preston looked at the phone, then at the Liquid Plumber.

"Do not leave the island," he said, and marched out of Dante's Landing, everyone at the bar watching with amused smiles. Moments later they heard his tires squealing on the pavement as he gunned the SUV cruiser and headed toward Cruz Bay.

"What was that all about?" Moonie asked when the Liquid Plumber returned to his seat.

The Liquid Plumber drained his shot glass and drank from the beer bottle. "The dumb cop's got it in his head that I might've killed those three guys that're dead."

"Most guys that get killed are dead," Nutty Betty said and laughed. "Did you make them dead?"

"Probably not."

"Probably?"

He shrugged. "Who knows? I'm a drunk. I fall into a stupor every night. I suppose a guy could do anything in a stupor."

"I don't think so," Nutty Betty said.

"Being in a stupor means you've got no critical cognitive function or level of consciousness," Robert said from behind the bar. "People in stupors are almost entirely unresponsive, responding only to base stimuli such as pain.

They could also be rigid and mute. The word comes from the Latin *stupure*. It means insensible and it's usually seen in people with infectious diseases and complicated toxic states, among other causes."

Nutty Betty hooted and slapped the Liquid Plumber's back with an open hand. "That's him, for sure. He's always in a toxic state."

The Liquid Plumber rolled his eyes and grinned at her.

Robert continued. "It's also seen in severe hypothermia; in mental illnesses such as schizophrenia and severe clinical depression, as well as in vascular illnesses like hypertensive encephalopathy, brain tumors and vitamin D deficiencies. There's more, of course."

"You sound like a medical dictionary Mr. Robert," Bethany said.

"Or like a doctor," Nutty Betty said. "Are you a doctor, or a nurse, something like that?"

"I'm a bartender," Robert said without lying. "I like to read medical thrillers and police procedurals, the kind with lots of forensic details."

"You must read some strange stuff," she said.

"Reams of it," Robert said with a careful laugh.

The conversation trailed off. Robert washed glasses. Skipper Dan busied himself painting the woodwork behind the bar. The Liquid Plumber and Nutty Betty drank.

Bethany brought Moonie his check.

"You must be careful," he said as he paid her with a twenty dollar bill.

"I always am."

"Especially careful. Carnival Festival is only two days away and the jumbies are getting restless."

She left and came back with his change. "The jumbies don't worry me."

"I hope not, but be very careful for the next few days. I am afraid that more bad things are going to happen around here."

"I'll be careful." She cleared his dishes from the table and carried them back to the kitchen.

Thirty

THE LIQUID PLUMBER left Dante's Landing less than half an hour after Sergeant Preston had questioned him. He walked along the road that followed the waterfront, waves from the choppy sea splashing high enough that their spray dampened his bare legs. After a few minutes he turned on to a gravel road leading out to the Fortsburg peninsula that jutted into Coral Harbor. A hundred yards along the road he passed a corral where a small group of donkeys and horses were penned. The roadway was covered with deep potholes full of red muddy water. With his unsteady gait he nearly stumbled and fell into several of them.

Wearier than he could remember feeling in a long time, he stopped and mopped sweat from his forehead. The sun was high and hot overhead, the still air heavy with moisture. Suddenly nauseated, he turned around, thinking he'd go back to Dante's Landing and settle his nerves with a cold beer and a shot of whiskey. He took two steps, stopped and turned again, continuing down the road toward the end of the peninsula. Sweat rolled down his forehead into his eyes. A small swarm of gnats followed him for a short while. Holding one hand over his mouth and nostrils, he lowered his head and slapped at the bugs, his eyes on the uneven road surface.

Five minutes later, he saw Miss Polly Moses coming toward him, walking from the outer part of the peninsula and going in the direction of the Coral Bay community. Dressed in a navy blue dress with small polka dots, a flat straw hat firmly on her head, the artificial flowers fastened beneath its band springing back and forth with each step, she walked carefully and briskly. When she was just a few feet away from him, he smiled.

"Good morning, Miss Polly."

She looked at her watch. "Drunk again, I see from your wavering steps. And it is not even noon. You should be ashamed, Mr. Plumber."

He tried to smile. "Yes ma'am, I suppose I should be."

She poked a finger at his chest. "Being a drunk is nothing to smile about, Mr. Plumber."

"No ma'am, but for some it is unavoidable. Being a drunk, I mean, not smiling about it."

She stood on her toes to bring her face as even with his as possible and glared at him. "Are you telling me that the Lord intended for you to be a drunkard and a wastrel?"

The Liquid Plumber kicked at a small stone in the road, sending it splashing into the water of a nearby pothole. "No ma'am. I don't suppose he did, but he and I aren't on speaking terms and I figure he doesn't care one way or the other about my drinking habits."

"That is nonsense, Mr. Plumber. He cares about each and every one of his children."

"Then why did he make me a drunk?"

"He did not. You made yourself a drunk."

"They say alcoholism is a sickness, a disease."

"Diseases can be cured, Mr. Plumber. There is a special cure for yours. Prayer and hard work."

He looked at her without replying, hoping she would walk on by and let him continue his hike out the peninsula. Instead, for the second time, she poked her finger at his chest. "Pastor Jensen, down at the Coral Bay Christian Church has started a chapter of Alcoholics Anonymous. My sister's husband, James, has been sober for eight weeks with the Pastor's help. I will send him around to talk to you."

"James or Pastor Jensen?"

"Both, if you wish."

The Liquid Plumber said, "I'll think about it."

"I will pray that you do, and I will pray that you do something about your drunken and wasteful ways. You know how to contact me, or James or Pastor Jensen, if you wish to change your ways. The Pastor will welcome you." She gave him a tight smile.

"I fear that I enjoy my drunken and wasteful ways."

Miss Polly's eyes narrowed and even the tight and reluctant smile she had given him vanished. With a single shake of her head she spoke through lips that barely parted for her words. "Good day, Mr. Plumber. I have much to do."

She walked on by. The Liquid Plumber stood in the middle of the road, watching her move farther way with each step. When she disappeared around a bend, he continued on his way, coming at last to a narrow rutted roadway on the left that led uphill. He followed it, panting and perspiring as he trudged upward under the hot sun, at times scratching his legs on grasping tendrils of catch-and-keep that grew out over the roadway. At the top of the hill he followed a barely visible path, increasingly overgrown with sting nettle and catch-and-keep. Several times he had to take the Leatherman out of its holster on his belt to cut his way through small branches and vines that blocked his way. The trail ended at a ruin where ancient rusted cannons stood in the crumbling stone and coral remains of a fortification overlooking the harbor.

It was one of his favorite places on St. John. Once a bulwark against invasion, the grounds covered with the remains of buildings and ramparts were one of the few places in the world where he could rest, at peace with himself. They forced him to consider the ruins of his life. No matter how fierce the battles that were fought here might have been, now quiet and peacefulness prevailed. Broken and open to wind and rain, battered by centuries of hurricanes and covered with vines and bush, the ruins and their useless weapons rested in cool shade, even on the hottest day. He sat on a large rock and laid his arm on the rusted and pitted barrel of a cannon. He smiled, thinking of Miss Polly poking her finger at him.

He had made light of her description of what she called his drunken and wasteful ways, when she was offering him the best advice she had to give. Sitting on the highest point of the peninsula, the waters of Coral Harbor far below, he watched three pelicans circling, their wings spread wide as they coasted on the thermals, gliding like living kites. One of them dove suddenly and seconds later he heard it splash into the water. There was a story about blindness among pelicans; that after years of diving, crashing really, into the sea, their eyes would be ruined from the repeated pressure. Blind, they would no longer be able see the food fish below and they would starve. He was sure it wasn't true, but the tale could describe his situation, blind from diving into too many drinks.

"Am I starving?" he asked himself, but he always ate enough to maintain the strength he needed to walk from his shack to the Landing and back. "And if I am, what am I starved for?"

Sitting on the hill in the sunlight, his drinks oozing out through his pores, it occurred to him that he was starving for was to be known as something more than the Liquid Plumber. Even Miss Polly called him Mr. Plumber. No one on St. John knew his name. At times he almost forgot it. He hadn't spoken it since coming here and moving into the one room shack he rented near the junkyard on King Hill Road in the flats of the Coral Bay Valley, a five minute walk from Dante's Landing, Skinny Legs Bar and Grill and the Island Blues Bar and Grill. After trying them all out on various days over several years, he'd settled on the Landing and made it his home away from the shack.

His fingers fell to the rope he used as a belt and moved upward to the beard that hung halfway to his chest, thinking that no one who might see him at this moment would guess that he had been raised in a wealthy suburb of Philadelphia. His father had been a successful architect in Bucks County, his mother a physician and professor of cardiology at the School of Medicine at the University of Pennsylvania. Nor would any of his Coral Bay barfly friends believe that he'd been an A student at George School and gone on to Swarthmore College with a full scholarship. Following a religious conversion at the end of his senior year, he disappointed his atheist/agnostic parents by enrolling in the seminary at Drew University, but dropped out after three semesters. Sure he had come to his senses, his parents were delighted, welcoming him home, assuring him he could stay with them until he felt ready to move on.

"I thought seminary would be simple," he had told them. "I was intrigued by Kierkegaard, but Heidegger—before he bowed to Hitler—confused me, and he repulsed me afterward. Sartre's existentialism was an interesting distraction for a while, but empty, and Tillich's theories on the failure of historical research to offer any kind of safe foundation for faith depressed me. Faith, it turned out, was elusive. It could not sustain me."

"I wouldn't know about any of that," his mother said. "I study the heart."

"That's what I thought I would study in seminary." He played with his right ear lobe for a moment before saying. "Albert Carver has agreed to take me on as an apprentice plumber."

"I see reason has prevailed," his father said.

He had grunted and said, "Seems so.

A year later his father kicked him out of the house, saying, "I was wrong about reason having prevailed when you quit that idiotic seminary. It was alcohol that prevailed."

Remembering his comment when his pleased father praised his reason, he said only, "Seems so."

He finished his apprenticeship but never got his license. Through the eighties and early nineties, he kicked around the country, working for plumbing contractors whenever he needed money to keep some kind of shelter over his head, a bit of food in his stomach, and enough alcohol glugging down his gullet to keep him numb. His parents were killed when his father crashed his Lear Jet into the side of a mountain in Colorado. As their only child, he inherited everything, stocks, bonds, and property worth millions. He instructed the estate attorney to set up a trust fund that would give him a guaranteed income for life. Then he moved to St. John to drink and be left alone and had spent nearly twenty years consuming what he insisted was the perfect drink, a shot of whisky chased with a beer.

The day progressed. The sun, ever hotter, leeched the alcohol from his system as he sat motionless, watching pelicans fly in circles, his arm resting on the rusted cannon. Desperately thirsty, he began having visions of a cold green bottle filled with beer, condensation streaming down the bottle's sides. The beauty of the scene faded, the peacefulness he always felt in the midst of the ruined battlements deserted him.

He needed a drink.

Bracing himself on the rusted cannon, he stood and made his way to the trail and began the trek back to Dante's Landing, where a barstool, a beer and a shot were waiting. He reached the lower road and turned toward Coral Bay. A mongoose darted in front of him, followed by a large black and white cat. They disappeared into the bushes and he continued walking. Three donkeys stood at the edge of the road, mutely watching as he passed, their swishing tails brushing away flies that swarmed around them. At the sound of a shrill cry from above, he raised his eyes and saw a hawk swoop toward the ground. As he watched it descend, he stumbled on a rock and fell face first into a watery pothole. Half conscious, he tried to breath, inhaling mud and water. Quickly, he sat up and blew it out, coughing and sputtering, his mouth filled with mud and grit.

Standing and spitting, he looked toward the waters of the bay, barely visible through the thick brush along the roadside. He shut his eyes and sobbed quietly. If some thought St. John was paradise, let them. It was opposite for him.

He laughed and shook his head. St. John was St. John. Hell was inside him and he was his own devil and torturer. He poured the waters of hell down his throat every day as he sat on his stool at Dante's Landing. Now that cop was trying to say that because he couldn't remember where he had been at specific times, he was a suspect in three murders. Could he have committed them?

He'd had dreams in which he had murdered someone and could not remember the murder; but they were dreams. Everybody must have them.

He stood in the full sunlight to let the muck on the front of his shirt dry. But if people did have such dreams, why wasn't there more discussion of them? Of course, he knew he had not killed anyone. He was too busy killing himself. Still, he hated the thought of there being times he could not remember. And then there was the matter of the cop and the way he had ordered him around with such disdain.

"You, come over here," the cop had said, and he had obeyed.

His mouth tasted salty. Raising a hand to his lips and pulling it away, he saw blood on his fingers. He felt like one of the last rag tags of humanity. Standing on that dirt road on the peninsula, his legs and arms scratched and scabbed from the catch-and-keep, his mouth bleeding, his clothes and bare skin covered with mud, he thought he must resemble a post-apocalyptic wraith stumbling through the waste land that some believe the earth will become following the Rapture, and other believe will be the inevitable result of mankind's environmental carelessness.

He knew it did not matter. There was nothing he could do to change the future of the world. He felt weak and ridiculous. What did matter was that he needed a drink. He buried his face in his hands, wondering how he could go on.

An hour later he was back on a stool at the crowded bar in Dante's Landing. Moonie sat next to him, a hamburger and a cup of coffee in front of him.

"A beer and a shot?" Robert asked.

About to say yes, two beers and two shots, the Liquid Plumber looked at Robert, his mouth half open, the words stuck in his throat. A man at the far end of the bar called for the bartender. Robert was too busy to wait for the Liquid Plumber to break through his paralysis, and left to attend to the other customer.

"Are you all right, mon?" Moonie asked.

The Liquid Plumber, hands shaking, looked at him and stuttered a reply. "I don't think so. I believe I might be in Hell."

Moonie coughed, as though choking on his food and then spoke with a shiver. "I have looked directly into the Pit of Hell and seen the darkness there."

He was about to say more when he saw Teach sitting at a table, glaring at Bethany who stood by a table of tourists asking her about Carnival and the upcoming Festival. Moonie coughed again and stopped himself from telling the Liquid Plumber about the pit on Bordeaux Mountain. The sound caught Teach's attention and his eyes shifted toward Moonie. Raising his right forefinger, he jabbed it several times in the air between them, his lip slightly curled; then he sighted along the finger and mimed shooting a gun, mouthing a silent "Pow."

Moonie looked away and said nothing. The Liquid Plumber, preoccupied with his own thoughts, noticed nothing. When Robert returned to him he ordered a beer and a shot.

Thirty-one

BETHANY AND ROBERT'S shifts were over. Christine sat at a table waiting for Robert to join her for dinner, an unlit cigarette in one hand, tapping her fingers on a half-empty pack lying on the table. Bethany and Robert walked over from opposite sides of the room and sat down, one on each side of her.

"Hey, X," Bethany said, looking from the cigarette to Christine's yellowed fingers on the cigarette pack. "Are you in a quandary over whether or not to light that thing?"

Christine turned it over in her hand and stuffed it back in the pack. "Call me Christine, please. Robert does."

Bethany looked as though she had received a gift. "Is that your real name, or just another St. John name that you've picked out for yourself?"

Christine grinned, "That's for me to know and you to find out."

Bethany cocked her head. "I haven't heard that expression since my brother Johnnie used to taunt me with his secrets."

Christine said, "It's my real name, Christine Grace St. Pierre, to be exact."

"Is that public knowledge now?"

Christine looked from Bethany to Robert, then back at Bethany. "I don't need to keep secrets about who I am any longer. I'm Christine Grace St. Pierre from Long Lake, New York, and I'd like to stop smoking those cancer sticks."

Bethany leaned forward and picked up the cigarette pack. Turning it over several times, she read the Surgeon General's warning aloud. "Do you like these things?"

"I love them. And I hate them. Robert has been trying to get me to quit." She made a nervous laughing sound. "I've quit three times in the past five years, once for two long weeks."

"Nicotine is one of the most addictive drugs we know of," Robert said. "Quitting's terribly hard to do."

"Anything you want, if you pray hard enough, you'll get it or you'll understand and accept why you're not getting it."

"I want Grace back in my life," Robert said.

"Grace is always with us, if we open our hearts," Bethany said.

"Grace is Robert's daughter," Christine said. "His ex-wife took her and walked out on him."

"Soon-to-be-ex-wife," Robert said.

Dropping Christine's cigarette pack into her purse, Bethany took his hand. Christine watched her cigarettes disappear into Bethany's purse, started to object, then sat back and smiled.

Bethany smiled back at her and shifted her gaze to Robert. "I'm sorry, Mr. Robert. Is that why you're down in these islands?"

"That's why I came here, to get away from the icy cold, both of Maria's heart and of Massachusetts winters, as well as to hide from my sorrows."

"Is that why you stayed?"

Robert looked into the blue of her eyes, then over at Christine, who waited for his answer with an apprehensive look.

"I stayed because I like it here." He smiled at Christine. "And because I found something worth staying for, as well as someone worth staying for."

"Y'all surely do make a fine looking couple."

Christine said, "I don't think you should call us a couple, yet. We're still getting to know one another."

Robert gave her a soft look. "There's a complication. I'm still legally married although I'm not married in my heart."

"She left you and took your baby?" Bethany asked.

"She did."

"Your wife broke God's law. People do that at their own peril."

Christine saw a hard light in Bethany's eyes, heard a cruel note in her voice when she spoke.

Robert ignored it. "I don't have any confidence in God or his laws."

Bethany coughed lightly and was about to respond. She stopped when Christine gave her a look that said, let it be. Rising, she rested a hand on each of their shoulders. "It's been a tiring day y'all. I'm headed for Love City Mini-Mart and then back to my boat."

As she left the Landing and walked outside, Bethany did not see Teach standing in the shadow under the canopy of a nearby flamboyant tree. He suddenly approached her and she had the discomfiting sense that he had been waiting for her. Startled, she took several steps back, away from where he stood still half hidden in the shadow of the tree.

"Going somewhere?" His voice was low, whispery and, she thought, heavy with menace.

"To the store."

"I don't suppose you'd like a ride?"

"I prefer to walk."

"That's foolish. A woman should not be walking alone at night."

"That's ridiculous."

He walked to his car and opened the passenger's side door, waving his arm as if to usher her in. "Please, allow me to give you a ride."

She did not like the way he smiled and the menace in his whispery voice seemed to deepen with each slowly and carefully enunciated word. "You're afraid of me."

"I'm not afraid of anyone."

"You're afraid of me. I frighten you to the very core of your soul."

"Sorry. Not frightened."

"You should be. If you are not frightened there is something very wrong with the way you perceive reality," he said and went around to the driver's side car and climbed in.

Bethany stepped onto the roadway and started walking. Behind her, she heard the sound of Teach's motor turn over and the crunch of his tires on the gravel parking lot. She did not look up when he pulled alongside her and rolled down his window.

"Sooner or later, you'll ride with me."

"I doubt that, Mr. Teach."

"I have something to show you that will test your faith."

She stopped walking. Taking a deep breath, she squared her shoulders. "My faith was tested a long time ago, Mr. Teach, and it was unshaken. I don't reckon that anything you've got to show me or tell me is going to make any difference."

"How do you know if you won't come with me?"

"I don't need to know anymore than I already know, deep in my heart."

"You're quite the coward, aren't you? A brave Christian would not be afraid to test her faith."

"My faith is beyond questioning."

Without another word, Teach rolled up the window and drove away. Watching his tail lights recede, Bethany stood unmoving for several long minutes, her heart racing, her blood pounding. When her nerves finally calmed, she went back to Dante's Landing. Christine and Robert's dinners had been served. They ate and were talking quietly. Bethany sat at their table.

"If it's all right, I surely would like to catch a ride to the store and back with y'all when you're ready to leave."

ROBERT STOOD ALONE in the dark center of Dante's Landing. Boozie had left an hour earlier, complaining of a stomach ailment. Skipper Dan, who had a date with a woman he knew in Cruz Bay, twisted Robert's arm until he agreed to finish Boozie's shift and stay after closing time to shut down the Landing for the night. When he and Christine finished their dinners, Robert returned to his post behind the bar. Christine drove Bethany to the Mini-Mart and dropped her back at the Landing. Tired, she said goodnight to Robert and went home. After the last customers left, he wiped down the bar, loaded the dishwasher and put the chairs on their tables so that Randy Hodge could sweep up and mop the floor first thing in the morning.

The televisions were all turned off, the wooden boxes holding them closed and padlocked. For midsummer, it had been a busy night. Skipper Dan had told him that he was grateful for the tourist business the last week of Carnival and his own pre-Fourth Festival party brought to the slack time.

"From now until mid-December things slow really down," he said, explaining that they would close the place for most of September and October, historically the worst months of hurricane season. If there were no damaging storms the time could be spent cleaning, painting and repairing the building. If a storm came along and did major damage, the time would have to be spent cleaning, painting and repairing the building. Either way, he had assured Robert that he would be busy.

Grabbing a club soda, he locked the building and walked outside to sit on the dock and relax after a long and hard day's work. He was surprised to find Moonie leaning against a piling near the end of the dock, a cigarette smoldering in his hand. The night was still, almost airless, and the smoke curled slowly upward in the moonlight.

"Nice night," Robert said.

"It is a beautiful evening." Moonie took a last few puffs and tossed the butt into the water. The fiery end glowed on the surface for a moment before going out.

Robert hunkered down on the dock beside him. Popping the top of his soda can, he took a drink and rested the can on his knee.

"I do not like that man they call Teach," Moonie said abruptly.

"What brought that up?"

Moonie shook his head. "I just do not like him. I believe he is a very bad man, and I believe he harbors bad thoughts about Bethany."

"Has he done anything?"

Moonie hesitated, as if he had something to say, but instead shook his head and said, "I do not like him at all. We should all be watchful around him."

"But you have nothing specific to say?"

Moonie thought of telling Robert about Teach's Pit of Hell, but he recalled Teach telling him that he would be within his rights to shoot him, and thought of how, earlier in the evening, Teach had sighted along his finger and mimed the sound of a gun firing. He was not about to trespass on Teach's land again, nor did he wish to be responsible for someone else going up there and getting shot.

"Nothing specific, mon. It is just a feeling I have. There is probably nothing to it, just my mind playing tricks on me."

"Sometimes that's because we know things without being able to explain them."

"Miss Rachel, my fifth grade teacher, used to say that I had an overactive imagination," Moonie said.

"Is that what's making you think Teach has it in for Bethany?"

"I do not like the way he looks at her."

"Then we'll keep an eye on him," Robert said.

"That would be good." Moonie lit another cigarette and smoked it in silence.

Drinking the last of his soda, Robert stood and stretched. "If you think of anything else, anything specific, let me know."

Moonie exhaled smoke through his nostrils. It hung in the still air, clouding his face for several seconds; then a breeze stirred and it slowly cleared. He scratched his head. "I will, if I think of anything."

MOONLIGHT SHONE through the trees surrounding Teach's property. Their branches and leaves cast moving shadows on the roof of the Pit of Hell. The hour was late, the night quiet, the last strains of music from the restaurants and bars in the valley had long ago ceased drifting up from Coral

Bay. With no rain for nearly a week, there were relatively few singing tree frogs, the only break in the stillness coming from the distant whine of a motorcycle engine echoing against the hills.

A rat sat on one of several moonlit bright spots on the Pit of Hell's roof, nibbling at the carcass of a lizard. Teach squatted on the ground beside the Pit, watching the rat, a net in his hands. Breathing slowly, he never took his eyes from the roof. The rat seemed oblivious to Teach's presence. Once it finished eating the lizard, only the tail sticking from its mouth, Teach stood and lowered the net. The rat squirmed and squealed but could not free itself. The net bounced at the end of its handle as the creature futilely struggled against captivity.

"Got you, my friend," Teach said, holding the net so close to his face that he could see moonlight reflected in the rat's eyes. He lifted the roof from the Pit of Hell and overturning the net, dropped the rat in.

"You'll have company soon." Smiling, he closed the lid.

Thirty-two

BY FOUR in the afternoon of the third of July, Dante's Landing was packed. People came early to get seats at tables and the bar. The Liquid Plumber and Moonie, among the earliest arrivals, sat side by side in the middle of the bar, equidistant from two small make-shift stages on either side of the exit leading to the dock where two different bands would be playing. One band, an acoustic country/rock group, had already begun setting up on one of the opposing stages. A steel drum trio was set up on the other stage.

Robert and Bethany had hung brightly colored decorations on the beams running from the Landing's center pole out to the edges of the room. Some were traditional Fourth of July pieces: buntings of red, white, and blue were draped over the bar; banners with stars and stripes bedecked the walls; images of Uncle Sam, from the famous Uncle Sam Wants You! poster, originally published as the cover for the July 6, 1916, issue of Leslie's Weekly, to more modern cartoon depictions of the iconic figure.

The patriotic theme was mingled with decorations more suitable for Carnival, table cloths and wall hangings with vivid colors, greens, blues, fuchsias and yellows. On the larger tables were floral centerpieces, with hibiscus and birds of paradise surrounded by greens. Smaller tables held clear glass lanterns anchored in white sand and surrounded by shells. Large cardboard jumbies were suspended from the highest beams.

Skipper Dan supervised the work, checked on supplies, and placed copies of the special menu he had prepared for the party in plastic holders at every table and at strategic places along the bar. He shook hands, hugged people, kissed bald men on the tops of their heads as he passed them, always thanking people for coming and promising them a rollicking good time.

"Gonna be jumbies here tonight," he promised. "Wait until you see the jumbies dance. It's going to be a night to remember, I promise you."

The steel drum trio began playing at five-thirty, opening with "Island in the Sun," their music barely audible above the talking and shouting people jostling for room at the bar. Robert and Boozie struggled to keep up with shouted orders from the bar as well as from the waitresses working the room.

At seven-thirty, Skipper Dan stepped to the stage where the trio had been playing. Taking a microphone from its stand, he cleared his throat and spoke into it.

"A big hand for the Coral Bay Steel Drummers," he said, and initiated the applause by clapping, the microphone in his hand, the sound of his hands amplified throughout the room. "Next we'll be hearing from another of our very own groups, the Hot Club of Coral Bay."

There was more applause and hooting from the audience, but Skipper Dan held up his hands. "First, who knows what time it is?"

"It's jumbie time," called the regulars, having been through many of Skipper Dan's pre-Fourth parties.

Skipper Dan laughed. "I was afraid someone might yell 'it's Howdy Doody time,' and I'd have to disappoint you."

"It's Howdy Doody time," Nutty Betty called. There was a loud chorus of good-natured booing and laughter from throughout the room. She raised her hands in a single fist above her head. "I didn't want to disappoint you, Skipper."

"You never do," he said. "But you're wrong and everyone else is right."

"The story of my life," Nutty Betty said, to more laughter and loud hoots.

"She's wrong, the rest of you are right," Skipper Dan said, and nodded to the band. They played a jazzy introduction and Skipper Dan yelled over the microphone, "It's jumbie time at Dante's Landing."

The crowd cheered and a group of jumbies danced through the door. The first one had a face painted white, its eyebrows and lips covered with black lipstick, wearing a black hooded cloak. Pale stringy hair stuck out from the hood and hung to the middle of its chest, partially covering the bloody heart on its blue tee shirt. It stomped around on stilts that clomped against the wooden floor. The other jumbies, six of them, all on stilts and equally as tall as the first, were dressed in bright colors. They paraded around the room, several of them handing women and men alike pink and yellow Mandevilla blossoms.

The pale-faced jumbie circled the outside edges of the restaurant, stopping from time to time to lean over nearby tables, as though leering at women and men alike. Coming back to where it started by the door, it stood still for a while, watching the others. After several minutes, it crossed the center of the room and walked toward the section of the bar where Moonie and the Liquid Plumber sat. It stood behind them, resting a hand on each of their shoulders before moving on to stand beside the computer terminal the waiters use to place their food orders.

"Funny," Skipper Dan said. "I got a freebie jumbie. I paid for six and got seven."

"That one's creepy." Robert's thumb gestured toward the figure towering over the computer terminal.

Skipper Dan gave him a quiet laugh. "A creepy jumbie isn't a bad thing. It's a reminder that all is not lightness and laughter in the supernatural world."

Robert did not reply.

When Bethany came to the terminal she had to shove the jumbie aside with her hip in order to get to the screen. It moved easily, but only a few inches. She looked up at it.

"You might could get out of my way."

The jumbie nodded but did not move.

"Jumbies," she muttered. "Tall skinny devils is more like it. Lord, but I don't know why we tolerate such pagan foolishness." The jumbie briefly rested a gloved hand on the top of her head and walked away.

When the Hot Club of Coral Bay began to play, six of the jumbies formed a circle and danced around the floor on their stilts, clapping their hands above their heads. One by one, they went to the center of the circle and danced with wide-spread arms. When the last of the six finished its solo dance, they joined hands and beckoned people to enter their circle and dance inside. Through all this, the first jumbie stood by the door, apart from the others, its eyes following Bethany around the room as she brought food and drinks to her assigned tables, cleared away dirty dishes and chatted with people, smiling as they laughed at her jokes and comments.

No one noticed when it slipped out of the room. Skipper Dan looked up at one point and saw that it was gone. "Hunh," he grunted to Robert. "I'm down one jumbie, not that it matters; I paid for six, had seven for a while, and six is what I have left."

The evening wore on. The jumbies finally came down from their stilts, took off their long pants and mingled with the revelers, eating, tossing down drinks and dancing in their human forms. The kitchen closed at ten. By midnight the crowd had begun to thin. All but three of the wait staff went home. Boozie left shortly afterwards, again claiming an upset stomach. Bethany stayed to help Skipper Dan and Robert clean up and close the place.

By two-thirty the work was mostly done and only she, Skipper Dan and

Robert were left inside Dante's Landing. They loaded all the trash into plastic bags and piled them by the door. Robert was cleaning up behind the bar and Skipper Dan was counting the day's receipts.

"As soon as I drag those trash bags out to the dumpster I'm going to call it a night and go out to the boat and fall into my bunk," Bethany said.

Robert gave her the OK sign and she picked up a bag in each hand. The air was fresh when she stepped outside. A light breeze was blowing and she could hear small waves breaking against the rocky shore line a few feet away. Halyards clanged against aluminum masts. She thought they sounded almost like wind chimes.

Opening the dumpster, she dropped the bags in. She turned to walk around the building to the dock where her dinghy was tied up when a gloved hand was clamped over her mouth and something crashed against her skull. Moments later, unconscious, she was bound and gagged. Teach threw her into his back seat and drove away.

SHE AWOKE and sat up, the only light coming from above, through the opening around what appeared to be an ill-fitting roof. It wasn't much, but it was enough that she could tell it was morning. Her head hurt.

"Lord, what do you have planned for me now?" She looked around in the gloom, quickly seeing that the walls surrounding her were earthen, as was the floor she had been lying on. Her eyes landed on the rat sitting a few feet away, its black eyes seemingly fixed on her. Overcoming a momentary revulsion, she smiled at it.

'Hey mister rat, you're in the same fix I am. Who put us in here, as if I didn't know? It was that Teach, right?"

The rat's whiskers wiggled, but it sat still, its dark eyes still seeming to stare at her.

Standing, she reached upward, but the roof was more than two feet above her outstretched arms. She walked around the hole, feeling the sides with her hands.

"We're in a hole, mister rat. Maybe a basement, something like that." She sat again, leaning against the wall. "Can't be a basement," she told the rat. "There aren't basements on St. John. Anyone that goes to the trouble of digging a basement is going to cement it in and cover it with Thoroseal so they can use it as a cistern. I reckon this is a hole that someone dug especially for me, and it surely wasn't done out of kindness."

"I'm not a kind person," said a voice from above and Teach lifted the roof to look in. His face was still painted white, his eyebrows and lips still black.

"Well, if you don't look like demon from the depths of Hell, Mr. Teach."

"You're the one in the Pit of Hell," he said.

"I don't hardly think so. This is a little bitty hole that you probably dug all on your own."

"It could be your grave," Teach said. "In truth, it will be."

Bethany said nothing. She stared up at him, silently praying as she did, not wanting to give him the satisfaction of knowing that she wasn't praying for herself, but for God to strike him down with a mighty sword, to pierce his heart and pin him to the ground where she could hear his dying cries before his soul slipped from his agonized body and dropped through the earth to the eternal damnation awaiting him in the true pits of Hell. She smiled at the thought.

"Hungry yet?" he asked, ignoring her smile.

"I've never been known to turn down a morsel."

"Does that mean you're asking me for food?"

She shook her head. "I was only saying that I'd eat it if you gave it to me."

"You'll have to ask for it."

"Not yet."

"Thirsty?"

"Only if you want to give me water."

"You'll be hungry and thirsty both before the day's over. Let me know when you want something."

"You let me know when you feel the need to give me food and drink, and maybe some for this little old rat you've thrown in here with me."

Teach laughed in reply and dropped the roof back in place.

Bethany slid back down the wall to a sitting position. She was surprisingly calm. She had been uncomfortable around Teach, not frightened as he told her she should have been, but she knew there was something terribly wrong about him. He smelled of evil.

She knew she was in a bad situation. With Dante's Landing closed for the Fourth of July Festival celebration in Cruz Bay, no one would have any idea that she was missing until she failed to show up for work the following day.

"Rats, mister rat. We're in a jam. Now don't you get the idea that you can nibble on my fingers and toes."

The rat inched closer to her. She flicked her fingers and it jumped back.

"Looks like we'll be doing this for a while," she said. The rat hunched its shoulders and sat unmoving, its eyes still glued to her.

Thirty-three

SHORTLY BEFORE NOON, Reverend Garry Jensen put down his broom. With a small congregation, only half a dozen people tithing and the regular Sunday collections meager, janitorial work was a necessary part of his pastoral duties, including giving the church a thorough cleaning at least once a week. There was a soft cough from behind him. Looking up, he saw the Liquid Plumber standing in the doorway, his arms hanging limp at his sides, his face drawn and pale, his hands shaking.

He waved him in, pointing to a bench. "You look like you need to sit down."

The Liquid Plumber took a tentative step inside and stopped, as though his forward motion had been halted by a force greater than his own. "Maybe I've made a mistake."

"It's never a mistake to enter here."

The Liquid Plumber clicked his teeth and looked around, his eyes settling on the plain cross hanging at the rear of the room. "I don't know. It doesn't feel right."

Pastor Jensen studied the man's face. His graying beard and mustache were stained yellow by nicotine. The skin on his cheeks and nose was deeply lined and red from broken blood vessels and his pale eyes were red-rimmed and defenseless looking.

"You're welcome here." Pastor Jensen crossed to where the Liquid Plumber stood.

There was a long and awkward silence as the Liquid Plumber seemed to be engaged in a struggle against unseen forces, at the end of which he nodded and spoke in cracked voice, "Miss Polly said I might be."

"Miss Polly Moses is a wise woman." Pastor Jensen took the Liquid Plumber by the arm and led him to a bench seat near the front of the church, by the pulpit. "Sit here. Would you like some water?"

"A shot and a beer would be good. I haven't had a drink since last night. I suppose that's not what you meant."

"We're completely out of whiskey and beer," Garry Jensen said with a laugh. "They're not the kind of spirits we're concerned with here."

The Liquid Plumber gave him a weak smile. "That's why I'm here."

"For the Holy Spirit?"

The Liquid Plumber combed his fingers through his hair. "To find out about your group for drunks."

"The AA group."

"That's the one," the Liquid Plumber said. "I'm here for that and I want a beer and Jim Beam." He laughed.

The pastor nodded, as if he understood. "I've got bottled water, half a quart of orange juice and maybe a can or two of soda."

"Water, please." The Liquid Plumber said with a low croak.

"Coming right up." Pastor Jensen went to the church's kitchen.

As soon as he was gone, The Liquid Plumber pushed himself up from the bench and started down the aisle toward the door. He was nearly out when Jensen, holding two bottles of cold water, caught up with him.

"You don't have to leave," he said, again taking the Liquid Plumber by the arm and leading him back toward the middle of the sanctuary.

"I don't have to stay."

"You don't. You came here of your own free will and you can leave of your own free will. Nobody has to come here, although everyone is invited. God keeps an open house." He held out a bottle of water to the Liquid Plumber.

"God isn't what I need. It's help with the booze, and you've got that group."

"AA," Garry said again. "You can say the words, Alcoholics Anonymous."

Uncapping the bottle and taking a long drink, the Liquid Plumber coughed and took a second, smaller sip.

"I know you," Garry Jensen said. "You're the one they call the Liquid Plumber."

The Liquid Plumber's shoulders sank and he stared into Jensen's eyes. "Not a very distinguished way of being known, is it?"

Jensen shook his head. "No."

"I wasn't always the Liquid Plumber."

"I'm sure you weren't. Not many people would christen a child Liquid Plumber."

They both laughed, although the Liquid Plumber looked as though the effort pained him. He sat down again. Resting his elbows on his knees, his head cradled in his hands, he coughed several times and cleared his throat before looking up at Garry Jensen. Twice he opened his mouth to speak.

Twice he stopped himself. After taking a deep breath, he sat up, his back straight, his eyes making contact with Jensen's, as though he was suddenly free of invisible restraints. When he spoke, his voice was clear and strong.

"I was born in Doylestown, Pennsylvania. My parents named me William Pitcairn Hastings. My father called me Billy. My mother always called me William. That was a long long time ago, a lifetime ago. I always introduced myself as Bill." He paused before continuing with a smile. "That was when I was still introducing myself to people. After a while, I was too ashamed to let anyone know who I was. When I moved down here I just let people call me whatever they wished. The name Liquid Plumber stuck, although no one really calls me that to my face. They avoid addressing me as anything except as except you, or 'hey you, would you like another beer and a shot?' To which I've always said, 'Yes.' 'How are you today?' they might ask, not that anybody cared what I said in return. But I knew what they called me and it didn't matter as long as I could drink and..." He stopped, his voice trailing off.

Pastor Jensen held out his hand. Bill Hastings grasped it. "I'm Garry, Bill, and I'm glad to meet you. I was just about to go home for lunch. Care to join me?"

Bill sighed, heaving his shoulders. "I don't suppose I could get a beer and a shot at your place?"

"Not a chance of it."

"That might be a good thing."

"It is a very good thing. We'll have sandwiches and I can tell you about the group we have here at the church for alcoholics."

Bill withdrew slightly. "I'm not an alcoholic. I'm a drunk."

"This group is good for both drunks and alcoholics."

"I'm not good with groups."

"Just try it."

Bill looked down at his shaking hands. "I suppose I should try something."

"You're welcome here for any reason."

Maybe I should try it. Miss Polly was right about me."

Garry did not ask what Miss Polly had said, although he could guess. He threw his arm around Bill Hasting's shoulders and led him toward his car. "It'll be hard work and take some time."

"Time is all I have, and I've wasted too much of it."

*

ANDREA HILLBORN was furious. She had waited two hours for Bethany to show up at the rental villa they were scheduled to clean. After the first half hour, Andrea tried calling her, but there was no answer and she left a voice mail message. She stripped the beds, gathered towels and wash cloths and did the first load of laundry, mumbling as she practiced the tirade with which she intended to berate Bethany when she showed up. When Bethany didn't return her first call, Andrea called four more times and left four more messages, each one more urgent and angrier in tone. Bethany did not respond. By noon it was clear to her that Bethany was not coming. Andrea tried calling several other women to pitch in. No one was available and she was stuck trying to clean the house and pool by herself. It took hours and the people scheduled to come into the villa were forced to wait an hour beyond the usual check in time.

Finished, Andrea drove down to Dante's Landing to see if she could find out what had kept Bethany from working with her and found the note Skipper had posted telling people that the Landing was closed for the day and urging them to go to the St. John Festival gala in Cruz Bay. Driving along the waterfront, she saw Moonie empty a sack of fish into a ten gallon galvanized bucket half full ice that sat beside his table next to the road. A sign was taped to the edge of the table, FISH SALE. She pulled over and leaned out the window.

"Have you seen Bethany?"

He shook his head. "It is Carnival and the day of Festival. I am sure she has gone to town to celebrate. Everyone is there. Everyone but me. I have other things to do." He pointed at the bucket of fish. "I have some good mahi mahi, and redfish."

"She was supposed to work with me today and never showed up, but I'd think she would answer her phone, even if she is at the Festival."

Moonie picked up a large mahi and held it by the tail for her to see. "If she is not at the Festival, perhaps she is still sleeping. It was a big night at Dante's last night."

"That's not like her. She's super responsible about things."

"And you are angry with her."

"Not angry," Andrea lied. "Frustrated."

"Frustration leads to anger."

"I'm not angry," Andrea yelled.

Moonie grinned at her. "Mahi is good food for calming you down."

Andrea had to laugh at his persistence. "You're impossible."

"But the mahi and I helped change your mood."

"You did."

Moonie bowed. "I am a magician."

"You're a rascal."

"That too," he said.

"If you see her, tell her to give me a call. Tell that I've got a bone to pick with her."

"I filet my fish very well. There are no bones, guaranteed."

"No bones, eh? Then I'll just have to give her a piece of my mind."

"Make it a nicer piece than you've been showing me so far. Do not go off on the girl."

"I can't guarantee that." Andrea clucked her tongue and gave Moonie a forced smile.

She drove off, giving him two quick toots on her horn and a wave. A mile down the road, she turned around, came back to his stand and bought a pound of mahi-mahi.

"You cannot find fresher fish than the fish you buy from Moonie," Moonie said. He wrapped it in waxed paper and wrapped that in four layers of newspaper. "Eat it tonight."

"Right now I'm going to Bethany's boat and yank her out of bed and give her that piece of my mind."

"Remember what I said about that. Be kind."

Eight minutes later she parked in the lot at Dante's Landing. Mechanic Mike was standing under the flamboyant tree, Bethany's Samurai parked a few feet away.

"I see you finally got it done," Andrea said.

Mechanic Mike patted the Samurai's front fender. "I got it so that it'll run pretty good until the parts come in from the States. There wasn't no point in me keeping it when she could drive it. I guess you could say it's as good as I can get it without them parts."

"Is that good?"

He laughed. "It's a piece of junk. Even with the new parts it won't be nothing else but a piece of junk with new parts."

"But you fixed it for her."

"I wouldn't call this car fixed. I'd call it a working wreck." He looked toward the restaurant. "She ain't around. Her dinghy's tied up at the dock and I yelled for her, but it didn't do no good. I don't know where she is. I was hoping I'd give her the car and she'd pay me some of what she owes me and drive me back to my place. Now I got to drive it back myself and bring it to her another time and wait for my money while she's off to Cruz and dancing at Festival."

"She's not exactly the dancing type."

Mechanic Mike said, "No matter where she is, she ain't here."

Andrea leaned against the side of her car. "Rats. I've got a bone to pick with her."

"She owe you money too?"

"She owes me an apology. She never showed up to work today."

"I thought the Landing was closed."

"We had a villa to clean. I ended up doing all the work by myself."

Mechanic Mike tilted his head to the side. With his thumbnail, he picked greasy dirt from under the fingernails of his right hand and flicked the residue on the ground. "That ain't like her. Bethany's someone you can count on."

"Not today," Andrea said.

Thirty-four

FOR THE FOURTH TIME since lunch, Sergeant Preston squelched his police radio as soon as he heard the Commander's voice come through the speaker. He was not about to be pulled back from his prey to do some petty office work, or to be called to a minor accident. He still resented having been called away from questioning the Liquid Plumber to help the passengers on the grounded ferry. Whatever the Commander wanted from him could not be more important than arresting a triple murderer. Solving this case would get him a promotion. Rumor had it that the Commander was about to be named Deputy Chief of the Virgin Islands Police Department. If that happened, Sergeant Preston believed with three solved murder investigations on his record he would be a contender for Acting Commander of the St. John Station, perhaps even Commander.

He'd double-checked the alibis of his suspects at Dante's Landing. The Liquid Plumber alone could not account for his whereabouts at the times of the murders. Sergeant Preston chose not to believe his statement that he had been drunk and asleep. Now he was headed for Coral Bay, to Dante's Landing, where it seemed to him that the suspect almost lived at the bar. He was about to make an arrest. His future was made. Soon he'd be a lieutenant, perhaps even a captain. No more Sergeant Preston. He would soon become Lieutenant Preston, Captain Preston. Best of all, Commander Preston. He looked at his reflection in the rearview mirror and saluted.

"Hello, Commander Preston." He smiled at his reflection. With such a title there would be no more Statesiders snickering when he introduced himself, making jokes about some ancient television show that he did not understand.

Returning his attention to the road in front of him, he saw the Liquid Plumber driving in the opposite direction, toward Cruz Bay. Turning on his lights, he made a U-turn.

Bill Hastings pulled over to the side of Centerline Road the moment he heard the siren and saw the cruiser, blue lights flashing, behind him. The cruiser came to a stop a few feet from the rear of his car. Sergeant Preston got out and walked toward Bill, who sat motionless in the driver's seat, his hands tight on the steering wheel.

"Get out," he said, his hand resting on his holstered Glock pistol.

"I haven't had a drink since yesterday," Bill said. "You can run all the sobriety tests you can think of and I'll still be sober."

"Get out now." Sergeant Preston reached for the door handle, the pistol in his free hand.

Bill lifted his hands from the steering wheel, raising them high enough for Sergeant Preston to see. "I've got nothing in my hands."

Yanking the door open, Sergeant Preston grabbed Bill's left arm and pulled him from the car. Forcing him up against its side, he began to roughly frisk him. "You are being arrested on suspicion of murder. You have the right to remain silent, as if a disgusting drunk like you knows how to keep your mouth shut. Anything you say can and will be used against you in a court of law where you will be convicted and sentenced. You have the right to an attorney. If you cannot afford an attorney, one will be provided for you, perhaps my cousin, Thomas Preston. Do you understand the rights I have just read to you? With these rights in mind, do you wish to speak to me?"

"I've never been particularly interested in speaking to you."

"Useless piece of garbage," Sergeant Preston said, shoving Bill so hard against the car that he felt as though his cheek bones were about to break. "Do not mess with me, Liquid Plumber, or I will flush you down like the trash that you are."

"I haven't killed anyone."

"Do not talk to me unless you want to confess. A confession is the only thing I wish to hear come from your lips." Sergeant Preston's barked words were so loud in his ear that Bill feared for his hearing. When the policeman finished frisking him, he pulled Bill's hands behind his back and cuffed him, making sure the cuffs were tight enough to pinch the skin on his wrists.

"Get in the back of my cruiser," he said.

"What about my car?"

Sergeant Preston smiled and laughed. "What about it? You'll never need it again. Murder will get you a lifetime in prison."

He opened the back door of the cruiser and grabbed Bill's hair, forcing him to bend over as he shoved him onto the smooth vinyl rear seat. The space was cramped and he had to bend his knees uncomfortably. The clear acrylic sheet separating him from the front of the car was smudged with nose and hand prints and the car smelled of tobacco, vomit and urine.

Sergeant Preston climbed into the driver's seat, rolled down the front windows and turned off the air conditioning. The rear of the cruiser began to heat up almost immediately and Bill saw that there was no way to open the windows.

"Are you trying to suffocate me?"

Sergeant Preston smiled at him through the acrylic barrier. "That would be criminal."

He pulled his cruiser onto Centerline Road and started driving toward Cruz Bay. Rounding a sharp curve they passed another cruiser backed onto a side road. It was one of the newer members of the force, Andrew Sprauve, obviously waiting to catch speeders. He tooted and waved. Sprauve waved back. Sergeant Preston did not notice him pull across the road behind him, blocking traffic coming from Coral Bay.

"It's awfully hot back here," Bill called, rapping on the acrylic.

"Do not worry. Soon you will be in an air-conditioned cell in our new police headquarters in Cruz Bay."

"I can barely breathe."

"It is quite comfortable up front here. Of course, I have my windows open and the breeze blowing through them."

"You could open the rear windows, just a bit. I won't jump out."

"That is against regulations."

"And you're a stickler for regulations."

"I am a serious member of the Virgin Islands Police Department. To do anything other than follow procedure would not be proper."

Bill was about to make a snide comment when Sergeant Preston suddenly slammed on his brakes. Bill's head crashed into the acrylic. Two cruisers blocked the road ahead. Two more were parked alongside them. In front of them were ten policemen, including Commander Whatley who stood next to a heavy-set man in a blue t-shirt, FBI emblazoned across the chest in large yellow capital letters. All stood with their legs apart. Their guns, held firmly in both hands, were aimed at Sergeant Preston's cruiser.

"I must be an important catch," Bill said, rubbing his forehead. "Are they going to take me down into the bush and shoot me?"

"Shut your mouth." Sergeant Preston's voice was a fearful snarl.

The Commander raised a bullhorn to his mouth. "Sergeant, get out of the car with your hands raised."

Sergeant Preston slumped in his seat and banged the steering wheel with both fists.

Bill asked, "How am I supposed to get out?"

"Not you," Sergeant Preston said. "Are you deaf as well as a drunk? They want me."

"Out. Now." The Commander took a step toward the cruiser and was restrained by the FBI agent.

"What for?" Bill asked.

"It's none of your business, murderer."

"Throw your gun out the window," the Commander said.

Sergeant Preston sighed. He took the gun from its holster and held it for a moment, as if he were about to use it. Then, with a second, much deeper sigh, he tossed the Glock out the window. Roland Marsh picked it up and opened Sergeant Preston's door.

"Be very careful of what you tell them," he said in such a low voice that even Bill could not make out his words. "Do not make trouble for your friends."

"Do not worry," Sergeant Preston said, heeding the unspoken 'Or else' in the detective's voice. "I know what is expected of me."

"Total loyalty to the force."

Sergeant Preston nodded, but said nothing as he got out of the car. He was immediately cuffed and led to another cruiser where he was surrounded by police. The FBI agent read him his rights.

Bill banged on the window of the abandoned cruiser. "Hey, how about me?" he called. Eventually one of the policemen noticed and told the Commander who came over and opened the rear door.

"You are the one called the Liquid Plumber?"

"Bill Hastings," he said.

The Commander unlocked Bill's cuffs. "You can go."

"I'm not under arrest?"

"You are not even a suspect. My sergeant was acting on his own when he arrested you."

"I need someone to take me to my car."

"Where is it?"

He pointed toward Coral Bay. "About four miles back."

The Commander lit a cigarette, tossing the match to the side of the road. "That is not far. You can walk."

Bill pointed at the cruiser behind them, the one that had pulled out from the side road. "He could take me."

"He is on duty."

"Isn't part of his duty to help people?"

"He is helping the people of the Virgin Islands by participating in the arrest of a corrupt police officer."

"I'm one of the people of the Virgin Islands."

"You live here?"

"For almost twenty years."

"You will never be one of us." The Commander looked at his watch. "Now, if you will excuse me, I have to make sure we get Sergeant Preston back to town and properly arraigned. He is a blot on the department's reputation."

"That must disturb you terribly."

The Commander scrunched up his face and stared at Bill. "It does. It disturbs me greatly and I fear this is just the beginning."

Bill walked past the cruiser, still parked across the road. The policeman inside seemed to look through him, as if he were invisible. Several cars were backed up behind the cruiser, waiting for the road block to be moved. A West Indian man who looked to be in his early forties driving a pickup was at the front of the line.

"Hey mon, what is going on up there?"

"The cops just arrested a crooked cop," Bill said.

The man smiled. "They will need a convoy of busses to take all the crooked cops in these islands to jail. Who did they get?"

"Sergeant Preston."

"Ah. He is a bad one. They say; if you need good cocaine, go to Sergeant Preston."

"He's a dealer?"

"Worse. I have heard that if you need someone to disappear, Sergeant Preston can arrange it for you. I saw them let you out of the back of his cruiser. You are lucky."

"I guess so, but they're still making me walk back to my car in the mid-day heat."

"Where is your car?"

"Four plus miles back."

"That is uphill almost all the way."

Bill sighed and mimed wiping sweat from his head. "Tell me about it.

And me just beginning to dry out after twenty-years of being drunk on my butt."

"No problem, mon, I will take you to your car." He reached across the seat and unlocked the passenger's side door.

Bill got in. "Thanks."

"No problem. I would just be waiting here for them to clear the road." He turned around and drove Bill back to his car. "You are trying to get sober, mon?"

"I suppose. If I'm able to do it."

"Have faith in yourself."

"Who else can a man count on?"

"Friends," the driver said.

They reached his car and Bill got out of the truck. "Thanks again." He took a twenty dollar bill from his pocket and handed it through the window toward the driver.

He pushed it away. "There is no need for that, mon. If people did not help other people out this world would be a sad place in which to live."

"It's pretty sad anyway."

"But we live in a beautiful place, this island of ours."

Bill smiled. "There is that."

"Indeed."The driver gave him a wide smile and drove off. Bill Hastings got into his car, turned around and headed back to Coral Bay.

Thirty-five

LIGHT LEAKED around the edges of the roof over the Pit of Hell. Bethany awoke, stiff, aching, her throat dry and sore. She gently patted the fur of the rat that lay sleeping nearby. It stirred but did not waken.

"I reckon you're better than no company, Mr. Rat. At least I can talk to you." She touched the sleeping rat a second time. "Heck, I can do better than that. I can sing to you."

She stood. Leaning her back against the wall of the hole, she began singing *Sinner, Art Thou Still Secure*, a John Newton hymn she had learned from a 1928 hymnal her mother had kept.

Sinner, art thou still secure?
Wilt thou still refuse to pray?
Can thy heart or hands endure
In the Lord's avenging day?

See, his mighty arm is bared!
Awful terrors clothe His brow!
For his judgment stand prepared,
Thou must either break or bow.

The rat opened its eyes, stood and snuffled the corners of the square hole looking for food. Finding none, it squatted and stared at Bethany.

She did not stop singing when Teach lifted the roof.

"Shut up. You woke me up with that yowling."

Ignoring him, Bethany kept on singing.

At his presence nature shakes,
Earth affrighted hastes to flee;
Solid mountains melt like wax,
What will then become of thee?
Who his advent may abide?
You that glory in your shame,
Will you find a place to hide
When the world is wrapped in flame?

"If you want me to give you any food and water you'll shut up," Teach said, the calm in his voice belying the menace in his face and eyes.

Bethany sang, a tremor of delight running through her with the words of her favorite hymn with its images of God's punishment of the wicked, the world melting in the flames of his vengeance. That was the God she loved, the God who would tolerate no wavering from his commandments.

Teach released his hold on the roof. It closed with a bang. A few minutes later he raised it again and threw a bucket of sand into the hole. "Try eating and drinking this."

Bethany sang.

Teach slammed the roof shut. Singing, Bethany did not hear him threaten to lasso her and hang her by the neck.

In his small home, Moonie was just getting out of bed when he heard faint singing coming from a distance. The hills surrounding Coral Bay valley create an amphitheater effect which is augmented by the prevailing winds. At times, music from the bars and churches in the valley sound as though they are coming from only a few yards away, rising and falling with the intensity of the breeze. Moonie guessed that the singing must be wafting up from one of the churches below, the Moravians or the Coral Bay Christian Church. Perhaps someone was singing at morning services in the Coral Bay Christian Church. Whoever it was, he thought it sounded peaceful and lovely.

"DID YOU HEAR about that cop, Preston?" Skipper Dan greeted Robert as they arrived at Dante's Landing the following morning.

"The nasty one?"

"They busted him yesterday, right on Centerline Road. Set up a road block just like you see on television." He took a newspaper from under his arm and waved it in the air. "According to this morning's newspaper he was working with an ex-cop, Randall Brady." Skipper Dan unlocked the door. Once inside, he and Robert quickly opened the shutters around the bar while Skipper Dan summarized the article in the *Virgin Islands Daily News*.

"A couple of years ago this Brady landed a job as some kind of high level muckety-muck enforcer for DPNR, the agency that oversees all laws dealing with everything along the coast, including boat registration, mooring and anchoring in the territory. Apparently the FBI was watching when Brady used a DPNR boat to meet with a couple of guys from Puerto Rico. They gave him a knapsack filled with money. He took it to Preston who was in an unmarked police car parked at one of the overlooks above Cruz Bay. Preston took the money and put almost eight kilos of coke in the knapsack and sent him back to the Puerto Ricans. They busted Brady and the Puerto Ricans just as he was handing it over to them."

"Nice guy, Preston."

"This was a big operation, in addition to the FBI, the investigation involved the DEA, the IRS, Homeland Security, the Coast Guard, Customs and Border Protection, the US Marshals, the Bureau of Alcohol, Tobacco, Firearms and Explosives and the VI Police."

"From what I've seen, using the local cops is like hiring the mob to guard prisoners."

"There's more," Skipper Dan said. "After they busted Brady and nailed Preston, the cops and the Feds went to Preston's house and found a huge cache of guns and narcotics in a safe there. Preston claimed they belonged to his mother."

"The guns or the drugs?"

"Both. Nobody believed him, of course, and according to the paper, his mother hit him with a shoe and nearly put out his eye."

Bill Hastings came up as they were talking. Taking his usual seat at the bar, he said, "I was there yesterday when they arrested Preston." He told them the story.

"Preston had you locked in the back of his cruiser with the air-conditioning turned off? Give this man a cold beer and a shot," Skipper Dan told Robert.

"Make it a burger and an iced tea," Bill said.

"I'll get the tea," Skipper Dan said. "Bethany hasn't shown up for her morning shift and I've been waiting tables. Fortunately, business is slow so far today." He chuckled. "And conversely, unfortunately, business is slow."

Moonie came in, his clothes damp and smelling of fish. He set a plastic bag on the bar. "I have some excellent fish for you," he said to Skipper Dan. "Red snapper, grouper, mahi. Enough for you to have fish specials on the menu tonight and tomorrow."

Sitting next to Bill Hastings, Moonie looked at his iced tea. "Do you have a hangover, mon?"

"With any luck I've had my last hangover. Tonight I go to my first AA meeting at Pastor Jensen's church."

"That is fantastic," Moonie said, shaking Bill's hand.

"Tell Moonie about Preston," Bill said.

Skipper Dan set the *Daily News* on the bar. Moonie read it, laughing as he did.

"Preston was always bad. He was a bad kid and he grew up to be a bad man and he was a bad policeman. I always figured that being bad is what attracted him to becoming a policeman."

As they spoke, Nutty Betty, Icebox Bob, Mechanic Mike and Pilgrim Jack came in and sat at a table.

"Got anything special for a late breakfast?" Nutty Betty asked.

"How about a burger and fries," Skipper Dan said. "Any of you see Bethany this morning?"

"I was looking for her yesterday," Mechanic Mike said. "I got her car done good enough for her to drive around until I get the right parts, but I couldn't find her nowhere to give it to her and Andrea said she never showed up for a house cleaning job earlier in the day."

"That's not like her," Robert said.

"She may be at church," Moonie said, thinking of the singing the breeze had carried to his home earlier.

"I'll check," Bill said, swallowing the last of his hamburger. "I've got to go there to find out the time for the AA meeting."

"Tell her I need her," Skipper Dan said.

"Will do. By the way, you can call me Bill. Bill Hastings."

"I never thought I'd see him sober," Skipper Dan said when he was gone.

"Never underestimate the body's need to preserve itself," Robert said.

Moonie laughed. "He was preserving himself all right, mon. In alcohol."

Skipper Dan said, "I just hope he sticks around the Landing and eats as much as he used to drink."

"Always the cynical business man," Robert said.

"That's me."

"About these fish I have for sale," Moonie said.

"I HAVEN'T SEEN her for a couple of days," Garry Jensen said when Bill stopped by to get the schedule for AA meetings and to ask if the minister had seen Bethany.

Bill scratched his beard. "She didn't show up for work today and Mechanic Mike said she missed a villa cleaning job yesterday."

"Maybe she's home sick."

Bill shook his head. "Andrea and Mechanic Mike were at her place yesterday. She wasn't there."

"Strange," Garry said. "She's the most reliable, responsible person I know."

"Well, she's blown off a couple of jobs and nobody's seen her since the night before last."

Garry looked concerned. "I'll ask around. She was instrumental in getting the church started. I couldn't have done this without her, and I couldn't continue to make it work without her. She's the guardian angel of this place, that's for sure."

Bill nodded.

"We can help you here with more than your drinking," Gary Jensen told Bill and handed him the schedule of AA meetings.

"You've helped me, and I appreciate it." He waved the schedule in the air. "But what you provided for me was practical, not spiritual."

"Don't be so sure," Garry said, forcing a smile.

"I am sure, but I do appreciate your help and thank you for it."

The minister gave him a sad smile and turned away as Bill left the church and returned to Dante's Landing.

"Pastor Jensen hasn't seen Bethany for days," he said, sitting next to Moonie, who was counting the money Skipper Dan had paid for his fish.

"Do you think something's happened to her?" Skipper Dan said.

"They haven't caught the murderer yet," Robert said.

"I know who it isn't," Bill said, pointing at his chest.

The others laughed, but it was nervous laughter, all of them fearful that Bethany might have been a fourth victim of the killer, no one willing to mention the possibility, as if talking about it could somehow make it more than just a terrible and random thought.

For a time no one spoke as they sat and stood in place, each waiting for someone else to change the subject.

Moonie was the first to break the stalemate. He shrugged and pushed away from the bar. "I have to get moving. I have more fish to sell and work to do for my brother's father-in-law's sister."

"Let me know if he needs a plumber," Bill said.

Over the next twenty minutes the others finished their drinks, ate their meals and left. Robert and Skipper Dan were left to clean up, after which they sat at the bar and watched a Red Sox game. One or two people stopped by for burgers and beer, but business remained slow.

"Probably people are still sleeping off their Festival hangovers," Robert said. "Maybe things will pick up at dinner time."

"Maybe. Maybe not. It's summer and Festival is over. The island's emptying out. There won't be a lot of business until Thanksgiving and then it'll slack off again until Christmas. It's just as well that Bethany didn't come in. I wouldn't make enough to cover her salary, cheap as it is to pay people to wait on tables."

"I hope she's all right."

"Me too." Skipper Dan's lips were drawn over his teeth and he fiddled with a pen, flipping it repeatedly over and through his fingers.

Between waiting tables and tending bar, they busied themselves with other chores. Skipper Dan cleaned and rearranged the store room while Robert put together an order for bar and restaurant supplies. The cook cleaned the grill and scrubbed down the appliances.

Finished with the store room, Skipper Dan poured himself a glass of iced tea and sat on a bar stool. "At this rate we won't have any work left to do during the autumn shut-down."

"We could go to the beach. They say the water's lovely and warm in the fall."

"That's why we have hurricanes," Skipper Dan said. "The warmer the water, the worse the hurricane season."

At five-thirty, the time the Landing usually began to fill up, not a table was taken. Two men sat at the bar, Leander Benjamin, who drove the refrigerated truck that brought meats and produce to the restaurants in Coral Bay, and Pilgrim Jack who nibbled at a BLT, his beer sitting beside it.

"I say if it's still this quiet at eight, we'll call it a night," Skipper Dan said. "That should get us out of here by eight-thirty."

"I won't argue," said Robert.

Leander Benjamin paid his bill and said, "It is this way all over Coral Bay. Cruz Bay is almost as bad. The ferries this morning were filled with people leaving the island. Carnival and Festival are over. We will have our island back until the snowbirds start coming in December."

He left the Landing. Only Skipper Dan, Robert and Pilgrim Jack remained, and Pilgrim Jack signaled for his check.

Thirty-six

BETHANY SANG. She had sung all day and into the evening. She did not stop, no matter what was in the buckets Teach threw at her, and the first bucket filled with sand was by far the least noxious. Nor did her voice falter, no matter how vile his threats were. The rat seemed pleased with the garbage that Teach tossed into the Pit of Hell. It nibbled contentedly. Bethany sang, ignoring the increasing stench in the hole with each fouler and fouler bucket load from Teach. Her only song was Newton's hymn with its promises of eternal damnation for those who do not turn to God. The words and tune lifted her spirit.

"You're going to die," Teach snarled down at her as he emptied a bucket of rotting fish in the Pit of Hell.

Bethany sang. "*In the Lord's avenging day, see his mighty arm is bared.*"

"Your death will be the most unpleasant one I have ever brought upon a person," Teach said. The bucket he upturned contained human refuse.

Bethany sang. "*For his judgment stand prepared; thou must either break or bow.*"

"You're only alive because I'm not ready for your suffering to end."

Bethany sang. "*At his presence nature shakes; Earth affrighted hastes to flee.*"

"I will wreak such havoc upon you that your soul will shrivel and turn into little dry pieces of dust and blow away on the wind."

Bethany's voice rose, the notes pure, the words clear.
Then the rich, the great, the wise,
Trembling, guilty, self condemned;
Must behold the wrathful eyes
Of the Judge they once blasphemed:
Where are now their haughty looks?
Oh, their horror and despair!
When they see the opened books
And their dreadful sentence hear!

"There's nothing, girl. You'll die expecting your Heaven and you'll fall into eternal darkness, nothingness, and in the last instant you will know that, and you'll know that you've been a fool. Your last act will be to cry out in total despair, just like your Jesus did." He spoke in an exaggerated whine, "My God, my God, why hast thou forsaken me? You know what God answered? Nothing. Nothing."

Teach dropped the roof and tossed the cement weights on it. Lighting a cigar, he opened a beer and sat in front of his cabin, his hearing blocked by the rubber plugs foresters use when working with chain saws.

Moonie heard the singing when he returned home. There was no breeze and it came through the woods the moment he shut off his engine and stepped from the truck, the sound so clear and unwavering on the still air that he knew it could not be echoing up from the valley below. The singer had to be nearby.

He stood as still as a tree and listened. The voice seemed to come from the direction of Teach's place.

"Who's there," he called. There was no answer and the singing continued.

He walked to the edge of the woods. The singing was surely coming from Teach's place. Stepping onto an old trail that had led through what had become Teach's property, he walked until he came to three strands of newly strung barbed wire. Tacked to a tree was the sign:

Keep Off!

No Trespassing.

Trespassers Are Subject to Being Shot. This Means You.

Keep Off!

Recalling Teach's words, ""I'd be within my rights to shoot you. Sneaking through the woods outside my home like you are," he stopped, eyes fixed on the sign. It had frightened him when he'd seen it the first time. Now, combined with the barbed wire, he felt as though he stood at the edge of a war zone. Teach could be anywhere, hiding behind a tree or crouched in the bush, taking aim, waiting for him to step onto his land. Anything could happen. The ground could be mined. A misstep could result in his body being riddled with nails and broken glass. The wire could be coated with poison.

He thought of the jumbie beads he sold to local artisans for necklaces, bracelets, brooches from them, as well other ornamental trinkets. What if Teach had also harvested some, taken them out of their shells and after grinding them down and soaking them in water, painted them on the barbed wire? One ground up seed could kill a man. He shuddered to think what a bunch of them painted on the sharp barbs would do to him. One little scrape and he would be doomed. He'd probably die right there on the spot. Hawks and feral cats would feast on his body and the hot tropical sun would decompose what they left uneaten in a matter of days. The jumbies would truly have gotten him.

He stepped back. The singing tempted him to move forward, but it could be luring him to his death. He remembered the story from school, about the sailors drawn to the songs of the deadly sirens. Perhaps this was a trick of the jumbies. Perhaps they knew of Teach's deadly wire and wished to entice him onward. The jumbies were not mankind's friends. He looked again at Teach's sign and turned away.

He sat on a boulder near his house and was suddenly sure it was Bethany he heard singing. Teach must have taken her and was holding her captive. The hole, he thought, the one Teach called the Pit of Hell. That was what it was for.

He knew what to do.

Teach may not have contaminated the barbed wire with jumbie poison, but Moonie would. Back at his house, he put on a long sleeved shirt, draped a beach towel across his legs and set to work with elaborate caution. Wearing a carpenter's mask over his mouth and nose, eye protecting lenses and the latex gloves he kept for protection when wildcrafting in areas where nasty and toxic plants grew, he carefully removed the shells from a dozen jumbie beads and crushed their centers with a mortar and pestle. He put the crushed seeds in a large bowl and added water, stirring the mixture until the seeds were dissolved.

Still clad in protective clothing, he painted the poisonous concoction on the barbed wire stretched over the trail. With wire cutters, he cut the fencing in several places to loosen the wire so that anyone crashing into it would quickly be tangled in poisoned barbs and wire. When the job was done he stepped back and smiled, his arms folded over his chest. Teach might have guns and land mines for his side in this war. Moonie would fight with a quiet and invisible weapon.

BY EIGHT the last of a handful of customers had left Dante's Landing. "I say we lock up and take the rest of the night off," Skipper Dan said.

"I'll vote for that," said Robert and looked up as Moonie came charging through the door, talking breathlessly.

"I know where Bethany is. Teach has her in the Pit of Hell. I hear her singing."

"You're not making any sense," Robert said.

Moonie's eyes widened and he grasped his chest. "I make sense, mon. I heard her. She is a prisoner in the Pit of Hell and she is singing a hymn of some kind."

"You need a drink," Skipper Dan said.

Moonie shook his head wildly. "I do not need a drink. You need to listen to me."

Robert took three chairs from the table top where they had been placed for the morning cleaner. "Sit down and tell us what you think is going on."

Moonie told them about Teach's hole and the crudely painted Pit of Hell on the roof. "He said he would shoot me for trespassing and told me that he would be within his rights if he did it. That is a terrible thing to say."

"It is," Robert said.

Moonie described the signs on the trees and the barbed wire across the trail leading to Teach's place and told them about hearing the singing.

"It was Bethany, I am sure," he said.

"We've got no choice," Robert said. "We have to go up there."

"Teach has guns," Moonie said.

"Then we'll call the police," Robert said without thinking.

Skipper Dan and Moonie laughed and he joined in.

Skipper Dan said, "The police are too busy trying to figure out how to cover their own sins and crimes to care about our problem."

"We'll have to take care of it ourselves," Robert said.

"We will," Skipper Dan said. "And who knows, we might be putting an end to the St. John murders at the same time."

"You think Teach killed those people?"

"It's possible."

"So what do we do?"

"I have a plan," Moonie said. "But we must be very careful. Not only does Teach have guns, he may have land mines in the woods surrounding his place."

"So we'll avoid the woods, and guns are no problem," Skipper Dan said. "I've got quite a few guns of my own."

Robert and Moonie looked at him, surprise on their faces. Skipper Dan said, "I've always had guns. For my tenth birthday my father gave me my first one, a .22 lever action Marlin rifle. Before that I had to shoot his guns, pistols and rifles, until he figured I was old enough and careful enough to have my own."

"Why have guns?" Robert asked.

"Because I can."

"I've never needed a gun," Robert said.

"You are going to need one today," Moonie said.

Skipper Dan pointed a finger at him. "Moonie's right. If Teach has Bethany and if he's armed, we're going to need to be armed. Too bad you don't know how to shoot."

"I never said I didn't know how to shoot," Robert said. "From the time I was six until I was fourteen my parents sent me to Wallawhatoola, a summer camp in Virginia. We learned all kinds of survival skills there, including shooting. There was a shooting range and every kid in camp had to learn gun safety and how to be dead-eye accurate with rifles and pistols."

"Were you?"

"I won top honors five years running."

It was Skipper Dan's turn to look surprised. "So why not have a gun or two?"

"Never needed one," Robert answered in a clipped New England tone.

There was no mirth in Skipper Dan's laughter. "As the man said, you'll need one today."

"Do you wish to hear my plan?" Moonie asked.

Robert and Skipper Dan looked at him with expectation.

"You bet," Robert said.

Thirty-seven

"IT SHOULD work," Robert said after Moonie explained.

"It's a stroke of genius," Skipper Dan said.

Moonie looked pleased.

"Next stop, my armory." Skipper Dan raised his arms and aimed an imaginary gun at the far side of the room.

Robert's reaction was amused surprise. "Armory? You said you had a few guns; now you've got an armory?"

Skipper Dan stiffened at his reaction. "I'm a serious gun collector. They've always fascinated me. What's so funny about it?"

Robert's reply was quick as he held up his hands and shook his head. "There's nothing funny at all. It's just that you've never mentioned it."

Skipper Dan shrugged. "Having a gun collection isn't something to discuss openly, for a lot of reasons. There are people you thought were your friends who'd consider you a nut case if they knew you were a gun aficionado...which I am. I know people right here in Coral bay who'd ostracize me if they knew I own guns. Worse, there are low-lifes who'd try to steal them and sell them on the underground market. I don't want my guns stolen and I don't want them in the hands of criminals."

"Then why have them? Don't the advantages outweigh the disadvantages?"

"Like I said, they fascinate me. They can also be quite handy. If I didn't have guns we would be walking into danger going after Teach to save Bethany."

"We are walking into danger, with or without guns," Moonie said.

Skipper Dan grunted in agreement. "But we're lowering the risk factor by being armed."

"I guess that's possible," Robert said.

"It's an indisputable fact." Skipper Dan looked from Robert to Moonie. "Besides, having guns is a constitutional right."

Robert looked away for an instant. When he spoke, it was with a tentative smile. "From what I understand, there's some legitimate debate over how to interpret the wording of the Second Amendment."

"Not to my way of thinking," Skipper Dan said.

"Arguing over gun rights is not going to get Bethany away from that man Teach," Moonie said. "I am glad that Skipper Dan has guns and that we can use them."

Robert's mind flashed to the moment when he took his Hippocratic Oath, the phrase *Do No Harm* ricocheting over the surface of his thoughts. "If Teach has Bethany..."

Moonie spoke before he could finish. "He does. I am sure of it."

"Then he's like a cancer and we need to cut him out," Robert said.

They drove in Skipper Dan's Land Rover to his place, a masonry home on a high ridge overlooking Coral Harbor. He took them to a room secured by three locks, two of them operated by keys, one by a touch pad.

"Only my thumb print will unlock this one," he said.

The door opened into an air-conditioned room. Lining the walls were five locked gun-cases, their contents visible through thick shatter-proof acrylic windows on the cabinet doors. Some held antique weapons, ball and powder pistols, muskets and rifles, along with a smattering of swords and knives. Two contained guns of recent manufacture, one filled with rifles, the other with pistols. Skipper Dan unlocked them.

Handing a pistol to Moonie, he said, "Here's a Glock 17 nine millimeter."

"I have used them," Moonie said. "A fine weapon."

When neither Robert nor Skipper Dan said anything, Moonie added, "I was with the Special Forces in Afghanistan. It is something I do not wish to speak of. Something I will never talk about, to anyone."

Without commenting, Skipper Dan handed Robert a Sig Sauer 1911 Carry. "This beauty of a pistol is my latest baby," he said. It's got a rosewood grip and a shortened stainless steel slide, a stainless steel frame and a match grade barrel, hammer/sear set and trigger."

"I don't know what that means," Robert said.

"It means it's beautiful and efficient. All you have to know is that to use it you take aim and pull the trigger. The gun and the ammo will do the rest."

Thinking again of his oath, Robert said, "I hope I don't have to use it."

"Nobody in their right mind wants to have to use a gun. Anybody in their right mind should know how to use one."

"As I said before, I know how," Robert

"That's the point." Skipper Dan threaded a holster to his belt and placed a pistol in it. He took a rifle from the second case. "My Glock 34 and for good luck, a Colt AR-15, which is the civilian version of the M-16."

"Teach will feel like the Special Forces have descended on him," Moonie said.

"I hope your plan works," Robert said.

"It will work," Moonie said.

When the guns were loaded and spare ammunition passed out, the three men climbed into Skipper Dan's Land Rover and set out for Teach's place on the side of Bordeaux Mountain.

8:23 pm

A .22 Smith & Wesson pistol loaded with hollow points held loosely in his hand, Teach stood with a foot on the roof of the Pit of Hell, his face twisted in fury. Bethany had not stopped singing Newton's hymn since she first started. It was as though it came with her breath, a function of the very nature of her being. Seeming to arise from the Pit with supernatural intensity, its volume penetrated the roof and echoed against the hills as if the roof presented no barrier to her rising song.

He hated the sound. It had to stop. It would immediately stop if he put a bullet into her brain. Smiling at the thought, he visualized putting the barrel of his rifle against Bethany's temple. He would do it when he was ready, but the time to kill her had not yet come. She had not begun to suffer in the ways he wanted her to suffer, and the more she sang the more drawn out he wanted her suffering to be. Death would be a kindness following the completion of his plans for her, a kindness she would plead for. Even then he would not allow her death to be a gentle one. Maximizing her suffering was essential. He wanted it to last until her final tortured breath.

Stomping on the roof of the Pit of Hell, he called to her. "Shut your pie-hole. Your singing makes me puke."

Bethany sang.

Lifting the roof, Teach beamed a 250 lumen LED flashlight at Bethany's eyes. She shut them, but still sang. He shifted the light to the rat. It scurried to the far side of the Pit. In his other hand, Teach drew the pistol and took careful aim at the rodent. Bethany's eyes followed the line from the end of his pistol to the rat cringing against the far wall.

"You'll sing my praises in gratitude when I finally do this for you," he said to Bethany and shot the rat.

Bethany's voice faltered for the briefest of moments. She did not move, but her eyes filled with tears as she looked at the dead creature.

"Your knees will be my next target if you don't stop that infernal screeching." Teach's voice, a low growl, dropped into the Pit of Hell and died against the Pit's earthen walls.

8:57 pm

Skipper Dan pulled the Land Rover into Moonie's drive and shut down the engine. Over the chirping of the tree frogs they heard Bethany sing, lyrics and melody flowing through the thick bush separating Moonie's land from Teach's cabin and the Pit of Hell.

"Her singing is clearer and louder than ever." Moonie spoke in a near whisper.

"Time for action," Robert said, touching the butt of the pistol tucked under his belt. After synchronizing their watches, they briefly clasped hands.

"You will hear me at nine-fifteen," Moonie said. That should give you more than enough time to get into position."

"This would be a lot simpler if we could trust the cops," Robert said.

Moonie's laugh was short and bitter. "That is a pipe dream, mon."

Each of them clapping Moonie on the shoulder, Robert and Skipper Dan walked back to the road and along the asphalt pavement for several hundred feet, to the point where Teach's gravel drive led off to the left. Halfway down the drive they could see lights from his cabin. They separated, Robert slipping through the woods to the rear of the left side of the building, Skipper Dan to the right.

8:57 pm

Teach sat inside his house, a nearly empty bottle of rum on the table in front of him. His hands clamped over his ears did little to muffle the sound of Bethany's singing and he thought again of the pleasure it would bring him to blow her apart just as he had done with the rat. Deferring pleasure had never been his strong point, but he had taken a vow not to deviate from his plan to make her suffering last for as long as possible before giving her the release of death.

He would do it slowly, from the feet up. He would start by shooting a single toe. After all, there were ten of them; one every five minutes would take almost an hour. Then, as he promised her, he would shoot her knees. The first knee an hour after shooting her final toe, the other knee an hour later. The fingers would follow. He would stretch the time out, a finger every fifteen minutes, or every half hour. Half hour intervals would be good. Ten fingers, five hours.

That would be quite satisfying. It would, he was sure, put an end to her singing. He'd give her one toe, two at the most, before her song dried up in her throat. Not long after that, he believed, it would dry up in her heart. He smiled at the thought, wondering how long it would take before she begged him to kill her.

When you renounce your Jesus, he would tell her; when you curse God.

A shiver of pleasure ran up his spine at the thought of Bethany, agonized and wretched, turning her back on all that she believed was holy in a vain attempt at saving her life. He imagined her saying in those dulcet Carolina tones, Please, Mr. Teach, I have turned my back on all that religious clap-trap, that childish foolishness, that ridiculous God, so please please Mr. Teach, set me free.

I'll set you free, he would say. At the moment she renounced her faith he would fire three .22 hollow point lead missiles into her brain.

9:10 pm

Thick clouds covered the sky, the night as dark as night can be. Hoping that Moonie's plan was as good as it sounded, Skipper Dan stood inside the tree line waiting for Moonie's signal, Bethany's voice drifting on the still air. Closing his eyes he was surprised by finding himself thinking that God wouldn't let Teach truly harm Bethany. Someone like her must surely be special to him, an emissary to a fallen and corrupt place the world.

He buried the thought as quickly as it had arisen. Religion did not matter to him. He had seen how Bethany lived according to her faith, the work she put in with Garry Jensen to build the Coral Bay Christian Church, raising money to pay to have the old Expeditions restaurant converted and endlessly striving to recruiting people to join the small congregation. He was an admiring observer of her labors and commitment, but at the same time, suspicious of what she was hiding, or hiding from. As for him, religion got in the way of life.

And he had a good life. Dante's Landing was a successful business that had become a St. John destination. Tourists flocked to it. It was listed as one of the must go to places on the island. Along with Skinny Legs, The Tourist Trap and Aqua Bistro, Dante's Landing was one of the things that made Coral Bay a unique and colorful community. He had a lovely home on the Estate Carolina hillside, a new Land Rover and his ever-growing gun collection. He never wanted for food, and his daily life was filled with laugher from the patrons who surrounded him, sharing their stories with him and buying the things he had to offer: food, drink, tee shirts and baseball hats, souvenir mugs and glasses, CDs of "Music from Dante's." Profits from sales piled up in his bank account. What did he have to complain about or reach for? Life, as the tee shirt says, is good. He knew he was as content as he could be, knowing that life was all he needed.

9:10 pm

Moonie was frightened. He knew how wrong things could go. He'd seen it happen many times in the Gulf and Afghanistan. You never knew where the crazed jihadist that would kill you might come from, or what might lie in the ground beneath your feet. He considered the crude land mines he feared Teach might have planted around his land. If they were there, one wrong step and he would be nothing more than quivering and cooling meat.

He took a deep breath and forced himself to relax. If there were mines on the other side of the barbed wire, why had none of them been set off by the donkeys and deer that roamed over the land? A mine could conceivably explode even if a feral cat or a mongoose stepped on it.

You are afraid when there may be nothing to fear, he told himself. The land mines are no more real than the jumbies his teachers had told him were imaginary. Shaken by a sudden shudder, he hugged himself. What if all those teachers were mistaken? What if there were jumbies haunting the shadowy nights? His grandparents had claimed to have seen them. His mother had warned him about them. He had seen his father shaking, on moonless nights refusing to venture outside the clay and wattle cabin the family had lived in when Moonie was a small child, sure there were jumbies hiding in the dark. Moonie did not believe in jumbies. He did not believe in Teach's land mines. Still, it would be foolish to ignore them. Night shadows could hide all kinds of surprises.

But if he was fearful, he was also determined. He had survived two wars in which crazed fanatics wrapped themselves in explosives and threw themselves at soldiers and civilians; adults and children alike in pursuit of their warped ideals. If he could survive that, he could survive any danger that Teach presented. He had to. Most selfishly, to allow that man to harm Bethany would bring dishonor upon him. Worse, to have Bethany come to harm would be an affront to all that was good in the world. There might not be jumbies, he told himself, but there were creatures like Teach, and if such evil existed, perhaps souls such as Bethany must represent their opposite, people so exceptional in their righteousness that they were of a kind far beyond ordinary humans. He did not know what that might be, but he sensed it whenever he looked at her, whenever she bestowed her kindness on him or someone he knew.

"You are special," she once said to him when he had thanked her for bringing his cousin Althea to the Coral Bay Christian Church the time she was suffering from a sickness the doctor at the clinic said was incurable and fatal. Bethany had put her hands on Althea's head and kept them there for more than an hour, singing and praying while Pastor Jensen prayed with her. Three days later, when Althea died, Bethany had personally washed her body before the funeral home took it away.

Moonie thought of all the things that might go wrong with his plan, but he did not hesitate. Bethany must be saved.

9:10 pm

Robert listened to the night. Bethany's song rose above and mingled with the soft murmur of the tree frogs, the whisper of the breeze and the rustling of small creatures in the bush. A rooster crowed in the distance, belying the myth that they are reliable heralds of the dawn.

He marveled at his situation. A once prominent physician with a family and a western Massachusetts home that some considered a showpiece, here he was standing in the dark on a small island in the tropics, a pistol tucked under his belt, ready to help rescue Bethany from a man who might be the murderer of at least three people. Blood pounded in his ears and despite knowing it to be impossible, he felt as though it might burst through his eardrums.

Pinching the bridge of his nose with a thumb and forefinger, he took a deep breath and exhaled slowly. Words from Bethany's song washed over him, "Who His advent may abide? You that glory in your shame...." Picturing Maria walking into the blinding white cover of the blizzard, tears formed in his eyes, blurring the lights from Teach's cabin. Bethany's song continued, "Will you find a place to hide...when the world is wrapped in flame?"

He could not help but smile at the thought of her mobile in Dante's Landing, *The Lost Soles of Coral Bay*, and Christine's comments about her: *Bethany always has to save something, like it's her mission in life to keep people and critters from suffering. Bethany's a professional rescuer. She's got to take care of everybody. If I were you, Robert, I'd turn my life over to her.*

In some ways he had. He believed her outlook on life was distorted by extreme religious faith, but she was a good friend and had helped him in many practical ways. She found him a home, a car and she had goaded him into asking Christine to dinner. He had moved to the islands to get away from his former life, a life that had become unbearable in its loneliness and grief, and he had come to St. John by happenstance. The life we end up living, he realized, is often not the life we planned. We go along doing what we expect to do, what we have prepared ourselves to do, and things change abruptly. We meet someone who makes a casual remark that can result in dramatic changes of course.

If Maria had not left him would their lives together have been satisfactory, or would their marriage have deteriorated into a complete standoff? What if he had chosen Key West instead of St. Thomas as his destination upon leaving Keetsville? Was having that last gin and tonic at Hook, Line and Sinker the only thing that led to Gypsy Davy suggesting that he move to St. John?

He shook his head. There were too many what ifs in life for him to comprehend the complexity of events and encounters that gave rise to them. There was no purpose in following the myriad twists and turns in the chaos that makes up the human experience. What mattered was that his life was taking a shape he would never have predicted possible, and he was responsible for saving the person who had done much to influence that shape.

Still, he pondered the imponderable, playing with it. Was there a plan after all? Was meeting Bethany part of it? If so, what was his purpose in that plan? Was he an instrument of the plan, a cog in it, or the purpose for it? What part did he have in furthering it, if any? Most important, if there was a plan whose plan was it? Even as he asked it, he knew the question demanded knowledge beyond human understanding, but he had come to believe there was nothing beyond the moment. There was either a plan or there was no plan. He decided there was none. Existence was a chain of random events and the challenge facing everyone was to give meaning to those events that make up our lives. His immediate task was to concentrate on what he, Skipper Dan and Moonie had come out on the mountain to do: assuring Bethany's safety.

His hand dropped to the grip of the Sig Sauer. The rosewood at the top, near the rear of the barrel was smooth and he rubbed his thumb over it. Farther down it was checkered with a double diamond pattern, providing what he assumed would be a positive grip. There was comfort in the fact of the gun, the smooth cool steel, the texture of the grip, the solidity of the entire instrument. He hoped he would not have to take it from under his belt and fire it at another human being, but he would if doing so was necessary to save Bethany. It was time to rescue the rescuer.

9:15 pm

Robert and Skipper Dan heard Moonie call Teach's name. It was time and they began to move. With each slow step they took toward the cabin, Bethany's singing seemed to increase in volume. Robert briefly wondered how he could ever have thought of music as anything other than one of the great splendors of the world. His thoughts were broken by Moonie's voice.

"Teach, I am stepping on your land. I am going to burn your cabin to the ground. I am going to tie you up in a chair in the middle of the floor, spill gasoline all over the place and set it on fire and listen to you scream like the damned cry out from Hell."

"You'll die before you get within fifty feet of my house," Teach called back.

"You will have to come get me, mon. I am death and I am waiting for you."

"I'm coming." The rifle in his hands, Teach burst through the cabin door and ran toward the sound of Moonie's voice.

Robert and Skipper Dan emerged from the cover of night, one on each side of the cabin just as Teach moved out of the circle of light from the cabin and disappeared into the woods. They each fired a single shot into the air.

Moonie called out, "Hey, Teach, mon. You are surrounded it seems."

Teach's response was an inhuman scream, as if a vengeful demon had been released upon the earth and was rushing to destroy them. Robert heard him crash through the woods, screaming, cursing, his words venomous, his voice vibrating with hate and rage.

Moonie called again. "I am waiting for you, mon. Why are you so slow? Are you afraid of me? You should be, you know."

Teach screamed and cursed, a howl of rage that abruptly became a shriek of shock and pain.

"It worked," Moonie called. "He is down."

"Hold him there," Robert called. "We'll get Bethany."

Following the sound of Bethany's song, Robert and Skipper Dan quickly found her, the crudely painted words, Pit of Hell visible in the light from the windows of Teach's cabin.

When they lifted the lid Bethany stood in the middle of the pit. She appeared fresh and calm. She stopped singing and smiled up at them.

"Hey boys. I've been waiting for y'all. You doing all right?"

Lying on the ground, Robert reached into the hole and extended his hand to her. Grasping it, she arose from Teach's Pit of Hell as if floating on the air. Later, Skipper Dan swore that in the instant when they raised the cover from the Pit of Hell she had seemed to be sheathed in a brilliant golden light. Robert had not seen it and Skipper Dan soon admitted he had been mistaken, that it had been his imagination.

9:20 pm

The four of them stood at the boundary between Teach's and Moonie's land. Teach lay on the ground struggling against a tangle of the barbed wire fencing he had put up to keep Moonie from crossing onto his property. His face and arms were covered with gashes from the sharp barbs, a deep bloody cut running from what remained of his right eye down his cheek and disappearing in a slash that continued the line of his mouth two inches farther than normal.

"The jumbies got you, mon," Moonie said to Teach. "I painted the fence with jumbie poison."

"What does that mean?" Robert asked.

Moonie explained how he had cracked open the beads and dissolved their contents, painting the concoction on the barbed wire."

"Don't any of you touch that fencing," Robert said. "The scientific name for jumbie beads is Abrus precatorius. The beads are the seeds and they contain stuff called abrin. It's seventy-five times more deadly than ricin. It'll kill a horse, let alone a human being. Once abrin gets into your body's cells you're done for."

"What will happen?" Bethany asked.

Robert gestured toward Teach, who was already struggling for breath. "The symptoms are identical to those of ricin, but worse. He'll have difficulty breathing, eventually developing a fever along with a severe cough and nausea. He'll start to sweat heavily."

Bethany smiled at Teach. "Good."

"I'm already sweating," Teach groaned, and my chest feels tight."

"That's from fluid building up in your lungs. You might have hallucinations, seizures and there'll be blood in your urine. Abrin's nasty stuff and abrin poisoning is a particularly nasty way to die."

"Do something," Teach said, his voice filled with rage.

"There's no antidote."

"Y'all must be able to keep him alive," Bethany said.

Skipper Dan spat. "He was going to kill you."

"I still would if I could," Teach said.

"Dying is too easy. He needs to live so he can suffer more in this world before he goes to his eternal punishment," Bethany said.

Robert looked down at Teach. "Did you kill the others?"

"What if I did?" Teach's voice was flat and dull.

Skipper Dan nudged him with his foot. "What does that mean?"

"What do you want it to mean?"

"He wants to know if you're the murderer," Bethany said.

Moving with apparent agony, Teach reached his hand to his mouth and mimed zipping his lips closed.

Bethany smiled at the action.

"The humane thing would be to take him down to the clinic," Robert said. "Death from abrin poisoning is painful and horrible, the more so depending on the route of exposure and the dose received."

"He got a big dose of the jumbie poison," Moonie said. "I put a very heavy coat of it on that fence."

Teach's eyes blazed with hatred. "I will not be easily destroyed."

"We could give you pain medication at the clinic. That's about all anybody can do for you."

"We could let him lie here and die in total misery," Bethany said.

Skipper Dan cleared his throat. "It'll be pretty risky to disentangle him from the barbed wire if Moonie coated it with poison. I don't think we should risk it."

"He needs palliative care. I can't deny him that," Robert said.

"You surely do sound like a doctor, Mr. Robert," Bethany said.

Silent, Robert looked from Teach to her. Darkness and light, he thought.

With a knowing smile, she seemed to be looking into the core of his being. "You can say it, Mr. Robert."

Robert squared his shoulders. "I am a physician, or at least I was."

"And...?" Bethany said.

Robert looked quickly upward, then back at her. "And I guess I still am. I can't let him just lie here dying alone and in pain. I took an oath to do no harm."

Skipper Dan and Moonie stared at him.

"You did not do this, I did," Moonie said.

"But I would be doing him harm if I walked away."

"It would be God's will," Bethany said and sang, "Oh, his horror and despair when he sees the opened books and their dreadful sentence hears."

Skipper Dan took a step backward. "How do we get him out of that web of barbed wire without risking getting infected?"

"You don't." With a snarl and what seemed almost super-human strength, Teach pushed against the ground where he lay, launching himself toward Bethany. She did not flinch and he fell short.

Robert's throat nearly closed and he was sure his heart must have sounded to the others like an anvil. In that instant, as Teach snarled and fell back, Robert recognized him as the shadowy figure standing atop the tower he had seen in the dream that still troubled him. He remembered how it looked, clad in black robes as it pointed at him. Its face had been lost in the shadows of his nightmare, but he saw it now, clearly. It had been Teach.

Shaking, he turned away and barely heard Skipper Dan say, "Leave him here."

"Skipper Dan's right," Bethany said.

When the words registered in his mind Robert shook his head. "I can't."

"I know what to do," Moonie said.

Skipper Dan glared at Teach. Taking his Glock from its holster, he pointed it at him, the barrel inches from Teach's face. "So do I. Shoot him."

Robert reached over and touched the Glock's barrel, forcing it away from Teach's head. "A nice thought but a bad plan."

"My idea is better," Moonie said and walked toward his cabin.

A pair of long handled wire cutters in his hand, he returned wearing boots, heavy canvass long pants and a long sleeved shirt. A bandana covered his mouth and nose and he wore protective goggles. Under his arm he carried a large blue tarpaulin. "You have to know how to dress when going into the deep bush. There are many things in there you should not expose your skin to."

Cautiously, he snipped the wire into small pieces that with a little prodding from a stick fell from Teach's body. Using the same stick Moonie pushed the wires into a pile several feet away from where they stood. Throughout the process Teach lay surprisingly still and compliant. He did not struggle or complain when they wrapped him in the tarpaulin and carried him to the Land Rover. When they unwrapped him at the clinic he appeared to be unconscious.

At the reception desk, Robert identified himself as a physician and showed the Massachusetts physician's ID card he had never removed from his wallet. Following the doctor on call as they took Teach to an examination room, Robert described the nature of his injuries without any explanation of how they occurred. When the doctor pressed him, he said they had found him moaning in the woods on Bordeaux Mountain, barely conscious enough to explain that he had accidentally ingested crushed Abrus precatorius seeds and stumbled into the barbed wire fencing.

Teach lay still, as though already half dead.

"He's a goner," the doctor said.

Robert said, "All you can do is make him as comfortable as possible."

Teach opened his eyes and stared at Robert, but said nothing.

Thirty-eight

"IT WAS YOUR imagination," Robert said.

"At first I really did think I saw light surrounding you," Skipper Dan said. "Of course I couldn't have."

Thinking of the mysterious lights on Brown Mountain, Bethany looked at them in silence.

After leaving Teach at the clinic, Robert, Bethany, Moonie and Skipper Dan had returned to Dante's Landing and were sitting around a table, a tray filled with hamburgers and fries in front of them.

"Y'all shouldn't make too much of it," she said.

"It was a sign from God," Moonie said. "I did not see it, but I believe it was there."

"Why isn't your throat sore from singing?" Robert asked, changing the subject.

"Grace is an amazing thing, Mr. Robert."

"I suppose." He dropped his eyes.

"Things will never be the same for any of us," she said.

"They can't be. Nothing is the same from day to day."

"God is," Bethany said.

Again, Robert kept silent.

"You blew my mind," Skipper Dan said to him. "How is it that you're a bartender instead of working as a doctor?"

"It's a long story," Robert said, turning to Bethany. "How did you know?"

"I didn't know."

"You gave me that look of yours and said I could tell them."

"I knew you had a secret and I knew the time was right for you to let it out. I didn't know exactly what it was."

"Exactly?" he said.

"There are things I can't explain, Mr. Robert. Things I know that I know just because I know them."

"That doesn't make sense."

"It surely does. It just doesn't make sense in the way people are taught in school to think of how things make sense. Knowledge of that kind, knowledge of the ways of the world, is one thing. Spiritual knowledge—true knowledge—is another thing altogether."

No one spoke. After a long minute, Moonie said, "I think I understand."

"It doesn't make sense," Robert said.

Skipper Dan nodded, and another long silence followed. It was broken by Skipper Dan. He clucked his tongue and looked at Robert.

"What now?" he asked. "Will you go back to the States?"

"I like working here."

"You'll need the income from the job at the Landing to support your work," Bethany said.

"What work?" Robert asked.

"The free medical practice we're going to start at the Coral Bay Christian Church."

"Free medical practice is a contradiction in terms," Robert said.

"Not if you've got a decent job at Dante's Landing," she told him.

"You'll always have a job here," Skipper Dan said.

Bethany said, "With your help, Pastor Garry and I can convert the rear rooms of the church building into a small clinic and you could work there a few hours every day. There are so many people here with no medical insurance and they need you. I believe you were sent here to do this. You can help heal the lost souls of Coral Bay."

"Maybe I can heal," Robert said. "But it will be bodies, not souls."

"Healing bodies is a good start," Bethany said.

"And the end, as far as I go."

She smiled. "That might could be, but don't bet money on it."

"It'd be a safe bet," Robert said.

Thirty-nine

BETHANY STOOD in front of a microphone at the first Thursday open mic night at Dante's Landing. She strummed through three chords and sang the first two verses of Townes Van Zandt's, "If I Needed You," accompanied by Icebox Bob who played harmonica and sang harmony. As they finished, loud applause and cheers filled the crowded restaurant. There was standing room only at the bar where they were toasted with raised glasses and offers of free drinks.

"I'll have a ginger ale," Bethany told Boozie.

"A double scotch straight up and a beer," Icebox Bob said.

Sitting at a table next to the small covered stage with the slogan, *Hear the Music of Paradise*, Skipper Dan held a squirming Grace who patted his face, her hands sticky from the pieces of mango he had cut up for her to eat.

"Ginger ale's a good idea," Bill Hastings said, passing his full glass to Moonie. "Sloppy drunks can put a damper on the party."

Robert sat beside Bill. Christine was next to him. Robert's lawyer, Jeannette Evans, sat next to Skipper Dan.

"You look happy," Jeannette said to Robert.

"I'm still surprised," he said. "I was sure I'd have a long drawn out custody battle with Maria."

"John made a lot of money buying and selling gold and jewelry. He wants to travel. Maria told me that he said he wouldn't take her with him if she insisted on dragging the kid along, her very words, by the way."

Robert kissed the top of Grace's head. "I hope she'll be happy with Good Old John."

"She was happy enough to give you full custody of Grace," Jeannette said. "The last I heard they were going to spend six months in France."

"I think I'll do something like that someday," Bill said. "I know some people who rented a barge and lived in it as they traveled all over the rivers and canals of France. Now that would be a fine adventure."

"I hardly recognized Maria in court," Robert said.

"In my experience, the people we divorce look very different from the people we marry," Bill said. "And I've had a lot of experience with marriage—with marriages."

Skipper Dan nudged Robert. "Tell the truth. You're hoping she falls off a bridge and drowns in the Seine."

Robert gave him a quick smile. "There's no point in wishing her bad luck." He smiled again and shrugged, as if in surrender. "Not that I haven't had fantasies of terrible things happening to her, but even if I could wish them true, I wouldn't. I have Grace and Christine. I enjoy my job at the Landing and the free clinic will open in two weeks. Best of all, I don't have to live with Maria. What good would it do anyone if she drowned in France?"

"It would serve her right," Skipper Dan said.

Bethany joined them at the table and waved a hand in the air, flashing him a wry smile. "My gracious, Skipper, you surely do harbor a mean streak."

"Imagining bad things happening to bad people is one of life's pleasures."

Bethany nodded and smiled. "God takes care of that. He makes sure very bad things happen forever to bad people. I do take great pleasure in that."

"Maria isn't a bad person," Robert said.

"You should write novels," Jeannette told Skipper Dan.

"I could write a better ending for Teach," he said.

Bill laughed. "We all could do that."

"It's so weird," Christine said. "How did he disappear from the clinic?"

"That much abrin would have killed a team of horses," Robert said. "It should have killed him."

Christine shook her head. "And how did he manage to get away?"

"Evil isn't easily destroyed," Bethany said, a strange smile playing across her lips, as though she were hiding a great secret. "The poison in his soul might could have counteracted the jumbie poison. I reckon he's gone on to be an agent of chaos and destruction somewhere else."

"I think he went off and died somewhere out in the bush," Robert said.

Bethany rapped her knuckles on the sound board of her guitar. The strings vibrated and everyone turned to look at her. "God needs him. Having wicked people like Teach at large is part of his plan. Their evil deeds stand in such contrast to God's plans that people can't help but understand that to turn away from him is to loose a bloody tide of depravity upon the world. Teach's evil deeds serve God's purpose."

Moonie shook his head. "I believe he was not human. Jumbie poison cannot kill a jumbie."

Robert said, "I thought you didn't believe in jumbies."

"I believe in evil. I have seen its face in war and I saw its face right here on St. John."

"You can't destroy evil," Jeannette said.

"Perhaps we can't, Miz Jeannette," Bethany said. "But evil will be destroyed when the time of the world's end comes."

"I suppose it could be comforting to believe that," Robert said.

"It's true," Bethany told him.

"There are too many truths," Bill said. "How can anyone be expected to choose one and stick with it?"

"I did," Bethany said.

"Life is good," Skipper Dan said, pointing to the logo on his tee shirt. "That's my truth."

"It is a good truth, but there are better ones," Moonie said.

Christine closed her eyes and sighed audibly. "I'm not so sure of that."

Robert took her hand. "If there are better truths I doubt if anyone has discovered them."

Bethany shook her head but said nothing.

The child, Grace, looked at Robert and threw her arms around his neck. He kissed her cheek and held her close. For a moment his eyes met Christine's and a smile passed between them. Then his gaze shifted to the doorway beyond which sunlight shone on the water. A sailboat broke through the bright sparkles that danced across the surface of Coral Bay, its wake spreading out in an ever widening vee, its sails full.

He looked again at Christine who held out her arms. He leaned against her and she embraced him and Grace.

"Skipper's right," he said. "For now life is just fine."

"For now. Maybe for now is all we get," Christine said.

"Could be that's enough." He smiled, looking comfortable with the idea.

"It's all foolishness," Bill said.

"I'll believe that," Robert said. "But it's our foolishness."

Pilgrim Jack lit a cigar. A sudden gust of wind blew through Dante's Landing, taking up the smoke and dispersing it as quickly as he exhaled.

To the Reader

I PASSED Notre Dame as I slowly motored along the Seine in my barge early this morning. Cloaked in heavy mist that was just beginning to dissipate in the rising sun, I glanced at it and quickly looked away. By the time I reached the Louvre the fist rays of sunlight were reaching the buildings of Paris, the mist lifting like a curtain before a mystery play. My radio tuned to an audio feed from CNN, I heard a reporter describe the conflicts between Jews, Muslims and Christians over a piece of land in Jerusalem that all three claim as holy.

"It is perhaps the most holy place in the world," she said, ending her report and ceding the air to another reporter who opened with a description of a one-eyed cat found living in a church in Brazil. According to a small group of believers, it could foretell the future by the motion of its tail.

I turned the radio off.

Ah, the world; I wiped my eyes. The world's people venerate their prophets and ignore their messages, fighting over places where they believed the prophets were born, lived, died and ascended into whatever realms are imagined to lie beyond, all the while ignoring the one and only holy place in the known universe.

We ignore Earth: we take from it, pollute it, fight secular and religious and economic wars over portions of it. As individuals we lay claim to its land, buying and selling and trading it as the earliest humans surely gave one another shells and stones for goods and favors.

People worship Gods, gods, goddesses, as well as lesser beings they believe divine. I think of Bethany and Teach, of Robert Palmer, of Dante and the hangers-on at his Landing, and Christine St. Pierre, who was perhaps at her best when she was X. Some were kind. Some were struggling to live. Some were vicious and wicked as only humans can be. Dante's Landing: We were all there, as if in a waiting room, Bethany expecting Heaven and glory; Teach sure of annihilation and nothingness. Others of us drank to avoid the pain of too much thought and waited only for the following day.

Earth. Where all the sacred rivers flow into the singular oceanic body covering the planet, separating the land that has risen from it; continents, islands, islets and the smallest reefs. Earth, holy, standing alone, the only place in the universe inhabited by our kind, humans, and we fail to look out in awe at the faceless, incomprehensible and, ultimately, unnamable forces that over the millennia have resulted in each of us living on this holy planet for our moment in eternity.

Pirate Pete aboard *Clair de Lune*
The Seine
Paris, FRANCE

CPSIA information can be obtained
at www.ICGtesting.com
Printed in the USA
FFOW02n1810281014
8388FF